'With the hauntingly original backdrop of Orkney as a character in its own right, and enough twists and turns to keep the hardened thriller reader engrossed to its surprising end … [*Dark Island* is] a wholly satisfying reading experience. Freya Sinclair is a protagonist with mileage, and I cannot wait to see where she goes next.' **Wiz Wharton**

'A tense read played out over a gorgeous, unforgiving backdrop, with a protagonist you can't help but connect with. Freya is a triumph, written with genuine emotional honesty by Daniel Aubrey, and I'm looking forward to her next scoop.' **Callum McSorley**

'Sublime. *Dark Island* by Daniel Aubrey does for Orkney what Anne Cleeves does for Shetland. With beautiful and stark prose to match the unique louring landscape and a story that is every bit as tempestuous and powerful as an island storm, Aubrey's writing is both supremely pacy and deeply thoughtful. Moments of high tension are masterfully interwoven with moving scenes of introspection and intuition. Freya Sinclair is an absolute winner of a protagonist: beautifully and vividly painted, with doubts and fears that threaten to overwhelm but that she strives to defeat, and who has you rooting for her from page one. Without a doubt, *Dark Island* has to be my debut novel of the year. Please may there be many more in this series.' **Chris Lloyd**

'What a fantastic debut. I adored the complexity of Freya's character and I couldn't turn the pages fast enough to see where her investigations were taking her!' **Nasheema Lennon**

Daniel Aubrey is a former journalist based in Scotland. His debut novel, *Dark Island*, has been translated into four languages and is in development for TV adaptation. It is the first instalment of the Orkney Mysteries series.

Daniel's obsession with all things Orcadian led him to take up an MLitt in Orkney and Shetland Studies at the Institute of Northern Studies in Kirkwall. Learning about the history, archaeology, and dialect of Scotland's second most northern county, along with his repeated trips to the islands, influenced his decision to make *Dark Island* the first in a series of books set there. Daniel's experience of being diagnosed as autistic and ADHD in his early forties also inspired the journey Freya goes on throughout the series. When he's not writing or studying he's either reading, travelling (most likely to Orkney), playing guitar, or walking in the local hills with his dogs, Dylan and Maggie.

DARK ISLAND

DARK ISLAND

by

DANIEL AUBREY

Harper
North

HarperNorth
Windmill Green
24 Mount Street
Manchester M2 3NX

A division of
HarperCollins*Publishers*
1 London Bridge Street
London SE1 9GF

www.harpercollins.co.uk

HarperCollins*Publishers*
Macken House, 39/40 Mayor Street Upper
Dublin 1, D01 C9W8, Ireland

First published by HarperNorth in 2024

1 3 5 7 9 10 8 6 4 2

A catalogue record for this book
is available from the British Library

ISBN: 978-0-00-862440-8

Printed and bound in Great Britain by
CPI Group (UK) Ltd, Croydon

MIX
Paper | Supporting
responsible forestry
FSC™ C007454

This book is produced from independently certified FSC™ paper
to ensure responsible forest management.

For more information visit: www.harpercollins.co.uk/green

For Dylan and Maggie

who were no help at all

MONDAY, 19 DECEMBER

1

THESE ISLANDS ARE TERRIBLE at keeping their secrets. Nothing in Orkney stays buried forever.

Freya already knew that, didn't need the reminder, but she still got one this morning. She stood alone at the top of the steep bank of boulders that protected the dunes and she watched. She knew she was at a safe distance, a couple of hundred metres across the semilunar curve of the bay – not close enough to be seen, too far away to hear anything other than the rush of the wind and the roar of a bad-tempered sea. Away to the south-east a reluctant dawn was leaking into the sky, turning the clouds greenish-grey at the horizon and casting barely enough light to see the people in white paper jumpsuits, appearing and disappearing between the mounds in the earth where the Neolithic village lay. Last night's storm had passed, but as she watched a pair of the white figures struggle to put up a small tent, a gust caught on the tarpaulin and threatened to carry them both away. Freya couldn't make out what it was exactly, but through her cheap binoculars she could tell they were trying to cover something that had been unburied at the back of the beach.

Another secret these islands had failed to keep.

She ran her tongue over her dry lips and they tasted of sea salt. She hoisted the hood of her yellow raincoat over her head with her free hand, and with the other she adjusted the focus on her binoculars until the blobs in the field of view grew limbs. She had grinned when Tom had suggested buying bird-watching binoculars from the tacky gift shop at John o'Groats on the journey up here, but she had to admit they were coming in handy.

'What if we hear a corncrake while we're out walking Luna?' he'd said. 'Or what if … what if we spot a pod of whales off the coast? I'm telling you, we'll be gutted we didn't buy these when we could.'

His enquiry had seemed so genuine, his enthusiasm so innocent that Freya hadn't had the heart to tell her husband that in all the years she'd lived in Orkney growing up, she'd maybe heard a corncrake once or twice, but she'd never actually seen one. And even if they did, there wasn't a chance in hell they'd get a decent look at it through these piece-of-shit plastic things.

Her phone vibrated in her coat pocket, interrupting her thoughts, and even before she saw the screen, the anxiety she'd fought on the drive over here swelled in her stomach again. But it wasn't the number she had been expecting and she was almost glad to see the name *Kristin*. She thought about answering, long enough to let it ring through to voicemail, then she glanced at the clock above the photo of Tom and their black Labrador, Luna, on the home screen.

It was eight twenty-three.

Kristin was no doubt wondering why she hadn't checked in yet.

Freya put the phone back in her coat pocket; she would text Kristin back when she'd got where she was heading, but she wasn't quite ready to head there yet. Not for another minute or two. She returned the binoculars to her eyes and instinctively her free hand floated to the piercings in her right ear. She began to pinch them in order, from top to bottom then back again, counting as she did. *One, two, three, four, five. Five, four, three …*

The fog in her brain began to clear. Her breathing returned to normal.

That's when she saw it.

Down on the beach, something was moving. The wind was whipping the waves into a frenzy, sending clouds of white foam rolling across the flat, wet sand like tumbleweeds, and amongst the debris dumped by the retreating tide Freya saw something shift again. A black shape, like a shadow. Sand, sea, and rock swept past her eyes, making her feel seasick, as she swung the binoculars left and right before she landed on her target: a dog. A German Shepherd, its black and brown fur rippling in the breeze. It was a beautiful dog and it was still now, looking towards the shore, its jaw opening and closing like it was having a good old blether with someone. The faint sound of its bark reached Freya a few seconds later.

She followed the dog's line of sight to the rocks at the water's edge on the far side of the bay, where a man was standing with his back to the sea. Even from this distance and with his own set of binoculars obscuring his face, Freya could tell he was an older man. He was carrying a walking stick and his shaggy white hair was being blown this way and that. He lowered his binoculars and Freya adjusted the focus again on hers. He was watching the forensic team setting up arc lamps in the gloomy field beyond Skara Brae, like she had done.

He stood there for another couple of minutes, completely still, taking it all in. Then he whistled for his dog, turned back towards the headland, and hurried away.

2

THE WIND WAS BRINGING the sea with it, across the dunes to the single-track road.

Freya's windscreen wipers wailed like a tired toddler, the sound of them making her teeth hurt as she drove the short distance to Skara Brae. The gates were open, but a strip of blue-and-white police tape was pulled across the entrance to the car park. A middle-aged woman in a thin-looking purple coat stood on the near side of it, two uniformed police officers – an older man and a younger woman – were stationed on the other. Freya tried not to make eye contact with them as she drove past, but she heard their raised voices even over the snap of the gravel beneath her tyres and the howl of the heater that was trying to drag the temperature in her ageing Hyundai Getz above freezing. She drove on a little further along the track, past the small crossroads and an unmarked white Audi Q3 that was parked only slightly on the grass verge, almost cutting off the road entirely. She pulled over and killed the engine. Her wipers came to a halt halfway across the windscreen so she turned the key in the ignition again, the rubber blades juddering violently as they were dragged across the barely damp glass to their proper resting place.

She sat in silence, feeling the gentle rocking of the car in the wind, watching the three figures at the tape in her wing mirror. She guessed the woman in the purple coat was the person she was here to meet. Kristin had said her name was Gill.

'She can be a bit …' Kristin had told her during the unexpected phone call this morning, leaving the rest of her sentence hanging somewhere along the connection between them. 'Just … don't take her personally, okay. We're not all like her, I promise.'

That hadn't helped.

Freya closed her eyes, felt her hand float towards her right ear again. She had five small silver studs there – two in the lobe and three in the shell – and she pinched them hard so her fingertips burned. Usually, this helped untangle the wires in her brain, calm her nerves, but not this morning. There was too much at stake. She *needed* to get this right, but the change of plan was making her anxious to the point of being almost angry. This wasn't how today was supposed to play out. It wasn't what she had prepared herself for. She couldn't just—

Her eyes snapped open.

A sound like a swarm of angry bees had invaded her swirling thoughts, cutting her out of her spiral and commanding her full attention. She glanced through her car window and saw the police tape thrashing in the breeze like a plucked guitar string. Beyond it, blue lights strobed silently in the feeble grey half-light. The green LCD clock on her dash said it was after half eight now, but it was barely light, sunrise still another half an hour away. Freya tried to calm herself by counting the emergency vehicles in the car park. She determined five of them were police cars and three were vans, from their height, though she couldn't see them clearly for the drystone dyke. There were people coming out of the visitor centre too, barely visible in the low light. Two of them were dressed in green uniforms. Paramedics. They flanked a tall man with a blanket draped over his shoulders. He was walking without assistance so Freya assumed he must have been relatively unhurt. There were no police officers accompanying them, so he wasn't under arrest either.

The trio walked towards one of the vans behind the wall, then moments later an ambulance approached the cordon. One of the two green uniforms was in the driver's seat; the other, Freya guessed, must have been in the back with the tall man. The ambulance stopped and the male police officer approached and handed a clipboard through the driver's side window for the paramedic to sign. The record of everyone who had come and gone through the cordon, Freya thought. This was far from her first time visiting a crime scene, another reason it was daft she had been sent here to shadow this Gill. She wondered how many serious crimes her new colleague had covered in her career. Unless she had ever worked anywhere other than Orkney, it would only have been a handful.

A diesel engine roared as the policeman pulled back the tape and the ambulance drove out onto the single-track road, turned right at the end of it, and headed inland along the lonely shoreline of Skaill Loch towards Kirkwall. Its sirens flashed but they made no sound. Freya turned her attention back to the cordon. The three people standing there were looking at her now.

She couldn't put this off any longer. She needed to plan what she was going to say.

Hi, I'm Freya. I'm the new girl. Kristin sent …

The new girl? Christ, no. That made her sound like a baby starting nursery.

The new reporter, then?

Better, but probably too formal. And should she mention she used to write for *The Herald* or did that sound like a brag? Or was it somehow more conceited not to mention it, like she was trying to hide it because she thought it was a better job than working for a local paper like *The Orcadian*? Fuck's sake, this was why she hated having to talk to other people; the effort it took simply to work out what they expected you to say, how they wanted you to say it, was exhausting.

The trio at the tape were still gawking at her. Freya took a deep breath, pinched harder on her studs.

She swallowed the bile that had risen onto her tongue and got out.

3

FREYA THOUGHT OF TOM again as she stepped into the bitter wind.

'It won't be the same here, you know,' he'd said before she'd left the house that morning. 'A different place, different people. I promise, you'll be fine.'

Luna had leaned against her legs for moral support, leaving another dusting of black hairs on her jeans. Labrador glitter, Tom called it. The cottage they'd bought was a small place in its own plot of land near the village of Orphir, on the shore of Scapa Flow. It was warm, cosy, while outside the suffocating dark still smothered the windows. Freya hadn't wanted to leave.

Tom had hugged her tight, kissed the top of her head and, for a blissful, brief moment, things had felt like they used to between them.

'They won't be anything like those pricks at *The Herald*, you'll see,' he had said.

But even the pricks at *The Herald* hadn't been pricks to begin with.

Her car door slammed shut the second she let go of it, and it jolted her out of her thoughts. The three faces at the cordon were glaring at her in unison. Freya raised an uncertain hand in greeting then started walking towards them. She felt the cold air bite through her coat, sending shards of hot pain shooting through her left hip. It still hadn't fully healed. She put her hand into her coat pocket and pressed down as she walked, trying not to limp. She got her words ready, lined them up carefully on her tongue, took a deep breath.

'You're not supposed to be here.'

She stopped.

What did the woman say?

Silence followed. Nobody spoke again. It was left to Freya to say, 'Sorry?' Like she'd done something wrong.

'You're not supposed to be here,' the woman in the purple coat yelled over the wind. She pointed in the direction of the remaining emergency vehicles in the car park. 'There's been an incident. Visitor centre's closed to Joe Public this morning. Press and police only. Sorry, hen.'

Freya said nothing and that angry bee sound grew louder.

'Get back in your car and drive on, please.'

One of the uniformed officers this time. The female one. Freya felt so disorientated, and the request was delivered with such authority, that she almost obeyed it.

'No, you don't understand. I'm Freya. Freya Sinclair. The new girl.' The three faces in front of her crumpled in confusion and Freya cursed herself under her breath for coming out with that. 'It's okay, I *am* meant to be here.'

'Says who?' the policewoman asked.

'Kristin.'

'Who?'

'My editor.'

'Kristin Flett from *The Orcadian*?' the woman by the tape asked, still frowning.

Freya nodded. 'Are you Gill?'

'I am.'

'Kristin sent me to meet you. I'm the new girl.'

Freya screwed her eyes shut in frustration. Why the fuck did she keep saying that? When she opened them again Gill had left her post beside the police tape and was walking up the gravel track towards her. Freya could feel every fibre in her body tense with the crunch of each approaching step. Gill stopped only inches away from her face, so close that Freya could see the line at the corners of her cheeks where her foundation stopped. She could see small flecks of lipstick on her nicotine-stained teeth. Her breath smelled strongly of cigarettes and stale coffee, and it gave Freya the dry boak. Gill put her hand on Freya's arm and, even through her yellow raincoat and the thick fleece beneath, her touch felt contaminated. Dirty.

'Kristin never said anything to me about having to babysit this morning.'

The hell was she was supposed to say to that?

She didn't know, so she said nothing.

'Come on,' said Gill, nodding towards the white Audi. 'We'll talk in here.'

Gill dragged Freya by the arm to her car and they got in. The inside of the Audi was a crime scene in itself; everything was sticky, and the stench flooded Freya's nostrils so she could taste the remains of every crushed can of Irn-Bru in the footwell, every empty packet of crisps tossed on the back seat.

'So, what's your story?' Gill asked as her car door slammed shut, sealing them inside. She looked to be in her mid-fifties, late-fifties if Freya was being unkind. Her short brown hair framed a round face that flushed a deeper shade of purple than her coat, even out of the wind.

'What do you mean?'

'I mean, what am I dealing with here? How much do I have to mollycoddle you? Are you brand new in the job? Done it a few years? You don't look like you're long out of school, hen.'

Freya felt her frown deepen. She was thirty-two years old, hardly a fresh-faced novice. She decided to keep her answer brief. 'I've been a reporter off and on for the past ten years.' Almost too late, she remembered to add: 'How about you?'

Gill's facial expression changed. She puffed out her chest. 'I've been here at this same newspaper for thirty years now. Straight out of school, never done anything else.'

Freya nodded, unsure what to say. She was wishing she had asked Kristin if she could come into the newsroom this morning like they had initially agreed. Starting a new job was nerve-wracking enough, but the change of plan had thrown her and she was struggling to right herself. On top of that, this woman's abrupt manner, the assault on her nostrils, and the rasping hiss of the police tape were all combining to smother her brain in treacle.

Her thoughts jumped to a conversation she'd had with the counsellor she had been referred to after her accident. It was the first time anyone had ever suggested to her that she might be autistic. Freya hadn't really known what that had meant, but the counsellor had gone on to describe one aspect of it as feeling like all your senses were switched on at once, all of them cranked up to a hundred and ten.

'It can often feel like every little sound is an unbearable racket,' she had told her. 'The faintest smell can become an overpowering stench.'

Freya had understood that. *Deeply* understood it. That was how this felt now. She fought desperately to push all the intrusive sounds and smells to one side. Forced herself to maintain eye contact. Tried to appear engaged.

'Have they told you much?' she asked, nodding beyond Gill to the police at the cordon. She tried to sound natural. As far as she could tell, she was pulling it off. Her new colleague seemed oblivious to her discomfort.

'This lot? Not a chance.'

Gill followed Freya's gaze out of the window. The two officers were looking over at the car, their lips moving in conversation. Freya was pretty sure she lipread the policewoman say the word *Twat*.

'This one here's PC Flynn. Kate,' Gill said. 'Been on the force all of twelve months and thinks she runs the bloody place. Drunk on authority. And that one's Jim, or PC Brannigan. He's likely just drunk.'

PC Flynn looked young, probably early twenties, with blonde hair pulled back tight under her police hat and an eagerness in her expression that confirmed she was new in the job, while her colleague, PC Brannigan, seemed overdue for retirement. His dark grey hair was badly in need of a trim, and he had the wizened face of a man who had seen it all before and didn't much care for any of it.

'So who tipped us off about this?' Freya asked.

'Me.'

'Sorry?'

'They tipped *me* off, not us.' Gill turned back to face Freya, giving her another burst of nicotine breath. 'Is that what Kristin told you, someone tipped off the paper?'

'Kristin didn't say anything about it. That's why I'm asking.'

'Aye, well, it was me who got the tip. I got a call on my mobile this morning from a good source of mine, Michael Towrie. He's a crofter, lives up the way here in Northdyke. Said he'd seen the blue lights at about seven-ish, torch beams out near the shore. Me and Michael go way back – a heap of folk in these islands know me from the paper and know they can trust me with a tip, and I'll know if I can rely on them.'

Freya wondered, if this Michael had seen the lights around seven, then what time had he called Gill? How long had she been standing in the freezing gale getting stonewalled?

'I came straight over here,' Gill continued. 'Told Kristin I'd find out what was going on before word got out and every nosy bastard this side of the Pentland Firth showed up.'

There was a pause in the conversation. Freya got the impression Gill expected her to fill it. 'There's a forensic team here. They're investigating something in the field on the south side of Skara Brae.'

Whatever Gill had been expecting, it hadn't been that. 'What makes you say that?'

'I stopped at the car park behind the beach before coming here. You can see everything from the top of the tidal defences there. Crime scene tents, arc lamps, people in white paper jump-suits – I saw a lot of scenes like that in my last job.'

Gill's turn to stay silent now. Freya watched her eyes skipping over the features of her face, like she was searching for something. Whatever it was, she wasn't finding it.

'My guess is the storm last night either washed something up or unburied something, don't you think?'

Still nothing. The buzzing of the tape returned, the volume of it rising the longer the silence stretched out between them.

Gill's narrow eyes flicked between Freya's. In the end, Freya gave in to the urge to look away.

Eventually, Gill said: 'Okay, I've an idea.' She opened her car door and the wind whistled in. 'You say nothing, you hear me? Follow my lead.'

Gill climbed out of the Audi and was marching towards the cordon before Freya could respond.

As she got out of the passenger side, she could hear Gill shouting: 'Right, I know there's a dead body back there, so you lot have got two choices – you either go and get the DI to come out here and give me a statement or I go to print with what I know so far and we'll leave it up to Joe Public to speculate on the rest.'

Freya walked over to join Gill at the tape. PC Brannigan was smiling, shaking his head, but his young partner was failing to see the funny side.

'Just who the bloody hell do you think you are?' PC Flynn growled.

'I'm the most senior reporter in these islands, hen. I'm the voice of the people. My newspaper has been holding you lot to account for over a hundred and fifty years and I—'

'Holding us to account? Is that what you call that shite you wrote about us in the summer?'

'Hit a nerve, did it, sweetheart? I bet it did. Now look, this is your final warning. You either get that lazy swine DI Muir out here right now or I'll—'

'DI Muir? Is that Fergus Muir?'

Silence. All eyes turned to Freya. She felt their glare burning like sunlight focused through a lens, followed by the pull of her hand towards the studs in her ear. She stuffed her hands in her coat pockets to stop herself.

'How do you know Fergus Muir?' Gill asked.

Freya didn't answer. She looked at PC Flynn. 'Tell him Freya Sin … no, tell him Freya *Spence* is here and we just want five minutes of his time, then we'll go.'

PC Flynn glanced at her colleague, who simply gave her a nod. Maybe they were happy to shut Gill up, or perhaps it was the suggestion they'd go away and leave them alone, but whatever it was, PC Flynn stepped away from the cordon and, keeping her back to the wind, pulled the radio attached to the shoulder of her uniform to her lips.

'Spence?' PC Brannigan asked. 'Wouldn't be any relation to Neill Spence, would you?'

Freya nodded. She couldn't see Gill, but she could feel her watching her. She stole a glance at her out of the corner of her eye and thought she looked confused. Or angry. Perhaps both.

'I'm his daughter.'

PC Brannigan nodded too, looked down at his feet. He was smiling again but this one was different. 'I remember Neill well, worked with him when he was still in uniform. He was a good man. I had a lot of time for him.' He looked up. 'It wasn't fair what happened.'

Freya wasn't sure what to say to that. She simply smiled and nodded.

PC Flynn came back to the cordon, an eager grin playing on her lips. 'Looks like your new girl here's better connected than you are, *sweetheart*. Voice of the people, my arse.'

She turned to Freya.

'You've got your five minutes with the DI.'

4

GILL WALKED AHEAD, PANTING but seemingly desperate to stay in front. Freya could see the exertion peeling off her hunched shoulders like heatwaves on scorched tarmac.

They had been told to make their way to an officer by the outer cordon behind the visitor centre, on the sea-facing side. 'DI Muir will meet you there,' PC Flynn had said. 'He doesn't have time to be walking all the way out here for this.'

They cut across the top of the bank at the back of the beach, picking their way between the seaweed and other discarded sea-junk that been hurled this high by the storm. Bits of wood, chunks of plastic. Giant puddles pocked the ground. Freya lifted her head, took long, deep breaths of the invigorating air. They were completely exposed to the ocean here, nothing between them and Newfoundland save for a handful of skerries and a couple thousand miles of sea, and it showed in the strength of the gale that blew them sideways as they walked. It pulled several strands of Freya's red hair from her ponytail and sent it leaping around her face like flames.

Beyond Gill, Freya's gaze was drawn to the austere mansion of Skaill House, its stoic grey stone walls facing the relentless rush coming off the North Atlantic. The owners of the estate had found the remains of the Neolithic village of Skara Brae back in the mid-1800s after a storm, not unlike the one last night, had ripped away the top layer of land, revealing the warren of five-thousand-year-old houses and workshops huddled together underneath. Freya remembered trips here in primary school, the fizzy feeling she'd felt in her stomach upon hearing about the ornaments the archaeologists had found on the flagstone mantlepieces when it had been excavated. Intricate trinkets carved from whalebone and precious stones. A snapshot of village life from five millennia ago, all perfectly intact.

But something else had been found lying beneath the dirt today.

Freya swept her hair from her eyes, focused on the scene in the distance. In her last job on *The Herald*'s Crime and Courts desk, she had reported on hundreds of horrific cases, had almost grown numb to them in the end, but there was something different about a forensic team being in this place. This wasn't the same as Glasgow. And Skara Brae was the most visited tourist attraction in all of Orkney; if it was a body they had found out there, then whoever had buried it here was either really bloody stupid or they knew something Freya didn't.

About a hundred metres from the low chain-link fence around the Skara Brae site, they stopped in front of another line of blue-and-white tape. Two more officers were stationed here, both women this time. One of them approached the cordon, her chin tucked into her coat collar, eyes squinting against the blustery wind.

'He'll be right out,' she said to Freya.

She didn't look at Gill.

Seconds later, Freya spotted someone duck under the tape at the inner cordon, which was just beyond a stone warden's hut at the back of Skara Brae. A man peeled off his white jumpsuit and overshoes then walked slowly around the perimeter of the Neolithic village, head lowered against the westerly wind. As he got closer and looked up, Freya recognised him immediately. He had aged since she'd last seen him, of course – it had been almost fifteen years since she'd left Orkney, supposedly for good, but it looked like longer on his face. The grey hair, the pale, wind-weathered skin looked different, but the soft brown eyes were the same ones Freya remembered. The ones she recalled brimming with tears when she had crept down from her bedroom one night as a ten-year-old to find him sitting at their kitchen table with her mother, who had been too distraught to talk. Neither of them had been able to bring themselves to tell her what had happened.

But she knew.

One of the policewomen handed DI Fergus Muir a clipboard to sign as he approached, then he stepped under the outer cordon.

Freya had forgotten Gill was there until she spoke.

'I'll handle this.' Gill stepped forward, a Dictaphone in her raised hand. 'DI Muir, Gill Irvine from *The Orcadian*. How about you tell us—'

'Pipe down, Gill Irvine from *The Orcadian*,' DI Muir cut her off as he strode past her. 'I know all too well who you are, there's no bloody need to announce yourself.'

He left her in his wake, stopped about a metre in front of Freya. He was wearing a shabby black suit with a light blue shirt open at the collar, no tie, and now he was up close Freya could see grey stubble on his cheeks, maybe a few days' worth. He smiled before taking another step forward and wrapping her up in the tightest hug. She didn't mean to, because she really was glad to see him, but every part of her tensed in his grasp.

He let go immediately, stood back with his hands on her shoulders, still smiling. 'I forgot, you never were much of a one for hugs, even when you were in your peedie breeks.'

'Hi, Uncle Fergus.'

He chuckled and Freya realised what she'd said. Despite them being stung numb by the wind, she felt her cheeks flush.

'It's good to see you, Red. Your mam said you were moving back.'

Freya hadn't heard that nickname in years. Not since she was a teenager. 'We moved in about two weeks ago,' she said, tucking some of the hair that had earned her that name behind her ear. 'We've not been back long.'

'We? That'll be you and your new husband, aye?'

'Tom, yeah. Though he's not my *new* husband, exactly. We've been married almost ten years now.'

A pang of guilt struck her as she said that and she instantly wished she hadn't. She had meant to keep in touch with Fergus. Had done, at first. But she guessed as time passed and Orkney had grown smaller in her rearview mirror, her emails and texts back to the few people she knew here and tried to stay in contact with had shrunk to the point of disappearing.

'You still go by Spence?' Fergus asked.

She'd heard the question but needed a second or two before her brain made sense of it. 'Erm … no. No, I thought you wouldn't know who Freya Sinclair was.'

'Sinclair, eh? So your man's an Orcadian?'

'No, he's from Moffat. Near Dumfries.'

'A Doonhamer? Really?' Fergus raised an eyebrow. 'And this is who you want to spend your life with?'

Freya grinned, gave a small shrug. 'What can I say? There were no decent Orcadian men to be had.'

'Ain't that the truth.' He jerked his thumb over his shoulder. 'And you're throwing your lot in with this bunch?' He turned to look at Gill, who still had her hand out towards him, holding the Dictaphone. 'Turn that bloody thing off or I'll turn it off for you.'

Surprisingly, Gill seemed to do as she was told.

'Your mam's missed you while you've been away, you know,' Fergus said, turning back to Freya. 'I realise she's not the best one for showing it, but she has. She told me what happened too, about your accident. You're on the mend now, I hope?'

Freya's grin evaporated. She felt the wind sink its teeth into her left hip again. 'Never better.'

'And here you are, already up to your neck in mischief.'

'What's going on back there?'

'Wish I could tell you, but I'm under strict instructions from my boss, I'm afraid. "Not a word to anyone".'

'We know there's a body under one of those tents,' Gill shouted.

Fergus rolled his eyes, and Freya couldn't help but allow herself another tiny smile. He looked over his shoulder at Gill. 'Do you, aye?'

'Is this a murder case, DI Muir?'

'Take a day off, will you? I'll not be saying a word to you, of all people. I'm out here now because I was told my goddaughter was here, it's the only reason we're talking.'

Freya noticed him glance at the two uniforms behind the cordon.

'It's getting lighter, the wind's dropping off,' Gill said, unperturbed. 'You'll have dog walkers on the beach any time now. People are going to see this then they'll be getting the messages down the Co-op, chatting to their pals, coming up with all kinds of theories. You may as well tell us so we can set them straight.'

'Somebody's already seen it,' Freya said.

Fergus turned back to her. His face darkened.

'On the way here this morning I saw a man on the beach. He was watching you put up the tents. He had binoculars.'

'Is that so?' Fergus ran a hand through his thatch of slate grey hair. 'Look, the Area Commander will be putting out a statement later today. And you're right …' He looked at Gill. 'Folk will talk, they always do, which is why we don't want a word of this getting out until we know exactly what we're dealing with.'

'Off the record for now, then?' Gill asked. 'So we have a head start on everyone else when the statement comes out; that's only fair.'

Fergus glanced at the two uniformed officers again, then back at Freya. With the slightest flick of his head, he beckoned her and Gill to join him away from the tape.

'Fine, off the record,' he said, his voice low. 'But I mean it, none of this goes public until the second that statement gets released, you hear?'

5

GILL MADE A BIG show of putting the Dictaphone back in her coat pocket.

'We've found remains,' Fergus said, and before Gill could ask he added: 'Yes, the forensic archaeologist believes they're human. Last night's skreevar pulled the ground up at the back of the beach there. They weren't buried deep.'

'Recent?'

'Not especially. No flesh left on them. There's no telling how old they're likely to be until we get them looked at.'

'Just the one body?' Freya asked. She was looking towards the inner cordon. Now they were closer she counted three white tents trembling in the wind in the next field. One large and two smaller ones.

Fergus followed her line of sight. 'Aye, well, the storm's made a fair klatter back there. Bits and pieces have been torn out the ground, dragged all over, but it looks like it's just the one.'

As she looked across at the crime scene, a buzzing sound reached her ears again. Quieter this time, more high-pitched. It couldn't have been the tape at the cordon – she would have noticed it sooner.

Between the smaller tents she spotted two white-suited figures trying to get a drone airborne. In this weather, they didn't stand a chance. Every time it took off it was buffeted this way and that by the wind, unable to hover in one place. In the end the pair gave up, landing it safely on the ground before the gale could catch it and send it plummeting to earth to be smashed into tiny pieces.

'Come on, DI Muir,' Gill was saying. 'Surely you can tell us more than that. Is there any tissue on the bone? Any—'

'Look, you're lucky you've been telt this much. But if it's my best guess you're after, instead of waiting for the forensic examiner's report, then fine, I'd say it'll probably turn out to be one of the folks that lived in these.' Fergus nodded towards the stone houses at Skara Brae.

Freya was still half watching the Scene of Crime Officers attempting to get the drone in the air. 'I doubt it,' she said absent-mindedly. 'This whole area's been excavated several times since the first buildings were found. That field was dug up in the Nineties. If there were an ancient body out here at such a shallow depth, surely they would have …'

She stopped talking as she turned around, saw the look on Fergus' face.

He flashed her a resigned smile. 'Nothing ever did get past you, did it, Red?'

'So why fly a forensic team out here from Inverness in such a rush if you believe the remains are ancient?' Gill asked.

'Because look where we are,' Fergus replied. 'That sea is going to be coming back this way in twelve hours' time, and we've less than six hours' daylight to work with. I need to get as much forensic value out of that scene as possible before Mother Nature does her best to scupper me. I realise you don't have the first clue about police work, Ms Irvine, but surely even you can understand that, no matter what I think, I still have to investigate everything thoroughly.'

'Who found the body?' Freya asked.

'The lad opening up this morning. The site doesn't open to visitors until ten at this time of year, but he told us he was worried during the storm last night, so he came in early. He saw the hole in the ground from the fence there, caught it in his torch beam and scared himself to death.'

'This lad got a name?' Gill asked.

'Aye, but I'll not be giving it to you. He's a sensitive boy and he's had a rough morning. Last thing he needs is sight of you coming towards him, you hear?'

That buzzing sound drew Freya's attention again. The two SOCOs were making another attempt to get the drone off the ground, fighting a losing battle. They seemed desperate to use what Freya imagined must be a very expensive, very fragile piece of kit, despite the conditions making it impossible. She wondered about that.

When she turned back to Fergus he was looking at her with what seemed like a warning in his eyes, as if he'd read her mind and knew she was going to ask something he'd rather she didn't. Freya glanced between him and Gill.

It was her first day and Fergus was an old friend; she let it go.

'So that's it? That's all you'll tell us?' Gill was saying. 'The storm's uncovered remains, they're human, but you're not saying how old they are, and we can't report who found them?'

'You can't report a bloody thing for now other than there's a police operation underway and folk are to keep clear,' Fergus replied, still watching Freya. He turned to Gill finally as he said, 'Magnus will be repeating all this in his statement this afternoon. You know as much as we do just now, which is to say next to bugger all, but it's still more than anyone else. You can have your story written up and ready to print the second that statement comes out. I'm not asking you to keep anything secret, I'm simply asking you to be patient. Like you said, that's only fair.'

'Well, if that's everything, we'll let you get back to it. Thank you for your time, DI Muir.' Gill marched over and grabbed Freya by the arm of her yellow coat again. 'Come on, hen. Let's away back to base and—'

'Hold on a blink, Ms Irvine.'

Gill stopped, glanced back at DI Muir, looking hopeful.

'I need a minute or two longer with young Mrs Sinclair here.'

Gill's gaze flicked between Fergus and Freya, her face quickly beginning to redden again.

'I'll meet you at the car,' Freya said.

A few seconds passed, then Gill relinquished her grip on Freya's arm. She stomped away without saying another word, walking so fast in her rage she nearly tripped over the uneven ground.

Fergus watched her until she was far enough not to hear. 'I know you're big enough to take care of yourself now, and you certainly don't need advice from the likes of me, but I'd be neglecting my duty both as your godfather and as a half-decent human being if I didn't warn you to watch yourself with that one.'

Freya smiled. Fergus had always looked out for her, even before her dad died. 'I'll be fine.'

'I'm sure you will.' He smiled back, but it was weaker than the winter sun.

He turned to look at the two uniforms behind the cordon a third time. Something was up. He didn't make to leave, nor did he say anything else. Freya began to wonder if there was a question she was supposed to ask him, something else he wanted her to say.

'What about you? Are you okay?'

He was staring over towards the crime scene, eyes narrowed against the wind. He looked as though he was visibly ageing right in front of her – the bags under his eyes growing darker, the colour leaking away from his vein-riddled cheeks. 'Just stress, is all. I've been thinking about cashing in my pension soon. Never expected I'd be involved in something like this afore I did.'

'Something like what? I thought you said the bones were likely ancient.'

He didn't answer.

Instead, he asked, 'Why did you come back here, Freya?'

The question wasn't what she had been expecting. 'I don't know. Glasgow was … hectic. Pure chaos. It wasn't what either Tom or I wanted.'

'And what did you want?'

'A fresh start, I suppose. And this.' She raised a hand towards the sea. 'The open spaces, the beaches, nature. A quieter pace of life.'

That was a half-lie, but it was one both she and Tom had agreed to tell.

Fergus faced her now. Any warmth in his eyes had gone. Instead, he looked at Freya with a kind of pleading. 'If it's the quiet life you're after,' he said, placing a calloused hand on her shoulder, 'you couldn't have picked a worse moment to come back.'

6

FREYA COULD SEE GILL'S car had gone long before she got back to the gate at the Skara Brae car park.

She stood on the single-track road for a moment, turning to face the bay. Eyes closed, she let the sea-speckled wind brush her face as she tried to loosen the knot that had been tightening in her stomach all morning. She relished the chance for some time alone, but it didn't help her feel any less anxious. Fergus had been acting strange, and the fact Gill's car wasn't there had to mean she'd driven off in a huff. Freya had been in her new job just over an hour and already she was pissing someone off. So much for a fresh start. She opened her eyes, looked across the fields behind the beach towards the inner cordon. The SOCOs were trying and failing to launch the drone again.

Beams of brittle sunlight broke through the clouds as she drove across Mainland. The sky had been a shifting patchwork of pastel yellows and blues as she left Bay of Skaill, but by the time she reached the Hatston Industrial Estate on the edge of Kirkwall, less than thirty minutes later, the clouds were closing in again. The rain she'd seen moving in between the islands in the Bay of Firth began to spot her windscreen as she pulled into the car park, and the breeze-block walls and corrugated metal roof of *The Orcadian*'s newsroom were the same dull grey as the sky. The rapid change did nothing to settle the disquiet she was feeling. Nothing about today seemed structured or knowable. As she killed the engine and pulled on the handbrake, an image popped into her head of the T-shirts she used to see for sale outside the gift shops opposite St Magnus Cathedral as a kid, the ones with slogans on the front that read: *If you don't like the weather here, wait five minutes*.

At the reception desk, Freya introduced herself and asked for Kristin Flett.

'She'll be right down,' the smiling receptionist told her.

Freya twirled a strand of her hair around her finger as she waited, pulled it tight to make the tip go numb. She pretended to look at the display of old printing presses and framed front pages from decades gone by as she planned out a few lines of conversation for when Kristin arrived, and occasionally she sneaked a glance at the receptionist. The woman looked familiar, but Freya wasn't sure if she was simply imagining it. Around twenty-one thousand people lived in Orkney, most of them in Mainland, and while Tom had been half-jokingly asking if Freya knew everyone they had met during the past two weeks, she realised there was a good chance she would eventually run into someone from her childhood. They weren't encounters she was relishing. What she had told Fergus was mostly true; she and Tom had moved here looking for a change of pace. A fresh start. Though now she was here, she found she was increasingly questioning the logic of making a new life for themselves in a place where the veil between the past and the present had always been somewhat thinner than it was elsewhere.

'Freya?'

She jumped at a voice behind her. She spun around to see a smiling woman with long blonde hair and thin black-framed glasses.

'Oh, I'm so sorry, chick, I didn't mean to startle you.' The woman held out a slender hand. 'It's so lovely to finally meet you in the flesh.'

Freya recognised Kristin from the video call they'd had when she interviewed for the job. Now, as then, Kristin was impeccably dressed – her glasses looked designer, her pale blue blouse and grey pencil skirt expensive, but somehow the outfit didn't come across as showy. It looked natural on her, but it made Freya feel a little self-conscious about the blue jeans and Gore-Tex trainers she had chosen to wear when she had been told this morning she could dress any way she liked.

'Hi, I'm Freya. Yes, it's great to meet you too.'

Freya realised seconds after giving her rehearsed line that Kristin had used her name, so there was no bloody need to introduce herself. *What a prick.* She could feel she was blushing, but Kristin either didn't notice or she was too polite to let on.

Kristin led Freya through to a corridor that tasted of dry radiator dust, and up a dark staircase to the newsroom on the first floor. It was a large, open-plan room with a single, giant desk in the middle of the industrial grey carpet. The buzz of florescent strip lights in the lowered ceiling filled her brain. She felt the knot in her stomach tighten: was each reporter's spot at the desk assigned or would it be a nightmarish free-for-all? Or worse, maybe there would be no allocated places but everyone would have one seat they were precious about without giving any indication as to which one was 'theirs'. She had Gill pegged to be that sort.

Several computers were dotted around the desk but only one of them was occupied. Gill was staring at a monitor, her thin, purple coat thrown on the table beside it like she hadn't had the time to hang it up. Her fingers punched the keyboard in a staccato rhythm.

'I've already bollocked this one for leaving you behind,' Kristin said with a grin as they passed behind Gill.

'I've told you, I didn't leave her anywhere,' Gill retorted, eyes fixed on her screen. 'I've a big story to write up here and I wasn't to know how long she'd be talking to her Uncle Fergus.'

She heard that, then, Freya thought. *Fucking wonderful.*

Freya followed Kristin through one of two doors off the back of the room. It led into a small kitchen. The heating was cranked up high in here – there seemed to be one thermostat for the whole building – and the stuffy air was thick with the stench of dried food stuck to the Formica worktops and whatever meal had last been cooked in the antique microwave. She buried her nostrils deeper into her coat collar. Really, it was too hot to keep her coat on, but having it on, zipped up to the collar, felt safe, despite the beads of sweat blossoming on the back of her neck. It was also the only clothing she owned with decent pockets, and she hated carrying a bag. Kristin flicked on the kettle and took two mugs, a cafetière, and a small plastic tub of ground coffee from one of the cupboards.

'One of the habits I brought back with me from London,' Kristin said, holding up the tub. 'I cannot stand piss-poor coffee, but my God, I'm spoiled for choice here. Have you been into town much since you got back?'

Freya had, but she shook her head. It felt like the expected response.

'Honestly, I swear there are more trendy cafés in Kirkwall now than there are in Shoreditch,' Kristin continued. 'Wasn't like that when I last lived here.'

The thought of getting a decent cup of coffee, and Kristin's use of the word *trendy*, brought a smile to Freya's lips, as did the fact they had something in common. Kristin had mentioned during Freya's interview that she'd also left Orkney at a young age and had only returned within the last eighteen months.

A conversational question popped into Freya's head. In her delight at having thought of it she almost forgot to say it aloud. 'Where did you work in London?'

'A few places. I started out in print after uni, did my apprenticeship at the *Evening Standard* before moving to *The Guardian*.' Kristin leaned her hip against the counter, waiting for the kettle to boil. 'Then I switched to sub-editing for wire agencies. AP, Reuters. I thought it'd be more fast-paced but to be honest it got old fast. People thought I was mad to leave it behind to come back here, but then …'

Her thoughts seemed to evaporate into the steam as the kettle clicked.

Kristin began to pour the hot water into the cafetière. She looked a little older than Freya: mid-thirties, maybe. Despite having been away, her Orcadian accent had already made a strong comeback – a soft, lyrical lilt outsiders sometimes mistook for Welsh. Freya wondered how quickly her own accent would return.

'It put a few noses out of joint too, let me tell you,' Kristin continued as she passed Freya her coffee. She leaned in, lowered her voice to a conspiratorial whisper, and glanced towards the half-closed door. 'This is my first editor post. Gill's been here forever and thought she was a shoo-in when the last fella left.

Our other senior reporter, Keith, was here when Watergate broke too. Neither's taken my arrival well.' She shook her head, blew on her coffee. 'How about you? People must have thought you'd lost the plot when you quit *The Herald* to move to a local weekly.'

Freya smiled and nodded. 'Something like that.'

'Well, I'll be honest, it was a nice surprise for us too. Don't get me wrong, we're a bloody good team here. Small, but respected. But it's always nice to have a prize-winning journalist applying to join us.'

Freya felt her cheeks flush yet again. 'That was a while ago now.'

'Not that long. Scottish Press Award, wasn't it? For your story on that pervert doctor.'

Freya nodded. In only her second year at *The Herald*, while working the Health beat, she'd won a *Scoop of the Year* award for exposing a GP in Partick who had been convincing young women to undergo unnecessary breast examinations which he'd secretly been filming. The story had made headlines beyond Scotland and she'd been moved to the Crime and Courts desk. Freya considered whether or not she should say that, like Kristin, her success had put some people's noses out of joint, that the award had been the beginning of the end for her at *The Herald*, but giving so much away so soon felt uncomfortable. In any case, the pause lasted too long and Kristin filled it.

'I can see you're too modest to toot your own horn. Unlike some around here.'

Kristin nodded towards the newsroom and grinned, lighting another smile on Freya's lips.

'I'd introduce you to the rest of the team but, as you can see, we're a little thin on the ground just now,' Kristin said. 'Sophie's down at the courthouse on a story, and Keith's been off sick these past two months, so we've only Gill and Sophie writing for us full-time. That's why I was ecstatic when you said you'd get started before Christmas.'

They took their coffees through to Kristin's office, which was the next room along off the back of the newsroom. Like the kitchen, it was a poky room with a tiny window on the far wall which let in next to no light. Another fluorescent bulb buzzed and clicked in the low ceiling, but at least the smell in here was improved. The room was cluttered but not untidy. Freya's gaze landed on several framed photographs on Kristin's desk of two pre-teen kids – a boy and a girl – but no other family. No partner. She'd already spotted Kristin wasn't wearing a wedding ring. No photos of any pets either, disappointingly.

'My kids, Jordon and Alicia,' Kristin said as they sat. She must have spotted Freya looking at the frames. 'They were particularly thrilled to leave London. They think I've dragged them to the far ends of the earth. They call Orkney *The Rock*.'

She laughed so Freya did too.

'Gill tells me you're related to Fergus Muir, that he's your uncle,' Kristin said.

Freya's face warmed for the hundredth time today. 'No, we're not related. He was a close friend of my dad's.'

'*Was* a close friend?'

'My dad died in a car accident when I was little.'

'Oh Freya, my God, I'm so sorry. That was so insensitive of me.'

'No, it's okay,' Freya said and, even though she had stated a fact, she felt guilty for making Kristin feel embarrassed. 'It happened just before I turned eleven.'

'Was he on the force too?'

'He was a DI. He ran the CID here.'

There was a pause. Was Kristin waiting for her to fill it or weighing up asking more questions? Freya chose to keep silent, wait it out.

'Well,' Kristin said eventually, 'it'll be good having an in with the current detective inspector, especially with this latest story. A lot of our inside track comes directly from the station, and our relationship hasn't exactly been harmonious of late.'

'The constables at Skara Brae this morning seemed a bit annoyed with Gill.'

Kristin snorted a laugh. 'Travel to any of these islands, even the ones populated only by feral cows, and you'd find someone who was pissed off with Gill. We ran a story in the summer – a story I stand by, as it goes – which the police weren't happy about. The Area Commander's golfing buddies with Alistair Sutherland. He's our paper's owner.'

Freya nodded. She knew Alistair Sutherland from her research before taking the job. She had liked the fact *The Orcadian* was still in local hands rather than being owned by some faceless 'media group'. All across Scotland, weekly local newspapers like this one were dying out, but Orkney was perhaps one of the few places where such a thing could still thrive. People here rightly wanted to read about things that affected them, and that was more likely to be the closure of a community centre in Stromness than anything going on hundreds of miles away to the south. The paper had been owned by the Sutherland family for generations.

'Magnus had a word in Alistair's ear and that was that, he made us retract it,' Kristin was saying. 'He said we couldn't back up such accusations. But the accusations weren't ours, we were merely reporting what people were saying. That's the first and hopefully last time he's ever stepped in.'

'What was the story?'

'Oh, the kind of thing you'd only hear in Orkney,' Kristin said with a shake of her head. 'A farmer in Burray found almost half of his cattle with their throats slit one morning. It was bloody gruesome, to be honest. Heartbreaking. Anyway, he'd been in an ongoing feud with another farm in South Ronaldsay. He and some of the locals down there were convinced the boys from this other farm were behind it but the police said there was no evidence, never found who did it. The farmer claimed the police knew but were too scared to do anything, that there were certain folk in these islands who live outwith the law.'

'Was Fergus Muir involved?'

'He led the investigation.'

Freya shook her head. 'I've known Fergus all my life, I doubt he'd be involved in a cover-up.'

'And here I was thinking you were a hard-hitting reporter.' Kristin leaned forward and put her elbows on her desk. 'If there's anything you learn in this job, chick, it's people can always surprise you.'

Kristin moved the conversation on to her plans for making better use of the newspaper's digital platforms.

'You can bet what's happened at Skaill this morning is all over Facebook. We should've been posting from the scene, putting up some video, dragging readers over to our website. But Gill "doesn't do social media"' – Kristin made the quotation marks with her fingers – 'so it wasn't until she got back here that I was able to post something second-hand.'

Freya suddenly remembered Kristin had been trying to call her. That might have been why. She tried to apologise, she had meant to text her back, but Kristin waved her away.

'I just wanted to check you'd found Gill and she was behaving herself. But I'll be honest, when we took you on, I was hoping I'd be hiring an ally. I want to put you in charge of our social channels. Anything that happens with this story, you get it on there and break it before someone else does. Think you can do that?'

'Absolutely.'

Freya liked the sound of that word, *ally*.

There was a knock at the door. Freya turned in her chair to see a young woman, mid-twenties, standing in the doorway. She had chestnut hair that reached the shoulders of her black woollen coat. Her cheeks glowed the same colour as her pink scarf and gloves after coming in from the cold.

'Ah, Freya, this is Sophie Rendall,' Kristin said. 'Sophie, meet Freya.'

Sophie nodded a hello at Freya but quickly turned her attention back to Kristin. 'Is it true they've found a dead body at Skara Brae?'

'Gill's just pulling a story together. We've got a jump on this afternoon's statement, but she said we'd been asked to hold back any mention of the body for now. How did you hear about it?'

'It's on Facebook. Everyone's talking about it in town.'

Kristin pointed at Freya. 'See, this is what I mean. This is why we need to be a serious presence on social media. If people aren't getting their news from us, they'll find it—'

'There's a woman here too,' Sophie cut her off. 'I met her by reception on my way in. She wants to talk to us.'

'About?'

'She says she went over to Skaill just now but was told to head home. She says the police wouldn't listen to her, but she thinks we might be able to help.'

'With what?'

'The body,' Sophie said. 'She says she knows who it is.'

7

THE WOMAN GAVE HER name as Beth Campbell.

Sophie showed her through to the kitchen. Freya, Kristin, and Gill joined them. The room quickly grew hot and claustrophobic, the reek of old food still thick enough to taste. Freya buried her face in her coat collar again and tried to shut it out. Easier said than done.

Sophie sat Beth at the small round table while Kristin fired up the kettle again and Freya leaned against the chipped Formica counter. Gill took the chair next to Beth and made a big show of fussing over her.

'You look familiar to me, hen,' she said. 'We've spoken before, have we not?'

Beth nodded but didn't speak. Freya thought she looked like a sick bird that had fallen from its nest. The way her shoulders hunched as she sat at the table, cradling the warm cup of tea Kristin offered her, gave the impression she was trying to curl into a ball. The lines on her face put her at about seventy, but she probably wasn't even close. Her dark eyes were sunken, her face gaunt. When she blew on her tea, her breath was barely strong enough to cause ripples on its surface.

Kristin took the last seat at the table with Gill and Beth, leaving Sophie to stand next to Freya. Beth took a few sips of her tea before deciding it was still too hot for her to drink and set her cup down on the table. She raised her eyes to look at each of the women in turn before returning her gaze to Gill.

'You were the one who wrote about it when she went missing,' she said.

'Your peedie lassie,' Gill replied, a sad smile on her lips. 'That's right, you're Ola's mammy. I mind it well.'

Cold fingers wrapped themselves around Freya's heart.

Ola Campbell. She knew that name.

'Have you been out to Skaill this morning?' Beth's eyes widened as she spoke. 'Did you speak to the police?'

'I have and I did,' Gill said. 'I interviewed Detective Inspector Fergus Muir. He's the Senior Investigating Officer on this case.'

A frown creased Freya's forehead. That wasn't strictly true, and she wondered if Gill knew. If the remains turned out to be recent, the case would be handed over to Police Scotland's Major Investigations Team and they would assign their own SIO. The locals would be kept involved, sure, but Fergus wouldn't be running the show. Again, Freya was reminded that Gill likely hadn't covered any serious crime in a very long while.

'Did he tell you anything?' Beth asked.

Gill shook her head, pulled a face like she was in pain. 'Oh sweetheart, I know what you're thinking, but you mustn't. DI Muir told me the body was probably very, very old. It's not your wee girl, I can assure you of that.'

Beth made a sickening sound then, like she'd been punched in the stomach. Her face creased into tears and her body seemed to collapse in on itself. Gill reached across and squeezed her shoulder.

Kristin looked up. 'Soph, pop next door and grab the box of tissues off my desk, will you? Thanks, chick.'

Sophie nodded and left.

'Mrs Campbell,' Kristin continued in a soft voice. 'I'm so sorry, but I don't think I'm following what's happening.'

'It was long before your time here, Kris.' Gill answered for Beth, who continued to sob almost silently, her shoulders trembling. 'Beth's daughter went missing about twenty years back.'

'Seventeen,' Beth managed to force out. 'This October just passed.'

Those icy fingers around Freya's heart tightened their grip. Seventeen years ago, Freya had been at secondary school, and there were only two of them in all of Orkney: Kirkwall Grammar and Stromness Academy. Growing up in Birsay, in West Mainland, Freya had gone to the latter. When she was about fifteen, the county had been rocked by the disappearance of a girl in the year above her. She had gone missing with her boyfriend, an older boy from Kirkwall, and the pair had never been found. There had been a large-scale search across the islands and Freya remembered seeing the police down on the shore near their home several nights in a row after school, picking between the rocks in the dying light.

'You'd probably moved away south before it happened,' Gill was telling Kristin. Like she had this morning, she puffed out her chest as she spoke. 'I covered the whole thing back then. Her and that boyfriend of hers, wasn't it?' she said to Beth. 'I remember it like it was yesterday.'

'I remember it too.'

The words slipped out before she could suck them back in. Everyone turned to look at Freya, their eyes cutting into her. She wanted to shrink into her coat and hide.

Beth's sobs subsided. She looked at Freya with a hint of hope in her glassy eyes. 'Did you ... did you know her? She'd be about your age now. I mean, she would have been, if ...'

Sophie came back with the box of tissues as Beth broke down again. Gill took one and passed it to her and she wiped her eyes, her mascara blotting the paper in blooming black spots.

'No, I'm sorry,' said Freya. 'We didn't know each other, we just ... I remember when it happened, is all.'

But that was a lie. Freya knew Ola Campbell perfectly.

Ola had been notorious at Freya's school: blonde, pretty, popular. And an absolute fucking cow to go with it. She was the kind of girl who, despite being taller than most other girls and able to handle herself in a fight, didn't need to bully the other kids directly. She had her minions to do it for her. And although Freya had become adept at flying under the radar, she had landed in Ola's sights on several occasions.

One stood out: in third year a rumour had gone round that one of the popular boys, Harry Donaldson, fancied her. Freya did not particularly fancy him back, but to avoid any hassle she went along to the place where she had been asked to meet him: the harbour front near the lifeguard house. It was in the heart of Stromness, next to the quay where the ferry docked for Scotland. When she got there, as well as the usual tourists and locals who congregated in that old cobbled square, there was a crowd waiting. At the front of the pack, standing next to Harry, was Ola.

'Did you really think Harry could fancy a spaz like you?'

Around her, all Freya could hear was the acid-laced laughter of mocking teens.

'Go on, Harry, give her a kiss. Can't you see she's wet for you?'

In hindsight, trying to batter the living fuck out of Ola had been the wrong move. Freya had been kicked to the ground by Ola's friends before she could land a finger on her, but even so, given the chance a thousand times again, she still would have tried to take Ola Campbell's wicked eyes out. So would several other people she had known at school, which is why she hadn't been able to understand it when, after Ola had gone missing, many of those same people had cried and started acting like Ola was some kind of bloody saint.

Freya had said as much to her own mother when she had asked why she didn't seem as upset as everybody else by Ola's apparent death. There were rumours Ola and her boyfriend had both died by suicide, and according to her mother, having no visible reaction to that fact made Freya 'cold' and 'lacking in empathy'. But Freya didn't see it like that; she knew it meant everyone else was a fucking hypocrite. Even by that age, Freya knew what it felt like to think about ending your own life, feeling like nobody would particularly care if you did, and honestly, she wouldn't have wished that on anyone. Including Ola. But Ola had been a bully and a bitch; Freya wasn't suddenly going to pretend otherwise simply because she had supposedly killed herself. That didn't make any sense.

'So you thought, when you heard the news about the body, maybe they'd found your daughter?' Kristin asked.

Beth had composed herself a little now. She sat up straight and took a few nervous sips of tea. She nodded.

'Do you want to tell us what happened to Ola?' Kristin said.

Gill opened her mouth to respond on Beth's behalf, but Kristin shut it for her again with a glance.

Beth took a deep breath. Taking her time, and with frequent pauses to choke back tears, she told them how seventeen years ago last October Ola had gone to a house party with Liam, her boyfriend, and the two of them hadn't been seen since. Ola and her family had lived in Stromness, but the party was in Harray, a parish about ten miles inland to the north. Liam was a year older than Ola and had a car, so he had come to pick her up a little before seven. The nights were drawing in fast by then and it was already dark by the time they'd left. Beth told Ola to be back by eleven.

But eleven came and went.

'She did that sometimes, stopped out late,' Beth said, dabbing at her eyes again with her tissue. 'She was her own woman, even at sixteen, hard to control at times. But when it got to the small hours of the morning, I started to ring round some folk, parents of the other kids. They all were home, so I didn't know what else to do. I called the police.'

Patrols across the islands were put on the lookout for Liam's car. By daybreak the following morning, they'd found it abandoned at the clifftops at Yesnaby, a notorious suicide spot above the crashing waves of the North Atlantic, not far from Bay of Skaill.

'It wasn't suicide,' Beth said, the steel in her voice so sharp the word made Freya flinch. '*He* killed her.'

Beth looked up then, first at Gill, then everyone else, as if challenging them to say otherwise.

'I've always known it. He killed her then he vanished, and nobody's been looking for him since because they all think he leapt into the bloody sea. And this morning when I saw on Facebook the police had found a body at Skaill, so close to where his car was discovered, well I …'

Nobody spoke. The only sound other than the click of the refrigerator and Beth's feeble sobbing was the low, distant thrum of something heavy and mechanical that seemed to pulse through the walls and the linoleum floor. It had been creeping into Freya's brain since she'd entered the reception this morning, crowding out her thoughts, and it seemed louder now in the silence. She guessed it was the commercial printing presses, somewhere on the far side of the building.

The throb of it built as she waited for someone to ask the obvious question.

They didn't.

'What did the police conclude, Mrs Campbell?'

Beth seemed to shrink into herself. She dabbed her eyes again with her mottled tissue. 'They kept an open mind at first, carried out searches, spoke to the others at the party.'

'And what did they say?'

'They said her and Liam had been there but they'd left early. But nobody would say why or where they were headed.'

Beth looked up, and when their eyes met Freya felt a jolt, like an electric shock, but she stopped herself from looking away.

'There was more to it than that, but those kids were too scared to talk. Something happened at that bloody party. I should never have let … if I had the chance again, I wouldn't …'

'So this morning, hen, when you went over to Skaill,' Gill jumped in, 'what did the police say to you then?'

'I spoke to a young female constable, but she wouldn't let me in or tell me anything. They told me to go home and try not to think on it, that they'd come and see me with any news. But I've been waiting on them for news now for seventeen bloody years, and nothing. So I thought, maybe you …'

She looked again at Gill with pleading eyes.

Gill laid her hand on Beth's. 'If it's your lass who's buried out there, I'll get to the bottom of it, don't you worry.'

Out of the corner of her eye, Freya saw Kristin shift in her seat.

'Chief Inspector Magnus Robertson – he's the Area Commander for the Orkney police force – will be giving a statement later this afternoon,' Gill continued. 'He'll be telling me everything he knows so, if nobody has spoken to you by then, I'll pass whatever he tells me right along to you. How does that sound, sweetheart?'

Beth started to cry again then. Gill rubbed Beth's back and made cooing noises like she was soothing a baby. Freya noticed Kristin glancing over at her and she hoped she was keeping her thoughts from her face.

After she had gathered herself again, Beth thanked everyone for taking the time to listen. Then Gill stood with her and walked her out.

The second they were gone, Sophie jumped into the chair opposite Kristin. 'This is my story, right? I brought Beth in. You can't let Gill take this one as well.'

'What story?' Kristin replied. 'All we've got are the unfounded theories of a sad and desperate old woman. We can't print any of that if we can't stand it up.'

Sophie turned to Freya. 'Did you notice Gill spoke like you weren't even with her this morning?'

Freya nodded, but she hadn't. Her thoughts had been too consumed by the mention of Ola's name.

'She does that all – the – time. What do you think? Did you see anything while you there that might back up what Beth's just said?'

Freya didn't want to answer that, to be drawn into the argument between Sophie and Kristin, but actually she had. Thankfully, before she could be pushed further on the matter, Gill came back through the kitchen door with a sheen on her forehead, a purple flush to her face that suggested she had run back up the stairs.

'I'll type those lines up and add them to this piece I'm doing now, okay, boss?'

Thunder clouds drew over Kristin's face. 'No, not bloody okay. Firstly, Sophie brought Beth in, so if we run any of what's just been said, it's hers. Secondly—'

'But—'

'We didn't agree Beth was on the record.'

'Aye, but she never explicitly told us she wasn't. Bloody hell, she's a grown woman, Kris. This is a newspaper, what did she expect would happen?'

'And thirdly,' Kristin said, ignoring Gill's argument, 'as I've just told Soph, we don't print whatever anyone comes in off the street to tell us. Not unless we can stand it up first. You remember well enough what happened last time – I'm not having my knuckles rapped by Alistair again. Besides, you said DI Muir had told you the bones were ancient.'

'And *she* said he was wrong.'

All eyes turned to Freya again.

'You said that area had been excavated in the Nineties and the body must have been put there since, did you not?'

Fuck's sake, Gill was more observant than Freya had given her credit for.

An uneasy silence followed as everyone waited for Freya to weigh in. She didn't want to. What she was thinking would betray everything Fergus had asked of them. It would mean disagreeing with Kristin and siding with Gill, just as she seemed to be hitting it off with her new boss. But her bloody stupid brain wouldn't stop whirring, picking up patterns and spitting out theories she hadn't asked for.

'There's a chance …'

'A chance of what?' Kristin asked.

Freya's heart sank at her tone. 'There's a chance Beth's right,' she said. 'And I think there's a way to know for certain.'

8

GILL INSISTED ON DRIVING. That meant sitting in her foul-smelling Audi. On the bright side, they wouldn't be going far.

They took the road that rounded the shore of the Peedie Sea, the small lakes cut off from the harbour west of Kirkwall town centre. Freya sat on her hands to stop herself from playing with her ear piercings, but the leather seats felt sticky against her palms and that made her want to jump out of the moving car, so she balled her hands into fists and squeezed them between her knees instead. Thoughts raced behind her eyes, but she was unable to home in on a single one. The stench of stale cigarettes and the hiss of the radio filled her brain with fog. On the dark water beside the road, a flock of swans glided by. It was fitting. Outwardly, Freya was a picture of calm (or so she hoped) but beneath the surface everything was in perpetual motion. She had pissed Kristin off by opening her big mouth and there was pressure now. She *had* to be right. If she was going to get off to a good start with her new editor, she needed this to pan out.

But what if she'd fucked this up already?

'Kristin's right. Feels like a long shot, this,' Gill said beside her. She had been silent since they had left the newsroom. It was too much to hope she would stay that way.

'Maybe,' was all Freya could muster in reply.

The conversation they'd had in the newsroom played on a loop in her mind as they drove.

What makes you think Beth might be right?

Firstly, the drone.

Three faces had frowned back. Three sets of eyes, intense as spotlights, waiting for her to explain. She hated this, speaking in front of others, especially people who were essentially strangers. She hadn't had time to work them out yet, determine how to act around them. And being put on the spot meant there was no chance to plan what to say or how to say it. Her thoughts were chaotic and she needed a moment to organise them. She decided to let it go.

'You know what, I'm probably wrong.'

'No,' Kristin said, leaning forward in her seat. 'I'd like to hear it. What's so odd about them using a drone?'

Nothing, ordinarily. Freya had seen them used plenty on stories she'd covered back in Glasgow. Forensic teams used them to map a scene accurately, or investigate an area that was hard to reach, like a derelict building or an island in the Clyde. But there had been nothing inaccessible about that field at the back of the beach. Plus, there was no chance of getting accurate measurements, due to the high winds. That left one option.

'I think they were using lidar.'

'Lidar? What in God's name is that?' Gill asked.

'It's like radar but with light. Hence the *L, I*.'

Sophie choked back a laugh and Freya realised how cheeky that had sounded, but she hadn't meant it like that. She resisted the urge to reach for her ear piercings and gripped her coffee cup instead. The porcelain and the liquid inside it had already gone cold.

'What does that do?' Kristin asked.

'You can use it to take measurements, but it can also penetrate the ground, identify places where it's been disturbed.'

'Disturbed, as in …?'

'As in dug up.'

She watched her three new colleagues closely. Were they making the same leaps of logic she had? Those SOCOs had been exceptionally keen to use a very expensive piece of kit in weather it clearly couldn't fly in, but why? What had prompted them to keep trying? Having heard Beth's story, Freya thought she now understood.

Like a sheet of ice slowly melting in the sun, she saw the idea creep across the faces in front of her.

'You think they were looking for Liam,' Kristin said.

'Or Ola. We don't know which of them they found, if either.'

'Okay, so what next? You said there was a way we could find out for sure.'

Freya swallowed. 'We could speak to the man who found the remains.'

Her heart shrank with those words. Fergus had explicitly asked them to leave him alone. In return, he had given them more information than he'd needed to. Tracking down the man who had made the discovery this morning was going to damage her relationship with Fergus, but not finding him and hearing what he had to say now meant blowing her fresh start in her new job. What was she supposed to do?

'And how do you suggest we do that?' Gill asked. 'Your Uncle Fergus never told us where to find him. In fact, he said—'

'He's at The Balfour.'

A pulse beat in Freya's temples at Gill's repeated use of the word *uncle*.

'And how do you know that?'

'I saw him being helped into an ambulance this morning. They took him somewhere. My guess would be a hospital.'

Sophie didn't stifle her laughter this time. Freya's comment even brought a grin to Kristin's lips but, yet again, she hadn't meant it to be as smart-arsed as it had sounded, she was simply stating a fact. Still, felt good to get a jab in.

Gill's face flashed beetroot red. 'And say we track him down, hen, what's your plan, then? You think he'll speak to you, aye? And even if he does, what's he going to say? That he's seen a big mess of bones in the ground.'

'What if there was clothing on the remains, something that made them look more human?' Freya said, but to Kristin, not Gill. 'The man had a blanket on him, looked like he was in shock.'

When Freya had done her Highers, she'd known someone who'd worked at Skara Brae. She and the others working there were all either archaeology students or people hoping to go to university to study it. Freya's friend and her co-workers used to volunteer on digs, and it wasn't uncommon for them to uncover human bones. The sight of a skull or a bare femur wouldn't be enough to send someone like that into shock.

She explained this to Kristin, but her boss still needed convincing. 'It's one thing to find bones on a dig, quite another to see them sticking out of a hole in the ground on a dark, windy morning.'

'Sure, but still, I think the only reason he'd be shaken like that was if he saw a bone poking out of a coat sleeve of something. And if he did, maybe he could identify it.'

'It's a long shot,' Kristin said, shaking her head. 'It's been seventeen years, wouldn't everything have rotted away by now?'

'I don't know, maybe not.'

That was a lie, Freya knew it wouldn't. A few years back, she had become enthralled by a story she'd covered in which a teenager had been found dead in Kelvingrove Park with a strange puncture wound in his abdomen. The detectives were unsure what could have caused it. Forensic examiners had eventually worked out it was from a crossbow bolt, and from the shape and size of the hole they had been able to accurately determine not only the model of crossbow used but the angle and distance from which the bolt had been fired. Once a list of owners had been run down and a thorough sweep of CCTV had been completed, police had their suspect in custody within hours. Freya had been so obsessed with how such small details could yield so much information that she had signed up to a course in forensic science online. She even completed a master's degree in the subject in her own time. But doing a seemingly pointless degree outside of work, and talking passionately and apparently obsessively about something besides reality TV or gormless newsroom gossip, had become yet another thing her colleagues in her old job had poked fun at her for. Another item on a long list of reasons Freya was 'a fucking weirdo'. She decided not to share her love of forensics with her new co-workers for now.

At that point, Gill stood up and headed for the door.

'Where are you going?' Kristin asked.

'You heard the woman,' Gill said. 'The one man who can settle this for us is laid up in The Balfour. So that's where I'm headed.'

Of all the things that had changed since Freya had left Orkney, perhaps the most different was The Balfour Hospital.

Freya glanced through the Audi's windscreen as Gill turned into the car park. The Balfour looked like a flying saucer that had landed in a field between Scapa Flow and Kirkwall; a curved white facade sweeping along Foreland Road. It had only been moved to this site a few years ago and it was light years away from the small pebble-dashed cluster of buildings Freya remembered from the doctor's appointments her mother used to drag her to when she was little. She could almost smell the disinfectant as she thought about it, could hear the tinkling of the glass jar of lollypops they used to try and coax her into the treatment rooms.

Gill parked as close as she could to the main entrance without ram-raiding the front doors. 'Right, you stay here.'

Freya frowned. 'Sorry?' That word again.

'Listen, sweetheart, you might know about lidar and whatnot, but I know people. People who work in there and who can tell us where to find this laddie. And they're not going to talk to me with you listening in.'

'You can't go in there and ask where this guy is.'

'I'm not asking for his name and sexual history, am I? I'm simply enquiring as to which ward someone might be found on if they had been brought in with shock this morning.'

Freya shook her head, though she wasn't surprised.

'Like I said, you stay put and I'll—'

Freya unclipped her seatbelt.

9

THEY WALKED TOWARDS THE main entrance in uneasy silence. As they approached the doors, signs appeared for the various departments: *Accident & Emergency, X-Ray, Oncology*. That was when Freya felt the first twinge deep in her stomach.

Automatic doors glided apart with a sigh, giving way to a huge vestibule that looked more like an airport terminal than a hospital. A café with tables outside was to the right, a sweeping reception desk was dead ahead. Spotlights sparkled in the huge ceiling that curved above them. Everything gleamed clinical white.

But the smell … it hit Freya like a left hook she hadn't seen coming.

She froze in the doorway. Gill walked on a few metres before she noticed. She stopped and turned back.

'You coming or not?'

Freya couldn't move. She couldn't answer. Her feet were fixed to the floor. It was that stench, that heady combination of industrial cleaning products and death. The same in hospitals the world over, no matter how modern they looked. She had never considered how she would feel stepping into one for the first time since her 'accident'.

She was blindsided by a memory of the February night she had been rushed to Glasgow Royal, slipping in and out of consciousness, lights flashing past her eyes as she'd heard voices around her yelling. Faces falling in and out of focus. A snatched sound of somebody talking solemnly at her bedside:

Quite frankly, Mr Sinclair, she's lucky to be alive.

When she had fully come around in that strange place with the machines blaring and that god-awful smell crawling up her nose and down into her throat, she'd gagged until she'd almost vomited. She couldn't breathe. Doctors and nurses rushed in, pulled the tubes from her windpipe, and she'd cried and she'd shouted until finally they'd allowed Tom in to see her. Even in her panicked state, she spotted the police officer standing at her door. She and Tom hugged without talking for what felt like forever. Then he'd pulled back and looked at her.

'It was him, wasn't it?' he'd said. 'It was Damien Barber.'

And her grief and her guilt had eaten her alive from the inside.

'Freya!'

She snapped back to the present.

People were staring. Gill was a few metres ahead of her. 'What's the bloody problem now?'

Freya didn't say anything. She couldn't.

She turned and ran.

Outside, she couldn't get the smell out of her lungs quickly enough. She was taking rapid, shallow gulps of air. Her airways had shrunk, her nose and throat closing up. Gill hadn't followed so Freya stood alone in the middle of the path and tried to calm her breathing. But she couldn't. A weight pressed on her chest and she looked around her frantically, like a drowning swimmer searching for something to keep her afloat.

Fuck's sake, Freya, get a grip.

Focus on breathing. People were talking about her, they were staring, but fuck them, she needed to shut everything out and use the techniques her therapist had given her.

Breathe in slowly, count to four.

Hold for four.

Breathe out.

Again and again she did that until, after a few repetitions, the hammer in her chest calmed, her breathing returned to normal. Cupping her hands over her face like she'd been taught, she inhaled through her nose and exhaled through her mouth until the dizziness and light-headedness passed.

She took her hands away from her face. They were still shaking.

There was a sound to her left. At the children's play area, the parents and kids at the swings were gawking at her, making comments under their breath. She wanted to yell at them to get away to fuck and mind their own business but instead she started to run again, her footfalls clapping heavily on the concrete. At the end of the path there was a bench, far away from everyone. She ran to it and threw herself down.

She hadn't had a panic attack like that in months.

A few small drops of rain began to fall. The clouds were growing heavy again, closer. Freya shut her eyes and pinched hard on her ear piercings, counting them forward and back. All she wanted to do was go home to Tom and their little house by the sea. She wanted to hug Luna. She wanted today to be over and to curl up on the sofa eating pizza in front of a show she'd seen a thousand times and she didn't want to have to think about anything else. She took her phone from her pocket, longing for the comforting sight of Tom and Luna on the lock screen, but instead she was met with two notifications. A missed call and a text. The call was an 0141 number. Glasgow. It wasn't a number she had saved in her phone, but she knew who it was. It was the person she had been expecting earlier when Kristin had called. The text announced she had a voicemail.

She deleted both.

That was the fourth voicemail they'd left this week she hadn't listened to.

Footsteps neared. Freya glanced up, saw Gill walking down the path towards her, a grin smeared across her lips. But it shrivelled and died the second she saw Freya's face.

'Jesus, hen, you all right? You're looking peelie-wally.'

'I'm fine,' said Freya, standing.

'What was all that back there?'

Freya didn't answer. They started walking to the Audi. As they did, Freya realised Gill hadn't been in the hospital long. 'So, what happened?'

'He's not there. Discharged home a half-hour ago.'

They got in Gill's car, the reek of cigarettes and sweat now playing second fiddle to the headache brewing behind Freya's eyes.

'What do we do now?'

'We pay him a house call.'

Freya shut her eyes, pinched the bridge of her nose.

'I didn't ask them to give me his address, okay? They just did. It's not my fault if some of the staff in there like to gossip.'

Freya said nothing to that either. She had closed her eyes, not because of anything Gill had done or said, but to shut out the light, ward off the headache rumbling towards her like an articulated lorry with its brakes cut. She was still feeling the lingering fog of the panic attack, but it wasn't just that – it was having to deal with Gill, and coping with this constantly changing day that was going nothing like she had planned, but how could she possibly explain that?

'Look, sweetheart, if you don't like the way I do things, I can drop you off back at the—'

'No, it's not that. It's …' Freya sighed and opened her eyes. She pulled on her seatbelt. 'Let's go see what he knows.'

10

GILL'S CONTACT WITH THE slack attitude to patient confiden-
tiality had given her the name Kyle Laughton. They had also
given her an address in Dounby, a twenty-five-minute drive from
Kirkwall back in the general direction of Skara Brae.

The house was a street back from the main road through the
village. A red Vauxhall Corsa sat on the driveway. Gill pulled to
a stop at the kerb then reached into the back seat for her handbag
and took out her phone.

'Here,' she said, holding it up. Freya had to squint past several
long scratches down the screen. 'This is the story I wrote way
back when. Beth and Liam's granny gave us those photos. That's
what the pair of them were wearing on the night they vanished.'

Two photographs had been placed side by side in a composite
image at the top of the article. On the left, a blonde teenaged
girl with light grey eyes smiled at the camera like she didn't have
a care in the world. On the right, a boy with black hair falling
over dark brown eyes glared out of the screen, like he was trying
to look deep and cool and brooding. Ola wore an unzipped red
puffer jacket with a fur-rimmed hood, and a pale woollen jumper.
Liam was wearing a green bomber jacket and a white New York
Yankees baseball cap. Freya wondered who'd taken the shots.
She'd always been morbidly fascinated by photos used in the
media following some life-altering event – what the people in
them were thinking, if they had any inkling what was in store
for them. Looking at these two young faces, it was hard to
imagine either would contemplate taking their own life, though
of course she understood all too well you could never tell. In her
darker moments, Freya had wondered which photograph of her
the press would have used if she hadn't survived her 'accident'.

'If you're right,' Gill was saying, 'our boy Kyle should recognise
one of these items of clothing. I'd say they're pretty distinctive.'

Gill put her phone back in her purse. As she did, a grin crept out of the corners of her lips.

'You know, hen, since we left the office, I've been thinking about what you said about that lidar thingy. About how it would tell them whether or not the ground had been dug up anyplace.'

Freya said nothing, unsure where Gill was going with this. She still hadn't shaken off her headache. If anything, it was getting worse.

'Well, didn't you also say they'd done excavations in that field quite recently?'

'The Nineties,' Freya said. 'Ninety-eight, to be exact.'

She remembered it well because her dad had taken her to see the dig. It had been open to the public, like the Ness of Brodgar was now.

'Aye, well, if that's the case, wouldn't your lidar whatsit show that?' Gill said, her grin growing into a full-blown smirk. 'Surely it'd show nothing but big holes in that field.'

A red-hot pain pulsed behind Freya's forehead. Gill was right. But the SOCOs probably hadn't known that. They weren't local – they were flown in from Inverness – they wouldn't have been aware of the dig. Freya wanted to say that, but couldn't muster the words, though something else dawned on her then. This morning, she'd wondered if the person who had buried a body at Skara Brae had been stupid or if they had known something she didn't – perhaps it was the latter. Gill was right: the excavations would have hidden a grave from lidar and, even if the body had been put there before lidar had been invented, burying someone at a site that had already been excavated and filled in again made sense in a landscape that was constantly being dug up because of new archaeological finds. It meant it was unlikely to be disturbed again.

'Seems to me we may have spent the past hour on a wild goose chase,' Gill said.

Freya swallowed down the two-word response that immediately sprang to mind and reached for the door handle.

They walked up the path to Kyle's front door in the usual formation. Freya's head was still throbbing and she was struggling to get her thoughts together, let alone summon the energy to turn them into words. She was more than happy for Gill to take the lead. Gill knocked on the door and a few seconds later an angry-looking woman in her late forties opened it. Short black hair framed a face with pale, paper-thin skin. The woman had bags under her eyes you could sleep in.

'I hope you're here to apologise,' she snapped. 'Yous have left my Kyle high and dry this morning. He's not like other boys his age. He shouldn't have to …' She stopped, narrowed her tired eyes at the two women on the doorstep. 'You're not the polis.'

'No, Mrs Laughton, I'm Gill Irvine with *The Orcadian*. I'd like to speak to your Kyle about—'

The door swung shut, but Gill stuck her foot in it, causing it to bounce open again. Mrs Laughton's pale face flushed purple with rage. 'Get your foot out of my doorway or you'll have my foot up the crack of your arse.'

'Mrs Laughton, we're here on behalf of a poor, desperate woman whose daughter went missing some time ago. Ola Campbell. Maybe you remember?'

Gill held up her phone to show her the article.

Mrs Laughton glanced at the screen. She folded her arms. 'What's that got to do with my boy?'

'We have reason to believe the body he found this morning might have been Ola, and that some of her clothing might have survived. We just want to ask him about it.'

'No, forget it.'

'Mrs Laughton, you'd be helping a woman who—'

'Look, I'm sorry about this poor woman, but my boy's got Asperger's and he doesn't do well talking to strangers, especially ones from the press. He's already been through enough for one day.'

That knot yanked tighter at the sound of that word, *Asperger's*.

'Those doctors should never have left him as long as they did without calling me,' Mrs Laughton continued. 'Those detectives should've known better too. So I'm sorry, you'll have to find another—'

'Mam?'

Mrs Laughton fell silent and turned to the sound of the voice. Behind her, along the dark hallway, was the man Freya had seen this morning. He looked taller than before, at least a couple of inches over six feet. He had a mop of black hair hanging over his eyes and he looked ghostly white, like he was on the verge of vomiting. Maybe the hospital had let him go too soon. Or perhaps being there had made him like this.

He glanced past his mother at Freya and Gill on the doorstep. 'I want to help.'

'Can we show you a picture?' Gill asked. 'It's of a peedie lassie whose mammy wants to know what happened to her.'

Freya's palms stung as she clenched her fists. That voice. That fucking tone. Kyle worked at the busiest tourist attraction in Orkney, was senior enough to be opening the place up by himself, and here was Gill talking to him like a sodding five-year-old who couldn't wipe his own arse. She thought about the missed call and the voicemail and wondered if this was how people would talk to her once they knew.

Kyle pulled at a loose flap of skin next to a fingernail. As he moved into the light, Freya saw the ends of each of his fingers were red raw, like they had been picked at again and again. Was this Kyle's way of stimming, of regulating his emotions? Freya had been asked if she did anything similar when she had undergone her autism assessment a few weeks ago back in Glasgow. She hadn't been sure. She had thought about the way she liked to count her ear piercings and press on them till her fingertips burned, and how that always seemed to make her feel better, but she wasn't sure if that was what the assessor had been looking for and so she never mentioned it.

'I don't want my name in the paper,' Kyle said. 'There's a term you use, isn't there, when you don't want what you say to be printed?'

'Off the record,' Freya heard herself say, surprising herself with the sound of her own voice. 'We won't print what you tell us, certainly not with your name or anything that could identify you. If what you see in the photograph confirms the body is Ola, we'll tell the police and let them speak to her mother and we won't print anything until that happens.'

She ignored the look that earned her from Gill.

'You don't have to do this, Kyle. Not if it's going to be too much for you,' Kyle's mum said. Freya noticed she spoke to him in the same tone as Gill.

Kyle tore a long strip of soft flesh from his finger, making Freya shudder.

Gill didn't seem to notice, she simply held up her phone. 'What do you say, young man? Will you tell us if any of the clothing in this photograph matches what you saw?'

Kyle took a few tentative steps towards the door. As he drew level with his mother, she put her arm around him and squeezed his shoulders tightly. It was evident how much she cared for him, how much she wanted to protect him, and right then Freya thought about Tom, and that knot in her stomach became so tight she thought she might double over. The whiff of Gill's perfume and nicotine breath caught in her nostrils, like it had suddenly grown stronger, and for the first time she noticed the smell of damp coming from inside the house. She began to feel faint and fought an overwhelming urge to run back to the car, but that wasn't far enough. She didn't want to be here, and she felt her hand go for her ear. Kyle's mum saw it, and Freya snatched her hand away quickly, put it in her coat pocket.

She no longer cared if Kyle saw anything in the photo, she just wanted to go.

But Kyle was taking his time. He showed no emotion as he stared, unblinking, at the faces on the screen. His eyes shifted over their features, taking it all in, but nothing sparked a reaction.

A curtain twitched at the house next door.

This was taking too long.

Gill glared at Freya, who realised her leg was twitching. She was hopping from one foot to the other. She forced herself to stand still and focused again on Kyle and, as she did, something cracked. It started with his eyes. They fixed on a single point on the screen, didn't shift. Next, his bottom lip began to quiver, like the first barely perceptible tremors of an earthquake. Something so small, it could easily have been missed.

Kyle reached for the phone and pinched his fingers to zoom in on the photo of Ola. Not on an article of clothing, but of jewellery – a gold necklace hanging around her neck. Freya hadn't spotted it before against the pale colour of Ola's jumper. It looked like it spelled out her name.

Kyle left his sore and mangled fingers resting on the pixellated image of Ola's necklace as a single tear rolled down his cheek. He opened his mouth, but like Freya before, he couldn't summon his voice.

Eventually, he found it. 'She's still wearing it.'

11

SHE HATED USING THE phone, yet the first thing Freya did when they got back to the newsroom was call Fergus.

He was silent a long time before he spoke. 'How did you find him?'

'Gill knew somebody who knew him.'

'Aye, I bet she did.'

She could feel his disappointment seeping out of the receiver, but he wasn't as seething as she had expected. Maybe, given Gill's reputation, he had anticipated this. Which begged the question, why had he told them anything at all?

Even now, Freya was surprised to find Fergus relatively forthcoming.

'We'd already made the connection between the necklace and Ola Campbell,' he told her. 'We'll be sending someone round to her mother's place this afternoon.'

'We won't print anything until you do.'

Freya hoped that might appease him a little. All she got was static.

'So, what happens next?'

'We get the bones out of the ground and we go from there.'

'They still haven't been excavated?'

Another pause, then: 'It's a delicate process.'

Freya waited for him to elaborate. He didn't.

'How long do you think it will take?'

'I doubt we'll be done before dark now. Most likely we'll have to pause until the morn.'

'Then what?'

'Once they're up, they'll be sent away to Aberdeen for examination. We don't have the facilities for that here.'

More silence filled the line.

'It goes without saying you can't quote me on any of this,' Fergus said eventually.

'Why did you tell us about the body this morning? You didn't have to speak to us at all – you and I could've caught up another time. Or you could've "no comment"-ed every question Gill asked you.'

'You said it yourself. Someone had already seen it. Word was going to get out sooner or later. It always does here.'

That didn't explain why he had told them about Kyle. They had only been able to confirm the body was Ola's because of him.

She heard a deep sigh on the other end of the line. Several more moments of silence passed between them before finally Fergus said, 'MIT will get involved now. It'll be taken out of my hands. Congratulations on your big story, Freya.'

Then he hung up.

Later that afternoon, he surprised Freya by calling back again to tell her officers had spoken to Beth, so they were free to print whatever they liked. He was as curt as he had been earlier, but the fact he had made the call meant he couldn't have been too angry. Freya knew it was her default to assume everyone was pissed off with her for some reason she didn't understand, and often she was wrong, like she had been about Kristin. Her editor was all smiles now as she handed out assignments and made last-minute changes to the week's print edition, which would go to press in the next twenty-four hours.

Once the story hit the internet, *The Orcadian*'s social media channels lit up. Talk turned from who the body might be to who had put her there. Judging by the comments, there was no point discussing anyone else. The outpouring of hatred towards Liam took Freya aback, although he was the obvious suspect – two people go missing, one body gets found; doesn't take a genius to make the next leap. But Freya was going to keep an open mind. One of the pieces she'd been given to write for the print edition was a sidebar on the original investigation. Before starting it, she wanted to get her hands on every last piece of information she could, so she took herself down to archives to read through the old stories. Gill's byline was all over them like stains on a rag. She moved quickly through each article but made sure she read every last word, keen to absorb as much information as possible. Most of what she read had been cobbled together from party-line police statements, or generic soundbites the Chief Inspector at that time – a man named Allan Tait – had thrown Gill's way. Fergus was mentioned too – though he had been *DS* Muir then – and a DI Jim Shearer. Freya didn't recognise Tait or Shearer from the photographs that went with the articles, but she knew their names; they were men who had worked with her dad, and she had heard him talking about them around the dining table.

Another name jumped out at her as she read: Sergeant Magnus Robertson. His wasn't a name she knew from her dad; Gill had mentioned him earlier. He was the current Area Commander. According to the story, he had found Liam's blue BMW abandoned at Yesnaby. The ignition had been on but the engine was dead, having run out of petrol, and the doors had been left open. Liam's and Ola's wallet, purse, and mobile phones had been left inside on the leather seats. This had led the police to a conclusion of suicide and, judging from Gill's reporting, they had reached it quickly. The same day that Liam's car had been found, in fact. The search had continued for several days afterwards, but each statement from the police had included the same line from Chief Inspector Tait: 'The sad truth of the matter is, we have to consider the strong possibility that the couple tragically took their own lives at Yesnaby.'

Beth and the community had disagreed. They had blamed Liam.

They still did.

12

FREYA FELT LIKE SHE had done a full week's work by the end of her first day.

She had excuses ready when Kristin and Sophie invited her out for a drink at the gin place by the harbour in town. She liked them both, but she had nothing left in the tank, was all small-talked out, and she especially couldn't face trying to act sociable in a loud and unfamiliar bar. She didn't tell them that, she simply said she had plans with Tom and they accepted it. Though she knew there would come a time when they wouldn't.

For everyone else, it seemed, being around people was the thing they craved most, and nobody ever understood it when Freya tried to tell them she preferred to be alone. She didn't know how to explain that if she was sitting in a bar, she overheard every conversation, she could smell the collective alcohol breath of everyone in there, she could feel whatever it was that had been spilled on the floor and was now sticking to the soles of her shoes, and while she was being bombarded with all of that unwanted information she was having to remember to make eye contact – but not too much – and she was processing what was being said to her, then trying to think of the appropriate thing to say back, then anticipating what she might get as a reply. And when your whole world was like that, sitting in a bar wasn't so fun anymore. But people either couldn't or wouldn't understand that, so it was easier for them to chalk you up as anti-social.

A loner.

A fucking weirdo.

It had happened to her before; she knew it was only a matter of time until it happened again.

On the drive to Orphir, a familiar, unsettled feeling stirred in her stomach. She couldn't place it, but then she never could – it was more a general inkling she'd said something wrong or somehow acted weird during the day, and now Kristin and Sophie would be sipping gin and talking about what a freak the new girl was, banging on about lidar and drones and other freaky shite. Past the edge of town, the world beyond her headlights disappeared into the inky night, bringing the imagined demons more vividly to life. The feeling in her stomach didn't settle until she turned onto the track to their house and she caught sight of the lights in the windows.

After living in a flat in Glasgow's Southside for the past five years, she and Tom decided they wanted to stay somewhere more rural. They had found a two-bedroomed former croft close to the shore at Orphir Bay. It had the calm waters of Scapa Flow on one side, rising moorland on the other, and the nearest neighbour was a five-minute walk away. Luna had heard the car on the uncovered track and was waiting by the front door when Freya opened it, tail wagging so hard her whole back end wriggled from side to side. When she jumped up and planted her paws on Freya's chest and licked her face, Freya only half pushed her away.

'That you?' Tom called from somewhere.

'No,' Freya yelled back, making herself grin.

She found him in the kitchen at the back of the house, taking two huge homemade pizzas out of the oven. She leaned against the doorframe and smiled as she watched him juggle the two trays before plonking them down on the worktop. Making meals from scratch, eating less carry-out, was all part of their plan to enjoy a quieter pace of life here. And to be fair, Tom was getting pretty good at it. He wasn't starting his new job as an engineer with the European Marine Energy Centre in Stromness until after Christmas, so he'd had time to practise. Freya noticed he'd set the table already and had put drinks out for them both. She also spotted he'd packed away some of the stuff that had been lying around in boxes. As he had been for the past few months, he was doing everything he could to make sure Freya didn't have to lift a finger. Like a candle caught in a sudden draught, Freya's smile flickered and dwindled as she remembered why.

Tom set the pizzas down on the kitchen table then came over to her and wrapped her up in the tightest hug. His soft, woollen jumper smelled of woodsmoke from the log burner in the lounge.

'How was your first day?'

'Eventful.'

They kissed then Freya went to the bathroom, swapped out her contact lenses for her glasses and put on her pyjamas, then she came back through to the kitchen to eat. Luna had placed herself on the floor next to Freya's chair; no matter how hungry Freya got, or how good the food tasted, she wouldn't ever finish a meal without sharing some with Luna, and that dog knew it.

'So, I've been keeping up with your stories on the website all afternoon,' Tom said as they tucked in. 'I can't believe how much has happened.'

'How do you know they were mine? We don't get bylines on the website, only in the print edition.'

'Aye, well, I figured yours were the good ones.'

'Smooth.'

'That wasn't bad, was it?'

'Cooking me pizza, coming out with lines like that. If I didn't know any better, I'd say someone's trying to get lucky tonight.'

'How am I doing?'

Freya took a sip of the beer Tom had bought. It was from the local Swannay Brewery and, like the pizza, much to her liking. She held up her bottle. 'Couple more of these and we'll see.'

She felt herself relax as his grin lit up the room. When things were like this, like they used to be, she could almost trick herself into believing nothing had changed.

She told Tom how they had discovered the body was Ola's, plus everything she had read that afternoon. 'Everyone's saying Liam must have killed her.'

'Makes sense,' Tom said while chewing. 'If they've found her but not him.'

'Yeah, but they've been saying it since they first went missing.'

'People must have a reason to think that, though, right?'

Not as far as Freya could tell. In the articles she had read, people complained there had always been something off about Liam. They called him cold, distant, aloof, but that was hardly damning evidence – Freya had been called the same before now. What had really caught her eye were the accounts that said, before he'd got with Ola, Liam always seemed to have a different girlfriend each month. And people had rightly questioned how a seventeen-year-old studying for his Highers, living with his nan, could afford a brand new BMW M3.

Freya had wondered the same thing, but she still doubted how much stock she could put in these stories, given all of them had been written by Gill. Her new colleague had seemingly only bothered to speak to Beth and people who had been friends with Ola, all of whom had described her as a saint, of course.

'So, this Ola and Liam, did you know them?'

Tom was grinning again. This was the same bloody joke he'd been making since they had crossed the Pentland Firth, which took the piss seeing as he was from a small town in the Southern Uplands that was home to more sheep than people.

'Actually, yeah, I knew Ola.'

'Seriously?'

'We went to the same high school.'

'Were you close?'

'Not exactly.'

She told him how Ola had been in the year above her and had occasionally picked on her, without going into specifics. She didn't mention the Harry Donaldson incident.

Tom's grin slipped away. He reached across the table and held Freya's hand. 'She sounds like an absolute bitch.'

'That's what I said.'

'Well maybe someone besides Liam had a motive for doing her in.'

Freya shuddered as she considered that. The feeling took her by surprise and she needed a moment to work out what had caused it, but she soon figured it out: someone *she* knew had been murdered. Freya had covered some horrific events in

Glasgow, had met the families and (in the cases that weren't murders or suicides) the victims themselves. But thinking about someone she had known personally, even someone she had never liked, meeting their end in such a savage way made her feel funny in a manner she couldn't describe.

She looked up. Tom was staring down at his plate, lost in his own thoughts too. She felt a tightness creep across her shoulder blades. 'What is it?'

He lifted his head, met her eyes. 'Hmm?'

'What's wrong?'

'Oh, nothing, it's just …' He smiled, but there was no joy in it. 'It's crazy, isn't it? All this.'

She knew what was coming. 'This isn't the same as what I had on in Glasgow, you know.'

Tom pushed some pizza crust around his plate. He nodded but said nothing.

'It isn't. Sure, this is all I've been writing about today, but give it a week and I'll be covering county fairs and council meetings and fights down the Co-op like we expected.'

'How do you figure that?'

'Because where has it got left to go? There's going to be a press conference tomorrow morning, the Area Commander will be trying to get us to turn the heat up on Liam, get the public's help with finding him. But he's long gone.' She squeezed Tom's hand. 'It's been seventeen years since the last development in this story, it could be another seventeen until the next.'

Tom nodded, though he didn't seem convinced. 'Unless Liam decides to come back, get revenge on the journalist who discovered it was his girlfriend buried under the sand.'

He tried to laugh, like he was joking again, but Freya knew he wasn't and she wanted to scream.

The Tom she had met in a dank student bar in Edinburgh fourteen years ago was the most laid-back guy in the world. He had always been the calm yin to Freya's chaotic yang, and it worked, they levelled each other out. One of the many things she loved about being with Tom was she never felt the need to apologise for who she was. He not only accepted but loved all the little things that made her different, and so when she was with him she never felt like a freak or a fucking weirdo.

But since February that had changed. Ten months ago Freya had been hit by a car and almost killed – she had just left the glass-and-steel offices of *The Herald* after yet another argument with her editors and she had found herself wandering the pavement in the pouring rain, watching the traffic stream down Fullarton Road, when the next thing she knew she had heard car horns wailing, the shriek of tyres unable to grip. A witness said they'd noticed a man fleeing the scene on foot. As Freya had told the police she couldn't remember how she ended up in the road, the witness had to be taken seriously. Tom knew Freya had been writing stories about some dangerous people, people who wouldn't think twice about pushing a person they disliked into traffic. One man in particular had stood out.

It was him, wasn't it? It was Damien Barber.

Tom had begged Freya to tell the police about the man she had been investigating for a series of sexual assaults, and Freya had finally agreed. There was more to the whole situation than Tom knew, but since then he had been terrified to let her out of his sight. He had wrapped her up in cotton wool. It made her feel like she was incapable of looking after herself.

An image sprang to mind then of Kyle's mother putting her arm around her son as Gill spoke to him like a dribbling baby.

Something must have shown on her face because Tom tried to rally himself. He squeezed her hand and smiled. 'Hey, go check the fridge.'

He stood to clear the dishes away while Freya went to the refrigerator by the back door. Inside, she found two slices of Orkney fudge cheesecake on a plate on the top shelf.

'Oh, you definitely are trying to get lucky.'

'Told you I'd find us some.'

She took out the desserts then nudged the door shut with her hip. As she did, an envelope on the counter by the back door caught her eye.

'Careful!'

Tom dashed over and grabbed the plate from Freya's hand before it fell. He followed her gaze to the worktop. 'It was on the doormat when I got home.'

Freya took the letter off the counter. In the top right-hand corner was an *NHS Greater Glasgow and Clyde* logo. Beneath that, the words *Adult Autism Team*.

They sat back at the table. Tom put the desserts to one side while Luna began to lick at Freya's hands. Maybe she could sense her unease and wanted to soothe her. Or perhaps it was because her fingers tasted of pizza. Probably the latter, but Freya didn't mind. It felt nice.

'I didn't think you'd want to open it tonight,' Tom was saying. 'I mean, after everything you've had on today.'

Freya simply nodded.

'I can't believe they didn't do this over the phone. I know they would've done it in person if we hadn't moved, but they could've at least called to let you know it was coming.'

She said nothing to that either.

'It doesn't matter, you know,' she could hear Tom saying. 'Whatever it says, it doesn't matter.'

'It does.'

'There's nothing wrong with being autistic. It doesn't mean you're any less capable than any—'

'I know! Christ, that's not what you think I'm worried about, is it?'

'Then what?'

Freya turned the envelope over. She picked at the seal with her thumbnail but couldn't bring herself to peel it open. She didn't answer Tom's question, she wasn't sure how to explain what she was feeling. She still didn't completely understand it herself.

Tom left his chair, came to kneel beside her. He put his arms around her, pulled her in close.

'What's in there doesn't change a thing,' she heard him whisper by her ear. 'It won't change who you are, who you've always been. You're the kindest, smartest, most incredible person I know.'

Freya wiped her cheek with the back of her hand and smiled. 'You're still trying to get laid, aren't you?'

Tom leaned back and looked at her. He smiled too. 'Well, you've got to respect me for trying.' He stood up, took the envelope and placed it on the table, then he held out his hand. 'Come on, you don't need to open this tonight. We'll do it whenever you're ready.'

Tom put the cheesecakes back in the fridge and they went through into the lounge, curled up on the sofa together in front of the fire, and watched episodes of *The Good Place* until Tom fell asleep.

But Freya couldn't.

She sat awake in the glow of the dying embers, thinking about the past, worrying about the future. She stared into the hearth and she stroked Luna's soft ears and she slowly spiralled into a panic over a multitude of newly imagined demons that would be waiting for her tomorrow.

* * *

It starts pissing down as I reach the factory car park. I've been expecting it, the sky's looked threatening all afternoon, yet somehow it's still caught me unprepared.

I don't rush upstairs. My heart sinks and water pools on the lino-leum floor with every begrudging step. In the break room I'm hit by the heat. At least I'll be dry by the time my shift starts. Glynis, the elderly shift manager whose office is the room next door, keeps the thermostat cranked up on this floor.

'Thin skin,' she always tells me. 'The price of getting old. You'll know that yourself someday.'

I always smile back, always wonder, 'Will I?'

This is just temporary, I tell myself – a job to keep me afloat while I get back on my feet. It's been keeping me afloat for five years now. Barely. I remember seeing the regulars huddled together in the break room on my first day and thinking I'd fucking kill myself before accepting this as my life. Only one's left now: Digger. He's in his usual spot at the regulars' table and he nods at me as I take my place across from him, jerks his chin at the TV. He's watching Countdown, *the volume turned up so loud over the background moan of machinery that the TV rattles as the music plays and the large clock ticks down to the deadline. Two grown men are on the screen, furrows in their brows as they search for a nine-letter word in the jumble* CENEVAGEN. *Neither manages it.*

'Some tough ones the day,' he says.

I ask him if he got it, but he's turned back to the TV already and doesn't hear me, doesn't reply. I rub my eyes, look around the room. It's filling up, people ready to start their shift. Most of them temp workers, by the looks of it. They're not so much younger than me and I see the glances they give me and Digger. There was a time that would've angered me, but that time has passed. I don't get angry like I used to, these days. I don't feel anything much like I used to. I sit back in my plastic seat, close my eyes for a second, and let their inane chatter and the drone of the factory floor wash over me as I prepare myself for another shift. Another twelve hours of my life pissed away stuffing clinical wipes or sachets of sauce into tiny boxes. The fuck am I doing here?

Where the fuck else would I be if I wasn't?

I hear Digger talking as I'm on the edge of a dream.

'Terrible business, this.'

I peel open my eyes.

Countdown *has gone, replaced by the news. Shots of a windswept beach scarred by police tape. Mounds in the earth where old stones are laid.*

A shiver travels the length of my spine.

Digger says, 'You don't expect it. Not in a place like that.'

'No. You don't.'

The picture switches to show a photograph of a teenaged girl. Blonde hair, grey eyes. A smile that tells a thousand lies.

I recognise that red jacket.

The necklace.

The newsreader talks over the image in a voice so loud I feel it in my teeth, yet I don't hear a single word he says.

Digger's talking too, might've asked, 'Whit's the matter? Dinnae tell me she was a friend of yours?'

I hear myself say, 'No. Not really.'

I've been expecting this day for seventeen years, and yet it's still somehow caught me unprepared.

The story changes as the bell sounds for the start of the shift and folk start heading for the factory floor, and it's funny how the mind works. Right there and then, I know what word the men on that game show had been searching for.

TUESDAY, 20 DECEMBER

13

THE CRAMPED MEETING ROOM on the first floor of Kirkwall Police Station smelled of bad coffee and morning breath.

Between the table at the far end of the room and the camera crews from BBC Scotland and STV News setting up by the door, there was barely space to cram two rows of plastic chairs, only some of which matched, most of which must have been hastily snatched from elsewhere in the building. Kristin had already told Freya there was no dedicated media briefing room here, no local media relations team like there had been at the stations down south. Ordinarily in Orkney, there was no need for such things.

Freya sat in the centre of the front row, struggling to keep another headache at bay. The room was hot but she didn't unzip her yellow raincoat. She had the collar pulled over her mouth and nose again, partly to block out the smell, mostly because it soothed her, but not much. She hadn't slept well, had maybe managed an hour or two that had been disturbed by fitful dreams. It had tired her out more than staying awake would have done. Fatigue was making her paranoid, she knew that, but in the darkest hours she had convinced herself that Gill had noticed something about her was 'off', that somehow she knew about her autism assessment. Freya wasn't worried about being diagnosed as autistic; in fact, the opposite was true. After she had been referred, she had scoured the internet for information, had watched videos and read blogposts by so many people who said getting a diagnosis had transformed them from feeling like a failed human being to understanding they were a perfectly normal autistic person, and Freya had felt that so deeply it had made her cry. So, what did it mean if she wasn't autistic? Tom was right in a sense: that letter wouldn't change who she was, the difficulties she faced, but it would surely help explain them. She desperately wanted answers. She wanted to tear that envelope open and know. But what if she opened it and it didn't give her a diagnosis, what then?

After what had happened at Kyle's house yesterday, the way his mother told them he'd 'got Asperger's', like it was some kind of fucking disease, and the condescending voice Gill had used, Freya knew that getting a diagnosis wouldn't be a silver bullet. How were people going to treat her once they knew? Tom was already behaving like she was some kind of fragile ornament, would this only make him worse? Her hand crept into her coat pocket for the thousandth time that morning and she ran her thumb along the sharp edges of the unopened envelope. One way or another, whatever was waiting inside it was going to present a challenge she knew she wasn't ready to face.

She only realised her eyes were closed when Gill's voice roused her. She could hear her somewhere behind her, talking shite to some poor bastard who hadn't been able to get away in time. She'd dragged Freya to the front to hold their seats then gone off to blether. Still, better she was bending someone else's ear than feeding Freya's burgeoning headache.

She turned and took a tentative glance around the small room, saw it was filling up, but she didn't recognise any of the faces other than Gill's. She didn't think *The Herald* would bother sending a reporter so far north when they could simply lift copy off an agency wire, but that had troubled her during the night too. The Ola Campbell story had attracted significant attention since they had broken it yesterday afternoon, so there was every chance someone would come. Whoever they sent, Freya wanted to make sure she saw them first.

'Morning, all.'

The sound of a booming voice snapped her from her thoughts. Turning, she saw a man in full police uniform striding past reporters to the table at the front, a stack of briefing notes tucked under his right arm. The odd flecks of grey in the neatly trimmed black hair beneath his peaked cap put him in his early-to-mid-forties. His rank as Chief Inspector, and Kristin's mention of

Magnus Robertson being Alistair Sutherland's golfing buddy, had conjured an image of someone much older.

Fergus followed Chief Inspector Robertson a few seconds later carrying a scuffed and battered-looking laptop. He wore the same black suit as yesterday and the scruff on his cheeks was quickly becoming a beard. He was joined by a middle-aged woman in a grey trouser suit with her mousy brown hair pulled back into a long ponytail. Fergus and the woman joined the Chief Inspector at the table, which had been set up in front of a white backdrop with the Police Scotland insignia and the words *Orkney Islands Area Command* emblazoned across it in blue. There was a dirty smudge in the top right-hand corner. No doubt it had been left unused in a storage room somewhere for years before being plucked out into service this morning.

Gill came scuttling back over. She plonked herself down, got her pen and notepad ready as everyone took their seats. An expectant hush fell over the room as Robertson surveyed the gathered press with a tight grin. Fergus unbuttoned his suit jacket, opened the laptop. He was sitting only a few feet in front of Freya and seemed to be doing his best not to catch her eye. The woman in the grey suit unscrewed one of the bottles of water on the table and poured some into her glass and one for each of the men. She looked the kind of heavy tired that came from years in a tough job, but she exuded a calm authority and seemed the most relaxed of the three. Freya guessed she was with MIT.

'Good morning, ladies and gentlemen. For those of you who don't know, my name is Chief Inspector Magnus Robertson, Area Commander for the Orkney Islands. With me are Detective Chief Inspector Jess Macintosh from the North Command's Major Investigation Team, and Detective Inspector Fergus Muir of Kirkwall CID.'

A camera flashed. Someone coughed. Chief Inspector Robertson explained there was a lot to go over and therefore it would be appreciated if the good folk of the media would leave all questions until the end. He began by running through the events of yesterday morning, all of which were in the previous day's statement. He added that, due to the painstaking forensic processes which needed to be followed, the excavation of the bones was still ongoing and he asked the press and public to keep away from Skara Brae.

Freya should perhaps have tweeted some of it, as per her brief from Kristin, but she was struggling to focus. It wasn't only the heat from the TV lights and the stench of stale breath; her dad had been stationed here, had brought her in once or twice when she was little to see where he worked. She remembered these long, grey corridors and pokey dark rooms which didn't look much different from how they had when he was alive. She could feel his ghost everywhere.

'Following the rumours reported in yesterday's press,' Robertson continued, 'I can confirm that items of partially decomposed clothing and jewellery have been found on the remains which appear to match those worn by Ola Campbell when she was last seen on 1 October 2005.'

There was the clatter of camera shutters, the scuttle of fingers across keyboards. Everybody had this information, of course, but confirmation from the investigative team was still a big deal. Freya unlocked her phone to post the news on social media, knowing she was about to get the same slew of replies as yesterday – people pointing the finger at Liam, folk angry at the police for letting him get a seventeen-year head start.

Her thumb was poised over *send* when Robertson said, 'Furthermore …'

The sound of clicking keys subsided.

'Earlier this morning, after resuming the forensic investigation of the scene, a second set of human remains was found. Once again, partially decomposed clothing and items of jewellery were found on these remains which appear to be consistent with those worn by Liam McDonnell when he—'

The room erupted with questions.

14

THE CHIEF INSPECTOR RAISED his hands. He waited for the voices to settle, the burst of camera bulbs to subside. Once they had, he handed the reins to DCI Macintosh.

'Thank you, Magnus. Good morning, everyone,' she said. 'There will be a chance for questions in a moment, but first, I want to ask the public for your help.'

DCI Macintosh glanced over the reporters' heads as she spoke, looking directly into the cameras at the back of the room. She explained, given the clothing and jewellery that had been discovered, the fact the bodies had been found together, plus their location near the site where Liam's car had been abandoned, there was enough for the police to proceed on the assumption that these were the remains of Ola Campbell and Liam McDonnell, pending formal identification from the forensic anthropologist. As a result, the case had been referred to MIT, as was protocol with any complex investigation in Scotland.

'We will be working alongside Kirkwall CID because their local knowledge is going to be crucial, as is yours,' DCI Macintosh continued. 'In any investigation, the first forty-eight hours are key, but in this instance, the person or persons we're looking for have had seventeen years to cover their tracks. That's why we need your assistance more than ever.'

She nodded at Fergus, who pressed a key on the laptop. A large TV had been set up beside the table and this now showed a satellite image of West Mainland taken from Google Earth. The locations of Harray, Yesnaby, and Bay of Skaill were all marked with small yellow dots, roughly forming a long, sharp triangle, like a spearhead, lying on its side. Harray lay at the tip, inland to the east, while the short distance between Yesnaby and Bay of Skaill along the Atlantic coast to the west formed the base.

Referring only occasionally to her notes, DCI Macintosh recounted the events of Saturday, 1 October 2005, as they had been described in the original investigation. According to witnesses, Liam and Ola had attended a house party at an address in Harray, hosted by friends of Ola. The pair were seen leaving together, sometime between nine and nine thirty, in Liam's blue BMW M3, which was then discovered by police at Yesnaby with the doors open and the ignition still on at ten fourteen the following morning.

'We want to know what happened in those thirteen hours,' Macintosh said. 'Crucially, we need to understand Ola's and Liam's movements. Did they go directly to Yesnaby, or did they travel elsewhere first? Were they going to meet someone? And how did they subsequently end up two miles away to the north at Bay of Skaill?'

Fergus clicked the laptop again and the image changed to the photographs Freya had seen yesterday, the ones of Ola and Liam that the media used when they first disappeared. A third picture showed Liam's car with a clear view of the front registration plate.

'Somebody out there knows the answers.' DCI Macintosh knotted her fingers together, leaned forward. 'Maybe you saw them that night. Or perhaps you saw something else; a person or a group of people acting suspiciously which you never thought to report before. Any detail, no matter how small, may prove significant.'

Another laptop click and information appeared on screen detailing how to contact the investigative team. DCI Macintosh wrapped up by stating that, where possible, all witnesses from the initial investigation would be reinterviewed, and she appealed again for anyone with any new information to come forward.

After that, Chief Inspector Robertson opened the floor to questions.

'How were Ola and Liam killed?'

DCI Macintosh took it. 'Because of the level of decomposition, we may never know for certain, but we should hopefully get some idea in the next few days, once the remains have been examined by the forensic anthropologist. In the meantime, there are a couple of lines of enquiry we'll be pursuing based on the forensic findings so far, but we won't be sharing those publicly.'

'Why not?'

'Because you don't need to know them yet,' the DCI replied. 'And because it might be hurtful to the families of the deceased.'

'Before, you said person or *persons* responsible,' someone directly behind Freya said. Her heart lunged at the sound of their voice. It sounded familiar, but she told herself it was just her fatigue-induced paranoia. 'What makes you think there may have been more than one killer?'

Again, the DCI answered. 'A couple of things, some of which I can't go into, but needless to say, killing two young, fit people who may have been trying to defend themselves, then burying their bodies, is no easy feat for one person. So at this stage we're simply keeping an open mind.'

The distance between the car and the burial site probably meant the victims were moved after they were murdered, Freya thought, which wouldn't have been straightforward for someone on their own. The police had quickly jumped to an incorrect conclusion of suicide due to how the car had been found. Had that been planned? It seemed that way. Surely it was more likely Liam and Ola had been killed at Bay of Skaill, or somewhere else, then the BMW had been dumped at Yesnaby after the fact.

She felt a familiar flutter of butterflies in her stomach as she began formulating the right words to ask the question, putting them in order, but someone else beat her to it.

'Is it not possible the car was dumped at Yesnaby by the killer or killers to throw the police off the scent, make you think the couple had killed themselves? A tactic, it seems, which worked quite well.'

Freya saw Fergus' eyes narrow at that jab, but if there was an emotion on Chief Inspector Robertson's face, she couldn't read it.

DCI Macintosh fielded the question a third time. 'It's entirely possible the car was moved, yes, and it's something else we'll be looking into. Though I do believe it was something that was considered during the original investigation.'

Macintosh glanced past the Area Commander to Fergus, who shifted forward in his seat. 'It was …' He coughed, cleared his throat. He took a sip of water and continued. 'It was something we looked at, yes. We had a forensic team go through the car with a fine-tooth comb and nothing was found that couldn't be accounted for.'

'What does that mean?'

'It means your smart comment wasn't as smart as you thought it was, boy.'

'What DI Muir is saying' – Robertson stepped in – quickly, 'is that the car was fully examined and, other than a few prints and fibres, none of which proved to be suspicious, there was nothing to indicate anybody else had been inside the vehicle. There was no sign of any attempt to clean the car down, no traces of blood. And look, we all know hindsight is 20/20, but given the evidence available to the detectives at the time, I believe it was reasonable for them to reach the conclusions they did.'

'What about the reports at the time that Liam was mixed up with drugs coming in from the south?' someone else asked. 'Is that being investigated as a possible motive?'

'Those were rumours, nothing more,' Chief Inspector Robertson said in a level voice. Unlike Fergus, he was managing to respond without becoming ruffled. 'There was no evidence of Liam being involved in criminal activity of any variety. The witness testimonies and evidence seventeen years ago suggested that Liam and Ola were young lovers who tragically took their own lives.'

'But clearly mistakes were made,' someone else added. A voice coming from beside Freya. 'Is the Chief Inspector now willing to admit that the tragic deaths of Ola Campbell and Liam McDonnell are yet another case the Orkney police has failed to investigate properly?' Gill asked.

Fergus pushed his tongue against the inside of his cheek, leaned towards the microphone.

Luckily for Gill, the Chief Inspector got there first again. 'Ms Irvine, let me be clear, no stone was left unturned in that investigation. As you may recall, I was a sergeant at the time, and I well remember the long days and nights we spent looking for these two youngsters. I myself volunteered to help detectives by trawling through CCTV footage. I joined folk combing our shorelines, part of me hoping we'd find something, a larger part of me praying we wouldn't happen upon a body. I know DI Muir did the same.'

Fergus was glaring at Gill. He nodded.

'So, as I said, it's easy to judge us now, but we did our best. You have to keep in mind, we're not exactly used to these things here.' He raised his gaze to the TV cameras for his next line. 'Thankfully, these islands remain the safest place to live in the whole country, and that's largely thanks to the excellent work my police officers do in the community. But, if mistakes were made, we'll gladly learn from them.'

Freya saw Fergus reach for another sip of water, but his glass was already empty.

The questions continued for another minute or so before Robertson wrapped up with a reminder of how the public could contact the team. 'I would also like to make a personal plea to members of the press to respect the privacy of Ola's and Liam's families and friends at this time.'

Outside, a morale-sapping mist had rolled in off the sea. It was getting on for eleven, but fuzzy orbs of light still glowed along the row of lampposts in the police station car park. They had arrived together in Gill's car and Freya wandered across the tarmac towards it in a trance, still deep in thought. The discovery of Ola's body on its own had painted a tragic picture of a young girl killed by her boyfriend; Liam's death made this something much bigger, more sinister. Two people – two teenagers – had been murdered. Magnus Robertson was right; that didn't happen here.

As she neared the car she became aware of Gill talking to her.

'You'll need to catch the bus back to base, hen. I'm away to Stromness just now.' Gill leaned in close as they walked, like she was about to share a secret. Freya fought the instinct to pull away. 'I'm doing an interview with Beth.'

The idea of changing plan so suddenly made Freya's skin itch. A hundred thoughts hit the back of her eyes at once – what was she going to do now? Where would she even catch a bus? Which route did she need for Hatston? Did she have any change? And how …

'Well?' Gill snapped. 'Did you not hear me, sweetheart? The bus is that way.'

'Can't I come with you?'

Much as Freya hated to admit it, speaking to Beth was actually a good idea. Anyone who wanted to read about Liam's body being found would have their pick of stories already, and, by the time their paper was published on Thursday, it would definitely be old news. An interview with Beth was a unique angle at least, something that would make their coverage stand out.

Or maybe she was trying to talk herself out of an unexpected bus ride.

Gill unlocked her Audi and eyed Freya over the bonnet. 'You'll be there to shadow me, that's it. No butting in.'

Freya nodded, made a gesture like she was zipping her lips.

'Aye, fine,' said Gill. 'Come on, then.'

Freya reached for the handle on the passenger-side door. As she did, she heard a voice behind her.

'Freya?'

She turned. A large middle-aged man with a pockmarked face was walking towards her. Greased-back hair, brown out of a bottle with flecks of grey where the truth got through. He was wearing a jeans-shirt-leather-jacket combo that made him look like he was auditioning for *Top Gear*. Her chest tightened as she realised his was the voice she had heard during the press conference, the one she'd hoped she hadn't.

'Freya Sinclair, that *is* you.'

Of all the people *The Herald* could have sent, Martin Fletcher – or Fletch, as he insisted on being called – was possibly the worst. Fletch was part of a group of men who had worked for *The Herald* for so long they should have named one of the conference rooms at the newsroom after him. He hadn't taken Freya's rise to the Crime and Courts beat well, didn't think she had been there long enough to earn it. One story didn't make her a proper reporter, he'd once said. Freya had found that ironic, because the more stories she got, the more Fletch had grown to resent her.

'Small world, eh? We all thought you'd ended up in witness protection, the way you left in such a hurry, no proper goodbye. Or maybe a padded cell.' He laughed, then glanced at Gill. He nodded. 'Pleased to meet you. Martin Fletcher with *The Herald*.'

'Gill Irvine, senior reporter at *The Orcadian*.'

Fletch grinned. 'The local rag?' He looked at Freya. 'This is where you ended up?'

Freya wanted to say so many things, but they all became tangled on her tongue and she said nothing.

Martin chuckled. 'Bloody hell, how the mighty have fallen.'

Freya looked at Gill, saw her face was glowing purple again. 'We'd better go.'

'Seriously, we've all been taking bets on what had become of you,' she heard Martin say as she opened the passenger door. 'And after everything that went on between you and Damien Barber we reckoned—'

She got in the car and slammed the door.

15

THE HEAVENS OPENED AS they reached Stromness. The sky had grown black on the drive across Mainland, and, as they stopped at the roundabout, the high peak of Ward Hill towered into the clouds across the Hoy Sound ahead of them like a wall of solid granite rising out of the sea, making the town appear even darker than it already was. The NorthLink ferry was in the harbour, cars steadily streaming out of it with their headlights lit. They had to wait until there was a gap in the traffic.

Gill had the radio on, heaters turned up high, augmenting the smell. She had been relatively quiet, but now she asked, '*The Herald*. That where you used to work, was it?'

Freya was resting her head against the cool window. 'Yes.'

'You must've had a fair few big stories there.'

It might have been a question, but it sounded to Freya like a statement. She chose not to respond.

'There a long time, were you?'

'Sorry?'

'I said, were you there a long time?' Gill didn't turn down the radio, merely shouted her question over the top of it. The sound of it rattled inside Freya's head like loose coins inside a tin.

'Five years.'

'So that man we just met, he a friend of yours, was he?'

'No.'

There was a break in the flow of vehicles and Gill put her foot down, pulled out with a jolt. 'Not much of a talker, are you, hen?'

'There's not much to tell.'

They took Back Road, which as the name suggested climbed the brae at the back of the cluster of small stone buildings around the harbour before turning onto the estate on Grieveship Road. A clutch of grey, pebble-dashed semi-detacheds and bungalows surrounded a small patch of grass. There was an old fella trussed up against the heavy rain in a thick coat with a tiny Jack Russell straining on its leash, but nobody else was in sight. Gill came to a stop outside one of the houses and switched off the engine, but she didn't make any move to get out. The sound of the downpour pummelling the roof grew louder.

'I don't mean to pry,' Gill said, a phrase Freya knew meant the exact opposite. 'But what was all that about before?'

'All what?'

'Whatever your man back at the cop shop was on about. Something about a David Barker?'

Freya rubbed her left eye with the palm of her hand. 'Damien Barber.'

'Aye, that's it.'

She bit back a sigh. There was going to be no avoiding this. She had always known she would be talking about it at some point, and she had planned what to say, figured there was no harm in telling the truth. Or the truth up to a certain point.

'It was nothing really. He owned a production company in Glasgow and a few other businesses – a couple of bars in the West End, a few restaurants too, I think.'

'Sounds like a big deal.'

'He thought he was.'

She unclipped her seatbelt, hoping Gill might take the hint. She didn't.

'So what happened?'

Freya felt the pull of her hand to her ear piercings. Instead, she began to wrap a strand of hair around her fingertip. 'A woman who worked for him claimed he'd sexually assaulted her, but nobody would believe her.'

'And how did you get involved?'

'Do you remember a story about a GP in Glasgow who had been filming his female patients?'

'Aye, I do. Dirty bastard. He'd been at it for years, hadn't he?'

'I broke the story.'

'That was you?'

Freya nodded.

Gill said nothing for a long time. She stared at the windscreen; the glass had become opaque due to the rain streaming down it. If Freya had known this was all it would take to stun Gill into silence, she would have told her this story first thing yesterday.

Eventually, Gill asked, 'What does that have to do with this Barber character?'

'The woman he assaulted came to me because of that story. She hoped I could do the same thing for her, I guess. Get people to believe her.'

'Did you?'

Freya pulled her hair tight. 'I tried.'

She looked out of the passenger window and saw Beth had opened her front door and was waiting for them.

'We should go,' she said.

They ran up the garden path but were still soaked by the time they reached the house. Beth showed them through to a small lounge where all the lights were on, but it didn't help. The room was decorated with old-fashioned wallpaper and dark wooden furniture which, like the mist back in Kirkwall, seemed to suck the life out of it. Beth sat in a floral-patterned armchair to one side of the TV while Freya and Gill took seats on the sofa opposite the fireplace. It wasn't lit but it should have been. Freya was freezing even with her coat on, and the layer of sweat that had formed under her clothes in the car now felt like frost against her skin.

'Thank you so much for speaking to us, sweetheart,' Gill began in her most cloying voice. 'I know how hard this must be. Your Ola would be so proud of you for wanting to share her story.'

Freya noticed a hoard of TV magazines piled up beside Beth's armchair, listing programmes that had no doubt been cancelled decades ago. There were several wooden cabinets on the wall behind her head, lined with row upon crowded row of figurines whose sad porcelain faces peered out from behind the glass, trying to listen in on the conversation. Everything smelled musty and damp.

There was a small side table by the door with a landline phone on it and a phone book – Freya didn't know they still printed those. An artificial Christmas tree was in the opposite corner and tinsel was strung across the mantelpiece over the gas fire, which seemed like a bad idea. Maybe that was why it wasn't lit. Freya wasn't sure if the decorations had gone up recently or if they had been there for the past seventeen years. Either was possible.

'We took that at Rackwick, the summer afore it happened. It was the last time we went anywhere together.'

Freya glanced at Beth, who had followed her gaze to the fireplace. She must have thought she had been looking at the framed photograph above the tinsel, the one showing Beth and her husband flanking three teenaged children – Ola and a younger-looking girl and boy. Ola was standing next to her dad, his arm around her shoulder. The sand stretched out behind them to the giant cliffs that tower over that bay. From the angle it was taken, Freya guessed they'd placed the camera on one of the boulders at the back of the beach and set the timer. She hadn't been to Rackwick in years, but she remembered what it looked like. The sun was at their backs, casting the family in silhouette, so it was hard to see their faces. It wasn't a great shot but that wasn't why Beth had kept it, of course.

'Have your bairns moved away south?' Gill asked.

'One has. Hannah. She's down in Fife now. Our Stevie's still here, works on the ferries like his dad did.'

'Did? Oh sweetheart, you don't mean he's …?'

Beth's face darkened. She shook her head. 'Oh, no. He left soon after they stopped looking for Ola. Convinced himself she was still out there, went away to Scotland on a fool's errand to find her. He had a group running on Facebook, asking for sightings of her. Last I checked, that's still going.'

'It must've been so hard for you both.' Gill cocked her head to one side, put a hand on Beth's knee.

'Ola's been a memory now longer than she was with me,' Beth said, placing her own hand over Gill's. She looked her in the eye. 'Have you got weans yourself?'

Gill beamed. 'A fourteen-year-old girl. Peedie madam she is too. Thinks she's seen it all already and knows better than her mammy.'

Beth smiled a forlorn smile. She turned to Freya, whose stomach sank. 'And you?'

'No. Not yet.' Experience had taught Freya that adding 'Not yet' was more acceptable than simply saying 'No' for some reason.

Beth turned back to Gill. 'You'll understand, then.'

Freya clenched her jaw.

'We'd never really fought until then,' Beth continued, referring, Freya assumed, to herself and her husband. 'I know people say that, but for us it was true. After it happened, we struggled to be in the same room.' She exhaled a tired laugh. 'Funny, you'd think a thing like that would bring you together – you're going through something very few folk can comprehend, and all you've got for support is each other, but it was like we were living two different lives.'

The words struck a chord with Freya. She remembered how she and her mother, Helen, had reacted in their own ways to the death of her dad. That in turn reminded her she and Tom had agreed to meet Helen for dinner tonight in town and she wondered if it was too late to come up with an excuse to get out of it.

Gill proceeded to ask a string of questions about Ola's life – what she was like growing up, how popular she'd been at school. Beth portrayed her daughter as an angel, of course. Freya wondered how much of this was the same shite she'd told Gill seventeen years ago; they'd have been quicker going to the archives. Later, when she was replaying the events of the day, she would feel guilty as it dawned on her that Beth had only recently received confirmation that her daughter was dead and had been for a very long time, and maybe she just needed to talk about her daughter with someone. She might even have believed the things she was saying about Ola. But in that moment Freya was focused only on the task at hand and Gill was making an arse of it. She asked nothing about Beth's reaction to the news about Liam. If Freya had been in charge, she would have been digging into Ola's relationship with him. Had Liam been caught up in something that had got them both killed? A number of the reporters at the presser seemed to think so; it would've been interesting to get Beth's take on that too. But Freya followed orders and kept her mouth shut. Her headache had only grown worse as the morning had worn on and she didn't need any extra hassle.

She found herself tuning out, distracted by the sound of the heavy rain against the glass and the strange smells in the house that were making her wonder if there was a cat somewhere. Her leaden eyelids were beginning to draw shut when they were snapped open by the sound of Beth's voice becoming animated.

'I can show you. That's if you'd like to see?'

Freya roused herself, glanced at Gill. She wasn't sure what the last question had been. Something about Ola's friends.

'There's photos up in her room. Hundreds of them. If there was one thing our Ola loved, it was taking pictures.'

'Ola's room?' Freya asked.

'Aye,' said Beth. 'I'll show you.'

16

THEY FOLLOWED BETH UP a dimly lit staircase made darker by the dour wallpaper. Ola's bedroom was the last door off the landing on the left. It was closed. The only one that was.

'I left everything as it was,' Beth said, pushing it open gently, as if someone might be behind it. 'You know, in case she ever …'

Her voice broke when she looked inside the room. Her shoulders buckled, her face crumpled into tears. Unable to cross the threshold she took a step back, allowing Freya to see past her. The room looked like a time capsule, sealed up and frozen on the day Ola last walked out of it almost two decades ago. Gill fished a tissue out of her purse and passed it to Beth, then she put her arm around her and made no motion to go inside the room.

Freya stepped past them both and went in.

Like the rest of the house, the room smelled musty, but a hundred times worse. A smell so thick Freya felt it in the back of her throat, like even the air in here was the same as it had been seventeen years ago. The view from the window looked down the hill towards the sea, but the rain was so heavy she couldn't see past the rooftops in the next street. It plunged the room into an eerie half-light. Freya's gaze landed on the posters on the walls, their corners frayed and their colour faded by years of sunlight. They showed pop groups from when Freya was a teenager: *The Pussycat Dolls* and *The Black Eyed Peas*. Everything was decorated white and pink and silver.

Freya couldn't name the way she was feeling right now. It simply felt odd, but she wasn't entirely sure why. An unnamed dread danced on her chest as she took in the photographs stuck with Blu Tack to the walls and the wardrobe doors. Beth hadn't been lying: there were hundreds, each filled with faces of young girls pushed together as they pouted for the camera. Some of them Freya recognised; she remembered only deeds, no names. Most of the photos were taken outdoors, sitting on benches in Stromness town centre or with groups of boys at the beach. Only a few looked like they had been taken at a house party. There were merely a handful of Ola and Liam together.

'How long had Ola and Liam been seeing each other?' she asked, thinking aloud more than anything.

She turned to see she had cut Gill off mid-sentence. She had been so engrossed in her thoughts she hadn't heard Gill start to question Beth again. That earned her a scowl from Gill, and she remembered the orders she'd been given back at the police station. She parted her lips to say sorry, but Beth spoke first.

'Not very long. At least, not that I was aware of.'

Freya decided against any follow-ups. She smiled and nodded, then Gill and Beth got talking again. Freya turned back to the room. There were yet more photographs Blu-Tacked around the mirror on the dressing table. Ola was with Liam in most of the these. He even cracked a smile in some. There were three drawers beneath the dresser, and Freya's eyes were drawn to the bottom one. It had a lock on it, but the wood around it was splintered.

She walked over to the drawers and ran her fingers over the fractured wood.

'The police did that,' she heard Beth say behind her. She turned to see her and Gill looking at her again from the doorway, the latter with a face like thunder, even though Freya hadn't said anything this time. 'They forced it open in case there was anything inside that might help.'

'Do you mind if I look?'

'Go ahead, love. There's nothing in there the police haven't been through already.'

There were some notebooks in the drawer, as well as several more packs of photographs with the logo of Sutherland's – the local pharmacy – on the paper folders. A lot were shots of the landscape, no people – sunsets, close-ups of flowers, black-and-white photos of the old cobbled lanes around Stromness. There were only a handful in each pack and Freya wondered if Ola had put only the pictures of her and her friends on display because she didn't want anyone to see these other ones. She didn't want anyone to know she had taken them. It mustn't have been cool in Ola's circle of friends to have had interests and hobbies.

Freya returned the photos to the drawer and picked up the notebooks. She was surprised to discover Ola had tried her hand at poetry. It was terrible, full of teenage angst and loaded with clichés, but between this and the photography there was clearly a side to Ola she had hidden from the rest of the world. Freya shuddered at the thought the two of them actually had something in common.

The second notebook contained more of the same, along with a few doodles, only the work took a creepier turn. Rifling through the pages, she stopped as they fell open in the centre of the book, on a drawing scrawled in black biro across both pages. A large spider sat in the centre of a web while dozens of tiny ones spread out across the paper. Looking more closely, she saw each of the tiny spiders was carrying a person bound in web, their eyes closed, their mouths smothered. The web where the giant spider was sitting seemed to emanate from a corner high up on a bare brick wall, halfway down which faint letters spelled out the words *Play Pen*, with the second *P* written backwards as though scribbled by a child. Ola had pressed so hard with the biro as she had coloured in the giant spider's black body that she had torn the page.

She dropped the notebooks with a clatter as a shiver thundered through her, earning her yet another derisive glance from Gill. She gathered them up and dropped the first two back in the drawer. She saw then the final one had a small clasp on it that could be locked but, like the drawer, it had been forced. Freya opened it. It was Ola's diary.

She almost dropped it again. She turned to see if Beth and Gill were watching. It felt wrong to be looking at this, although logically she knew it didn't matter now, and it was hardly more of an invasion of privacy than she had already committed.

She began to flick through the pages, not really reading, but skimming, hoping something might leap out.

About halfway in, something did:

There was a boy waiting for me after school tonight. He knew who I was, but I didn't know him.

Freya stopped. Her stomach tightened. She glanced up and saw Gill and Beth were still deep in conversation in the doorway. She read on:

He said we met at Katie's party last week, but I don't remember him being there and, when I asked Katie later, she didn't know him either, so I was either absolutely hammered (probably!) or he's full of shite. He said his name was Liam and he asked me out to another party on Saturday. He was fit, but that's not why I said yes. I don't know, he just seemed different somehow. Sounds stupid when I say that, but he wasn't like the pathetic farmers' boys at school. He was more grown up, not so small-minded. And super confident. I liked that ...

Freya vaguely remember someone called Katie in Ola's circle of friends. She glanced at the photos surrounding the mirror, recognised some of the girls who had kicked and spat at her, but she couldn't put any names to them. Years of trying to forget the bastards had paid off. Something stirred in her chest; part embarrassment, part rage. She wondered which one was Katie and whether she was still in Orkney and what she was doing now. Something told her she wasn't performing brain surgery or trying to cure cancer. And there was little chance Katie remembered the Harry Donaldson incident as clearly as she did.

She read on. Liam had picked up Ola for their first date but there'd been a change of plan. They hadn't gone to the party – Liam had decided they should blow it off to get fish and chips and a couple of bottles of wine instead, which they ate and drank in his car.

When Freya saw where they had gone, her pulse quickened:

He drove us to the clifftops at Yesnaby, which sounded so lame when he suggested it, but it was kinda romantic. I thought he was going to try something but he was actually really sweet. And if I'm honest, I'm gutted he didn't. I know I would have been okay with it if he had …

Freya flicked through the pages. She wanted to absorb as much as she could before Gill was finished, but there was too much here to get through now.

'Mrs Campbell, would you mind if I—'

'Freya, for the love of God, will you please stop butting in? Show some respect.'

The words were a slap in the face.

Freya turned to see Gill glaring at her from the doorway. Beth seemed to be shrinking into herself beside her.

'Beth here is trying to talk to me about her beautiful daughter. Do you have any idea how raw that still is for her? And all you can do is keep interrupting.'

Freya's heart raced. Her cheeks burned. Her head filled with comebacks, but the words became knotted and tangled and none would come out.

'It's … it's okay,' Beth said, offering Gill an apologetic smile. 'I'm sure she didn't mean to.'

No, she didn't mean to.

Of course she didn't. She had simply been so wrapped up in her thoughts she hadn't realised Beth was talking.

And Gill reprimanding her like a petulant child who had done something naughty on purpose sparked a feeling in her she knew she would struggle to contain.

Gill and Beth still watched her from the doorway, their eyes burning holes in her skin, and suddenly she was flooded with an urge to run, to get as far away from this tiny, airless room as possible. But the exit was blocked, and the walls seemed a lot closer now, the air much thicker. She was struggling to breathe.

The two older women began talking again. Freya's free hand had unconsciously gone to her right ear and she was pressing hard on her piercings, might even have been counting them out loud. But it wasn't calming her down and she needed to stop herself, so she shoved both hands in her coat pockets and started to pace, but that earned her another glare from Gill, so she tried to stand still and the urge to tap her feet became overwhelming.

She felt her body filling with a cocktail of unnamed emotions and she knew the only way to make it stop before she burst was to remove herself from this situation, but there was no way out. She needed to fucking leave. Now!

Finally, Gill was done and it was time to go. Outside, the downpour was still biblical. Gill scuttled down the path ahead of her and jumped in her car, started the engine, but Freya stopped on the pavement.

Gill glared at her through her car window. After a second or two of no movement from Freya, she wound it down.

'Get in, you bloody lunatic. You'll catch your death.'

Freya didn't want to. She couldn't be in that confined space with that smell and that brain-mincing howl coming from the radio, but what else could she do?

Reluctantly, she got in. Gill started on her as soon as they drove out of Beth's street. 'There's something you need to learn, missy, and you need to learn it quick.'

Freya screwed her eyes shut. She was sitting on her hands. She felt herself begin to rock.

'You're not bloody Jessica Fletcher and this isn't *Murder, She Wrote*. I don't know what you got up to in Glasgow, but here we leave the detective work to the police.'

There was a spark. Moments later the suffocating stench of cigarette smoke filled Freya's nostrils, flooded her throat.

'I don't care how many big scoops you've bagged in your time,' Gill barked. 'What did you think you were playing at, going through those drawers like that?'

She couldn't breathe.

'I'm talking to you. Have you nothing to say for yourself?'

The windscreen wipers thrashed across the glass, the *thrum, thrum, thrum* of them reverberating around the inside of her head.

'And constantly jumping in on me. Think you can do a better job than I can, is that—'

'I didn't—'

'The bloody nerve! You're doing it again.'

The car slowed to a standstill. Freya opened her eyes, unbuckled her seatbelt, threw open the door.

'What the bloody hell do you think—'

A hand grabbed her forearm. She thrashed against it. There was a scream, sounded more like shock than pain.

Freya jumped from the car, slammed the door, and ran.

17

FOR THE FIRST FEW moments after jumping from the car, Freya could think of nothing else but getting as far away as possible. Then, she became conscious of the rain exploding like firecrackers against her hood. She looked back. Gill had stopped at the North End Roundabout and Freya had run a good thirty or forty metres away from her, back along the road towards Beth's house. Gill's Audi was still stationary, just for a moment. Then with an over-rev of the engine Gill shot out of the junction in front of another vehicle and sped away up the hill towards Kirkwall.

The smell of diesel reached Freya on the damp air from the petrol station across the street. It made her feel giddy. The rain was coming down so hard it was bouncing back off the pavement. It ran off the shell of her yellow raincoat and soaked through her jeans. It breached her trainers too. Her thoughts shifted from escape to realising she was stranded – her car was back at Hatston and she had no idea how to get to it. And in about thirty minutes, Gill would be back at the newsroom without her and she was going to tell Kristin what had happened. Then Kristin would try to call her. Freya couldn't face that. She didn't know what to do.

The tears came like a river bursting its banks. The force of it so great it shook her. Anger, fear, exhaustion. She was well aware she was alone in a public place and breaking down in tears was going to attract unwanted attention, and again all she wanted to do was run but she had no idea where.

She had no idea of the time either. It couldn't be later than one but the heavy cloud made it seem much later. A car turned the corner and caught her in its headlights, and she flinched. She flashed back to that February night in Glasgow when she was standing out on Fullarton Road in the pouring rain, her mind swirling with dark thoughts, as it was now. She'd just lost another battle with her editors over Damien Barber – they weren't interested in pursuing a sexual abuse story against a man who did so much good for the city, they'd said. A man who had a family. A man who was being considered for a future tilt at a seat at Holyrood, it was rumoured, and whose businesses had recurring adverts plastered across the pages of the newspaper. There had been no such concerns about the Partick GP.

Freya remembered standing on the edge of the pavement in the cold and the rain, just like now. She had closed her eyes, the brightness of approaching headlights feeling strangely comforting as it fell on her eyelids, and she had longed for her swirling brain to fall silent, just for a moment.

Now, as then, fatigue spread to her bones. The emotion and the adrenaline were draining away and, as they always did, feelings of anger and desperation were giving way to guilt and embarrassment. How the fuck was she going to explain this to Kristin? She shivered as the rain reached her skin. She needed to find shelter.

There was a café open across the street from the quay where vehicles board the NorthLink ferry. The concourse was empty now, the next sailing not until the evening. Maybe not at all, if the weather worsened. The café was quiet, only a handful of folk sitting by the large windows. Freya took a seat far inside, away from everyone else. Despite the weather, it was a bright place with old black-and-white photos of the town on the walls, their frames strung with fairy lights or gold and silver tinsel. There was a shot of the square where Freya's encounter with Ola and Harry Donaldson had taken place – a group of old men were sitting on a bench in front of the lifeguard station and she recognised one of them as the Orcadian writer George Mackay Brown, who had lived not far from this spot. The square wasn't far from here either, she probably could have seen it from the window. But she couldn't be bothered to find somewhere else. There were few places in this town that didn't trigger bad memories and she needed caffeine. Really what she wanted was to go home and sleep, but she couldn't call Tom and tell him what had happened: he'd only panic. Christ, her second day, and here she was.

She ordered an oat milk latte. The woman behind the counter told her to take a seat and she would bring it over. Freya found a table and wiped her eyes on her sleeve, hoped they didn't look too red and puffy, and her hand went to her coat pocket. She needed to keep her mind distracted. She felt the envelope that was folded up in there and the same thoughts as earlier flashed across her mind. Was that why she had reacted the way she just had? Was it something to do with being autistic? Of feeling overwhelmed by everything all at once and this was how it all came out? But again, what if that letter said she wasn't autistic, what did that mean? That she was just a grown woman who didn't know how to cope with life, how to handle her emotions? These weren't questions she wanted to deal with right now so she left the letter where it was and instead she took out Ola's diary.

She hadn't meant to steal it. Or maybe she had, but the act hadn't felt conscious. It had ended up there when she had stuffed her hands in her pockets in Ola's room. She thought about taking it back, but she couldn't face seeing Beth again. She didn't want to see anyone. She ran her thumb across its pages and watched them fall open. Reading this now, in her current state of mind, was a bad idea but she was intrigued. As she flicked quickly through, she noticed the pages turned blank about two thirds of the way in. Her fingers were shaking – partly from cold, mostly from emotion still coursing through her system – making it hard to turn the pages, but she found the last one with writing on it. There was an entry from the ninth of September, more than three weeks before Ola and Liam had been killed:

Liam gets so depressed sometimes and it breaks my heart. He'll go quiet, stare into space. Other times he can get so angry and his whole face changes, it's hard to describe, like he's gone for a while and there's someone else inside his head. I know he won't hurt me though, I'm never scared of that. He says it's nothing to do with us and that he loves me, that all he wants to do is protect me, but he won't tell me what from.

As soon as school is done we're getting the fuck off this rock. He says we'll go someplace where it will only be us, but how can I while there's something he's hiding from me? So this is it, when we meet tonight I'm giving him the choice: either he tells me what the fuck's going on with him, or we're through.

That was it. Freya riffled through the pages again to the end but there was nothing more.

The waitress came with her coffee. Freya felt ashamed to have been caught reading someone else's diary – the woman probably had no idea she was doing that, but she felt funny anyway so she decided to put it away. She sipped at her coffee, felt its warmth spread through her, but she still couldn't relax. A million thoughts were barrelling through her brain, making her legs jump, her wet shoes slapping the stone slab floor. She needed another distraction.

Beth had mentioned a Facebook group Ola's dad had set up, as well as a brother who still lived in Orkney. These seemed like good next steps. She took out her phone and felt sick when the screen came to life with dozens of notifications. Instantly her mind went to Kristin. These must be texts from her. But there was no way Gill had got back to Hatston already, and she soon saw they were notifications from Facebook and Twitter. Replies to her posts on *The Orcadian*'s account from the press conference.

Despite his body having been found too, there still appeared to be little love for Liam. While he could no longer be considered a suspect, the majority still held him responsible. Freya thought about Ola's last diary entry. They might have had a point.

It occurred to Freya that while she knew a little about Ola, Liam was a complete mystery. She had never met him, hadn't exactly hung out in circles Liam would have mixed in. There were several possible avenues for finding out more about Ola, but how was she going to look into Liam? Scrolling through the replies, she found only one that had a good word to say about him: by a man named Scott Connelly. He claimed to have been school friends with Liam and said the anger against him was because he was a *ferry-louper* – an Orcadian term for someone who had moved to the islands from elsewhere. Scott reckoned that because Liam had no family here after his nan died, there was nobody to stick up for him. Freya checked Scott's profile but there was no picture, no location details. She replied anyway, asking if he would like to tell her more, off the record if needs be. She then decided to do that with all of the replies.

As she went through them one by one, a name jumped out at her.

A woman called Katie Marwick had posted a message saying she was Ola's best friend at school. Freya wondered if this was the same Katie from Ola's diary, the one who held the party where Ola and Liam had supposedly first met. Like she had with Scott, Freya checked Katie's profiles. There was a photo of a tired-looking woman with dark, shoulder-length hair, trying her best to smile next to two young children, but Freya didn't recognise her from the photos in Ola's bedroom.

Katie's Twitter profile gave her location as Kirkwall. Freya sent her a direct message, asking if they could meet to chat, then waited for a reply. As she watched her phone, refreshing the screen and hoping for an unlikely instant response, it dawned on her that Kristin could call any minute.

Texting her first was probably the right thing to do, but some familiar force was stopping her. It wasn't just that she was nervous, or didn't know what to say: she simply didn't *want* to. Bothering about Kristin was a waste of her energy when all her focus now needed to be on this story. But she knew if she didn't, it could land her in trouble, and she'd liked what Kristin had said about her being an ally. She'd never had that before. She fired off a quick text, simply saying she was chasing down a lead and everything was fine. Half of that was true, at least, and the best way to bounce back from what had happened this morning was to get something to wipe the floor with Gill's inane interview with Beth.

Maybe there was another way to contact Katie. An image of Beth's dour living room flashed behind her eyes and gave her an idea. She checked Google to see if there was an online version of *The Phone Book* and was surprised to find there was. She got a further surprise when it turned up both a landline number and an address. But there were four Katie or Katherine Marwicks listed in Orkney, two in Kirkwall, and no way of knowing which was the right one.

Time to bite the bullet and phone them both.

She was dialling the first number when her phone pinged.

18

It was quarter past two by the time Freya arrived back in Kirkwall. Thankfully, the rain had stopped, but the temperature was plummeting as the clouds were clearing and the light drained out of the day. She was exhausted, her taxi driver having been relentless in his pursuit of small talk, even though Freya had flat out ignored him since Finstown. When she paid him, he'd given her a 'Smile, love, it might never happen' with her change. She wished she could've summoned the energy for something more than a scowl.

Katie Marwick hadn't arrived so Freya had a few minutes to herself to recover. She stood on the steps in front of St Magnus Cathedral, watching the Christmas lights in the trees along Broad Street. They reminded her she hadn't bought any presents yet for Tom or her mum, and that made her anxious. It wasn't what she needed to be focused on right now, so she pushed the thought away and instead came up with some questions for Katie.

When she finally showed up a little before half past two, Freya didn't recognise her at first – the years since high school had not been kind and she looked even more tired and run-down than she had done in her Twitter profile. Like Ola, Katie had been in the year above Freya, but now she had dark lines around her eyes and the resigned slump in her shoulders of someone twenty years her senior. Her hair was thin, mostly black but showing a few flashes of grey. Her skin was pale and gaunt. It was like the spiteful soul she had been in high school had turned her insides rotten and it was beginning to show on the outside too. Freya found it hard not to stare.

'I've only got fifteen minutes on my break,' Katie said. She'd already explained she worked as the assistant manager in the Poundland a short walk away on Albert Street. Under her coat, Freya saw she was wearing a blue polo shirt with a logo on to prove it. 'I won't be able to talk longer than that, sorry. They'll need me back.'

Freya couldn't imagine what the staff of Kirkwall Poundland would need her for so desperately, but she nodded anyway.

There was a café across the street, *The Daily Scoop*. It seemed appropriate. They decided to talk there.

Freya bought them both drinks – another oat latte for herself, a mocha for Katie – and they sat at one of the tables near a window, looking out through the glow of the Christmas lights strung around the glass. As in Stromness, the café was quiet, the lunch crowd having tailed off by now. Despite occupying one of the old buildings in this part of town, it was modern inside – polished oak floors and spotlights in the ceiling. Freya sat across from Katie, her phone on the table between them set to *Do Not Disturb* so as not to receive any calls or texts from Kristin. She asked if it was okay to record their conversation.

Katie nodded, tried a smile, but the downturned corners of her mouth didn't seem up for it. 'It's quite exciting this, speaking to a journalist. I don't recognise your name from the paper, though.'

'I'm new. This is only my second day.'

'You seem like you know what you're doing.'

Freya didn't know what she was supposed to say to that. She smiled and nodded. She was eager to cut to the chase, but she knew people always liked to make small talk first. She was also unsure how she felt about Katie not remembering her from their school days. She had guessed she wouldn't; Freya had kept a low profile and her run-ins with Ola's crowd had mercifully been rare. It was only now they were sitting opposite each other that Freya recognised Katie from the crowd that day in Stromness. She wondered if Katie even remembered it.

'You know, it still hasn't sunk in yet,' Katie said, staring into the foam on her coffee as she spoke. She stirred it slowly with a small silver spoon. 'I suppose it's no shock though, really.'

'Which part?'

Katie looked up. 'Sorry?'

'Which part isn't a shock? That Ola was murdered or that Liam was too?'

Katie gave her answer some thought, like she had said what she had simply to put a hole in the silence. 'Ola, I suppose. I've always had an odd feeling deep down that something had happened to her.'

'But you were surprised to hear about Liam?'

Katie nodded. 'Yesterday, when I first saw the news on Facebook, I assumed Liam must've done it. I'm still not convinced he's not to blame somehow.'

'What were they like together?' Freya asked.

The corners of Katie's lips curled as a memory passed behind her eyes. 'She was obsessed with him. I'd never seen her like that with anyone else, and she'd had plenty of boyfriends.'

'Was it mutual?'

'She seemed to think so. She said they were in love, that he was going to take her away from here. I guess, in a sense, she was right.' A violent rush of air that might have been a laugh escaped her nostrils. 'Sorry, dark sense of humour.'

'They met at a party at your house, didn't they?'

'Who told you that?'

'Ola's mother.' Freya thought that was better than saying she'd read Ola's diary.

Katie's eyes flicked away to the left. 'Could've been. I'm not sure.'

'Is it likely you would have invited him?'

'I doubt it. Before he and Ola started seeing each other, I'd never met him. He went to school here, at the Grammar.'

'Would someone else have invited him, do you think?'

'Who knows? But I'm sure you remember what parties are like when you're a teenager. People used to gatecrash all the time. Everyone was either too steaming drunk or too busy shagging to care.'

Katie laughed, so Freya pretended to as well.

'What about the night they …' Freya stopped herself from saying what she was going to. She figured she needed to be a little less direct. 'The night you last saw them both, there was another house party, right?'

Any remnants of laughter on Katie's lips vanished. Her eyes flicked a glance at the phone. 'Uh huh.'

'Were you there?'

'I was, aye.' She took a long draw of her coffee, looked like she was trying to hide behind her cup.

'And did anything happen? Was there some reason Ola and Liam left around nine-ish?'

'Are you asking about the fight or …?'

Freya hoped her surprise didn't show on her face. No, she hadn't been asking about any fight, but she was now.

'Can you tell me about that?'

Katie looked at her watch. 'It's nothing I haven't already told the police. They said they looked into it, so I suppose it didn't turn out to be important.'

'Did you see it?'

'I heard it from the kitchen.'

'Was this a physical fight? Between her and Liam or—'

'No, it was nothing like that. Just yelling and screaming, you know?'

'Ola was yelling?'

Katie took another sip, nodded. 'Ola was outside, and I heard her voice raised, so I went out to check she was okay. She was screaming at this boy, some friend of Liam's. She was calling him all the names under the sun, and he was smiling back at her like he didn't give two fucks. Then she started on Liam too, yelling, "We've got to go, we've got to go".'

'Go where?'

'Not a clue.' Katie glanced at her watch again. 'All I know is I watched her get into that bloody precious BMW of his and I never saw her again. I let her drive off with him. Then yesterday I find out she's been buried in the sand this whole time over at Skaill and I …' Freya heard a slight crack in Katie's voice. 'I told the police all of this at the time. They said they would check it out, so maybe it was all nothing, but …'

'But what?'

Katie wiped her eye with the back of her hand, sat upright. 'But I know he had something to do with this. Liam. Even if he didn't kill her himself, something he did got her killed.' She checked her watch a third time. 'I'd better get back.'

'Do you know what Liam's friend was called?'

'I didn't even know for sure he was a friend of his,' Katie replied. 'Only that none of us knew him.'

'And what did Liam do during all this? Did he get involved?'

'Nope, just stood there mute, like always.' Katie downed the last of her coffee, reached for her handbag on the chair beside her. 'He never said all that much, to be honest. One of the reasons I didn't trust him. He was too quiet, know what I mean? Like he was hiding something, or thought he was too good to speak to the likes of us.'

Freya felt her hands bunching into fists under the table, but she smiled and nodded. Being deemed untrustworthy just because you didn't incessantly chat or stare into people's eyeballs when you talked was something she was sick of hearing.

'Do you remember what he looked like, at least?'

Katie stood up, her eyes pointing at the ceiling as she thought. 'He was really tall, I remember that. Had a shaved head, looked kinda scary with these real intense eyes, not that Ola seemed to be afraid of him. But she was like that, Ola, you know? Wasn't scared of nobody.'

Outside, it was now almost completely dark, but the Christmas tree on the cathedral green and the lights in the trees cut through the gloom. The wind had picked up too and it sliced through Freya's still-damp jeans. Katie didn't leave right away; she thanked Freya for the drink then asked if her interview would be in the paper this Thursday. Freya had forgotten that had been the whole point of talking to her.

'It might not make it before the deadline now,' she said, knowing she had no intention of going back to the newsroom today. 'It'll probably go on the website, though. Are you happy for me to name you in the piece?'

Katie thought about that. 'Actually, on second thoughts, maybe not. Is that okay?'

Freya nodded.

'It's just …' Katie chewed at her thumbnail. 'Well, thinking about it, I don't know where that friend of Liam's is now. I'm sure the police found him back then. I was told they'd spoken to him, but I never heard of it going any further, so …'

'It's fine, I'll say you're an unnamed source.'

Katie smiled, nodded, but she still didn't leave. The fifteen minutes were long up by now. Freya got the impression there was something else she wanted to say.

Eventually, Katie said, 'I got a call earlier from a detective. They've asked me to come down to the station.'

'They said they would be interviewing all the witnesses from back then.'

Katie nodded again, swept her hair from her face. Freya couldn't work out what was going on in her head, but it was clear there was something she was keeping back. She remembered something Beth had told them yesterday when she had come to the newsroom. She'd said she thought something else had happened at the party.

Those kids were all too scared to talk.

Freya tried to think of the right question, the correct combination of words to unlock whatever it was that was stored away behind Katie's tired eyes.

But before she could, Katie pulled her handbag up her shoulder, tucked her black hair behind her ear. 'It was lovely to meet you, Freya,' she said before leaving, as though it was the first time in their lives they ever had.

19

GETTING THE BUS BACK to Hatston wasn't as difficult as Freya had feared.

She didn't go into the newsroom. Instead she waited until she was sure she wouldn't be seen, then she collected her Hyundai from the car park and drove away. Quickly. She'd had a reply from Kristin but she had no intention of reading it. She told herself she'd send her a text later explaining her phone had died. It wasn't a total lie: she only had something like twenty per cent battery left. She couldn't face any contact with her now. The Molotov cocktail of emotions she'd felt earlier had all burned out and only one remained: shame. She had no idea how to explain to Kristin why she had acted how she had. People didn't get it. At best, they thought she was being 'difficult' – a term often used by her editors at *The Herald* – or immature, unable to cope with the world. At worst, people accused her of making it up to get attention, which was ironic because attention was the last thing she wanted. Attention only made it worse.

She was at a loose end now, unable to go home because Tom would wonder why she had finished work so early. She felt untethered. Having structure and routine helped, but her days here lacked that as yet because everything was new. Everything was happening *to* her and nothing seemed within her control. She needed to change that. The best way was to remain focused on the story, but the next step was the most difficult. She had thought about tracking down Ola's brother – he was still local and might have given a less rose-tinted view of his sister than Beth had. She also considered looking for Ola's sister, Hannah, or her dad, who was still out there somewhere on his quest to find his daughter. That seemed like a good angle, but really she wanted to speak to someone who had known Liam. Everything they had on this story was coming from Ola's side, but nobody was speaking for him. The one person who had, Scott Connelly, still hadn't replied to Freya's request to talk further, and Liam had no surviving family in Orkney.

It was coming up on quarter to four and fully dark as she drove back into town. On the pavements she could see streams of teenagers in near identical dark clothing which all bore the same crest. It gave her an idea.

Five minutes later she pulled into the car park at Kirkwall Grammar. There were several cars dotted about, meaning some of the teachers were hopefully still inside. Her mother had worked as a classroom assistant at Freya's primary school in Dounby so she knew staff rarely left when the students did.

Automatic doors swept open as she approached them, giving way to a large, bright atrium similar to the one at the hospital, minus the smell. There was nobody behind reception, simply a printed page of A4 saying *Back Soon* stuck to the glass hatch, so she glanced around the airy entrance hall for a place to wait. Her gaze landed on a section of wall filled with framed photographs; pictures of sporting events and academic achievements from down the years. She walked over, and beside a densely decorated Christmas tree that stretched from floor to ceiling she found photos of all the previous year groups who had graduated and left. Liam had still been a pupil at the school when he was murdered, having started his Highers here, but he had just finished the last year of compulsory education. Freya hoped that was the year these photos showed.

In a picture dated June 2005 she found him, standing on the far left of the back row of three. As in the other photographs of him, he was stony-faced, no smile. The look in his eyes reminded Freya of something:

… his whole face changes, it's hard to describe, like he's gone for a while and there's someone else inside his head.

Ola's description of Liam from her diary could have been written about this photograph.

Freya glanced over her shoulder. The receptionist had returned but there was a woman and a teenage boy talking to her now. She turned back to the picture, and her conversation with Katie came to mind, the part about the boy who had been seen arguing with Ola at the party. Katie had said he was tall with a shaved head and intense eyes. The tallest kids in the year were standing along the back row, but nobody stood out. She checked the other rows of faces too but drew a blank.

The woman and boy were winding up their conversation with the receptionist. Freya was about to walk over when someone in the next photograph along caught her eye. A picture of the year group who finished S4 the year before Liam. On the back row, standing an inch or two taller than the other students, was a kid with a severe buzz cut and the most intense stare Freya had ever seen, like he could actually see her through the lens. The grin on his face sent more of a chill through her bones than the Arctic wind whipping up outside.

'Excuse me?'

Freya turned. The receptionist was calling to her from the desk.

'Are you waiting for a student?'

Freya walked over to the reception window, preparing the lines she had planned in the car as she did. 'No, actually I'm here to see a teacher.'

The receptionist, a middle-aged woman in a floral blouse with glasses perched on her head, smiled. 'Do you have an appointment?'

'No, I'm … it's an odd request, I know, but I was hoping to speak to someone who worked here seventeen years ago.'

The receptionist's smile faltered. 'What, anyone who was here … sorry, how long ago did you say?'

'Seventeen years. And yes.'

'Are you a parent? A former student?'

'No, I'm a reporter with *The Orcadian*. I'd like to talk to someone who—'

'I'm sorry,' the receptionist cut her off. There was no shutter that could be pulled down over the reception desk window, but one had been drawn over her face. 'I don't think I can help you. Now if you don't mind, we close the school at four.'

'It's about Liam McDonnell,' Freya persisted. 'I want to find someone with something positive to say about him. I'm not here digging for dirt.'

In the background, inside the reception office, there was a tall, slim man with thinning grey hair talking to another woman in a floral blouse who was sitting at a computer. They both turned at the mention of Liam's name.

'I take it you've heard the news?' Freya asked.

'I have. And it's terrible. But I don't think this is the best—'

'I've already spoken to Ola Campbell's mother,' Freya said, employing Gill's trick of using the first person singular. 'There's nobody to add anything about Liam. His nan is gone, there are no friends coming forward. Everyone on social media seems to think he's to blame for what happened. I just … I hoped someone here might be able to add some balance.'

The tall man had come forward and was standing behind the receptionist now. He wore a brown suit and a garish tie that looked out of place in these ultra-modern surroundings.

'Sheila, who's this?' he asked the receptionist.

'This is …' Sheila looked at Freya. 'I don't think I caught your name.'

'Freya Sinclair,' she said, looking directly at the tall man behind the reception window. 'I'm a reporter for *The Orcadian*.'

'And you want to talk about Liam McDonnell?'

Freya nodded. 'Like I said, I'm not here to dig up dirt. Everyone's blaming Liam for what happened, but right now, as far as we know, he's a victim, same as Ola. I honestly just want to quote someone who knew him, that's it.'

The tall man thought for a moment. He looked down at Sheila, who gave him the slightest shrug.

'Come around to the door,' he said to Freya. 'We can talk in my office.'

20

IN TRUE TEACHER FASHION, the man introduced himself as Mr Henderson. He was the headteacher. 'But not back then,' he told Freya. 'Seventeen years ago, I was head of the English department. I taught Liam McDonnell several times over the years. I suppose I knew him as well as most here.'

His office, like the rest of the building, was airy and bright and modern. White walls and a large window which looked out over the car park. The glass had become a giant mirror thanks to the blackening sky outside. On the other side of the room, a glass wall gave a view of the 'Street', as Mr Henderson called it – the giant atrium that ran the length of the building. It made this place look more like the huge shopping centre she hated back at Braehead in Glasgow than a secondary school.

There were more photos here of what Freya assumed were former students, many of whom seemed to have gone on to great things. There were certificates and letters in frames too, the latter Freya once again assumed were from past pupils. The two of them took seats either side of the headmaster's large desk, and Freya, as she often did, sat with one leg folded underneath her on the chair. She instinctively corrected herself when she saw the headmaster looking at her.

'Are you local?' Mr Henderson asked. 'I'd say your accent puts you from somewhere in the Central Belt.'

'I'm from Orkney originally, but I've been living down south for a while.'

'You didn't attend this school, I take it? I should recognise you if you did.'

Freya wondered if that was true. He must have known so many students in his time, he couldn't possibly remember all of them.

Mr Henderson was closing in on sixty, with receding grey hair on the top of his head, but it was still thick enough in his eyebrows. He wore glasses with thin, black metal frames on his slender face. His smile seemed relaxed and he had a brightness in his eyes that made him look more like someone's well-read granddad than a grammar school headmaster.

Mr Henderson asked what people had been saying about Liam, and Freya told him. On hearing it, he steepled his fingers beneath his chin, leaned back in his chair and shook his head.

'Liam was a complex character,' he said. 'A bright boy, though somewhat troubled. But I recall he always seemed to be very popular.'

Freya smiled and nodded, though her insides twisted in rage. Why was popularity always the metric by which the worth of the dead was measured? She would like to think she was kind, loyal, at least passably intelligent, but nobody ever mentioned those things when someone died. She thought about how, if she had been killed by that car back in February, anyone reporting on her death would have struggled to find someone who described her as popular.

'What do you mean by "troubled"?' she asked.

'Well, he didn't have the easiest of starts in life. You mentioned his grandmother before, so I take it you're aware of his familial situation?'

'I only know he wasn't originally from Orkney and he lived with his nan. That's why I was hoping to be able to find out something more meaningful to say about him in our coverage.'

Mr Henderson nodded. 'Liam was from Wick. He came to Orkney after his mother died – an overdose, I believe. He was thirteen. It's not the easiest age for any child, of course. It was a terrible thing for him to have to cope with so young.'

'What about his father?'

'He was in prison in Aberdeen when it happened, but I don't think he'd been involved in Liam's life a great deal before then anyhow. His maternal grandmother took him in, but then she fell ill not long afterwards. I remember he seemed very devoted to looking after her. Nowadays he would be recognised as a young carer and hopefully given some support, but these things weren't so readily identified in those days.'

'In what way did that make him troubled?'

'Well, he …' Mr Henderson stopped. He glanced at Freya's phone on the desk between them. 'I'm worried my answer to that question might be twisted in your story.'

'Mr Henderson, I promise you, I'm not here trying to prop up the angle that Liam was somehow to blame for what happened to him and Ola.'

Mr Henderson thought for a long while, tapping his steepled fingers against his chin. 'As I said, Liam was very close to his grandmother. There were occasions over the years when Liam got into physical altercations, and usually these started when somebody said something derogatory about the fact he lived with her. But I really want to get across how rare those occasions were. Like I told you, Liam was very well liked. He was friends with all the popular children, although he always seemed to have much more about him than they did.'

Freya made a mental note to ask on the way out if the tall, shaven-headed boy in the year above Liam was one of those popular kids Liam hung out with.

'May I ask,' Mr Henderson said, 'who exactly is saying these things about Liam?'

Freya explained they had been put on social media in response to her posts from the press conference earlier. 'There were some journalists there too who mentioned rumours from seventeen years ago about Liam possibly being caught up in something illegal.'

Mr Henderson shook his head and Freya felt like one of his pupils who hadn't turned in her homework. 'Rumours and internet hearsay. It's hardly conclusive, don't you think? What's that famous quote about journalism? Something like: "If someone tells you it's raining and someone else tells you it's not, a journalist's job is not to report them both but to look out of the window and determine which is true."'

Freya shifted in her seat again. 'That's why I'm here.'

Mr Henderson smiled. 'Well, I can only tell you that from what I knew of Liam, I don't believe he would have been mixed up in anything that would have caused what happened to him and that poor girl. Though I can't imagine anyone in Orkney being involved in something that would lead to a double murder. Things like that simply don't happen here.'

He was the second person today to say that.

And yet, it *had* happened.

'Why do you think none of Liam's friends are coming forward to defend him?' Freya asked.

'That's impossible for me to answer. Maybe they've moved away from Orkney and don't follow your newspaper online.'

'All of them? You said he was well liked, surely some of those people still live here and have seen the comments, but so far only one person has stuck up for him.'

Mr Henderson leaned forward. 'The people who are posting these things, are they friends of Ola Campbell?'

'The ones I've spoken to, yes.'

He nodded. 'I'm not aware of the reason, but I do remember their relationship wasn't particularly well received.'

Mr Henderson explained that when Liam had returned for his Highers in the August before he and Ola were killed, something had changed. He no longer seemed to be as close to the people he had been friends with before.

'We get to hear in the staffroom of the various dramas that are going on in the schoolyard, and I do recall his relationship with a girl from Stromness was causing some friction.'

'Because they went to different schools?'

'Could be, though you hear of that happening and it never seems to be an issue. Personally, I believed it was jealousy.'

'People were jealous of him and Ola?'

'I believe the girls here were, yes,' Mr Henderson said. 'You have to understand, Liam was a quiet, sensitive young man. Quite introspective, I'd say. And yet he still managed to be one of the so-called "in crowd". I don't know how well you remember your time in high school, Ms Sinclair, but that's quite rare.'

Freya simply nodded.

'The plain and simple fact of the matter is he was popular because he was good-looking. All the girls wanted to be with him, and all the boys wanted to be him, as the saying goes. I think they saw his relationship with a girl from Stromness as him rejecting them.'

Freya wasn't convinced it was as 'plain and simple' as that.

She tried to think of another question but couldn't. She wished now she'd had more time to prepare – the idea to come here had sprung itself on her and usually she would have spent more time putting her questions together. With the conversation winding down and the time now well after half past four, the interview drew to a close.

On the way out, in the reception area, she remembered to ask about the tall boy in the picture.

Mr Henderson leaned in close to the photograph, lifted his glasses from his face and squinted his eyes. His breath clouded the glass in the frame.

'Jason Miller,' he said. 'And no, as I recall, he wasn't in Liam McDonnell's circle of friends. In fact, he finished here a few weeks after this photograph was taken. He didn't go on to take his Highers, so he would have left the school over a year before Liam went missing.'

'I was told he was seen at a party arguing with Ola and Liam on the night they were killed.'

Mr Henderson hiked his shoulders. 'Much as we like to keep our ear to the ground, I was never aware of those two mixing in the same circles. Though I suppose, if it were to turn out …'

He stopped himself again, like he had earlier, even though Freya was no longer recording their conversation.

'What is it?' she asked.

Mr Henderson sighed. He glanced towards the reception desk. The window was now closed and the lights were off inside. 'We're no longer speaking on the record.'

Freya didn't think it was a question, but she nodded.

'I always like to think I can find positives in every student, but with some it's harder than others.' He paused, then: 'I'm not proud of this, but teaching isn't always the easiest of professions. You have to take the stress out of it somehow.'

Freya began to worry what he was about to confide in her.

'We don't do this anymore,' he continued, 'especially not since what happened to Liam, but years ago we used to have a mock end-of-year awards ceremony. We kept it among the teaching staff, never told the students, of course. It was puerile stuff – we'd have categories such as *Most likely to trigger an international crisis*, or *The first Kirkwall Grammar alumnus shot into space*.'

He looked at the photograph of Jason Miller. Freya had thought his expression betrayed embarrassment, but now it seemed to slip towards concern.

'Jason Miller was voted most likely to be handed a life sentence without parole,' he said. He turned back to Freya. 'Usually, it was all done in jest. But when it came to Jason Miller, I don't think anyone was joking.'

21

THE FIRST THING FREYA did when she got home was sleep.

These last two days had left her completely drained and she knew it was only going to get worse. Tomorrow, she would have to explain the Gill incident to Kristin. She hadn't replied to her text yet, but at least, when she did, she wouldn't be lying about her battery dying – it had run out shortly after ending her conversation with Mr Henderson. She had a charger somewhere that plugged into the cigarette lighter in the car, but she only ever remembered she needed it once she was already out in her vehicle somewhere. Really, she should have set herself a reminder on her phone to take it with her, but experience had taught her she wouldn't, or she'd forget the second she cleared the reminder from her screen. That same experience had taught her she wasn't going to read Kristin's reply to her text when she got home. That was very much a tomorrow problem.

It was pitch black in the bedroom when she woke up. She had no idea of the time, but the smell of food reached her under the door, as did the sound of music playing. She recognised the band – a Glasgow group called *Moy* she had gone to see once with Tom and some of his friends. She figured Tom would be in the kitchen cooking dinner and a sharp spike of anger pierced her stomach, followed by those familiar feelings of guilt. He was just being nice, trying to take care of her after a hard day. But she hated herself for how it made her feel.

There was a light scratching sound at the bedroom door. God knows how, but that dog always seemed to know the second Freya opened her eyes.

They had pizza for a second night in a row, but Freya wasn't complaining. She welcomed it, in fact. She would eat it every night given the chance – it was her favourite, so why not? You knew where you were with pizza. As they sat at the table, Luna strategically placed for scraps at Freya's feet as usual, Tom explained that he had called Freya's mother and postponed their dinner plans for another time.

'You called my mother instead of texting her? That was brave.'

Tom shrugged, looked away. 'It's not like I've got anyone else to talk to all day.'

'What did you tell her?'

'I said you had food poisoning from my cooking.'

'I think we used food poisoning when we cancelled on her last week.'

'Well, she didn't question it. She must know how bad my cooking is.'

He grinned and Freya smiled too. She leaned across the table and kissed him, still fighting that lingering sense of guilt. 'Thank you.'

'No bother. She took it better than I was expecting, to be honest. She seemed more disappointed she wouldn't get to share the "big scoop" she had for you.'

He made the quotation marks with his fingers.

'A big scoop, aye?' Freya grinned. Her mother was forever coming home from work full of tales when Freya was little. No doubt this would be something similar. Freya and her dad would grin at each other across the dinner table as Helen explained some staffroom drama like it was the Cuban Missile Crisis. Freya's dad would egg Helen on with a 'You're kidding?' or a 'Never', then he'd glance over at Freya and wink. Freya smiled at the memory.

'So, you want to hear this big scoop, or did I take notes for no reason?'

'You actually took notes?'

Tom laughed and shook his head. 'No, but do you want to hear it?'

'Aye, go on then,' said Freya. Anything to take her mind off work and the Gill incident. She had already decided it was best not to mention it to Tom.

'So apparently, last night your mam went to a Christmas lecture about archaeology.'

'She's into archaeology now?'

'Something about the Ness of Brodgar, a talk by the guy who'd overseen the first digs there after it was discovered. Sounded pretty interesting to be fair. I wouldn't have minded going.'

It did sound interesting, hence Freya's surprise her mother had been there. Freya had gone through a fairly intense phase of wanting to be an archaeologist when she was little, after that first school trip to Skara Brae, in fact. That was why her dad had taken her to see the dig, but Helen had never encouraged her fascination with the topic or shown any interest in it herself.

Freya didn't actively dislike her mother, but they had never been close. When her dad died, Freya had gone further into her shell than she had already been; she had no interest in playing with other children, she was more than happy being on her own, but her mother didn't think that was right.

'It's not normal,' she would say. 'A bairn should want to be with other children. You should go out and play with your friends. Make an effort.'

Helen had taken Freya to endless doctor's appointments, trying to figure out what was 'wrong' with her, but they had put her behaviour down to the sudden loss of her dad. Her mother would cry and get angry any time Freya was reluctant to be affectionate towards her, so, after a while, Freya forced herself to hug her just to be left in peace. It was safe to say the two of them had never understood each other, and probably never would.

'Well, if you want to go next year, I'm sure she'll take you, if you ask,' Freya said with a grin.

'Aye, well, anyway,' Tom said, brushing quickly past that. 'Turns out the guy never showed up. He hadn't cancelled. Everyone was expecting him to be there, but he simply never arrived.'

Freya waited for him to say more. 'Is that it?'

'Pretty much. She said her friend is married to one of the secretaries of the Archaeological Society and they've been trying to reach the fella since last night. Nobody can get hold of him. She thinks it's too big a coincidence.'

'What is?'

'That he should go missing on the same day a body was found.'

Freya shook her head. She could just imagine her mother coming out with those words. 'Has anyone been to his house to check on him?'

'I'd imagine so. She didn't say.'

Freya felt a twinge of concern for the man. She wasn't making the same connections her mother had, but she did think there might be a story there if he did turn out to be missing. Mostly, though, she hoped he was okay.

When they finished the pizza, it was time for the cheesecake they never got round to eating last night. It was worth the wait. After that had gone down, Freya and Tom took Luna for a gentle walk down to the shore. The rain had turned to sleet in the early evening, but it had stopped now and the clouds were clearing in small patches. No moon broke through, though, and the darkness was unyielding, but Freya didn't mind. She preferred it. When the cold and the dark set in, that was when the three of them got the world to themselves. Tom wore a head torch, and they walked along the deserted lanes until they reached the sandy beach at Swanbister Bay. The tide was out and Freya stood listening to the waves lapping the shore out in the black, her face buried in her coat against the biting cold. As she did, thoughts of the day crept back in and another pang of embarrassment struck her when she replayed the episode with Gill. She tried to forget it and concentrate on the other things instead.

She was still unsure what to make of Katie Marwick. There was clearly something she was holding back about the party in Harray, something she seemed reluctant to tell the police. They should have reinterviewed her by now. Freya considered how she might find out what it was and wondered if she should raise it with Fergus. She wondered too about Liam and Jason Miller – were the two of them involved in something together, and if so, why was Jason arguing with Ola and not Liam? And where was Ola so keen to go after speaking to him?

'I'm never going to get to see the Northern Lights, am I?'

Tom's voice interrupted her thoughts. He was standing only a few feet away, but he had turned off the head torch and Freya could barely see him in this moonless dark. She made out his shape, his face pointed upwards into the empty sky where the clouds obscured most of the stars.

She forgot about work and stepped closer to him, wrapped her arms around his torso. Her head only reached his chest and she liked the feeling of his warm winter jacket against her cheek. She could feel his chest rise and fall with his steady breathing, hear Luna rummaging around out in the darkness nearby. There was no other sound but the wind and the waves and, for perhaps the first time since she'd been back, she felt glad to be here.

'We call them the Merry Dancers.'

'Sorry?'

'The Northern Lights, that's what they're called in Orkney.' She looked up at him. 'The Merry Dancers.'

'I like that.'

'And you probably won't see them looking straight up in the sky. At this latitude you'll likely need a clear, low northern horizon. You're a scientist, right? You really should know that.'

'Yeah, okay. I studied engineering, not astronomy.'

'Well, lucky for you, I was interested in astronomy when I was a little girl and I know all the best places to go looking for them. First clear night we get, we'll go, I promise.'

'Was there anything you weren't interested in as a little girl?'

'Boys. I'm still not, really.'

Tom grinned. 'Good call. Boys suck.'

Back at home, she changed into her pyjamas and they curled up on the sofa with Luna in front of the open fire again. The heat made Freya's hands tingle after being out in the cold, and the room was filled with the sweet smell of the smouldering logs and the pine scent from the Christmas tree by the window. Freya fought the urge to read more of Ola's diary – she wanted to see if it made mention of a Jason Miller – but she decided she had done enough for one day. Not bringing work home was a good rule for her mental health and she intended to stick to it. She did, however, check one last thing.

There had been no replies to the direct messages she had sent on social media earlier, but there had been more replies to her earlier posts from the press conference, most of them saying the same thing as the others. She looked for a Jason Miller among the profiles but didn't spot one, so she decided to search for him instead. Nothing came back when she searched for 'Jason Miller Orkney', and there were far too many other Jason Millers elsewhere in the world to be able to track the right one down.

She glanced over at Tom, reached out her hand to run her fingers through the hair on the back of his head. He was reading something on the iPad, holding it in one hand and stroking Luna's head in his lap with the other. Freya smiled at the sight. She took a quick glance at what he was reading. The lamp at the end of the sofa was reflecting back off the screen so she leaned closer to him, put her head on his shoulder to look. A photograph caught her eye.

'What's that?'

Tom was so engrossed that he read on a second or two before responding. 'It's about that fella your mam was on about. Gordon Tulloch.' He glanced down at her and grinned. 'Thought I'd look him up. I've got to admit, she's got me intrigued. I see where you get your storytelling ability from.'

He was reading what looked like a blogpost on the website of the archaeology department at the University of the Highlands and Islands, a college of which was based in Orkney. It wasn't about the man her mother had mentioned, as such – it was a history of the excavation work carried out at Skara Brae.

'How did you find this?' Freya asked.

'I googled the guy's name, and this was one of the first things that came up.'

He scrolled further down as he read, pushing the photograph that had caught Freya's attention off the screen.

'Wait. Can you go back a second?'

Inset within the text was a black-and-white shot of a group of men and women dressed in T-shirts and shorts, kneeling in the dirt and squinting into the sun. She recognised the semilunar stretch of sand behind them. Beneath the photo, a caption read: *Prof. Gordon Tulloch, third from left, led excavations during the 1990s.*

Her mouth went dry.

She sat up, put her finger over the man third from the left in the picture. She knew he was the one her mother had been talking about before she read the caption. He had long hair flowing down to his shoulders beneath a sun hat, and something about him seemed so familiar, but Freya couldn't place it.

'I know this guy.'

'You know him? How?'

'I don't know. Can I …?' She put her hand out for the iPad. Tom gave it to her. 'Yeah, sure. Here.'

She pressed to go back to the search results list. Tom had simply googled the words *Gordon Tulloch Archaeology* and the first result was for the staff profile of a Professor Gordon Tulloch at Orkney College. She clicked it. It was a few years out of date – Prof. Tulloch had now retired, having been Dean of the archaeology department for a number of years, and the page had been archived. But there was a photograph of him, one taken much more recently than the Nineties. He looked at least sixty in the picture.

Freya felt pins and needles in her fingers as she recognised his shaggy white hair. She *had* seen him before.

And she remembered where.

* * *

I grip the folded slip of paper in my cold, clenched fist. I've been staring at the single name on it for so long that when I screw my eyes shut I can still see the blue ink on the crumpled white page.

It's been raining almost the whole way up here, only stopped once I was somewhere along the A9 between Inverness and Thurso. It's dry now but, when the clouds cracked, the wind lifted and within minutes of leaving the harbour at Scrabster, the ferry begins to rock and sway. I remember the last time I made this trip, heading in the opposite direction; the Pentland Firth was as unaccommodating then, but I don't think I felt it. After that night, it was a long time before I felt anything again.

The boat begins to tip to the left and it keeps going. Feels as though it's going to capsize before there's a crash, a dull thud of deep water against metal, and the world lurches the opposite way. I feel the boat fall from under me and my stomach goes with it. When I open my eyes, I'm gripping the seat so tight my knuckles have blanched. Two auld boys in woollen hats and hi-vis vests across the aisle are watching me, don't even try to hide the fact they're taking the piss. I think about saying something, but I swallow it down, like I've got good at, and I turn away, look out the window. There's nothing but spots of water and my own reflection in the black glass.

I hoped my stomach would settle when we made dry land, but driving off the boat into the streets of Stromness only doubles my nausea. I drive steady until the streetlights run out then I put my foot down, speed quickly away. Being back in Orkney after all this time is a headfuck, like stepping behind enemy lines. Someone's going to spot me, recognise me, call the police. Realistically, I know there's not a chance of that, but I'm not going anywhere near Kirkwall tonight.

Five guesthouses in, I wonder if I should change my mind. Every one is either closed for the winter or fully booked. Tourists here for Christmas. Fuck knows why. I haven't missed this place for a single minute. I don't want to be back, but I made a promise I intend to keep. Without closing my eyes, I see that face from the news again, but as soon as it appears it's replaced by the name on that list. Seventeen years I've had to prepare for this, and that single name is all I have to show for it. I should've done more, I shouldn't have given up, got sidetracked with stupid ideas about building some kind of life for myself. Any chance I had at happiness was crushed by the man whose name is scribbled on this piece of paper. Him, and others besides. Fuck, I haven't even worked out how many of them there are but, now I'm here, I'll do whatever it takes find out.

He *is going to tell me.*

At the sixth guesthouse I almost don't bother to knock. A large wooden house not far from Houton, so still too close to Stromness for my liking. There's not a light on in a single window as I drive up the gravel track. I stop, kill the engine. There's only one other car parked in the driveway; another dead end. I glance at the clock. It's only just gone nine but it feels closer to midnight. The silence here is so dense it's unnerving, like the islands themselves are holding their breath. An image of Digger in the break room comes to me, the TV turned up so loud I might be able to hear it from here. I almost miss it. What the fuck am I doing? How the hell am I going to pull this off? Not for the first time, an urge swells within me to turn the fuck around and go home.

White halogen light comes through the windscreen.

I raise a hand to shield my eyes.

Someone's standing on the deck at the front of the house, rendered nothing more than a shape by the bright light at their back. No way to tell if it's a man or a woman until they speak.

'Can I help you?'

A woman. American accent. Not a surprise.

I get out of the car. 'I was hoping you had a room.'

'Just for tonight?'

'Longer, if you have it.'

A pause. I can't see her face. Then: 'You're in luck. We had a cancellation only this morning.'

I fetch my small bag from the boot and follow the woman inside.

She looks friendly enough – round face flushed red from the wind. She relaxes a little once she gets a look at me in the light.

'Awful night to be without a place to stay. Not many folk turn up here without a booking at this time of year.'

'It was a last-minute thing.'

She leads me up a wooden staircase that creaks with every step. At the top: a common room with a TV, couple of sofas, kettle and cups. Three doors lead off it. She opens one with a heavy-looking iron key.

'I take it it's business that brings you here in a rush?' she asks.

'That's right.'

'Must be important to come here so urgently this close to the holidays.'

'It's something I've been putting off, can't wait any longer.'

She nods like that makes sense.

I take in the room – plush double bed, desk, large en suite bathroom. Thick rugs on the floor and a picture window with a view into the night. The floors, walls and ceiling are all pine wood, like a hunting lodge in the middle of a Swedish forest. It's nicer than I had in mind.

'How much?'

She gives me the price for one night. 'How long will you be stopping?'

'How long is it free?'

'The people who cancelled had it for the week. They were due to stay with us for Christmas, but the price goes up for—'

'A week's fine.'

I hand her a credit card I have no intention of ever repaying and she looks at it like she's not sure what to do. Then she tells me she'll fetch the card reader. I smile, nod, close the door behind her.

I throw my bag on the bed, sit on the edge of the firm mattress, and take in the room again. I need a plan, a way to find out the other names in case he doesn't know them – or claims he doesn't – but I can't sit here all night trying to think of one, I'll go out of my mind. Or come to my senses and leave.

Unfolding the sheet of paper one more time, I stare at the name. This bastard took everything from me, and he didn't do it alone. And now, the clock is ticking.

I make up my mind.

I'll find this prick tonight.

WEDNESDAY, 21 DECEMBER

22

FREYA LEFT HOME BEFORE Tom was out of bed. She'd barely slept a wink again and there was no point lying there tossing and turning. She'd got dressed, given Luna's velvet ears a rub, then put some kibble in Luna's bowl and headed out without eating her own breakfast. She left in such a hurry she forgot to leave a note telling Tom that Luna had already eaten, though she very much doubted that greedy dog would mind a second helping.

It was a little after seven and still nowhere near daylight. The clouds had cleared overnight and there was the slightest turquoise hue on the south-eastern horizon .The entire sky was alive with stars. It was so cold the air made her lungs hurt. Freya drove as steadily as her impatience would allow, heading west along the winding road from Orphir, hoping not to hit a patch of black ice. Although it was still dark, the landscape was illuminated by the moon and by blue starlight, and there was a dusting of snow on some of the higher ground. Yesterday, when the weather had closed in, these islands had felt like a prison but, when the sky looked like this, the horizon became infinite.

She was heading for Quoyloo in West Mainland. Last night, she'd remembered why she recognised Prof. Gordon Tulloch – he was the man she had seen walking on the beach at Skaill on Monday morning with his dog, watching the SOCOs set up the crime scene tents. He observed them investigating the area where the bodies had been buried then, later that day, he disappeared without telling a soul. Last night, Freya used the online phone book again to look up his address, discovered there were three G. Tullochs listed in Orkney, two of whom lived close to Skara Brae. Only one used the title *Professor*.

The road straightened out a little once she passed the ferry pier at Houton and she picked up speed. There were no cars ahead of her, only the occasional vehicle heading the other way.

Oil-terminal workers bound for the morning crossing to Flotta, no doubt. Less than thirty minutes later, she passed Bay of Skaill and kept driving, past the lonely stone chapel at Northdyke, and up to a junction where the road split in two. The cottages and farmhouses scattered in the general vicinity made up Quoyloo. Lights were on in only a handful of the houses. On the passenger seat beside her, her phone was displaying Google Maps, and a robotic female voice told her to take a right. She bounced along an uncovered road for about a quarter of a mile, heading inland until she reached a large detached house set in a sizeable plot of its own land. She came to a stop by a closed gate, the other side of which there was a wide gravel driveway leading to a garage. There were no lights on in any of the windows here either. It didn't look like anybody was home.

She felt stupid being here now. Lying awake in bed, she'd told herself coming this early was a good idea because, even if Gordon was keeping a low profile, he was likely to be in. But why would he be keeping a low profile? His presence on the beach on Monday morning and subsequent failure to turn up to a lecture might not mean anything. There *was* his connection to Skara Brae, but was she putting two and two together and coming up with eighteen? Christ, she was as bad as her mother.

Now she was here, she figured she should at least go and knock. There was a car in the driveway, so maybe someone was home after all. The curtains weren't drawn, though, and in the silence with the engine off she heard a repetitive hollow tapping, a metal bar banging against a post, and she noticed the gate across the drive hadn't been shut properly. It was blowing open in the breeze.

Freya grabbed her phone and got out. She pulled her coat up over her chin, tucked her hair behind her ears, and took a moment to allow her eyes to adjust to the dark. It felt much creepier being out of the car with the sound of the gate creaking in the wind. It occurred to her now that it might have been a good idea to have brought Tom's head torch. She hadn't told him or anyone else where she was going. She checked her phone.

No signal.

She pushed open the gate and locked it behind her, then she stood on the driveway and listened. No sound now but the wind and the distant, rhythmic crashing of the waves. There was the faint smell of woodsmoke on the frozen air and she looked around – the nearest neighbours were a few hundred metres away. There were lights on there, pale smoke drifting from the chimney. People awake and getting ready for work. She turned on the torch on her phone. The crunch of her footsteps on the gravel sounded loud as cannon fire in the early morning hush. As she approached the house, the cold making her teeth chatter, she noticed there were four ruts in the gravel: two sets of tyre tracks. One set led to the car, the other to the garage.

Freya knocked on the front door – not too hard – and waited. Nothing.

She rang the doorbell, but no lights went on, nobody stirred.

She tried the door handle and was relieved to find it locked. She didn't think she dared go inside, but her sense of curiosity wouldn't have allowed her to simply walk away.

The glass in the front door was frosted so she couldn't see into the hallway. The next set of windows looked into the living room, which stretched back into the gloom. The light from her phone reflected off the glass and made it impossible to see anything but her own reflection so she turned it off, put it back in her coat pocket, cupped her hands over her eyes to peer inside. She saw an unlit open fireplace with an empty dog bed in front of it, and photos on the mantelpiece, but they were small and it was much too dark to make them out. Two sofas, a rug, and a coffee table. At the back of the room there was the outline of a Christmas tree in the corner, next to what looked like an open doorway. There was a faint light coming from the other side.

Her heart was thumping in the side of her neck. She crept to the back of the house, passing the garage. There was a window in the side of it so she looked in. Her eyes adjusting to the darkness, she saw it was more or less empty. Shelves filled with junk, a few cans of paint. There was what looked like a dark shadow on the concrete floor. An oil stain, probably.

She left the window, her breath still on the glass, and carried on to the rear of the house where the sigh of the wind subsided. No traffic. No birdsong. She saw the faint glow coming from one of the windows and, peering inside, she saw it was the kitchen. The light was coming from the refrigerator, the door of which had been left open. There was barely any food inside and Freya could see some of the cupboards were open too, their shelves looking bare.

A sound.

Faint, but she heard it.

Metal scraping on metal. She stood, frozen, her heart in her ears now. She had her eyes fixed on the corner of the house next to the driveway, but nothing happened. Nobody coming. No further sound.

She took her phone from her coat pocket again.

Still no signal.

The silence grew heavier. The longer she stayed here, the more chance there was of being seen. She walked slowly back around the side of the house and looked straight into the eyes of a man standing on the driveway.

She screamed.

The man yelled too, clutched his chest.

A light went on, straight in her eyes. Freya shielded her face with her hand. She wanted to run, but she was blinded and the man was standing between her and the gate.

'What the bloody hell are you playing at?' a voice asked.

'I'm sorry.'

'Who are you?'

'Freya. Freya Sinclair, from *The Orcadian*.'

'A journalist?' The light was lowered. 'What are you doing sneaking around Gordon's house?'

Freya kept her hand raised, tried to blink away the yellow patches floating in front of her eyes.

'I said what are you—'

'I'm looking for Gordon Tulloch.'

'Looking for Gordon? Why?'

She wished she could get her thoughts together more quickly, come up with a response, but the light and the shock were making it impossible to think straight.

When she didn't say anything, the man emptied his lungs in a long, loud exhale. 'You scared the life out of me just now. I thought you were looking to burgle the place.'

'Do you know where Gordon is?'

The orbs in her field of view were fading and she could make out some of the man's features. He wore a thick coat, a woollen hat, jeans and wellies. He looked in his forties, maybe. He had a weathered face that made Freya think he was likely a farmer, or at least someone who worked most of the day outside.

'Why do you want to know?' he asked.

'I was supposed to be reporting on his lecture for the Archaeological Society on Monday evening,' Freya said now she'd had some time to think. 'He never showed up. People were worried about him.'

The man nodded now. He seemed to soften slightly. 'I saw him and Thorfinn – that's his dog – walking back up the road from Northdyke Monday morning. Haven't seen him since.'

'Did you speak to him? Did he say where he was going?'

'Didn't get the chance. He's getting on a bit now, uses a stick, but he was marching up the brae there like a man in his twenties. Thorfinn was lagging behind him, which is rare to see. I was on the quad, and I waved as I went past, but he mustn't have seen me. Twenty minutes later, I saw his van on the track here, heading for the road.'

'His van?'

'An old VW camper. He kept it in the garage. Don't think it'd been out in years. I was surprised to see it could still go.'

Freya thought about the gate being unbolted when she had arrived. He hadn't even stopped to shut it behind him.

'How long have you known Gordon?' she asked.

'We've been neighbours since I was a boy. My family owns the farm over there. Gordon's been in this house since afore I took things over.'

'Have you seen the story about the bodies being found at Bay of Skaill on Monday?'

'Of course.'

'Do you know if Gordon knew either of them? Their names were Ola Campbell and Liam McDonnell.'

The man straightened his back, folded his arms. 'I thought you said this was about some lecture or other.'

'But do you know—'

'Unless they were students of his, I don't know why a man like Gordon would have any connection to two teenagers,' the man said, his voice now changed. 'I think it's time you were on your way.'

Freya decided not to push it.

'Freya,' the man said as she reached her car. She didn't like him using her name and she cursed herself for having given it to him. 'I don't want to see any of what I've just said in your newspaper. Gordon's a good man – whatever reason he had for rushing off on Monday morning had nothing to do with those poor bairns, you hear?'

Freya nodded. She got in her car and locked the doors as the man bolted the gate behind him. He stood on the track with his arms folded as she reversed down the lane and was still watching her as she pulled onto the main road.

23

FREYA GOT TO *THE Orcadian* a little before half eight. The sky overhead was turning pink, but the car park out back was still empty.

Freya reversed into the space furthest from the road where she would have a good view of the others arriving and she sat for a while listening to the ticking of the cooling engine, her fingers drumming on the steering wheel, her heart still thumping in her ears. Could have been because of what had happened at Gordon Tulloch's house, or because now she was finally going to have to deal with the fallout from yesterday.

She had never got around to texting Kristin. She hoped it wouldn't matter once she told her what she had found out. She planned to play down the Gill incident, make out like she'd forgotten about it, then quickly bring Kristin up to speed about Gordon and Jason Miller.

She looked up at the sound of an engine. A car drove past, heading into the industrial estate. She counted her studs forward and back and thought about what had happened this morning. So, Tulloch had left home in a hurry immediately after seeing the forensic team at Skara Brae digging up the field in which he had led excavations a few years before Ola and Liam were killed. That felt significant, but she couldn't connect it to Ola's fight with Jason Miller, and that had to be important too.

Her hand left her ear, and she took her phone out of her coat pocket. She planned what she was going to say and dialled before she could chicken out. A tired-sounding woman answered the phone. 'Kirkwall Police Station.'

'DI Muir, please.'

'What's it regarding?'

She had already decided not to mention Ola or Liam in case the call handler put her through to one of the detectives from MIT instead.

'My name's Freya Sinclair. He asked me to call him back.'

There were no follow-ups. Freya was put on hold. A few seconds later, she heard a dialling tone again. Fergus answered on the second ring.

'I don't remember asking you to call me.'

'I didn't know what else to say to make sure I got you.'

'Well, it worked. What can I do you for?'

He didn't sound as annoyed as he had been on Monday afternoon. He didn't sound as amiable as he had been that same morning either.

'I've been speaking to a few people, and I've come across a couple of things I thought I should share with you.'

'Okay.'

'Did you know Ola had an argument with a guy called Jason Miller on the night she and Liam were killed?'

Technically, she didn't know it had been Jason – that was still an educated guess at this stage – but there was silence on the other end of the line. Freya could hear voices in the background. The station was a hive of activity. Did that mean there'd been a development, or was the level of chatter down to so many detectives being crammed into Kirkwall CID's tiny office?

'You have been busy,' Fergus said.

'Is that a yes?'

'Can I ask a favour?'

That wasn't the flow of conversation she had anticipated. 'Sorry?'

'Can I ask a favour?'

'Er, sure.'

'Keep that under your hat for now.' Fergus spoke more quietly now, his tone less abrupt. 'We might need you to report that later, but for now … hold off a blink, okay?'

Freya knew what that meant. The police were looking for Jason and didn't want him getting spooked by seeing his name in the press. Maybe there had been a development. She had been asked to keep leads out of stories before. Her stomach fluttered;

there was something in this. Perhaps one of the witnesses the police had reinterviewed in the past twenty-four hours had given them something more than Katie had.

'No problem,' she said. 'Listen, my source said they told the police about this seventeen years ago. They said you'd spoken to Jason back then.'

Fergus didn't respond. She heard the voices again. They sounded close. That was probably why he was keeping quiet. She remembered the story Kristin had told her on Monday, the one *The Orcadian* had run in the summer questioning how well the police in Orkney upheld the law. Was Jason someone they had let slip through their fingers seventeen years ago or had his involvement been actively overlooked? Either would be a huge story. But if she was the one to break it, Fergus would never speak to her again.

'Is there anything else?' Fergus asked. She noticed he wasn't using her name.

'Yeah. Do you know the name Gordon Tulloch?'

Another pause, then: 'I do. Why do you ask?'

His answer surprised her. Not because he knew Gordon, but because it was the first time he had answered a question. 'How do you know him?'

'He used to run the digs at the Ness, if I'm not mistaken. Taught at the college. He's done a heap of charity work too. He's well known in these islands.'

'Remember on Monday I said someone was watching you from the beach?'

'Uh-huh.'

'It was him. And now he's gone.'

'What do you mean, gone?'

Freya explained she had been to his house this morning to speak to him but he wasn't there. 'His neighbour told me he'd seen him leaving in his campervan that same morning, as soon as he'd got back from the beach. It looks like it wasn't planned either. He'd packed and left in a hurry.'

'And how do you know that?'

'He didn't even bother to shut the gate behind him, and I ...' She stopped, wondered if she should continue, decided it was hardly a crime. 'I looked through his windows and saw his cupboards and his fridge open. He'd emptied them.'

She was surprised and a little relieved when Fergus laughed.

Headlights swept through the cabin of her car. She looked up as a vehicle pulled off the road into the car park. As it turned and its beam was no longer blinding her, Freya could see its shape. It wasn't an Audi Q3. It wasn't Gill.

She exhaled slowly.

'Listen, what are you doing for lunch today?'

Another question she hadn't been expecting. She didn't answer right away, and Fergus continued: 'If you're free, it would be good to catch up properly. We didn't really get the chance the other day.'

A woman got out of the car and stood looking in Freya's direction. From the light of the streetlamp, she could make out it was Kristin. She was staring, trying to see if Freya was in her vehicle. Maybe she saw the light from her phone, because she waved. Freya hoped that was a good sign. She waved back.

'You there?'

'Er, yeah. That'd be nice,' Freya said.

'Okay. I'll see you later.'

Fergus hung up.

Kirstin was standing beside her car, seemingly waiting for Freya. Freya wanted to throw up and thought she might when another vehicle pulled in, but this one was too small to be Gill's monstrosity of an Audi.

She realised then that Fergus had hung up without agreeing a place or time to meet. As she got out of her Hyundai, her phone buzzed in her hand.

Burger van in Finstown. 12pm.

She didn't have Fergus' mobile number, it wasn't saved in her phone, but she guessed this was him.

Another text came immediately after it.

Next time you contact me, use this number. F.

Freya tried to calm the storm of emotions stirring in her as she crossed the car park. Nothing about that conversation had gone as she had expected, and it left her feeling unsettled. She didn't need it on top of everything else. She put her phone in her coat pocket and tried to focus on her facial expression as she walked, aiming for sufficiently contrite for not responding to Kristin's text yesterday but not so sorry that she looked guilty.

Sophie was standing with Kristin. Hers had been the small car that had just driven into the car park. Freya would rather have done this without anyone else there.

'Muhammed Ali, you're back!' Sophie exclaimed with a grin as Freya approached.

Freya laughed. Not because she found it funny – she didn't even understand what Sophie had said – but because Sophie had said it in such a way that it was clearly a joke, and in her nervous state Freya had responded how she thought she ought to. She immediately realised it was the wrong reaction.

Kristin slapped Sophie lightly on the arm. She looked angry.

'Kristin, I'm so sorry about yesterday,' Freya began. 'My phone battery died before I could read your text, but I've been busy speaking to some good sources. You'll not believe what I've found out.'

Kristin didn't look as impressed as Freya had hoped.

Headlights caught her eyes again and she turned to see a large car entering the car park. This had to be Gill. But, as she shielded her eyes against the light, she saw it wasn't an Audi. It looked like a Mercedes.

'It's bloody freezing out here,' said Kristin as it parked up. 'Come on, let's get away inside.'

24

FREYA WAS HEADING FOR the large desk in the middle of newsroom when she felt a hand on her arm.

'In here, Freya,' Kristin said, nodding towards her office.

Kristin closed the door and immediately the room shrank. Freya took the same seat as she had on Monday, and she could hear the throb of the printing presses through the floor again. It mirrored the thump of her heart in her ears.

Kristin didn't sit, preferring instead to perch on the edge of her desk. She was towering over Freya and was far too close. Her perfume filled Freya's nostrils. She could taste its sweet scent on her tongue.

Tears brimmed in her eyes, but she tried to hold them back. She'd run through several imagined versions of this conversation in her head since yesterday afternoon and they had all ended with Kristin forcing her to apologise to Gill before Freya told her to stick her job and stormed out. She knew she couldn't do that in reality. She had to keep it together.

She failed immediately.

'Freya, yesterday I—'

'I'm so sorry.'

Hot, salty tears streamed down her cheeks. She wasn't sad, wasn't even angry or embarrassed anymore. She was simply overwhelmed.

Kristin picked up the same box of tissues off her desk that she'd offered to Beth. She passed them to Freya, who took one and dried her eyes.

'What happened?'

Freya wanted to answer. She opened her mouth, but her mind was scrambled, and she couldn't summon the right sequence of words.

'Gill told me you got upset with her.'

Freya looked up. 'That's what she said?'

'I'm paraphrasing. "Went fucking mental" was closer to her appraisal.'

Okay, so now Freya was angry again. She felt her hands ball into fists, her fingernails pinch the soft flesh of her palms.

'I want to hear your version of events. I know what Gill can be like. She's had …' Kristin stopped, pushed her tongue into the inside of her cheek. 'She's not had the easiest time over the years, but that's no excuse. She can be right a pain in the arse so, if she did or said something to provoke you, I want you to tell me.'

Freya wiped her eyes. What could she say? That Gill had told her off for butting in when she hadn't? That didn't seem enough to make a person break down the way Freya had.

But it wasn't just that, it was *everything*.

It was how close Gill stood to her and the stink of her breath and the way she kept grabbing at her fucking arm all the time. It was the constant undermining and the repeated references to her *Uncle* Fergus and the incessant howl from that bloody radio. It was the tone in Gill's voice when she'd spoken to Kyle, and seeing Fletch again, and that letter in her coat pocket, and the sight of all those faces in the photographs in Ola's room.

It was a lifetime of snide comments and small things that on their own didn't seem like much, but together they added up to something immeasurable, and they had all come roaring back at once.

But Kristin wasn't going to understand any of that, so what was the point in saying anything?

There was a knock at the door.

A tall, grey-haired man Freya didn't recognise opened it, poked his head into the office. Behind him, through the crack in the door she could see Sophie sitting at her computer in the newsroom, craning her neck, not even trying to hide the fact she was hoping to catch a glimpse of what was going on inside.

'Okay if I join you?' the man asked Kristin.

Kristin nodded and he stepped into the room in an ambush of aftershave. He wore a tailored blue suit, soft leather loafers, a smart grey shirt open at the collar. The smoky smell wasn't terrible, but it was too strong and the combination with Kristin's sickly-sweet perfume made Freya's face crumple.

The man rolled a chair in from the newsroom, sat down so close to Freya his leg was almost touching hers. She could feel his proximity like static on her skin. He smiled and offered his hand.

'Nice to meet you at last, Freya. I'm Alistair.'

Alistair Sutherland. *The Orcadian*'s owner.

Why the fuck was he here?

Alistair was slim, his grey hair and beard closely cropped. She knew he was in his sixties but something about him made him seem younger. He had that confidence that came from either money or good looks, and Freya supposed some might say he had both.

Perhaps he saw the panic on Freya's face, because he said, 'Don't worry, I'm not here to sack anyone. I usually let Kristin handle the hiring and firing. Don't let her friendly demeanour fool you: she's like a peedie terrier, this one.'

He smiled again, gave a small laugh which Kristin reluctantly returned. Freya thought her boss seemed nervous. She imagined Alistair's appearances here were rare.

Alistair glanced at Kristin. 'How far had you got?'

'Freya was about to give me her side of yesterday's events.'

He turned back to Freya, watched her through powder blue eyes accentuated by his suit. Neither he nor Kristin said anything further. Freya guessed that meant it was her turn to talk.

'It's like I said before, I was out all afternoon following a lead and my battery died. I lost track of time.'

'A lead in the *Bodies on the Beach* story? Anything juicy?'

Alistair was still smiling. Freya didn't think he was asking because he doubted her, he seemed genuinely intrigued. His relaxed mood combined with the obvious seriousness of his presence here was confusing.

Without naming Katie, Freya explained how she had tracked down one of Ola's school friends.

'Remember how Beth told us Ola and Liam had been at a party on the night they were killed?' she said to Kristin. 'My source was there. They told me Ola got into an argument with someone then she and Liam left in a rush, and nobody saw them again.'

'Did your source know who this other person was?'

'No, but I found that out too.'

She told them about speaking to the headteacher at Kirkwall Grammar School and getting the name Jason Miller.

'Jason Miller?' Kristin said. 'Bloody hell, I knew him. He was in the year below me.'

'Mr Henderson said all the teachers were concerned about him.'

'Mr Henderson, from English class,' Kristin said, shaking her head. 'Christ, this is a trip down memory lane. And aye, concerned is an understatement – he was a psychopath. He had the nerve to ask me out once, got really scary when I told him to fuck right …' She glanced at Alistair. 'When I said no.'

Kristin looked at the floor awhile, lost in her thoughts.

Eventually, she said, 'Well, I'll tell you what, if he's in any way involved in this, I wouldn't be the least bit surprised. I take it the police are aware of this?'

'I've spoken to DI Muir this morning,' Freya said. 'He didn't confirm or deny he knew about it when I asked him, but he's asked us to hold off on reporting it.'

'And does that mean what I think it means?'

Freya wasn't sure if Kristin had reached the same conclusion as her, but she nodded. 'I think they're looking for him, yes. Whenever the police asked us to withhold something like this at *The Herald* it usually meant they were tracking the guy down and didn't want him alerted before they had got to him. If they find him, we'll have the jump on everyone else, and if they don't, they'll no doubt come to the press for help. And we'll be able to report why.'

For the first time that morning, Kristin's face melted into a genuine smile. She looked at Alistair. 'Told you she was good.'

'And I never disagreed.' He turned to Freya. 'Did the person you spoke to know what the fight was about?'

'No, but …'

She stopped short of telling them Katie had spoken to the police when Ola and Liam first went missing, and how it could turn out the police had let a murderer slip from their sights seventeen years ago. Alistair had been the one to shut down Gill's story into police failings in the summer – she decided to keep quiet.

'But what?' Alistair asked.

'But it seemed like my source was holding something back,' she said instead. 'I think, if I talk to them again, or maybe speak to a few more of Ola's friends, I can find out what it was.'

Alistair gave a Kristin a look then. An unspoken message seemed to pass between them.

Kristin said, 'Look, chick, maybe it's best if you hand over what you've got so far to Soph.'

Freya frowned. 'Why?'

'When we asked you what happened yesterday,' Alistair said, 'we weren't only asking why nobody had heard from you all afternoon. What we meant was, what happened between you and Gill?'

Freya shifted in her seat. 'Nothing happened. She was yelling at me, I asked her to stop, she wouldn't.'

'So you hit her?'

Alistair's question floored Freya. It knocked the wind from her lungs, and she couldn't respond.

'When Gill got back here at lunchtime yesterday, she had a scratch under her left eye,' Kristin took over. She kept her voice low and calm. 'She said you'd been interrupting her during Beth's interview and, when she raised it with you on the drive back here, you screamed at her and jumped out of her car while it was still moving.'

Freya's head was spinning. Every single word of what Kristin had just said was like a knife to the stomach.

'She said she tried to stop you, but you … she says you slapped her face and ran.'

The scream she'd heard when she'd pulled her arm away from Gill – Christ, had she caught her? She hadn't meant to. It was an accident. She was trying to get away and the stupid bitch kept grabbing at her.

Freya wanted to say this out loud, wanted to yell it, but the words got lodged like a fishbone in her throat.

'We understand why you might have done it,' Alistair said. Kristin snorted a laugh and Alistair gave her look. She held up a hand in apology. 'We know why you came back to Orkney. I spoke to your previous editor before you joined us. Standard procedure, obviously, nothing more in it than that. Everything he told us about your work was exemplary. But he mentioned you'd spent some time in hospital.'

'Freya.' Kristin now, her voice still aiming for calm and soothing. 'Your last editor said there were rumours a man you were investigating for a story tried to have you killed, that he had someone push you into a busy road and you were struck by a car. They said you were lucky to survive. I mean, that's just … it's awful. I can't even begin to imagine …'

Freya screwed her eyes shut, felt the warm tears come again. She couldn't believe she was hearing this.

'We support each other here, Freya,' she heard Alistair saying softly beside her. 'We want to look out for you. We know you had counselling for a few months after your discharge, but something like that, it's not the kind of thing you forget in a hurry. So …'

'So, with that in mind,' Kristin continued for him, 'we think, from now on, you should avoid working on the Ola Campbell story.'

Freya eyes snapped open. 'What?'

'It's for the best. It surely can't be easy to—'

'No. That's bullshit! I've …'

She realised what she'd said, slammed a hand over her mouth. She looked from Alistair to Kristin with wide eyes. She wanted the ground to open and swallow her whole. She wanted to disappear. She wanted to go back in time and reset everything and start this day, this whole fucking week, from scratch.

'We're sympathetic to your situation,' Alistair said, breaking the silence. 'I imagine you're roughly the same age as Ola would have been now. I hear you went to the same school. Kristin said you remembered her disappearance well when her mother stopped by here on Monday. Dragging this up can't be doing your mental health any favours, but we cannot tolerate aggressive behaviour of the type we had yesterday—'

'But I didn't—'

'Please, let me finish.' Alistair's tone made Freya feel two inches tall. 'When I said we look after our own here, it's true. And Gill Irvine has been part of our family for longer than I care to admit. You've only been with us a couple of days. You're still in your probation period here, remember that.'

Perhaps seeing the look on Freya's face, Alistair tried a reassuring smile again.

'As I said, I'm not here to reprimand you. This chat is nothing formal. But I think it would be best for everyone if we can all agree you don't work on this story any longer. Does that sound fair?'

No, it fucking didn't. But it did sound familiar.

This was the Damien Barber debacle all over again.

Alistair stood and left the room. He was back ten seconds later with Gill Irvine.

Gill pulled the most contrite face her mean features could muster. 'I'm willing to accept we were both at fault yesterday. I pushed your buttons, you reacted. No hard feelings, eh, hen?'

Freya saw the scratch under her eye. It was barely visible, even though Gill hadn't caked herself in makeup today.

Gill pushed a hand towards her and, like she had yesterday, Freya wanted to run. She wanted to scream. But she couldn't. She shook Gill's hand and it felt clammy, the sensation of it against her skin bringing bile to her throat.

Freya was told to bring Sophie up to speed with what she had found out about Jason Miller, then this afternoon there would be a new story for her to cover.

'It's midwinter,' Kristin said in a tone that Freya guessed was supposed to spark some kind of excitement. 'They'll be hoping to see the sun light up the chamber at Maeshowe later today. For the first time in years, it's actually bloody clear out there for it, so it might happen. I want you there, it'll be a good change of pace for you.' She smiled. 'It's not all murder and mayhem around here, you know.'

Freya excused herself as soon as she could and immediately went downstairs to the bathroom. She couldn't be around people and needed some space, some time to readjust. She locked herself in the stall furthest from the door and sat on the toilet seat, listening to the sound of machinery pulsing through the walls. She had thought she was all cried out, but she was wrong.

She took out her phone, saw the photograph of Luna and Tom. She was about to call him, but she stopped herself. If he knew she was already having the same problems that had driven her over the edge in Glasgow, he would spiral into a panic, and that wasn't what she needed from him right now. She sat with her phone in her lap, and she heard the bathroom door open.

Heels clicked on the tile floor. Two feet came to a halt outside her cubicle.

'I hope you understand your situation now, hen.'

Gill's disembodied voice echoed around the room. A malignant air of stale cigarette smoke came with it.

'You can turn on the tears all you like. It might work with Kristin, but you don't fool me, nor Alistair. So you mark my words, sweetheart, if you ever pull anything like yesterday's stunt with me again, I will bloody end you.'

25

FREYA KEPT HER LUNCH appointment with Fergus. There was a queue at *Leigh's* – the burger van permanently parked in the waterfront car park in Finstown – and a steady flow of people replenishing the line. She looked down the row of cars that were parked facing the water. It was five to twelve and she couldn't see anyone waiting, so she got out of her little turquoise Hyundai and sat at one of the picnic benches on the grass, tapping the nail of each finger against her thumb and watching the sea while she waited.

Sunlight blinked back at her off the sapphire surface of the bay. There was no warmth in the day, though, and patches of snow still lingered on the north-facing slopes of the Firth Hills where the sun couldn't reach. The smell of fried onions on the crisp air made her stomach growl. To any of the people standing nearby she no doubt looked as serene as the sun-kissed sea, but her mind was a swirling vortex.

Before her autism assessment, she had watched autistic people talking on YouTube about their lived experience. She'd read blogposts and tweets too, and one of the things that had come across loud and clear was how nothing was automatic. Everything was an effort. At any one time, your head could be filled with a million different thoughts and feelings, each taking up space and demanding attention and making it impossible to focus on even the simplest of tasks. That was how she felt now.

She thought about Tom.

She thought about life growing up here.

She thought about Ola and Liam and Glasgow and Damien fucking Barber.

The irony of her situation wasn't lost on her. She and Tom had uprooted their lives in Glasgow to avoid stories like these, and here she was throwing herself into one right off the boat. The parallels between this morning and her experience at *The Herald* were staggering, only there it had taken three years to reach this point; here she had managed it in under three bloody days.

About eighteen months ago, Freya had been contacted by a woman named Amara Choudhry. Amara was a senior executive at Damien Barber's production company before she reluctantly resigned. She came to Freya after seeing her byline on the stories about the Partick GP a year and a half earlier. Amara claimed Barber had made several unwanted advances towards her, beginning with messages on WhatsApp and escalating to a point whereby Amara had to physically flee the office after Barber tried to grope her. She went to the police but, because the only evidence she had were the messages, and because Amara had not immediately shut Barber down, afraid about what would happen to her job if she did, the police refused to take the matter further.

'It can't just be me,' she told Freya. 'There must be other women out there he's done this to.'

Freya agreed. So she went looking for them.

Within a few weeks she had tracked down four more women, all of whom had reams of messages from Barber, but again the police hadn't acted and the women had all since left Barber's employment. Freya took their story to her editors, but they were reluctant to print.

'It's a "he said/she said" situation,' they told her. 'We need solid, irrefutable proof if we're going to run this.'

With the GP story, that had been relatively simple. Freya had posed as a patient and recorded the doctor trying to talk her into an intimate examination she clearly didn't need. She had managed to get staff who worked at the practice to search for the cameras the dirty bastard had hidden in his consultation room. She knew she needed a mole inside Barber's company if she was going to nail him, so she approached someone one of the women had recommended. Not only did they refuse to help, but they told Barber.

From that point on, as far as *The Herald* was concerned, the story was dead. Barber made a formal complaint of harassment, and a disciplinary note was put on Freya's personnel file. Her editors told her to back off Barber, anyone who currently worked for him, or anyone he had employed in the past. But she knew they were wrong, so she ignored them.

She told Amara and the other women to go public together. Put it on social media, get people's attention. It would mean missing out on breaking the story herself, but Freya didn't care, that wasn't the point. Then the women had changed their minds. Whether it was the fear of going it alone or someone threatening them, Freya never knew, but now nobody was willing to talk. Only, that didn't mean it was over.

Freya believed those women: Barber had abused them, and he would do it again. Freya couldn't understand why nobody was willing to do something about that. Her increasing frustration had come at a time when she was already losing faith in her chosen career, and her rapport with her colleagues, which had never been great, was coming apart at the seams. It was affecting her home life, her relationship with Tom, and she felt like her whole world was beginning to unravel. She had burned out and, at her lowest ebb, she had stood on the pavement's edge on a rain-soaked February evening and wished for everything and everyone to go away.

A car horn snapped her from her thoughts. A black Volkswagen Passat pulled in next to her Getz. Fergus was behind the wheel.

She still hadn't decided whether to tell him she had been taken off the Ola and Liam story before he walked over to her table. Fergus offered her a weary smile but no hug today. His grey scruff was becoming a beard, his eyes looked bloodshot.

'Ever eaten here afore now?' he asked her.

'I don't think so.'

'You'd remember. Best burgers you'll ever eat. Go for the Smoke Stack. You won't regret it.'

They made awkward small talk while they queued at the van. Fergus asked after Tom and how he was finding life in Orkney and how she was adjusting to being back.

'Must be lonely for the lad,' he said. 'No friends here, not starting work yet, and you out all day long.'

Freya answered like she was facing questions on a game show. They reached the front of the queue before she remembered she was supposed to ask questions back, but she knew Fergus had never been married and the only family he had was an elderly mother who lived in Westray. She surreptitiously glanced at his hand. Still no ring.

They went back to the picnic table with their food. A small family of eider ducks had left the water and were making their way between the benches, hoping for a bite. Having not eaten all day, Freya was starving. She took a mouthful of her burger and, bloody hell, Fergus was right.

'Wasn't lying, was I?' Fergus said, reading her mind.

Her mouth was too full to answer. She shook her head.

'Listen, Red …'

Calling her 'Red'. That was a good sign.

Fergus put his burger back in its cardboard tray, dabbed his lips with a napkin. 'I wanted to apologise for my manner on the phone this morning. If I was abrupt, it was only because I didn't want folk to know I was talking to you.'

'And I'm sorry we spoke to Kyle when you asked us not to. But, you know, it is kind of my job. And I did warn you before we ran it.'

'That you did. But it's my job to catch whoever murdered those two teenagers, and there's colleagues of mine who believe the press only get in the way.'

'But you don't?'

'Some of you have your uses,' he said with a grin. 'Speaking of, I'd like to hear how you came by the name Jason Miller.'

'I can't tell you my source.'

'Of course.'

'But I can say I spoke to some of Ola's old school friends.'

'As have we. Most of them remembered Miller being at that party in Harray, but not a one knew his name.'

'I went to Kirkwall Grammar and spoke to some of the teachers too. I found him on a photograph in the school foyer from a description I'd been given.'

Fergus smiled at that. 'You're your father's daughter, I'll say that.'

Freya felt herself blush. She took another bite of her burger.

'In any case,' Fergus continued, 'this is where you reporters make yourselves useful. There's every chance we'll be asking you to print a statement for us later saying we're looking for Miller.'

'You haven't been able to find him?'

'We know where he should be – he stays down in Aberdeen now – but he wasn't home last night when their CID went round for us. He wasn't back this morning either.'

'Have you got enough to get a warrant to check his phone?'

Fergus grinned at that and Freya felt her cheeks warm again. 'It came through this morning. His mobile's been off since yesterday afternoon for some reason. Last time it pinged, as they say, was off a tower along the A9 north of Inverness. Clearly our boy's on a peedie road trip.'

'Do you think he's coming here?'

'Not sure why he would, but we've got the ferries and airports alerted on the off-chance.'

'What do you think it means?'

'At this stage it doesn't mean anything. We just want a word with him, tie up a few loose ends.'

'If none of the witnesses from the party knew his name, how did you get it?'

'It was in the old case files. We had a sketch artist speak to the witnesses during the original investigation, got his name through that. We took a statement from him back then, but Jim …' He paused, ran his tongue across his lips. 'I should've said this sooner, but you understand we're off the record here?'

Freya wondered again if she should tell him that it didn't really matter, but she simply shrugged. 'Sure.'

As she had been on Monday, Freya was a little confused about why he was being so forthcoming with her when, at the same time, he seemed cagey about any of this getting out. She didn't know what his motivation was, but she decided to go with it. She was happy he was talking to her at all.

'Seventeen years back, our force was a very different place. You'll mind this from your dad, no doubt – there was no Police Scotland back then, no MIT. We were Northern Constabulary and, when those kids went missing, we were left on our own to find them.'

Freya nodded. She ate another mouthful of her burger, let him talk.

'I don't know if you recall, but my boss back then was a man named Jim. Jim Shearer.'

Freya did remember him. She'd seen his name in the archives on Monday too. 'He took over from my dad.'

'He was promoted to DI, that's right. And taking over from Neill, he had big boots to fill. Anyone would've struggled, but Jim was never up to it. Not even close.'

'So why did he get promoted?'

'That was the way it worked back then. He was pals with the Chief Inspector at the time, a fella named—'

'Allan Tait,' said Freya. 'I remember him too.'

Fergus nodded. 'Aye, well, Allan put Jim forward and that was all it took. Jim ran the investigation with myself and the two other detectives we had in CID at the time. We had the uniforms to call on too, but that was about it.'

'How does this relate to Jason Miller?'

'Jim spoke to Miller after we'd got his name. There's a statement from him in the files dated two days after Ola and Liam had gone missing. According to Miller, he'd been invited to that house party by Liam, and everything had been fine until Ola had reacted poorly to some joke or other he'd cracked. He said she'd been off with him all night and she took this joke the wrong way, then she and Liam scarpered and that was that.'

'And where did Jason go?'

'Well, this is it. Per the statement, he left soon after, went straight home to his mam and dad's house. Reckons he was there by ten and never left again that night. But there's nothing in the files to show that Jim followed that up.'

'So nobody corroborated his statement? They didn't check his alibi?'

Fergus shook his head. 'His mam and dad still live local. We've spoken to them and they tell us they're sure Miller was home with them.'

'Come on, we're talking about one night seventeen years ago. How can they possibly remember?'

'Hence us wanting a word with him again.'

Freya was convinced now – as was Fergus, it seemed – that Jason Miller had to be a suspect. He'd had means and opportunity; it was just a question of working out his motive. But if he had murdered Ola and Liam, how was Gordon Tulloch involved? The two strands didn't seem to connect. She kept back what she had found out about Tulloch when she was forced to hand over her work to Sophie this morning, hoping it was a line of enquiry she could pursue herself. She worried now it might be pointless.

'So,' Fergus said, 'keep an eye out for the statement this afternoon, okay? You can give your editor – what's the girl's name? Flett? – you can give her the heads-up it's coming.'

Fergus must have seen something in Freya's body language. 'What is it?' he asked.

She had to come clean. 'Technically, I'm not working on that story anymore.'

Fergus opened his mouth to say something but paused, gave it some thought. 'Let me guess. Gill Irvine?'

Freya nodded.

'I had a feeling you two weren't going to get along. Thought you might have been able to play nicely for more than a couple of days, mind. What happened?'

'I hit her.'

Fergus laughed. A wholehearted one straight from the belly. 'It was an accident.'

'Nobody hits Gill Irvine by accident,' he said, and Freya couldn't help but grin too. 'How did it happen?'

'She grabbed my arm. I was trying to pull away. I guess I caught her. Now Kristin and Alistair, he's the newspaper's owner—'

'Alistair Sutherland. I know him well.'

'He and Kristin think it's best I don't work the story anymore. They think it's triggering for me, or something.'

They went quiet for a while then. Fergus seemed distracted all of a sudden, lost in thought. In the silence that passed between them Freya could hear the chug of the generator firing the grill at Leigh's, the metallic ring of the ropes clattering against the flagpole by the jetty where an Orcadian flag – a blue and yellow Nordic cross on a red background – shivered in the breeze.

Finally, Fergus said, 'I take it this happened sometime this morning, seeing as you were out trespassing at Gordon Tulloch's house earlier?'

She looked at him, was glad to see him smiling. 'They told me soon after I'd spoken to you.'

'Well, nobody's reported Gordon Tulloch missing.'

So he'd looked into it. 'Do you think there's something in it?'

'I doubt it.' He wiped his fingers on his paper napkin, screwed it up and dropped it in the grease-stained cardboard tray. 'Though I am curious: how did you place him as the man you saw at Skaill on Monday?'

'I recognised him in a photograph in an article about Skara Brae.'

'That you just happened to be reading?'

'Tom was reading it. My mother told him about Gordon not turning up to the Archaeological Society's Christmas lecture.'

'And how did she know that?'

'She was there.'

'Helen's into archaeology now?' He chuckled. 'Wonders never cease.'

Freya smiled too. 'That's what I said.'

'Well, I'll have a word with John Denison over at the Archaeological Society, see if he's still worried,' Fergus said, stretching out his back. 'But, given what we've got on, I can't take a serious look at this without a missing person's report. That woman Macintosh would have a fit.' He checked his watch. 'Speaking of ...'

'Why don't I report it?'

Fergus shook his head. 'I'll speak to John.'

'But I could just—'

'Trust me, Red. I'll talk to John. We'll go from there.'

The sudden abruptness of his tone invited no argument. Freya wasn't sure where that had come from, but she nodded.

Fergus stood. It was time to go.

Freya still had dozens of questions as they walked across the grass, such as: had the police discovered how Liam could afford that car? And something had been bugging her since yesterday's press conference too.

'Can I ask you something?'

Fergus stopped by his Passat. 'Depends what it is.'

'At the presser yesterday, DCI Macintosh mentioned forensic evidence related to the circumstances surrounding Ola and Liam's death.'

'And your question is?'

'It can't have come from the bodies – she said they were so decomposed you might never know the exact cause of death – so I'm guessing there wasn't anything obvious on the bones themselves. Plus, they hadn't even been fully excavated by yesterday morning, had they?'

'We're finishing up at the site just now. Yesterday's weather didn't help. The remains should be on their way to Aberdeen about now.'

'Well, that makes me think it was something about the clothing, or something else you found right there in the grave sites, right?'

Fergus glanced around. There was nobody nearby to overhear. 'And if I tell you, what are you going to do with that information?'

'Nothing. I'm just curious.'

That was true, she hated not knowing things, puzzles she was unable to crack. It was another way in which she was her father's daughter, as Fergus had said. She thought about using those exact words with Fergus, thought he might understand and it might convince him to tell her, but there wasn't time before he spoke.

'So you wouldn't be looking to use it to get yourself back in your editor's good books?'

Her initial reaction was to be offended, but after a moment or two that passed. It was a fair question. After all, she had said it herself, it was her job. 'No. If Kristin thinks Gill Irvine can do a better job, good luck to her.'

'So why do I get the feeling you won't leave this one be?'

She didn't answer that.

Fergus ran his tongue across his teeth. 'It's not what we found in those graves, it's what we didn't.'

She hoped he wasn't going to leave it at that.

'Do you know much about how quickly clothing perishes on a body, Freya?'

Lots. 'A little.'

'Natural fibres – cotton and the like, leather – that doesn't last long, but metals and man-made materials like plastics, elasticated items, they can take decades to decay in the ground, even in the presence of organic tissue.'

Freya nodded but didn't say anything. Where was he going with this?

'In Ola's grave, we found no sign of any surviving elastic from any undergarments. No underwire either. As far as I'm aware, they still haven't.'

It took a moment, then: 'She wasn't wearing underwear?'

Fergus shook his head. 'No shoes, either. They had been buried on top of her, but the underwear was gone completely, far as we can gather. Her leggings were torn too, at the waist. I don't mean to bring your lunch up, Red, but even bloating during decomposition wouldn't have done that.'

He stared at her to see if she was putting two and two together.

There was no other solution that could be reached. 'She was raped?'

'We may never know for sure, but it's a fair assumption someone at least tried.'

The wind picked up off the water and blew a chill through Freya that reached her bones.

'What Jess said about the cause of death, it is strictly true that we might never know, but we can more or less guess.' Fergus rubbed his forehead with the palm of his hand, like he was trying to rub away something inside it. Some memory or awful piece of knowledge. 'The pair of them, they had plastic bags over their heads. I thought the boy Kyle might have told you that too, but he either didn't realise or he was trying to pretend he didn't see it. Can't say I blame him. The skulls were in fragments inside, caved in with a rock or something. Whoever did this ...' Fergus stopped, swallowed. 'Whoever did this to that young couple, he must have had a rage burning inside him like no other. Their heads came out in pieces. I mean, I've never ...'

He looked down at his feet, like he was back in Bay of Skaill seeing the bones being lifted out of the dirt.

Several moments passed before he gathered himself. He looked at Freya, the whites of his eyes cracked and red. 'This is why we'd very much like to speak to Mr Miller again. Your editor might have a point, you know. The facts of this case aren't pretty – no one would judge you if you wanted to leave this one to someone else.'

Freya said nothing to that, and a sorrowful smile grew across his lips.

He nodded. 'Aye. That's what I thought.'

26

From Finstown, Freya drove five minutes inland to the car park at Tormiston Mill. Across the busy A-road, a grass mound rose twenty-five feet out of a farmer's field. Inside was Maeshowe: the five-thousand-year-old chambered tomb that would be brought to life with golden light at sunset. If the conditions didn't conspire to ruin it.

To the south, the sun was already sinking into the saddleback dip between the two highest peaks on Hoy. As she'd left the coast behind, she had seen the first clouds begin to gather low on the horizon to the north, but the rest of the sky remained clear, a bright cobalt blue. It appeared this once-a-year-at-midwinter event might actually happen, but Freya didn't know how she was going to give it her full concentration given what she had just heard.

Another car pulled into the car park. Freya checked the clock on her dash and saw it was a little after one. People probably wouldn't start to gather in earnest for another half an hour yet. She had time to sit and think. She wrapped and unwrapped her hair around her finger as she replayed her conversation with Fergus. Far too often during her stay on the Crime and Courts desk she had reported on cases where women had been raped and murdered, and the killers, possibly in a fit of shame at their disgusting act, had covered or disfigured the bodies in some way after death. Freya thought of the empty eyes and sadistic smile she had seen in that photograph of Jason Miller and wondered if he was capable of such unimaginable things.

If he was, had he acted alone?

Had he left Liam alive to witness what he was doing to Ola or had he killed him first?

That didn't bear thinking about, so she tried to clear her head and focus on other matters, such as why the two of them were at Skara Brae. And why had Jason really gone to that party in Harray where nobody knew him? It seemed like he had gone there specifically to taunt Ola, but why? Something as simple as a crush? Maybe Jason wanted Ola and the feeling wasn't mutual.

Thinking of the party reminded Freya of something in Ola's diary. Three weeks before Ola and Liam had been killed, Ola had written that Liam needed to tell her something he was keeping from her or they were through. They had been at the party together that night so their relationship hadn't ended, which meant he must have told her. And whatever he had said, Ola had never written it down. In fact, she never wrote in her diary again.

Another vehicle arrived. Freya began to grow anxious she had misjudged this and the place was going to get busy quickly. She decided to walk over to the tomb's entrance, taking her phone out on the way, and she saw she had several notifications. Top of the list was a text from Tom with a photo attached. Luna was on a beach, seawater dripping off her glossy black fur and a yellow tennis ball in her mouth, and behind her the rusting brown hull of a ship was poking out of the shallow turquoise water. She recognised it as Inganess Bay on the outskirts of Kirkwall.

Fancy joining us for lunch?

A thought flashed through her mind. Only for a moment, but she hated herself for thinking it.

He's checking I've not had a meltdown today.

Hot on its heels, another idea followed: what if he actually was feeling lonely, like Fergus had said? She'd heard Fergus' words but not fully processed them at the time. Tom might have been missing her. Or perhaps he was longing for someone to talk to. That familiar incision of guilt sliced her insides. She needed to do better. Christmas was less than a week away and she still didn't even have a gift for him. But just the thought of finding time to sort something brought butterflies to her stomach and sent her hands into a flap.

She couldn't think about this now. She sent a text back apologising and saying she hoped they had a nice time. She would sort this out later.

She moved on before her guilt grew too strong. Next on the list was a notification that there were replies to the private messages she had sent yesterday. She opened *The Orcadian*'s Twitter profile and saw several people had got back to her. The first reply was from the only person to have had a good thing to say about Liam: Scott Connelly.

The message preview read: 'I knew Liam better than anyone. I can tell you …'

Intrigued, she opened the message.

'I knew Liam better than anyone. I can tell you everything you want to know, but how do I know you won't twist what I say?'

Not as exciting as she had hoped.

A small group had gathered on the grass by the gated entranceway to the tomb, but no sign of the rangers yet from Historic Scotland, so Freya stood to one side and tried to compose a reply. She began to type, stopped herself, deleted it. This thread was open to everyone in the newsroom, so if she replied they could see it. Gill 'didn't do' social media apparently, but someone would have to check it. Kristin might have already asked Sophie to pick this up, though all the replies were showing as being unread, so she mustn't have done it yet. Still, if Kristin caught Freya asking members of the public questions about Ola and Liam, there would likely be hell to pay. As Alistair had seemed so keen to stress that morning, she was still on probation.

She was about to close the app when another message appeared.

'You started typing, you there??'

Scott Connelly was online right now.

Fuck it. She quickly typed: 'I'm here.'

She had no idea why she'd done that, but it was at least worth hearing what he had to say. If it was useless, or if he was some faceless internet troll looking to take the piss, she would simply give him Gill's email address and mobile number.

Three small dots appeared next to Scott's avatar, meaning he was typing. 'You didn't answer my question.'

She sighed. 'I don't have an agenda, I simply want the truth. I know …' She paused, considered what to say. 'I know Liam wasn't like people are saying. He was quiet, sensitive, and some people mistrusted him because of that. I can relate. I want to make sure he's represented fairly.'

She pressed send then wondered if she should have bothered. She followed it up quickly with: 'How do I know you're a reliable source? Tell me something about Liam.'

The three dots returned. They stayed on screen a long time. Scott was clearly typing an essay. Freya's right foot began to tap – the longer this went on, the more chance there was of someone else logging on and seeing her. She made a mental note to delete this whole thread once the conversation was done.

She looked up at the sound of more people arriving. When she looked back at her phone, Scott had replied. He'd written that Liam's nan was called Eileen and he'd given the address where she and Liam had lived on King Haakon Street in Kirkwall. He'd told her Liam's parents were called Sharon and Mark and that Sharon had died of an overdose in Wick when Liam was a young teenager. Freya knew most of this from her conversation with Mr. Henderson. It was accurate, but it didn't mean Scott knew anything of any use.

'I know all this,' she wrote. 'What can you tell me that nobody else will?'

Three dots again. Freya decided this was Scott's last chance. She began to hop from foot to foot, a chill setting in from standing out in the deepening cold. Her fingers became numb where they were out of her sleeves, holding her phone.

Finally, Scott replied: 'I was at the party that night in South Ronaldsay. I know what happened there.'

She read the message a couple of times. Had this guy really just made such a basic mistake? She was surprised by how disappointed she felt to find this wasn't going to go anywhere.

'The house party was in Harray,' she wrote back.

She was composing a follow-up telling him not to bother wasting any more of her time when he replied: 'The first one was. I'm talking about where they went after.'

Her pulse quickened.

Before her frozen fingers could tap out a reply, Scott wrote: 'Do you know about the argument Ola had in Harray?'

Freya deleted what she'd typed, wrote: 'Yes.'

'It was with a boy named Jason Miller. He told Ola her younger sister had been taken to a house in South Ronaldsay by some friends of his. That's where Ola and Liam went. Bet you didn't know *that*!'

Freya fought to keep her excitement in check. How could she be sure this guy was reliable? She guessed she couldn't. But the fact he knew Jason Miller's name meant he was someone worth talking to further.

'How do you know about this?'

'I told you, I was there,' Scott wrote back. 'I was at the house when the two of them showed up. I spoke to Liam. I can tell you what happened.'

She thought for a second. It was clear from the presser yesterday that Fergus and MIT weren't aware of any of this.

'Have you told the police?'

Nothing then. No dots. No avatar.

There was a murmur of excited chatter among the crowd and Freya looked up. The rangers from Historic Scotland were walking along the track to the tomb, ready to get everything underway.

She looked back at her phone. Still nothing.

She needed to get this conversation off *The Orcadian*'s account, quickly. She switched to her own Twitter profile and sent Scott another message. This opened up a whole new set of risks – he would have a direct link to her personal life and she knew nothing about this man. But she decided she barely put anything personal on social media these days anyway. It was a risk worth taking.

'This is my personal account,' she wrote. 'We can talk here privately, nobody else has access to this. Forget what I said about the police. Anything you tell me will stay between us.'

She realised that last part was a lie; if he told her something incriminating, she would have to report it to Fergus. But for now, it was as close to the truth as it needed to be.

She changed back to *The Orcadian*'s profile. Still no reply there. She took screenshots of Scott's messages so she could keep the information then she deleted the thread. She went back to her own profile to find a message waiting: 'I don't want to talk to you here.'

Her heart sank.

Then the dots reappeared.

'Better to talk in person. The harbour front, St Margaret's Hope. 6 p.m. tonight.'

27

Freya held her breath and waited.

The clouds that had threatened the clear sky earlier never arrived and, as the sun dropped behind the ridge between the silhouetted hills on Hoy, something magical occurred. A fragile thread of sunlight, the last of the year's shortest day, was spun across the islands and turned everything it touched to gold. The Barnhouse Stone, a solitary monolith standing in a field a few hundred metres to the south of Maeshowe, was momentarily brought to life as the sun grazed its head, focusing the light, sending it in a beam down the long, narrow entranceway to the tomb. Freya had been fascinated with Maeshowe since coming here as a little girl, seeing the runes scratched into the stone walls a millennium ago by Vikings trapped in a snowstorm and immortalised in the *Orkneyinga Saga*. This place was clearly special, and as the day's last light painted a portal at the back of the dark chamber, illuminating the ancient stones in a spectacular, almost supernatural glow, a reverent hush fell over the crowd. Freya held her breath and, for one blissful moment, found herself entirely under its spell.

Then the darkness returned.

She had found it hard to focus prior to the sunset. But she'd got some good lines from the rangers and a few folk in the crowd, and by five she had a story ready for *The Orcadian*'s website. This might not have been the beat she wanted, but she was determined to show Kristin her talents were being wasted. After that, she had texted Tom to let him know she would be late home, that she needed to speak to a source in South Ronaldsay. She neglected to tell him it was a source she had never met and knew nothing about. He knew where she was going and knew to call if he hadn't heard from her by eight. She was sure it would be fine.

By the time she left the newsroom, the clouds had drawn in and the stars broke through only in patches. As she left Mainland behind and crossed the causeways over the Churchill Barriers, the world grew darker still. Here there were fewer settlements, more sea than land. Black water stretched out into the void either side of her – the deceptively serene expanse of Scapa Flow on her right, the churning North Sea on her left. Waves crashed against the giant cuboid blocks of the barriers and spilled over onto the tarmac.

Despite being connected to the rest of Orkney by road for more than half a century now, South Ronaldsay felt as cut off from the world as any of the other outer isles. Remote. Sparsely populated. Separated from Kirkwall in both space and time. It was getting on for six by now, but it could have been any hour after midnight. There were lights on in the crofts and farmhouses she passed, but they were so few and far between as to make no discernible difference. South Ronaldsay was a long, narrow island running almost exactly north to south along the lines of the compass. St Margaret's Hope, the island's only village, was at the northern tip – a tight huddle of old stone buildings around a small harbour in a sheltered bay. The ferry terminal for the catamaran to Gills Bay on the Scottish north coast was here, about half a mile out of town. Freya could see it across the water from where she parked on Front Road. The village was in almost complete darkness, only two streetlights illuminating the harbour front, but the modern ferry dock was fully lit and she could see a few workers in hard hats and hi-vis vests busying themselves in anticipation of the ferry's return. That made her feel a little better.

There were no other cars here, no signs of life. She glanced at the clock and saw there were still ten minutes until six. Still early yet. She considered doing some more research into Scott Connelly – his Twitter profile had given little away and she hadn't had time to look anywhere else online – but she was keen to save battery. Unlike yesterday, her phone had survived the day, but it was already under thirty per cent charged. So instead she sat in the dark cabin of her car, watched the lights from the ferry pier paint yellow streaks across the water, and she counted the piercings in her ear forward and backward, forward and backward while she waited.

And waited.

Six o'clock came and no sign of Scott.

At five past she checked her phone for any messages. Nothing. Across the bay she saw a car drive down the narrow lane towards the ferry terminal and it occurred to her that she might have misunderstood; Scott had said the harbour, but he could have meant the dock. It was a less intimidating place to meet. Perhaps he worked for the ferry company and six o'clock was the time he got off.

She took the binoculars from the glovebox and got out of the car. The wind bit into her; it was so much colder here than in Kirkwall. She looked across the bay, tried to pick out anyone waiting in a car or standing around on their own.

She saw neither.

Somehow, being outside made the village seem darker, quieter. There was a sign for a B&B across the road, but it was closed, notices in the windows advising the business had been put up for sale. This little village had probably been popular with tourists driving off the catamaran at some point in time, but no longer. The place seemed dead and lifeless.

The hairs on the back of her neck stood up as she felt eyes on her. But she could see nobody watching. She got back in her car, locked the doors. As it had this morning, the stupidity of what she was doing dawned on her – she had no idea who this guy was or what he wanted with her. She could have at least mentioned his name to Fergus. But when had she had time?

In the dark and the silence, silly ideas began to plague her.

What if Scott was really Jason Miller?

What if Jason was still in touch with Katie, or with someone at Kirkwall Grammar, and he had found out Freya had been asking about him?

What if he knew the police were looking for him and he blamed her?

Fergus had said Jason's last known location was north of Inverness yesterday afternoon; depending on what time the police had notified the ports, he could be here right now.

It was ten past. Freya tasted metal on her tongue, realised she had chewed her lip and it made it bleed. She sucked the blood, hoping the saliva would make it stop, as she reached for her phone. One last check.

Sure enough, there was a message waiting: 'This was a mistake. I've changed my mind.'

28

'FUCK!'

Her phone clattered against the passenger door then fell into the footwell. Scott wasn't a psychotic killer, just some prick wasting Freya's time.

She reached over and retrieved her phone. A giant crack ran the length of the screen. Fucking brilliant. It still worked, though, and she opened the Twitter app again and wrote Scott a message, her thumbs hammering the shattered glass in her rage.

'Tomorrow my paper's going to run an interview with Ola Campbell's mother on the front page. She still blames your pal Liam for Ola's death, despite the fact he's seemingly a victim in all of this too. Don't you want people to know his side of the story?'

To her surprise, Scott replied. 'What do you mean "seemingly" a victim? He's the biggest victim of all in this.'

Freya shook her head. The fuck was that supposed to mean? 'How so?'

She watched the screen, waiting for an answer, wondering why she was bothering. She was never going to meet Scott, never going to be able to confirm he was a reliable source. His performance tonight suggested he wasn't. He could have lied about there being a second party here in South Ronaldsay when Freya had called out his mistake.

He did know about the argument, though. And Jason Miller's name.

Eventually, his reply arrived: 'Why isn't your name listed in the paper with the other reporters?'

Not what she was hoping for. But his question did reveal something: he must have access to a print copy of *The Orcadian*. Whoever this guy was, he was likely here in Orkney.

She thought for a long time before replying, still undecided about writing this off as a bad idea and heading home. But what if he really did know where Ola and Liam had gone after leaving Harray? What if he had been right about the argument? All afternoon Freya had been thinking about what Fergus had said about using the information he'd given her to get back on the story – she would never do that to him, but what if she could get something else? If she discovered what happened to Ola and Liam between leaving Harray and ending up at Bay of Skaill, Kristin would have no choice but to change her mind. Not only that, but it would put Gill back in her place.

I will bloody end you.

'Yeah?' Freya said out loud to no one. 'We'll fucking see.'

'I'm new. This is my first week. Tomorrow's the first edition that will include my name.' She sent the message, then immediately thought of something else: 'Google me, you'll see I used to work for *The Herald*.'

'I did google you. You wrote the stories about that pervert GP. That's why I think you're the right person for this. But I'll only talk on here for now, take it or leave it.'

The right people for this are the fucking police, she thought, but having almost scared him off earlier she decided not to type it. She rubbed her eyes. She was tired and staring at this screen in the dark wasn't helping.

'Okay, deal. We'll talk on here.'

She noticed her screen dim slightly and saw her battery had dipped to twenty-five per cent.

'If we're not meeting here, I'm going home,' she wrote. 'My phone's almost dead. If you message while I'm driving, I'll reply when I get back.'

She put the phone down on the passenger seat and started her engine. As she did, she saw out the corner of her eye that he had replied right away.

'No! Wait!'

The three dots appeared beside his avatar again, which was merely a blue circle.

'What do you know about a man named Graham Linklater?'

She sighed, picked up her device. Why did she have to wait for that? Scott was seemingly stringing her along. Before she had answered to say she knew fuck all and to ask who Linklater was, Scott wrote back again. This time it wasn't text, it was a link.

Freya clicked it and Google Maps opened on her phone, showing directions to a place a seven-minute drive away. She looked at the destination, which showed as a pin in the map. It was in the middle of a field close to the shore on the east of the island, didn't look like there was anything there. She switched to satellite view and now the pin sat dead centre in a group of small buildings around a courtyard at the end of a private track, metres from where the cliffs fell into the North Sea.

Thoughts collided in her brain, tied themselves in knots. What should she do next? Did she know the name Graham Linklater? It was a common enough surname in Orkney but it wasn't ringing any bells. She thought about googling him but she barely had any battery left on her phone and still hadn't put her charger in the car.

She went back to the Twitter app. Scott had typed another message.

'If you want to know where Ola and Liam went that night,' he said, 'go and see for yourself.'

* * *

The adrenaline makes my skin itch.

My car's parked where nobody can see it but where I've still got a clear view of the house. It's in darkness, nobody home, but that's fine – the fucker's got to come back at some point, and I can wait. I've waited seventeen years, another hour or two isn't going to kill me.

It's another dark night, the clouds have drawn over the sky as the evening's worn on and I only know the house is out there because I came here earlier. Several times, in fact. The man on my list owns properties all over Orkney so I had to make sure I've got the right one, and the only way to do that was to see this bastard coming and going with my own two eyes. It's taken me the best part of last night and most of this morning to find him. The house is remote – a large, old farmhouse near the coast. Other houses are nearby, but at a safe distance. There's lights on in some, but I'm too far away for anyone to see. I shut my eyes, ask myself that same old question:

Can you do it?

The blue ink on white paper rises in my mind's eye. An image of his face joins his name. I've killed before in anger. Only once, but I am ready do it again. So yes, I can do it. No fucking doubt in my mind.

Lights up ahead, a car approaching the house on the single-track road.

Someone is coming.

29

FREYA LEFT ST MARGARET's Hope and headed south. Within seconds she was alone in pitch-black open country.

Five minutes along the main road she pulled off onto a single-track road which she followed for about a quarter of a mile before taking another turning on the left. Tarmac turned to dirt as she drove. Each road narrower than the last. From the map she knew she was near the high clifftops in the east of the island, but it was impossible to tell by looking through the windscreen. Nothing ahead of her but black.

She came to a fork in the road. The track to the left had a metal gate across it and she could see in her headlights it was locked with a heavy chain and padlock. There was a sign too, a wooden board with the words *PRIVATE, KEEP OUT* painted in thick capital letters. To the right, another track led to a farm-house about half a mile away. Lights were on in the windows and what looked like a large bonfire was burning in the yard. Freya checked her phone again; the pin in the map was along the track to the left, beyond the locked gate. She would have to leave her car here and go the rest of the way on foot.

As she looked at the screen a notification popped up: Low Battery Mode. She had twenty per cent charge left. No signal, either.

Perfect.

She pulled her car as far onto the grass verge as she could, so as not to block any traffic for the farm, and got out. The wind sliced straight through her jeans; the rolling, treeless landscape offering no resistance to the gusts howling in off the sea. A particularly strong blast blew her a step backwards as she closed her car door and locked it. Now her headlights were off she realised exactly how dark it was this far out in the countryside; a thick, claustrophobic dark that felt like someone creeping up behind her and placing their hands over her eyes. From where she was standing in the road, she could barely see the gate.

Maybe it was the darkness, maybe it was the thundering sound of the sea colliding against the cliffs somewhere nearby, but she felt overcome with an immense feeling of dread. She stood still, hoping her eyes would adjust to the low light, but it was taking much longer than she felt comfortable with. She thought very hard about getting back in her car and returning in daylight tomorrow, but that would mean she was more likely to be spotted. The sign on the gate left no room for doubt; she wasn't supposed to be here. If she got caught snooping around and it got back to Alistair and Kristin, she'd have to tell them what she was doing. She didn't have enough yet to make them side with her over Gill. If she was going to do this, it had to be now.

She didn't dare use the torch on her phone for fear that the remaining battery would be gone in seconds. There was a small sign by the track to the farm where the fire was burning. She squinted at it in the dark, made out the word *Cleat*. No doubt the name of the family who lived there. There was no sign by the locked gate other than the painted board, no name of any family here. She climbed the gate, dropped down onto the track on the other side, started walking.

She could smell the smoke from the fire on the neighbouring farm. It smelled toxic, like they were burning plastic or rubber. Bags of rubbish, perhaps. Ahead of her she peered into nothing, like she was floating in the void of deep space. But she could hear the thump of the sea pounding against the cliffs. It grew louder and louder, like a giant's footsteps echoing across the land towards her. She couldn't tell if it was the dark playing tricks on her or if the cliffs really were as close as they sounded. She made sure to stick to the track.

After a minute or so another shape emerged out of the night. She saw no detail nor colour, only the outline of what she thought was the side of a building. Others soon joined it. It looked like one larger building then a couple of other smaller ones nearby.

Closer up, she was able to make out a house, saw there were outbuildings and a barn across the courtyard. She stood and listened but heard no sounds of animals in the barn, only the cry of the wind through the empty spaces in the brick. The yard was empty, no machinery, no cars. This place was abandoned.

The house was a two-storey farmhouse: a relatively recent build, within the last fifty years at least. There was probably an older homestead out on the land somewhere that had been abandoned and allowed to fall into disrepair when this one had been built. Freya wondered if anyone still lived here: that Graham Linklater that Scott had mentioned, perhaps.

She heard a sound then.

Distant but growing louder. Sounded like the rattle of a small engine, like a trail bike or quad.

She looked around but saw no lights and pretty soon the sound faded into the sigh of the wind. She turned back to the house; it was built in a backwards *L* shape, taking up two sides of the square courtyard. Like at Gordon Tulloch's house, she peered in through the windows and was surprised to see the place was furnished. As she ventured further into the yard the wind dropped a little and the darkness grew thicker. Freya hadn't thought that was possible. She made out the shape of a door.

The cold metal of the door handle bit into her skin as she gripped it.

* * *

Headlights flood my car.

I duck down, wait till they fade again then poke my head up, slowly. A car drives past and on towards the house.

It's time.

I reach over the passenger seat and open the glovebox, take out the long kitchen knife I've brought with me from my dank, shithole flat. The one I bought years ago, originally for my own wrists. But, back then, as the cold metal had begun to burn, I'd had a better idea: I wasn't the one who should have been feeling this blade.

It wasn't me who caused this.

As blood spread across my palms, warm and sticky, I decided that if the bodies were ever found, if the clock ever began to tick, then that would be the time to finally do what I'd promised – come back here and kill every last one of those men.

An image enters my head of the giant clock on the TV in the break room, the booming sound of its tick, the heat that brings beads of sweat to my neck. That was never supposed to be my life. A fire breaks out in my chest as I think about what I had seventeen years ago. About what was taken. About what they did to ...

The car stops. Someone gets out. I watch them head for the house. I grip the knife in my gloved hand and open my car door.

30

THE DOOR PUSHED OPEN.

Freya jumped back. She'd half expected it to be locked. It swung in the wind, creaking on its hinges, only darkness beyond. A musty, mouldy smell rushed from inside and assaulted her nostrils. It stank of decay. It reminded her of Ola's bedroom.

A million different worst-case scenarios raced through her brain. The only thing she was afraid of was her own imagination, she knew that. But it didn't help. A gust blew the door backwards, sent it clattering against the wall. Freya could see into the hall where, now her eyes had adjusted, she made out the pattern of floral wallpaper. She crept forward, poked her head in and saw the hallway was small with doors off to either side, leading into each wing of the building. She turned on her phone to use the torch. The battery had dropped again, the cold draining its charge. Only sixteen per cent left.

She used a loose brick from the yard to prop the door. If she needed to, she wanted to be able to get out quickly. She was also worried about someone coming back and locking her inside, as though whoever lived here had simply popped to the shops and had forgotten to close the place up, but as she wedged the door in place she noticed the handle and lock had been broken. Someone else had been here. Looking at the rust around the lock, Freya decided that whoever it was hadn't been back in a long time.

She chose the door to her right.

It opened into what Freya sensed was a large room. She couldn't see the walls or the ceiling yet but the echo of her footsteps on the wooden floor told her it was a vast space. She felt a draught of cold air as she listened to the sounds of the house. She could hear the wind against the windows, the whistle of it coming down a chimney somewhere nearby.

Far off there was a faint tapping sound, hard to make out over the sound of her own pulse whooshing in her ears. She focused on it. Too rhythmic to be an animal. Or human. It came every time the wind blew, and Freya chose to believe there was a window open somewhere upstairs. It was a door banging in the breeze, she told herself, nothing more.

She turned on the torch and saw she was standing in a large open-plan kitchen. An oak table in the middle of the room was big enough for ten chairs around it. Faint white circles on its surface caught in the light; watermarks where drinks had been placed directly onto the wood. There was an Aga, an American-style fridge-freezer. Double doors ahead and a staircase immediately to her right. Freya lifted the torch and saw a mezzanine area running around the edge of the room. More doors led off it. This place was big and spacious, and she could imagine parties being thrown here, but couldn't imagine who would host them. Someone with a lot of money, that much was evident.

She checked the cupboards and drawers and found them empty. A thick layer of dust covered everything, and when Freya tried the taps over the sink the pipes rattled and groaned, and she quickly turned them off. She decided to try the doors at the back of the room before going upstairs – they led through to a lounge big enough for two corner sofas and another huge dining table. She couldn't see a TV. There were curtains at the windows and she spotted a light switch on the wall but, even though the darkness in here was terrifying, she decided against using the lights in case the house could be seen from the neighbouring farm. She heard the fireplace before she saw it, the wind howling in the empty grate.

The bluish-white light of her torch threw long shadows up the walls and they followed her as she climbed the staircase. It drew monsters that she saw out of the corner of her eye. When she looked back down into the kitchen from the mezzanine level, for one awful moment her mind played tricks on her and she thought she saw people sitting at the table. The tapping sound she'd heard was louder up here, the cold draught stronger too.

She tried each of the three doors leading off the landing. Bedrooms behind each of them, all furnished. The beds were made but the fabric on them looked faded, though it was hard to tell in this light. The knocking sound was coming from a shower door in an en suite bathroom off the largest of the three rooms and Freya saw the window here was still slightly ajar. She thought about closing it, wondered if anyone would notice if she did. She left everything as she found it and made her way back downstairs.

This felt like an anticlimax. Whatever happened here, there was no evidence of it now. Why had Scott wanted her to see this, though? What could she possibly gain from coming here? She went back to the vestibule where the front door was still wedged with the brick and she looked at the other door. Check the rest of the house, or cut her losses and leave?

She glanced at her phone: her battery was at ten per cent.

She'd come this far. Seemed silly to quit now.

31

FREYA OPENED THE OTHER door and immediately the atmosphere changed.

It was colder here, somehow even darker. She was in a cramped space with a low ceiling. Bare floors, stone walls, and black wooden beams. Despite being above ground it looked like a cellar and the smell of damp was potent.

This must have been the old farmhouse; the other wing was a newer, more modern extension. It wasn't furnished and, even with her torch on, it still seemed dark, like some force in here was sucking the light out of the room. She felt goosebumps creep across her flesh, the hairs on the back of her neck brush against her jacket. There was a door diagonally opposite her – bare wood with a round, iron handle. The dull echo of her footsteps was far too loud as she crossed the room to open it.

She came out in a corridor. A chill seeped through her blood as the torch beam fell on a row of old wooden chairs lined up side by side. It was so narrow in here there was barely space to walk past them. It reminded her of a hospital or a doctor's surgery. People sitting here, waiting to be seen. But for what? There were three more doors at the far end – one on either side of the corridor, one dead ahead – and no windows. The darkness was the deepest she had ever felt.

She walked slowly down the hallway, past the empty chairs. She reached the wooden doors at the end and she could feel her heart behind her tongue like a lump in her throat. She put her hand on each of the wrought iron handles, hoping to get a feel for what was behind each one, but she felt nothing but dread. She wanted to stop this, to go home to Tom and Luna and never find out what was on the other side of these doors, but she knew she couldn't.

Her hand had stopped on the door closest to her on the right.

She pushed it open.

She saw the figure on the mattress before her brain had time to work out what it was. She screamed, throwing her hands to her mouth, dropping her phone and plunging herself into darkness. She dipped to the floor, her fingernails scratching the floorboards as she scrabbled blindly for the device. Finding it, she lifted it quickly, shone it into the room to make sure the figure hadn't moved, but in the blue-tinted glow she saw it was still lying spreadeagled on the dirty bare mattress, arms and legs bound in place out to the sides with thick gaffer tape. It looked human in shape, but something wasn't right, and Freya's brain wouldn't process everything quickly enough to work out what it was. Something about the face. The eyes.

She scrambled backwards into the hallway, pointing the torch back into the room at the figure. It was then that she noticed the light catch on something on the walls. She forced herself to her feet and peered into the room.

The figure on the mattress wasn't human. It was an inflatable doll, saggy and wrinkled where the air had leaked out over time. Its legs were pulled apart, exposing a slit in the groin that had been daubed with what Freya hoped was red paint. Its mouth was gaping open as if in shock, its dead eyes fixed and staring at the ceiling. Freya lifted the torch beam to the walls – a message had been scrawled across the wallpaper in the same red paint, thin streaks of which had run down the walls beneath each letter:

We know your dirty little secret.

She fought to get her breath back, tried to take in what it was she was seeing. She needed to get a photo of this.

Her phone battery was at one per cent as she opened the camera.

She lined up a shot, there was a flash, then the screen went dead.

Darkness fell on her like a hood being pulled over her eyes.

Her breath caught in her throat. She pressed her hand over her mouth, desperate to keep calm, trying not to scream. Knowing that, if she allowed herself to start spiralling, she would never get out of here. She needed to retrace her steps to the front door. It wasn't far. It seemed like it in the thick dark that brought white spots of light to her vision, but it wasn't. *Just keep telling yourself that.* She put her phone in her coat pocket, felt along the wall with her hand.

There was a sound at the other end of the hallway. Something scraping across the floor.

32

For a split-second that felt like forever, Freya did nothing.

She froze, paralysed by fear, listening.

All she could hear was her heart firing in her ears, her heavy breathing. She screwed her eyes shut and part of her wished this wasn't real. She hoped to open her eyes and find she was at home and she'd fallen asleep in front of the fire and this was all a bad dream.

Then she felt a rush of cold air, like someone blowing on the back of her neck.

She snapped her eyes open and ran.

She collided with the chairs, fell and hit her head on the floor. An enormous clatter echoed down the corridor and her leg exploded in agony but there was no time to think about it now. She had the dreadful feeling she wasn't alone in this house, so she clambered to her feet and kept going, unable to tell for certain she was still facing the same way. Her hand thumped against the wall and she groped around for the door handle. Her hip was burning, her head throbbing, every single part of her was going to hurt like hell later but for now she could not have cared less.

Through the door, she ran across the room to the hallway. It was like running underwater. Like punching in a dream. Everything slower than she needed it to be. Her heart thumping in her ears.

The front door was almost closed, the brick having failed to hold. The scraping sound she'd heard, perhaps? Realistically she knew it was, that there wasn't really anyone in the house with her, but she wasn't going to wait around to find out. She threw the door open and ran out into the courtyard, filled her lungs with the frozen air and didn't stop to look for anything that might have moved it.

She just ran.

Her breath scratched in her throat. Her chest hurt and she wanted to cry but she needed to hold it together. Away to her right, the sea thundered against the cliffs. They must be so close. Any wrong step could send her tumbling to her death, but she didn't slow down. She felt stones beneath her feet: she was on the track again and soon she would be back at her car and she could get the fuck out of here.

She threw a look over her shoulder. Nobody there. Maybe it was relief, or perhaps she was sliding into shock, but at that moment she started to laugh. She slowed her pace, eventually came to a stop, and bent over, hands on her knees, panting for breath. She could taste the burning plastic from the fire, and she had to spit a thick lump of phlegm into the ground. She wiped her lips on her coat sleeve and stood upright again.

She was out.

She was safe.

Up ahead she could see the gate, could just make out the front of her car. She saw the dark shapes of people standing around it.

She froze, watched. Perhaps it was her eyes playing tricks on her.

Then the dark shapes moved.

Her heartbeat hammered in her ears again. She counted three of them – two tall, one much shorter. They were peering into her car.

She became aware her hands were clasped over her mouth. She was holding her breath again. The shortest of the three figures walked away from her car and came closer to the gate, stood there for a while, looking out into the darkness.

They were looking at her.

She didn't move. Perhaps she was too far away to be seen, but in her bright yellow coat, she doubted it. And if she could see them …

'Did you find what you were looking for?'

A woman's voice. Thick Orcadian accent. It sounded so calm, so non-threatening that Freya didn't know how to respond. She wasn't sure what was happening.

'You're not the first to come here,' the woman shouted over the wind. 'Doubt you'll be the last.'

'Do you own this house?' Freya yelled back.

She couldn't see the woman's face, could only see her shape. The woman was leaning on the gate while her two taller companions stood either side of her a few feet behind. They were looking at Freya now too.

The woman didn't answer her question.

'We've taken a note of your car and registration.'

Freya frowned. Her leg was throbbing violently now. She could feel blood running down to her ankle and it was sticky, starting to dry on her skin. She had no idea what was going on in this conversation. She wanted to go home.

The woman seemed to push herself off the gate. Freya heard the chain rattle against the metal post.

'Don't ever come back here.'

Someone whistled, like they were calling a dog, and in the next moment Freya heard the buzz of a small engine, same as she'd heard before going into the house. Lights came on, headlamps of two separate vehicles, bright as searchlights in the heavy dark. Freya covered her eyes, heard the growl of the engines, and when she lowered her hand, she saw the lights disappearing along the track to the neighbouring farm where the fire was still roaring in the yard. She watched a rush of red and orange embers escape into the empty sky and hurry away on the wind.

She became aware of her surroundings as though coming out of a trance. The roar of the sea, the bite of the howling breeze. The cold had spread to her bones and she realised she was shivering. She couldn't stay here a moment longer.

She started to run.

33

FREYA LOCKED THE DOORS and drove back along the uncovered track much faster than the surface allowed.

A ball of anxiety had grown in the pit of her stomach like a tumour and it didn't subside as dirt turned to tarmac. It was still there when she reached the main road and she was finally able to fully accelerate away. Her heart rate didn't start to settle until she had crossed the last of the Churchill Barriers and was back in Mainland where there were streetlights and houses and other vehicles driving by.

Then anxiety turned to excitement.

Free of the crushing dread, thoughts flooded her brain. Had Scott known what she would find? Had he sent her there to see it? She was too overwhelmed to piece this together and she wanted to ask him these questions, but couldn't. Her phone was dead. She needed to get home, charge it, then find out what was happening. And pray to God the photo had taken before the battery had run out.

From the track to their house, she saw the soft glow of Christmas lights through the living room window and her excitement receded, replaced by that familiar sense of guilt.

'That you?' Tom called out as she opened the front door. Same line as always.

Luna came hurtling across the hallway towards her. But, instead of dropping onto her back for belly rubs, she pulled up short, sniffed the air. She approached Freya cautiously, head low and tail down, then began to lick at Freya's leg.

'Did you get my text?' she heard Tom saying. 'Hope you've brought us something tasty for …'

He fell quiet as he came out of living room and saw her. He stared at her face, mouth open, his eyes tracking a path down to her feet, taking in the damage. Freya wanted to say something, to explain, but too many thoughts and feelings filled her mind at once and blocked the exits, stopped her from getting the words out.

Tom walked over, brushed a strand of her hair from her forehead and frowned at something, must have been a scratch or a cut she'd got when she had fallen over in the dark. His hand was shaking. He looked down and Freya followed his gaze to where Luna was licking frantically at a patch of blood seeping through her jeans by her left knee. Some of it had trickled down over her shoe. She pushed Luna away but she immediately returned.

'What happened?' he asked.

She heard the tremor in his voice. Anyone else, she might have missed it. She threw her arms around him, hugged him tight, buried her head in his chest. She heard him smelling the smoke in her hair. She shut her eyes and she wished this could be the end of it, that he wouldn't push her. That they could just go to bed and wake up tomorrow like none of it had ever happened. But it was Tom who broke the hug off first. He pulled back, looked her in the eye and she knew he was begging for her to tell him everything without him having to ask again.

She wanted to. She really did.

'Freya, what—'

'I don't want to talk about it.'

She pushed past him, took off her coat and hung it up and ran through to the bathroom. Her eyes were stinging from the smoke and she couldn't think about anything else. She needed to change her contact lenses, wash her face. Tom followed her down the hall. He stayed in the doorway while she stood over the sink, occasionally glancing at him in the mirror. There were black streaks of grimy dirt down her face and the scratch on her forehead was a lot worse than it had felt. It was more of a cut than a graze and it had bled into her hair.

'I don't understand,' Tom said. 'You said you were going to meet a source. Did they … did they do this to you?'

She closed her eyes, shook her head. 'I fell.'

'You fell? Freya, come on, your face and your leg are cut to shreds, and you smell like … what is that? Burning rubber?'

She didn't answer.

'Why aren't you talking to me? You're scaring me.'

Everything fucking scared him these days. She screwed her eyes tight as guilt twisted her insides at that thought. *Why does everything scare him, Freya? What did you do?* She didn't want to talk about this because she would have to lie, and she was sick of lying. Used to be that Tom was the one person in the world she never had to lie to, and now …

If she told him she'd been to some abandoned house tonight on the direction of a complete stranger he would panic, and he would do so because he still believed that less than twelve months ago someone had tried to kill her. Since February, he'd been wrapping in her cotton wool, treating her like some fragile object that needed to be delicately handled at all times, and it was driving her crazy. He had abandoned his friends, left his job, moved here, and it was all for nothing. And what was making it worse was it was all her fault. *She* had chosen to lie.

It was him, wasn't it? It was Damien Barber.

She'd had to say yes. The alternative was to tell him that she had walked out into traffic herself. She hadn't really wanted to die – at least, she didn't think she had – she had simply wanted all the noise and the light and bad thoughts to go away. Just for a moment. It wasn't just her editors and Damien fucking Barber, it was everything. She had wanted that feeling, so familiar to her, of frustration at never being understood, at never knowing why other people made the seemingly stupid decisions that they made, of pure and utter desperate helplessness at being trapped in a mind that never stopped, that wouldn't allow her to 'just let it go', to vanish if even for a second or two. She needed a break from a lifetime of seemingly talking in an alien language and never knowing why. She wanted a rest from herself. And so she had closed her eyes and stepped into the headlights like she was accepting the embrace of an old friend.

But she could never have told Tom that. It would have only scared him more. He wouldn't have understood, or he might even have taken it personally and decided to leave her, and she couldn't face that. And once the lie was out, there was no taking it back. Tom had begged her to tell the police and she had knowingly misled them, kicked off an attempted murder investigation she knew was a hoax, all so that she didn't have to tell him what she had done. How could she come clean after that?

'Freya?'

She opened her eyes. He was standing behind her now. He put a hand on her shoulder.

'You can tell me anything,' he said softly. 'You know that, right?'

Freya felt the walls of the tiny bathroom closing in. No space to breathe. There was a ringing in her ears and she had to get out. She pushed past Tom without saying anything and headed into the living room. Luna was on the sofa, but she jumped off when Freya sat down and ran into the kitchen. Freya shut her eyes again, put her head in her hands. She just needed a second, some space to think.

But he followed her.

'That cut on your leg looks bad. We need to clean it. Come on, I'll—'

'No, Tom. Just … just leave me alone.'

'Wait a second, how the hell am I the bad guy all of a sudden for being worried about you?'

'I can't take it. It's too much. You have to let me do my job.'

'*This* isn't the job!'

When she opened her eyes, she saw Tom had sat down on the sofa beside her. He tried to put his arm around her shoulders, but she shrugged him off and stood up.

'Why are you being like this with me?' he asked. There was a pleading in his voice that stabbed Freya right through the heart.

'I told you, I don't want to talk about it.'

'Yeah? Well, you know what, I do. Because we *never* fucking talk about it.' He stood too. 'There's been something gnawing away at you for months now. I mean, at first I thought it was shock from what happened so I didn't say anything, but I think … I think it's more than that. There's something you're keeping from me and that … that fucking terrifies me more than anything else.'

Freya felt her hands opening and closing, balling into fists. Her feet tapping so fast her ankles hurt.

'Christ, I thought that coming here would put a stop to this,' he said. 'I was happy to leave our friends behind and give up everything we had in Glasgow to move here because—'

'Happy? This was *your* idea.'

'Yes, because I wanted—'

'I never wanted to move back here,' Freya said. She was shouting now, didn't mean to. Didn't mean what she was saying either, but she couldn't stop it. 'I got away from this fucking place when I was eighteen and I never planned on coming back. I only did it to stop you going on and on and fucking on about it. We're only here because of you.'

That wasn't true and she hated herself for saying it. They were here because of her. Because of that fucking lie.

'It was the only way to protect you.'

'You can't protect me!'

The look on Tom's face was like she'd slapped him. He took a step back, seemed so startled that she wondered if she actually had.

'What happened to me in Glasgow, what happened to me tonight … it's going to happen to me again and again and again because *I'm* the problem. Me and my fucked-up brain. I'm always going to be like this and I'm not going to change. So, if that terrifies you, if you can't deal with that, then …'

'Then what?'

Tom spoke so quietly, so calmly, she thought she'd dreamed those words.

'Then what, Freya? What are you saying?'

Silence now. She heard the logs spitting in the fire, thought she could hear Luna whimpering in the kitchen. She knew she'd be hiding under the kitchen table, like she always did when she got scared, and that plus the look on her husband's face burned a hole inside her like acid in her chest.

She couldn't be here any longer.

She ran. Barged past Tom, ran back down the hallway. Back into the bathroom, slammed the door behind her so hard she felt the floorboards shake. She threw herself onto the floor against the bath and she burst into tears of anger, regret. A million other emotions she couldn't name raged inside her.

Her sobbing shook her, but she made no sound.

She stared up at the towels hanging on the back of the door, listening for the creak of Tom's footsteps in the hallway, hoping he would come to find her and put all of this right.

She fell asleep on the cold bathroom floor before he came.

* * *

A light comes on within moments of me knocking on the front door.

A silhouette appears in the glow behind the glass, growing larger as it nears. For the first time since getting out of the car, the chill from the wind reaches my skin, but in the next breath a gust of warm air brushes my cheeks. A short, fat man in his late sixties is standing in the open doorway staring up at me with a look of confusion. It quickly shifts gear to contempt.

'Yes? Can I help you?'

So many times over the years I've pictured this moment. I've fantasised about what I would do to him, what I'd say. Now, here I stand and my mouth goes desert dry, devoid of words. Sweat trickles between my fingers and I squeeze harder on the handle of the knife behind my back. He's still wearing a black woollen overcoat, smart black trousers, polished shoes – he's been out somewhere for dinner, perhaps, and has come back to this big, old house alone. His wife left him long ago and his kids have all grown up and moved away. I've read all about Graham Linklater online. They left because they knew what he had done. They knew, like so many other people on this shitty little rock know, and they didn't tell a fucking soul.

My silence changes his contempt to barely concealed anger. He shifts his weight from one polished shoe to the other. 'Is this some kind of wind up? The bloody hell do you—'

'You don't recognise me, Graham?'

I don't know why I asked that. Panic, perhaps. We've never met, I don't think. And even if we had, the damage wrought by the last seventeen years has changed me beyond all recognition.

But something registers.

A flicker of understanding in his eyes.

I like it. That flicker sends a spark through my veins. It's not recognition of someone he knows, more the use of his name. He's putting the pieces together to come up with the only obvious solution. The creases in his forehead, the anger etched across his face begin to fade and wither. It changes to fear.

He steps back. 'It can't … You can't possibly be …'

Maybe he's been expecting me since he heard about the bodies. Maybe he's been picturing this day for the last seventeen years too. Not like I have. Nobody has been waiting for this like me.

I bring the knife from behind my back, step over the threshold into the hallway, and the blood drains from his face. I calmly close the door behind me, hear it click.

I did have a plan – I was going to take my time with him, get him to talk, force him to tell me all the other names I want to know.

As seventeen years of pent-up rage catches fire in my stomach, the plan changes.

THURSDAY, 22 DECEMBER

34

FOR THE SECOND DAY in a row, Freya left the house while Tom was still asleep. She had found him in the spare bedroom when she had woken up on the bathroom floor. Or at least, the spare bedroom door had been closed. She had pressed her ear against it, listened awhile for any sign he was awake, had even raised her hand to knock. But she hadn't. She had gone through to the kitchen instead where she had found Luna who, not wanting to pick a side, was sleeping under the table. They had sat awhile together on the cold flagstone floor, Freya stroking Luna's ears, Luna licking Freya's injured leg, and Freya had silently cried again.

There were no stars this morning. The drive towards Kirkwall was cold, dark, and depressing. She got to town around seven thirty, plenty of time before she needed to be in work, but the thought of going into the newsroom filled her with nauseating dread. She had scratches on her face and a cut on her forehead and they were bound to ask why. She thought about calling in sick but didn't know if she could face phoning Kristin. Plus, if she didn't show, Gill was bound to see it as a victory. Freya didn't want to give the bitch the satisfaction.

She parked behind the Co-op on Albert Street. The sky was still black as midnight and the streets seemed supernaturally silent. Christmas lights strung between the buildings reflected back off the damp paving stones, but there were no lights on in any of the shops. Everywhere was closed. Maybe it was because she was tired or stressed, but the world seemed to be turned up several notches. The cold wind burned her skin, the lights streaked across the wet pavement slabs made her feel giddy, like the ground she was walking on wasn't solid. Even the silence seemed too loud. She tucked her chin into her coat collar and stuffed her hands into her pockets, her fingers finding the envelope, and her heart sank a little further at yet another thing she needed to deal with. She felt like tearing it to pieces. What difference was it going to make anyway? She'd said it herself last night, she was always going to be the way she was, whether that was because she was autistic or not. What would some words on a piece of paper change?

She walked past St Magnus Cathedral and the giant Norwegian fir dressed up in Christmas lights, until eventually she found a small café that was open. Despite not having eaten since lunchtime yesterday, she couldn't face the thought of food, so she ordered her usual oat milk latte and sat by the window, looking out into the dark, empty street. She had the place to herself and the young woman behind the counter wasn't interested in her, so she could think without distraction, but her anxiety was reaching fever pitch. Over the last few days, she had felt adrift at sea. Her days had no pattern here, no routine, and that always made things feel a thousand times worse. She needed something to cling to, a shore on the horizon to aim for.

She took out her phone, which thankfully she had remembered to charge when she had gone down to the kitchen. Her thumb hovered over Fergus' name on the screen. The police had been speaking to witnesses since Tuesday morning, they had been hunting for Jason Miller – surely something must have come out of one of those lines of enquiry by now. The preliminary findings of the forensic examination might be back too. Fergus might exchange some of that information for the photograph she took in South Ronaldsay. She had checked it this morning and it showed the room she had found clearly enough, but what would it really tell him? And if Scott caught on that she had spoken to the police …

She hadn't decided her next move before a notification flashed on her screen. A text from Tom, she thought, waking up to find her gone and wanting to reach out to her. She was disappointed to see it was from Twitter. A message from Scott: 'I imagine you'll have questions.'

She pushed her disappointment aside and began with the obvious one, happy to have the distraction: 'What happened at that house?'

'Did you see the room?' Scott replied immediately.

She didn't have to ask which room he meant. 'Yes. Did you put that doll there and paint that message on the walls?'

'No. From the look of it, I'd say that's been there a while, wouldn't you?'

She had thought that when she'd seen it. The paint on the walls was dull and beginning to flake. That meant at least one other person in these islands knew what had happened there, and for some reason they'd chosen to leave that doll in an abandoned house instead of going to the police.

There was another message when she looked back at her phone: 'They called that room the Play Pen.'

Freya shuddered. The words were vile, especially in the context of what she had seen there, but also, they were familiar. She'd seen or heard that phrase somewhere else this week. She couldn't bring to mind where.

'Who called it that?'

'The men who paid for the parties. Remember I asked you yesterday if you knew the name Graham Linklater? Back then, he owned a company called Sigurd Holdings, which in turn owned Eastwynd Farm and a bunch of other places. Linklater hosted parties there for rich old perverts who …'

Freya stopped reading and put her phone down. She felt like she was being hit with a lot of new information on top of what she already knew, and she needed a moment to process it. She took a sip of her coffee, noticed she was counting her ear piercings when she caught the woman behind the till glancing at her out of the corner of her eye. She didn't care. She kept counting, her foot tapping too as she went over everything she thought she knew so far.

Yesterday, Scott had said Ola and Liam had gone to that house in search of Ola's younger sister, Hannah, after being told by Jason Miller that she had been taken there by his friends. But, if Hannah had been taken somewhere against her will on the night Ola had gone missing, surely she would have told someone. Beth never mentioned anything happening to Hannah, nor had Fergus. So, was Scott wrong? Or had Miller been lying to Ola?

Freya picked up her phone again. Scott's last message, sent after he'd had no further reply, said: 'You there?'

'I'm here,' she wrote back. 'How does the "Play Pen" fit in to this? What exactly were these parties?'

The familiar three dots appeared. Freya expected another long answer. While she waited for it, she opened the internet browser on her phone and googled Graham Linklater's name. Until his retirement a few years ago, Linklater had been the owner and CEO of Linklater Ferries, a company that ran some inter-island routes in Orkney as well as a couple of boats across the Pentland Firth. There was an article from *The Orcadian* dated ten years ago about the opening of a new community centre in East Mainland that Graham had funded. As usual with a web story, there was no byline, but it smacked of the work of Gill Irvine. There was a photo with it of two overweight, middle-aged men in suits shaking hands, the caption beneath it identifying them as Linklater and the leader of the Orkney Islands Council at the time. Graham was the slightly shorter and balder of the two.

She went back to Twitter. Scott's reply was much shorter than she had anticipated: 'That's where they took the girls.'

Freya felt vomit rise onto her tongue. 'What girls?'

'Any girls the men wanted.' Several more messages came one after the next. 'That's what the guests were paying for. Linklater had a system – he paid a small group of boys from the Grammar to ask girls from school to parties. They were the fit lads, the popular ones, so of course these girls always said yes. They had no idea where they were being taken. They thought they were going on a date, but essentially Linklater was offering his guests schoolgirls to order. Want yourself a blonde fifteen-year-old? He'd get you one, for the right price. He was a sick fuck. He even had the balls to call these lads his "Talent Scouts".'

Freya's hand shot to her mouth. She thought she might actually be sick.

Scott continued: 'They took these girls to the parties, got them drunk, slipped a little something in their drink, then they took them down to the Play Pen. You're a smart woman, Freya, I'm sure you can figure out what happened next.'

Freya dropped her phone to the table and the woman behind the counter looked over.

'You okay, love?'

Freya nodded, though she wasn't sure she was.

Her thoughts were coming too fast for her to get a grip on them, but she knew things were finally falling into place. She reached into her coat pocket and pulled out Ola's diary, riffled through the pages to the part where Ola had described first meeting Liam:

He said we met at Katie's party last week, but I don't remember him being there and, when I asked Katie later, she didn't know him either, so I was either absolutely hammered (probably!) or he's full of shite …

Neither of them remembered seeing Liam at Katie's house because Ola's assessment of him had been correct – he *was* full of shite. Liam had been paid to lure her to one of Linklater's parties. He'd turned up one day after school specifically looking for her. The thought made Freya's skin crawl.

She picked up her phone again. 'Liam was one of these Talent Scouts, wasn't he?'

Scott's reply was quick: a simple thumbs up emoji.

A battle broke out between the disgust she felt at that moment and the surge of adrenaline than ran through her. It all fit. It explained where Liam's money had come from, how he could afford that car. Christ, it even accounted for all the people who claimed Liam had a different girlfriend each month. That prompted Freya's mind to race with further questions and theories, but she needed to focus. Still, she couldn't help but realise that if Jason had known about the party, he had to have been one of these Talent Scouts too. As must Scott if he had been at the party in South Ronaldsay on the night Ola and Liam were killed.

Speaking of which …

'What happened when Ola and Liam got to Eastwynd Farm?' Freya asked. 'You said you were there, that you spoke to Liam.'

'Liam told me about Miller showing up at Ola's friend's house in Harray. He said he'd come to Eastwynd looking for Hannah – Ola's sister – but she wasn't there. Miller must have lied.'

'What about Ola? Did you see her too?'

'No, just Liam,' Scott wrote back. 'He told me Ola had stayed in the car. He didn't want her going in that house. I'm sure you can guess why.'

'And Miller, was he there?'

'No, I didn't see him.'

So, Jason Miller lied about Ola's sister to get Ola and Liam to that house. But why? She thought about what she had seen in that room last night – the doll and the mattress – and what Fergus had said about Ola's underwear being missing, her leggings being torn.

'What happened next?' Freya asked. 'After you'd spoken to Liam and told him Hannah wasn't there, did he leave?'

There was a pause. The three dots didn't immediately return this time. Freya checked her watch and saw it was after eight o'clock. She'd barely touched her coffee and now it was stone cold.

'Not right away,' Scott finally replied. 'I saw him about five minutes later, arguing with one of the old perverts.'

'Who?'

'I don't know. We never knew names. Linklater used a go-between – a guy he paid who then paid us and gave us a list of girls to find. Sometimes they gave you a specific girl's name, other times a general description of what the perverts wanted, but we never knew anything about the men themselves. I only knew Linklater's name because he was listed as Sigurd Holdings' owner, and I got the company name from the land registry. It wasn't hard.'

Something occurred to Freya then. She went to the web browser again and searched for an image of Gordon Tulloch, found one from when he was a few years younger. She copied and pasted it into the chat.

'Was it him?'

Another long pause. What was Scott doing? A rush of cold air brushed her skin as the door opened and a couple came in, rubbing their hands together to get warm. It was getting slightly busier out in the street now too, though no lighter.

'No,' came the reply.

'Did you ever see him at any of the parties?'

'No. I don't recognise him.'

That had been a long shot, but it had been one worth taking. Though she found it odd Scott hadn't asked who Gordon was or why she was enquiring about him.

A sharp pain shot through her jaw and Freya realised she was grinding her teeth. 'Talent Scouts', the 'Play Pen' – this was beyond a story now, much bigger than getting back in Kristin's good books. It was bigger even than finding out who had killed Ola and Liam.

She knew what she was about to type might scare Scott away, but she needed to say it.

'You've got to go to the police.'

There was no pause this time. 'I can't.'

'This is bigger than you, Scott. You need to face up to what you did to those girls. These men need to be punished.'

She was hammering the cracked screen so hard as she typed, she risked shattering it further.

'That's not why I haven't told the police,' he replied. 'They already fucking know!! Some of the men who attended the parties *were* the police. It doesn't matter if you take this to them, or I do, or anyone else does, it will simply get buried. That's why I'm telling you, Freya. A journalist. YOU need to expose this!'

'How do you know they were police if you don't know names?'

Nothing then. Maybe she had frightened him with her threat to go to the police, but she was past caring. It wasn't actually a threat. She had always protected her sources – wouldn't have got very far in the job if she hadn't – but if she was made aware of something illegal, especially something like this, she was duty-bound to report it.

Scott eventually replied, 'Everyone knew, it was hardly a secret. All the lads said there were high-ranking policemen involved. Councillors, MPs, anyone with any kind of power. The whole lot of them were fucking in on it. How do you think they've got away with it all this time?'

Freya's heart sank at the reply. Scott was beginning to sound like a conspiracy theorist, and she turned her anger inwards as she realised she'd allowed herself to get excited by nothing but the word of an unknown source. Scott's story had been convincing, and it did make a lot of sense in terms of explaining how Liam had got his money, how he'd met Ola, and what he'd been hiding from her too, but Freya had never met this Scott guy and couldn't simply take him at his word. She put her phone down and flicked through Ola's diary again, to the very last entry:

… either he tells me what the fuck's going on with him, or we're through.

This was what had been going on with him. Freya knew in her heart that what Scott had just told her was the exact same thing Liam had confided in Ola the night she had given him this ultimatum. But although she was willing to believe it, she needed proof.

She picked up her phone again, did another quick Google search for *Eastwynd Farm South Ronaldsay*. It brought up a website that listed the dates properties had last changed hands and the prices they had gone for. Eastwynd Farm was on there, last sold in 1997, but it didn't say who the buyer had been. There was a photo with the listing; a detached farmhouse with a new extension prominent in the foreground, the old wing of the house behind it. There were outbuildings surrounding the yard and, beyond them, clifftops dropped away to a wild and angry sea. Even though she'd only seen it in the dark, she knew it was the right place. At least Scott had been telling the truth about that.

She googled Sigurd Holdings too and found them listed on the website of Companies House, but Graham Linklater was no longer the owner. The company had changed hands a few years ago, which could have been when Linklater retired. But it was a real company – Scott hadn't made that up either.

Another cold draught ran its fingers down her spine. An old woman in a thick winter coat and a bright woollen bobble hat had entered the small café and hadn't closed the door behind her. With only four customers inside, the place was filling up. Freya would have to go soon. She went back to Twitter and found another private message waiting for her.

It was as though Scott had read her mind. 'Look, I know you'll probably want more to go on than just my word, and I think there might be a way to get something more concrete, but it's risky.'

'Then it's time to take a risk. You owe it to Ola and Liam. You owe it to every girl who was ever raped at one of your sick parties.'

She was past mincing her words.

'You don't understand,' Scott replied. 'It'd be risky for you.'

Freya sighed, rubbed her tired eyes. She thought of her fight last night with Tom. Still no text; she was sure he would be awake now. She couldn't remember the last time they'd had an argument that had lasted this long without one of them apologising. And since February, it had always been Tom who cracked first. Not this time. Maybe this time she had really gone and done it, pushed him too far away.

She looked at Scott's message. He was waiting for her reply. 'Tell me what I need to do.'

35

SHE DROVE EAST OUT of Kirkwall into a gathering fog.

'There's a man in Deerness, Paul Thomson,' Scott had written. 'He owns a garage out that way now. He should be there today. Go and see him and tell him I sent you.'

'What will he be able to tell me that you can't?'

'It's not what he can tell you. It's what he can show you.'

It was getting on for half past eight and the sky wasn't growing lighter so much as becoming a bit less dark, turning from black to deep grey. After St Ola, the road dipped and curved. Ahead, the red-and-white approach lights for the runway in the fields near the airport appeared and disappeared into the murk. She was going to be late to work but she hadn't been able to muster the energy to call Kristin. She'd written and deleted several texts too. It didn't matter; if this paid off, Kristin wouldn't care she was a few minutes late. Though it did mean nobody but Scott knew where she was going.

'What is he going to show me?'

'Photographs.'

Scott had explained the man he was sending her to see owned a cameraphone seventeen years ago, before they had become popular. The guests at the parties hadn't realised what it was.

'I don't know if he took them with blackmail in mind or if they were simply insurance. Maybe he figured if he ever got caught for what he was doing, tricking these girls, he'd have enough high-powered people on camera to make any charges go away.'

'What makes you think he's still got them?'

'Like I said, they were probably his insurance policy. He'll have them.'

'So why do I have to get them?' Freya had asked. 'Why don't you get them and send them to me?'

'Because you want proof, and this is the quickest way to get it. And don't worry, he'll hand them over. If you tell him I sent you, he'll do anything you ask.'

Freya had read that message back a few times. She had come to accept that Scott Connelly was a pseudonym, but if Scott reckoned his name was going to open doors with Paul, it couldn't have been.

The mist tightened its grip on the landscape as she drove further east. Farmland rolled away either side of her into nothing. She reached the narrow isthmus that marked the crossing into Deerness, the calm water of St Peter's Bay lapping the road on one side, the dunes of Dingieshowe beach towering over the other, before the road climbed again. A tiny hamlet with no sign to announce its name lined its flanks. A post office, a handful of small houses. Right at the end, before the road ran back out into open country, Freya spotted the garage.

She slowed but kept driving. She wanted to take a good look at the place first. There were two cars outside the workshop, the roll-up doors of which were open, and she could see another vehicle up on the ramp inside. It wasn't big; a single petrol pump, a few tyres stacked on the forecourt. She pulled onto the verge about a minute out of the village and tried to gather her thoughts, think about what she was going to say.

'So why is this risky?' she had asked.

'Paul is Jason Miller's cousin. That whole family's a set of nasty bastards. But don't fall for his shite, it's all show.'

That hadn't filled Freya with confidence. It hadn't been enough to put her off either. This was bigger than her feud with Gill, than wanting to get back on a story. Nobody had listened to the women who had raised the alarm about the Partick GP at first. Nobody had listened to the women who had spoken out against Damien Barber at all. Nobody ever fucking listened, which was why this happened again and again and again. Freya felt like she had failed Amara Choudhry and the other women whose lives Damien Barber had destroyed, and that still burned her. If Scott was telling the truth, she wasn't ready to fail again.

'What if he calls my bluff?' Freya had written before setting off. 'What if he asks how I know you, what you look like? I don't know a thing about you.'

'He won't.'

'But if he does?'

'Then tell him I'm five ten, blonde hair, brown eyes, a wee skinny bastard. That'll be enough, but you won't need it – the second you mention my name, he'll do what you ask. Trust me!!'

She supposed she had no other choice.

She could barely see the garage in her rearview mirror now for the fog. There wasn't another car on the road, nobody out walking in this weather. It was silent, the mist somehow sucking all the sound out of the atmosphere to the point that Freya could hear a ringing in her ears.

Before her nerve abandoned her, she put the car into gear and turned around. She drove back to the village, parked on the garage forecourt. She heard a radio playing as she got out of her car, an old song from her uni days she couldn't place. The only sound for miles around. She saw the vehicle up on the ramp ahead of her on the right, but nobody was working underneath it. A thick odour of motor oil caught in the back of her throat, making her light-headed. She'd prepared what she was going to say, but the sound of the radio, the stink of metal and fumes clouded her brain like the fog cloaking the landscape outside.

'Can I help you?'

She turned. To her left, a small area of the garage was sectioned off to form an office. A tall, thin man with thick black hair was standing in the doorway holding a mug, steam rising from it into the cold air. He looked to be early-to-mid-thirties, about the right age for one of Liam's old school friends, though there were lines at the corners of his eyes which suggested he'd not had the comfiest of lives so far. And the eyes themselves, the lightest blue Freya had ever seen. They were like Jason's. She made eye contact and a violent shudder ran through her. She couldn't help but look away.

'I'm looking for Paul Thomson.'

'You're in luck, you've found him.'

She tried to remember the line she'd planned but faltered.

Paul glanced out at the forecourt. 'Trouble with the Hyundai? They're usually good little runners, those Getz. What's the issue?'

'I'm not here about my car.'

'No?'

'I'm here because someone sent me.'

'A recommendation from a happy customer, aye? Who was it?'

'Scott Connelly.'

Paul swore as the mug he'd been holding shattered at his feet. He snapped his head up, said nothing, just stared at Freya.

She swallowed, hoped he hadn't seen. 'Scott sent me to get some photographs you took at a party in South Ronaldsay seventeen years ago.'

His icy blue eyes widened. A thought flashed across his face. Then he started coming towards her.

She stepped back, took out her phone and held it up. 'This conversation is being recorded. The file's saved remotely and can be accessed even if you delete it from my phone. Anything happens to me, they'll know it was you, Paul Thomson.'

Saying his name again for the recording had the desired effect. He stopped where he was, impotent rage steaming from his nostrils as he took deep, measured breaths. Maybe he was trying to decide if she was lying. She wasn't – she'd started recording as she'd got out of the car and everything on her phone backed up to the cloud. Whether or not anyone would think to check it if she disappeared was another matter.

'Who the fuck are you and how do you know Scott?'

'I'm a reporter, I work for *The Orcadian*. I'll make you the same offer I made—'

He laughed, but there was a tremble in it. Freya couldn't tell if it was fear or relief. 'A journalist? Get to fuck, I'm not talking to you.'

'That's fine, Scott's told me enough already. I'm running a story about those parties. I'm telling everyone about the Talent Scouts, about what happened in the Play Pen.'

Paul's face drained of colour.

It was taking every ounce of Freya's focus not to squirm. She was sweating profusely under her heavy jacket, hoping the cracks didn't show in her voice. But from the look in Paul's eyes, it was working.

'I told Scott I'd leave his name out of it if he helped me. He's led me to you, told me you took pictures, so I'll make you the same offer. Give me copies of those photographs and I promise never to reveal you as the source.'

Paul shook his head. 'You trust him, do you?'

Freya thought of Scott's final message: *Trust me!!*

She nodded, knowing the lie would show on her voice if she spoke.

'You can't leave Scott's name out of your story. He's the beginning, middle, and end of it.'

'How so?'

He snorted a laugh. 'If you don't know, then Scott hasn't told you everything. Not by a fucking mile, and why doesn't that surprise me? How did you even find the radge bastard anyway?'

Freya didn't answer, cracking Paul's face into a smile without a drop of joy in it.

'Let me guess, he's come crawling out of the woodwork since they found those bodies at Skaill, am I right? Ola bloody Campbell. The big catch. The one they all wanted, and Liam wouldn't give her to them.'

'Do you know what happened to them?'

Now it was Paul's turn to stay silent.

'Do you know who killed them?'

A chill crept over her, like a cloud passing in front of the sun, when Paul smiled again. Was he giving her his answer?

'Write your story. Name me if you want. Scott's lying about the photos anyway, so I'll deny it,' he said. 'But just know, if you go public with these things, you'd better be prepared for the consequences.'

'Is that a threat?'

'A warning. You come in here, saying these things out loud, and you've no idea the lengths certain people have gone to to keep this all hushed up. A story like this could make them feel cornered, threatened. They'll come for you.'

He walked towards her again. Slow, measured steps. This time, Freya didn't move. He towered over her, so far into her personal space she felt his presence like strips of barbed wire against her skin. She could smell the shite coffee on his breath.

'If you think this is a game, a mere *story*, you're wrong.'

He raised a hand and she flinched. When she opened her eyes, he was smiling again, clearly pleased with himself at scaring a woman, like maybe he'd got a kick out of it. He'd reached past her and taken a broom that was leaning against the wall. He walked back to the office doorway and began to sweep up the broken pieces of porcelain off the floor.

Freya cleared her throat. 'So you won't give me the photos?'

'What photos?'

Freya nodded, not sure what else to do. She started walking towards the roll-up door. The radio seemed somehow louder now, the cheerful pop song echoing through the workshop completely at odds with the atmosphere. She wanted to run but she forced herself not to. She needed to think. As she stepped out into the forecourt and the fresh air and relative light of the dreich day, her confidence grew.

She turned back. 'Out of interest, these people you say will come for me if I print my story, what will they do to you when they find out you've got photographs that can identify the men who fucked all those schoolgirls?'

The words landed a punch. Paul glared at her but said nothing.

'I'm running this story. It's my job to expose scum like you and the men you worked for, and I'll face whatever consequences come with it,' she said. 'But if you don't want to, then my offer stands. You can find me at *The Orcadian* newsroom in Hatston. Bring me those photos. I'll give you one hour.'

36

A MINUTE DOWN THE road she pulled into the car park behind the dunes at Dingieshowe, got out of her car, and retched over the sand. She was trembling, her hands shaking so badly she'd struggled to change gears. She sucked the sea air into her lungs like she'd had her head held underwater, and she tried desperately to calm down.

That was fucking intense.

Her muscles ached like she'd spent the last ten minutes in a sprint. She dragged herself up the wooden steps to the top of the dunes, hoping the sight of the crashing waves on the other side might clear her head, but the tide was out, and the mist was so dense that she could barely see as far as the water's edge.

Now what?

She hadn't got the photos, Paul had called her bluff, and he'd drastically called into question everything she thought she knew about Scott. Maybe he was trying to get inside her head, but Freya knew deep down there was something in it. She'd spent so much time lying to people these past ten months, but she couldn't lie to herself – Scott was only giving her the side of the story he wanted to tell, and she'd allowed herself to go along with it in the hope it would lead her somewhere.

He's the beginning, middle, and end of it.

The fuck did that mean?

Her phone vibrated in her coat pocket. She took it out and saw Kristin's name on the screen, an incoming call. It was quarter past nine now. She was late for work, and now she was going to the newsroom empty-handed. She didn't know if what she had so far would be enough to convince Kristin to let her keep her job, let alone run the story. She waited for the call to ring through to voicemail, then she opened the Twitter app and checked her private messages. There was one waiting from Scott.

'Did you get them?'

'No.'

Scott replied quickly. 'Go back and tell him you know about Becca.'

'Paul says you're lying. That you're way more involved in what happened than you're letting on.'

Again, the reply was rapid, like Scott had been expecting that. 'He's trying to scare you off. Don't listen.'

Freya looked up, towards the North Sea. She could hear it churning out there beyond the fog, the crack and hiss of it as it sucked in the rocks beneath the clifftops at the far side of the bay. Droplets of ice-cold water in the air covered her hair, her skin, slowly reviving her. She thought about the way Paul had reacted when she had said Scott Connelly's name, the evident fear in his eyes and the way he had dropped his mug. Who the hell was she getting herself mixed up with?

When she looked back at her phone, Scott had written to her again. 'Go back, mention Becca. He'll do anything then.'

'Who's Becca?' Freya asked. The damp air had coated her cracked phone screen, making it hard to type. She wondered if she really wanted to know.

'She was a decoy,' Scott replied. 'The go-between had the idea of bringing a few other girls to the parties who weren't on the list. Lads, too. We were told not to get these decoy lasses as drunk as the others, don't slip them the roofies, and they'd never see the Play Pen either. To them, it was a regular party, but see, they witnessed how wasted the girls from the list were. The idea was, if word ever got out ...'

More messages were coming, but Freya didn't need to read them. What Scott was saying was crystal clear – these other kids were there so that, if any of the victims ever spoke out, the decoys could undermine their story. They would say they had seen these girls at the party and they'd been steaming drunk, up for anything. They'd say how no one had tried anything on with them, it had simply been a mad party. It would sow just enough doubt in people's minds that the abused girls would soon drop their accusations, and others would be less inclined to come forward. Same as had happened with Damien Barber.

Like her editors at *The Herald* had told her: 'It's a "he said/she said" situation.'

And what *she said* wouldn't mean a thing.

The level of coordination, the steps these people had taken to cover their tracks and to perpetuate an operation that allowed teenaged girls to essentially be ordered for rape lit a fire in Freya's stomach again. She didn't need to read the rest of Scott's messages, but she saw as she looked at her phone again that Paul had tried to assault Becca.

'That had nearly blown everything, and the go-between was pissed,' Scott had written. 'I'm guessing that's when Paul started taking photos, in case they did anything to him.'

'What about Becca?' Freya wrote. 'Where is she now? I want to talk to her or any of the other girls who were taken to these parties. Bollocks to Paul and his photos, we don't even know if he still has them.'

'He has them, Freya! And we need them!'

'Give me the names of the girls. Let me speak to them.'

Her screen stayed blank this time. She waited for almost a minute. Scott didn't reply.

Freya rubbed her forehead, took a deep breath. She didn't relish the idea of going back and threatening Paul, but she didn't want to go to the newsroom either. Not until she had what she needed. She thought about calling Fergus again, regardless of what Scott had said about police involvement, but something stopped her. She knew Fergus would never have been mixed up in such things – the idea that he might even have known about it, let alone that he could have been present at one of the parties, was ridiculous. It was as insane as thinking her own dad might have been involved. But something Kristin had said to her on her first day kept coming back to her: *If there's anything you learn in this job, chick, it's that people can always surprise you.*

More than two minutes had passed. The conversation with Scott was clearly over. She turned around, looked at the shallow water in the bay over the road and the mist floating on its surface, then she glanced back up the hill towards the garage. The first houses in the village were only a minute's drive away across open country but were invisible today behind the haze.

She heard the car before she saw it.

A blue Subaru Impreza emerged from the fog, its engine roaring, haring down the road far quicker than the speed limit. It flew past the car park at the foot of the dunes before slamming on its brakes and skidding to a halt. The tyres screamed as they dragged across the tarmac. The white reversing lights went on.

Freya ran down the wooden steps over the sand, jumped in her car. She had just locked the doors as the Subaru reversed over the exit, blocking her in. Paul leapt out, ran around his vehicle and stood in front of Freya's.

'I've changed my mind,' he shouted, panting for breath. 'I'll help.'

Freya's heart hammered her ribs. Paul came to stand by the driver's window, peered down at her through the glass with those ice-cold eyes.

'I'm sorry I scared you before. You shocked me, okay? When you said Scott had sent you I just …' He shook his head. 'Look, I'll not let that prick land me in it. Not when it's him you should be writing about. If I give you what you want, you have to protect me. Keep my name out of everything. I'd be, like, a confidential source or something, yeah?'

Freya thought for a second. She nodded.

'And you can't go to the police, right?'

'If I grassed all my sources up to the police, I wouldn't last very long as a journalist.'

Another lie, though this one came dressed as the truth.

Paul nodded, running his hand through his hair. 'Okay. Okay. And I never want to see your face around my garage ever again, you understand me?'

That was a deal she was more than happy to make.

Paul let out a long, slow breath. 'All right.' He was still nodding, thinking. 'All right. I stay up the road there. It's not far.'

He pointed back the way he'd come, where the road would eventually run out at the clifftops at Mull Head.

He turned, jogged back to his car. 'It's a little off the beaten track,' he shouted over his shoulder. 'Follow me.'

37

DESPITE THE FOG, PAUL drove with no lights on. Freya had to stay much closer to the back of his car than she would have liked, or she'd lose him, though she wasn't sure there were too many places he could go out here.

Her phone was on the passenger seat beside her. She touched the screen to bring it life and glanced at it quickly. Sixty-five per cent charged. Better than last night. She also had two missed call notifications and two messages saying she had voicemail. Both from Kristin, none from Tom.

She turned her attention back to the car in front of her. The road rose again but the fog showed no sign of lifting. She could see nothing but grey emptiness beyond the wire fences at the side of the carriageway. She was comforting herself with the fact they were still on the main road when Paul suddenly signalled and turned, Freya braking hard to avoid going into the back of him. A million and one scenarios played out in her head at once as they drove along a single track, and not one of them involved her leaving here with those photos. She needed a strategy, a way to get what she wanted without putting herself in danger. Nothing came to mind.

They passed a couple of lonely pebble-dashed houses, kept going.

A cow's inquisitive face appeared at the fence by the roadside, the only other living thing she could see out here in the ether.

She jumped, almost swerved into a ditch as her phone vibrated and bounced across the seat. Probably Kristin again, but glancing down she felt a stab in her chest. It was Tom. She wanted to pick up but couldn't drive and talk at the same time. Stop, and Paul would vanish into the haze. There couldn't be a lot out here, maybe if she pulled over she could catch him up again, but as soon as she reached that conclusion the buzzing halted. She stole a look at the screen, saw the bars had vanished. She'd driven out of signal. Tom would think she'd rejected the call.

The main track turned ninety degrees to the right, but Paul kept going straight onto a narrower uncovered road with nothing nearby that she could see. No landmarks to discern where they were heading. The sea would be nearby, it always was here, but she could neither see nor hear it over the sound of her car rumbling over the loose gravel. Thirty seconds later, the silhouette of a house emerged ahead of them. A grey pebble-dashed cottage, bleak and lonely like the ones she'd seen further back down the road. Two-storey, nondescript. There was a large yard outside littered with tyres and old mechanical parts. A corrugated iron shed with one door ajar showed the remains of a vehicle, bonnet open, headlights missing like its eyes had been gouged out.

Paul pulled over to one side, clearly attempting to force Freya to drive past him into the yard. Instead, she stopped directly behind him, blocking the track. Nobody was getting in or out except for her.

Paul climbed out of his car, walked slowly across the concrete yard to the front door. As he reached it, a key in his hand, he looked back. 'You coming, or what?'

She stayed in her car, doors locked, engine running.

He grinned. She didn't like that. Like maybe he enjoyed the thrill of the chase. He unlocked the house and left the door slightly ajar as he walked over to Freya.

'The photos are saved on an old computer inside. It doesn't connect to the internet. Better that way, you know, so nobody can hack it.' He rubbed his oil-stained hand over his mouth. 'Listen, I'm not comfortable with you making copies to take away. I don't think I can agree to that. You can look at them here instead.'

She fought to keep her fear and anger from her face. 'Bring the computer out here. I'll look at them from the car.'

She wondered if Tom had checked her location from his phone before he'd called her.

'I told you, the computer's old. It's a PC, not a laptop. It's up in the spare bedroom.'

Fuck, everything about this was wrong. This had stopped being a good idea several bad decisions ago. But she needed those photos. Nobody was going to believe any of this without proof.

Paul began walking away. 'Suit yourself. I'll be upstairs setting up the computer when you make up your mind.'

She pinched at her ears. Indecision clotted her brain. There was a correct course of action she could take that led to her getting what she needed and getting out of here unscathed, but she couldn't decide what order she needed to do things in to make it happen. If she went in, she needed to be able to get away quickly; was it safer to leave her car unlocked and the engine running? That way she could make a rapid escape. But what if someone else was here and they took the keys?

Paul had disappeared inside the house by now.

Freya shut off the engine, decided to take her keys with her.

38

It was raining as she got out, the mist condensing into a dour, icy drizzle. She pulled up the hood of her yellow raincoat and ran across the yard. Black paint was peeling off a wooden front door that opened into a narrow, dank hallway. Even before she crossed the threshold, she noticed the smell; damp and something equally as unpleasant she couldn't place. A staircase rose into the gloom on her right, dark carpet, dark wallpaper. A landing window shed a little light at the top, but not much. She could hear Paul moving around upstairs.

She put her foot on the first step and it groaned under her shoe.

Her heart raced. She felt it in her throat, could hear the blood rushing past her ears. Her mind was going just as fast, but she was fighting to stay focused. At the top of the staircase, three closed doors led off the landing. A fourth one was open. Beyond it she heard the whirr and hiss of a hard drive spinning as a computer booted up but, from where she was standing, she couldn't see inside the room. The light cast against the part of the wall she could see seemed unnaturally bright, lit by a bulb rather than daylight. A second later a shadow moved across it. Then Paul's long body filled the doorway.

He nodded sideways. 'It's ready.'

Freya stayed at the top of the stairs.

Paul sighed. 'Look, you fucking begged *me* for this. Do you want to see these or not?'

'After you.'

He shook his head, like she was being pathetic, and stepped back.

Freya watched him closely as she crossed the landing. She peered around the door, making sure to keep herself between Paul and her escape route, and looked into a room filled with decades-old junk. It was cold and cramped, made smaller by the boxes and piles of paper that spilled from the unmade bed onto the floor. The smell, whatever it was, was stronger here. She could taste it on her tongue and it was giving her a headache, making it impossible to concentrate. She couldn't keep her disgust from her face.

As she battled to keep a clear head, she saw she'd been right: the threadbare curtains had been drawn and the light came from a naked bulb hanging from the ceiling. With the assault on her senses from the rancid room, she almost lost sight of what she was doing here until her gaze landed on the computer.

She forgot herself, took a step away from the door.

The PC was on a desk against the far wall. Paul hadn't been lying about one thing: it was ancient – a chunky CRT monitor sat on top of a horizontal computer unit with a floppy disc drive and one for a CD-ROM. No sign of any USB port, and it definitely didn't have Bluetooth. It was that cream colour all computers came in back in the Nineties, but over the years the shade had shifted somewhat closer to brown. Without connecting it to the internet, Paul couldn't have got the photos onto the hard drive from his phone without burning them to a disc with another device. He definitely had copies of these files somewhere. She glanced around at all the mess but the sight of it only made her feel dizzy.

She focused on the screen, like a seasick sailor fixing their eyes on the horizon. The grey Windows 98 desktop was giving her flashbacks to her primary school days, filling her head with more unwanted thoughts. There was a window open on screen, a file browser. A single folder was in it simply labelled 'X'. She suddenly realised she no longer knew where Paul was. She spun around to see he hadn't moved, but she had. They were now standing level with one another an equal distance from the door. The look he was giving her sent a chill crawling across her flesh.

'I want to look at these on my own, please.'

'No.'

'I don't feel comfortable being alone with you in this room.'

His upper lip twitched. He gritted his teeth. 'I don't give a fuck how you feel. I was minding my own business and you came to me, so either look at these pictures or get the fuck out of my house. Your call, woman.'

Her fingernail snapped between her teeth. Bitten too close to the quick, it started to sting. She couldn't have her back to him while she looked at these photos. There must be a way to get rid of him, but while her senses were being bombarded she couldn't think of one. Her mind skipped like a scratched record between wanting to see the photographs and not wanting to lower her guard and thinking about a way she could leave here with a copy of whatever was in that file, while simultaneously a toxic smog smothered her brain because of how badly this room smelled and how cluttered it was and how the light wasn't right and how she was now too far away from the front door. She could feel grit and dirt in the carpet through the soles of her shoes, as if it was inside her socks. She felt like she could taste the stains on the grubby bedsheets. She had to get out.

But she couldn't. Not without proof.

'Please, I just need five minutes.'

'What difference does it make if I'm here or not? Unless you're planning on trying something.'

'Like what?'

'I don't know, you could take photos of the screen with your phone.'

That was actually a good idea and in her overwhelmed state she'd not thought of it. She reached her hand into her coat pocket but felt only the crumpled envelope. Her heart sank. 'I've left my phone in my car. It's on the passenger seat.'

'Is it, aye?'

'It's true, go check.'

'Sure, nice try.'

'I know about Becca,' she said next, not really thinking. 'That's why I'm uncomfortable being in here with you. I know what kind of man you are.'

His nostrils flared. He ran his hand through his hair then launched his fist at the wall and Freya heard herself scream. He stepped closer. 'You don't know the first thing about me, you stuck-up peedie cunt, so don't act like you do!'

Freya moved backwards, the back of her legs touching the desk now. She was fully inside the room with this man between her and the way out.

'I honestly don't care what you did,' she said, the crack in her voice clear. She wasn't lying, wasn't trying to talk him down: it was true. 'You're not who I'm here for. The men in these photographs are. Please, give me five minutes to go through them, then I'll leave and you'll never see me again. Your name will never appear in my story.'

She saw his eyes flick to the right then back to her. Quickly. He might not even have known he'd done it.

'Please. Five minutes. Then I'm gone.'

He rubbed his hand across his mouth again. 'You've got the time it takes me to go and check your car for your phone.'

Freya nodded, relief rolling through her like a noose being removed from her neck.

'I'll be right back,' he said. 'I'm leaving this door open.'

'Leave the front door too.'

He nodded and left. Freya listened to the creak of each step on the staircase.

When she was certain he was at the bottom, she got to work.

She threw open the curtains and dust plumed into the air. She coughed, choking on decades of dead skin as she tried frantically to get the window open. Unless she got some fresh air, she couldn't think straight, but the two small openings on both sides were locked, no key in sight. She felt like she was swimming under ice, looking for the cracks that would allow her up to breathe.

And by now, Paul must've made it to her car and seen her phone.

She'd just wasted half her time.

Trying to shake off her sense of crushing dread, she turned her focus to the photos. But not the computer, not yet.

She looked to the right of the desk, where Paul had unconsciously glanced. There was a pile of old shoeboxes. Freya threw them open. There were floppy discs and CDs inside but no labels on any of them. Envelopes too. Each was sealed and Paul had written names and addresses on them but for some reason never sent them.

A name on one of them caught Freya's eye.

She couldn't work out why that person's name would be scribbled on an envelope in this box, but beneath her fog of confusion she knew. There could only be one reason. She reached for it but a noise downstairs reminded her there wasn't time.

Paul was already back inside the house.

Fuck it, the best she could do now was look at as many photos as possible. She hovered the mouse over the folder marked 'X' as she heard Paul's first step on the staircase.

She double-clicked and the file opened, revealing dozens of thumbnails. The scroll bar at the side of the window showed there were dozens more further down the screen. Paul had taken hundreds of photographs. There was no way she'd have time to go through more than two or three. His footsteps grew louder on the stairs. She was about to click one at random when her eye caught the filename of the folder at the top of the window. The root was D:\

She pressed to eject the CD drive.

There was a disc sitting in the tray.

No markings on the disc, same as the others in the shoeboxes. Were they all copies? Had he made hundreds for some reason?

No chance to consider that now. She took the CD from the drive, stuffed it in her coat pocket, thought about replacing it with one from the shoeboxes but there wasn't time. She turned around and ran.

She stepped onto the landing as Paul reached the top of the stairs.

'Done already?'

Freya nodded.

'Find what you wanted?'

Her heart was pounding. White spots appeared in front of her eyes. She just wanted to go. She didn't say anything, she simply tried to push past him onto the top step.

He grabbed her arm. His grip was like hot iron searing into her skin.

'The fuck did you do?'

She yanked her arm away. To her surprise, he let go.

For a second, she was floating. She wasn't sure what was happening until her stomach dropped and she realised she was in free fall. She thrashed her arms out, grabbed for whatever she could, snatched hold of the handrail just in time to stop her tumbling down the stairs but she still stumbled, felt something in her ankle go *pop*. She didn't stop to think about it.

She ran.

Down into the hallway, she slammed against the open front door and bundled herself out into the yard, her momentum throwing her forward.

She didn't look back.

No sound in her wake.

All at once she became aware of fresh air filling her lungs, rain on her face, the icy wind biting her skin. Her left ankle was on fire, but she kept running.

Now the commotion came. The howls of a wounded beast close behind, screaming at her to stop. She fumbled for her keys as she reached her car, her ice-cold fingers moving several seconds more slowly than her brain but finally the door unlocked and she fell into the driver's seat. She pulled the door shut, punched the lock, got the key in the ignition at the second attempt and as the engine roared to life there was the first sound of something pounding at the side of her head.

She looked up to see Paul, his face folding in on itself in anger, imploding with all the energy of a dying star as he pummelled the glass with the base of his fist.

His saliva speckled the window as she threw the car into reverse, the gearbox crunching like crushed glass. She stepped her foot on the accelerator and the vehicle flew backwards, sending Paul crashing to the ground.

He leapt to his feet, chased her down the uncovered track, but Freya didn't see him. She kept her head turned and her eyes locked on the road behind her as she reversed far quicker than she was capable of controlling, her vehicle clipping the grass either side of the track and swerving left and right as she fought the steering wheel with one hand.

Somewhere out there, someone was screaming.

Her engine squealed in pain.

No time to think about that. She focused on the turn in the road where Paul had driven straight ahead earlier.

Something thudded against the bonnet.

An object hit the windscreen with a sickening crack.

At the turn she spun the car to the right, the shift in momentum throwing her phone from the passenger seat and bouncing her head off the window. She slammed the car into first gear, sped away.

As she glanced in the rearview mirror, she saw the shape of a broken man standing on the track, launching futile missiles in her direction, gradually becoming smaller and smaller until he was nothing.

39

HER PHONE WAS RINGING. It reached her like the chime of an alarm clock creeping into a dream.

Freya became aware of herself sitting in her Hyundai in the Albert Street car park in Kirkwall again. She had driven here on autopilot and her engine was still running, the windscreen wipers still going. It must have stopped raining a while ago and they were juddering as they scraped across the bone-dry glass. She was gripping the steering wheel like she was trying to snap the thing in two.

She turned off the wipers, killed the engine, waited for her phone to fall silent, then she glanced at its cracked screen. Another missed call from Kristin. A notification of a new voicemail followed a few moments later and that familiar knot tightened in her stomach again. She checked the LCD clock on the dash – it was almost eleven. She was two hours late for work and Kristin had called nine times. Looking at the list of messages on her phone, she noticed Tom had tried to reach her five times as well. Maybe Kristin had phoned home, asked Tom where she was, and sent him spiralling into a panic. The right thing to do was contact them both, let them know she was okay, but that wasn't what she had planned to do so now her brain wouldn't give the command. It wasn't going to let her change course until she had finished what she'd started.

Her hand went to her coat pocket. She pulled out the CD.

There was no fog in town. The air seemed fresher now, renewed, and there were narrow canyons of blue in the slate grey sky. Her ankle throbbed but she ignored it, certain it was nothing more than a sprain. Fatigue clung to her limbs like a drowning man clutching at the riverbank, but the crisp sea air revived her as she walked. She wasn't going far.

The Orkney Library was on Junction Road, where Kirkwall had once met the sea. A young girl with pink hair and a silver nose ring smiled at her as she approached the front desk. Freya asked if there were any computers she could use to read a CD-ROM and the girl looked at her like she had just arrived in a time machine.

'CDs? Retro. I think our computers still have CD drives. Follow me.'

As the girl led Freya away from the desk, she spotted a stand filled with newspapers out of the corner of her eye. There were several copies of today's *Orcadian*, Gill's interview with Beth splashed across the front. Old news already.

Freya chose a computer on the far side of the table, with its screen facing the wall. Going through these images in a public place was far from ideal but she needed to know exactly what she was taking to Kristin. There was only one other person at the table – an elderly man who seemed enthralled by a story on the *BBC Orkney* website. As Freya walked past him, she could have sworn she saw a photograph of Graham Linklater's flushed fat face in the article, and she was struck by the idea that maybe she wasn't the only journalist Scott had been talking to. But the old man scrolled on before she could take a good look and she told herself off for caring who broke this first. The important thing was the truth coming out, not that she be the one to tell it.

The girl set her up with a guest account then left her to work. Refocused, she loaded the disc, felt a rush of adrenaline as she heard it whir in the drive. The file browser window opened and she clicked on the single folder marked 'X'.

The long list of thumbnails appeared again. On this newer computer they showed as small images so she could see what she was looking at before she opened it. She noticed how dark they were and her excitement waned – Paul had opted for quantity over quality, snapping these as discreetly as he could, only getting something usable maybe twenty per cent of the time. She thought back to the discs and the envelopes she'd seen in those shoeboxes and considered Paul's motivation for taking these. Blackmail? Revenge? Whatever it had been, he clearly hadn't had the bollocks to go through with it. The name she'd seen on one of the envelopes appeared in her mind's eye and she wondered what she'd do if she saw him in these pictures. If she did, what she planned to do next would become a whole lot harder.

The first photo was an anticlimax. The image was blurred and pixellated, though the faces in the foreground were clear enough. It looked like a regular house party – three teenagers on a sofa, two boys either side of a blonde-haired girl in a short red dress. She looked no older than sixteen. She didn't seem that drunk; maybe she was a decoy rather than a girl from the list. Thinking this lit a fire inside Freya again. The cold calculation that had gone into this was beyond sickening. She noticed the filename was a series of nine numbers with .jpg at the end. From the format, Freya guessed the first six digits corresponded to a date while the subsequent three denoted the number of pictures taken that day. The photo she was looking at was titled *030704001. jpg*, the next was *030704002.jpg*, and so on. These had been taken in early July, 2004, fifteen months before Ola and Liam were killed. That could have been when this whole sick operation started, or simply the night Paul had first taken pictures.

Freya closed the preview and looked at the list of thumbnails again. She scrolled through them quickly, studying the dates. They were in three-monthly intervals. Was that how often these parties took place or merely the times when Paul had been there? There was still so much she didn't know, not least how this connected to Ola's and Liam's murders.

She logged on to her Twitter account through the web browser and opened her private messages. No new ones were waiting for her from Scott.

'You there? I've got the photos.'

She waited a full minute. Nothing.

It didn't matter. If she could find something on this disc to stand up what he'd told her, that would be all she needed for now.

Freya opened some of the photos from the other parties. Nothing in them reminded her of Eastwynd Farm, but Scott had said Linklater changed the location each time. If Paul had been intending to use these to blackmail the men who'd paid to be there, he wouldn't have got very far – they were conspicuous by their absence. The photos were getting clearer as Paul was improving his clandestine shots, but they still only showed gangs of teenagers at varying stages of drunkenness. Occasionally, a shadowy figure or two was lurking in the background, but the camera wasn't advanced enough to pick them out in any detail in the low light. She was growing anxious, her foot taping wildly on the floor, when she came across a photo that stopped her in her tracks. Yet again, it showed only a group of young people drinking together, but one of the faces stood out.

Several teenagers sat around a table littered with bottles and cans. The picture had been taken from tabletop height, up through the clutter on the surface. Paul must have been trying to hide the phone beneath the table when he'd taken it – a large part of the bottom half of the photograph showed only the dark, blurry shape of the table itself – but between the dirty glasses and bottles of cheap vodka, two faces were in clear focus. One was a thin-faced, blonde-haired man, brown eyes, who looked somewhat older than the others. Not old enough to be one of the men, but certainly not a teenager. Early twenties, probably. She'd seen him in some of the other photographs and wondered if this was Scott. He matched the description he'd given of himself, although he was clearly too old to have been at school with Liam.

But it wasn't him who'd caught her eye. It was the boy sitting beside him.

The blonde-haired man had his arm around the shoulder of a kid next to him. Tight, almost as though he was gripping him in a headlock. He was laughing, but the boy wasn't – he stared straight ahead, his face devoid of emotion as the blonde-haired man slurred something into his ear. A mop of black hair fell forward over the boy's face, covering moody brown eyes.

Liam.

Her foot-tapping spread to her fingers. But this wasn't proof of anything. Not yet. A photo of a teenage boy at a party gave no indication of the horrors that happened there. She moved more quickly through the photos. Liam appeared several times, as did the man she thought was Scott. Nobody else in these images seemed to match his description so closely. Clicking between photographs, she felt a weight pushing on her chest, growing heavier, like each image added another rock to the pile. She thought it was rage but, as it built in her, she realised it was something closer to sadness. Or pity.

Or fear.

The faces of different girls flashed by, their expressions slipping from giddy excitement towards a comatose state, and she couldn't help but think of the photos on the wall in Ola's bedroom. These girls could have been any one of them. They could've been one of Freya's own friends from school.

They could have been her.

The pictures blurred in front of her as her mind slipped back to that day in Stromness with Harry Donaldson. She hadn't wanted to go because her anxious brain had already forewarned her it was an obvious hoax. She really hadn't fancied Harry, but she'd gone because the idea that a boy like him might be attracted to her had been too much to resist. She hated to admit it now, but it had been exciting. On the bus into town that day she'd been petrified, but deep down there had been a tiny seed of hope. If Harry had shown interest in her that day, asked her out to a party, told her he'd come by and pick her up in his car, would she have agreed to it? She wanted to think not, but she knew the answer was yes.

As Freya looked at these girls, she couldn't help but wonder who they were, where they were now. What they remembered of these nights. What had happened to them since. Every three months, a handful of lives had been casually ruined forever by these dirty old bastards who thought they had enough money and influence to do anything they pleased. She just needed one clear image. Something she could use.

Her phone rang again. It was silenced but the sound of the vibration was loud enough to make the old man on the other side of the table lift his head and tut. Freya ignored him, checked the screen – it was Tom.

She closed her eyes. A deep, dragging sensation rolled across the pit of her stomach. She desperately wanted to talk to him, to make up for last night, but again she couldn't make her thumb answer the call. It was like her brain was on a fixed track, focused only on the photographs, and there was nothing she could do to switch it to another line. When the call ended and the home screen appeared, she caught sight of the notifications waiting for her and saw a text from Kristin. She didn't need to open it to read it. It was only three words long. The entire message fit in the preview:

Call me IMMEDIATELY!!!

The old man was tutting again, this time at Freya's fingernails snapping between her teeth.

She ignored him, and Kristin's message, and pressed on.

In the photographs from a party in January 2005, she finally hit on something. Paul was perfecting his technique – the shadowy figures lurking in the background had faces now.

More than that, they were faces she knew.

Several shots in a row showed two men standing in a doorway. In the clearest of the bunch, she recognised the ruddy round face of the man on the right as Graham Linklater. But the man on the left was familiar too.

She closed her eyes again, tried to picture where she'd seen him. Another photograph she'd seen this week, in an article she had been reading. It wasn't the council leader from Gill's article about Graham Linklater. She opened the web browser again and searched for the article Tom had found about Gordon Tulloch and Skara Brae. She scrolled down to the picture of Tulloch squinting into the sun at Bay of Skaill with a group of other archaeologists around him, but their faces didn't match. She racked her brains – what else had she been reading? There were the old articles in *The Orcadian* archives from when Liam and

Ola had been reported missing. She found them again online, began to trawl through them, but before she got to the right picture it dawned on her.

She found the photo, just to be sure.

There was no mistake.

She went back to her messages. Still nothing from Scott. She sent him the photo of the two men.

'The one on the left, is that who you saw arguing with Liam?'

To her surprise and relief, the three dots appeared. 'No. Who is he?'

She slumped back in her seat, felt the creeping realisation of what she was up against. For the first time, it frightened her.

'You were right, the police were in on this,' she wrote back. 'That man's name is Allan Tait. Back then, he was *Chief Inspector Allan Tait.*'

The head of the Orkney police force – her dad's commanding officer – had been right at the heart of this whole disgusting affair.

Scott was typing a reply, but Freya's mind was elsewhere now. She thought about the articles she had read, how readily the police had concluded Ola and Liam had died by suicide. Tait must have known they were both dead right from the start, and he had known why.

A question she was still too afraid to ask kept creeping into her mind: did Fergus know?

She replayed their conversation from yesterday in her head. He'd told her about the previous DI, Jim Shearer.

He was pals with the Chief Inspector at the time …

Shearer had never checked Jason Miller's alibi. He'd led the investigation into Ola and Liam's disappearance and he'd taken it in whichever direction Tait wanted. The entire case had been a giant cover-up – Fergus *had* to have known. He would have been an idiot not to. Which again begged the question she had been asking herself all week: why was he being so forthcoming with her?

Freya's phone rang again. She didn't even bother to look.

The sheer scale of what she was sitting on began to overwhelm her and she needed to get a grip or it would send her into a meltdown. She counted her ear piercings, forward and backward.

One, two, three, four, five. Five, four, three …

She must have been counting out loud, because the old man was staring again, but fuck him. It was working. She had almost everything she needed now, but not quite. One final piece was missing.

She opened the photograph labelled *011005001.jpg*.

The first image from the party at Eastwynd Farm.

She recognised the large kitchen immediately, the giant oak table, the double doors to the living room beyond. It sent goose-flesh crawling up her arms. She clicked quickly through the images because she was searching for something specific. She caught glimpses of men who may have been Linklater, Tait, Scott Connelly, but no sign of Jason Miller. Nor the person she needed to find.

Towards the end of the list, almost the very last picture, she stopped. It wasn't the face she had been looking for. It wasn't even the face that had caught her eye.

It was the hair.

Long, down to the man's shoulders. Blonde turning to silvery-grey.

The man was standing side-on to the camera in an empty room. A cramped space with a low ceiling. Bare floors, stone walls, and black wooden beams. It was the first room inside the old wing of the farmhouse, and now, as it had last night, the mere sight of it sucked the warmth from Freya's blood.

Even in profile, she could tell this was Gordon Tulloch. He was looking towards the door on the other side of the room. The one that led to the corridor to the Play Pen. Freya was still processing the significance of this when she spotted what Gordon was looking at.

Two men in the doorway: one had hold of the other one, like he was pushing him back. Away from the Play Pen. From the angle the shot had been taken, the men were in profile too, but she knew who they were.

She sent the photo to Scott. 'Is this what you saw?'

The one on the left, the boy being pushed back from the Play Pen, was Liam.

'Yes!!!' Scott wrote back. 'That's the fucker who was yelling at Liam. Who is he? Do you know his name?'

She did.

He was the man whose name had been scrawled on an envelope in Paul's dank room.

The very last man she had hoped to see.

40

FREYA STOOD ON THE dark landing outside *The Orcadian* newsroom, summoning the courage to go inside. Over the familiar thrum of the building, she could hear a commotion the other side of the door. Gill's voice boomed above the others. It sounded like they were having an argument.

Freya was no stranger to feeling utterly and completely isolated, cut off from everyone else in this world. Sometimes she was okay with it, other times it truly frightened her. This was one of those moments. Even if Kristin believed what Freya was about to tell her, was there anything they could do about it? Perhaps not, given what she had just seen.

Her phone vibrated again in her pocket, the third time since she'd left the library. She let it ring, pushed open the door. Sophie and Gill were at the desk, the latter barking something over the top of the monitors at Sophie. Kristin was leaning against the table next to Gill, impeccably dressed as ever, a phone receiver against her ear. She eyed Freya over her black-rimmed glasses and hung the phone up, and the buzzing in Freya's coat pocket fell silent.

'Where the bloody hell have you been?'

The voices hushed. Everyone turned to look. Freya scratched the back of her hand where her skin had begun to prickle from the heat.

'We need to talk.'

'Too right we do. What do you …' Kristin stopped. Her gaze travelled from Freya's face to her ankle. 'What happened? Where in God's name have you been? We've all been worried sick, and with good reason too, it seems.'

Freya's hand went to the cuts and scratches on her face. She had forgotten about that. Looking down, she saw a small patch of fresh blood seeping through the bottom of her pale blue jeans.

She must have reopened the gash on her leg when she had stumbled on the staircase at Paul's.

'I fell. I'm fine.'

'You don't look fine, Freya.' The tone in Kristin's voice seemed to have softened from anger to concern. 'I've given your poor husband the fright of his life too. I called you at home when you didn't show up this morning – he didn't know where you'd got to either. Have you bothered to pick up the phone to him yet, or is it just me you've been avoiding?'

Freya shook her head. She had hoped she wouldn't cry but she could feel the tears building.

'Oh, chick,' Kristin sighed. She pushed herself off the desk, walked over to Freya and hugged her, and that only made things worse.

Kristin pulled back, looked Freya in the eye.

'Are you … okay?'

'Can we talk in your office?'

'Sure, but Alistair's in there just now.'

Freya's heart missed a beat. 'Why?'

'If you'd bothered to turn up for work this morning, hen, you'd know,' Gill said. 'We've been a bit preoccupied here. Would've been nice if you could've given us a hand. Not like it's your job or anything.'

Kristin rolled her eyes. 'Have you heard?'

'Heard what?'

Freya wanted to reach for her ear piercings, but Kristin still had hold of her arms.

'A man's been killed out at Swannay,' Kristin said. 'MIT were supposed to be giving us an update on the Ola and Liam investigation this morning but all of that has gone out of the window. Looks like it was deliberate – word is more MIT detectives are on their way from Inverness.'

'It doesn't *look* like it, Kris, it was,' Gill said, turning back to her computer screen. 'That poor lassie who found him said it was a bloodbath in there.'

'Who was it?' Freya asked.

'A friend of Alistair's,' said Kristin. 'He's a little shook up, as you'd expect. That's why he came over. His wife's out of the county and when he heard, I suppose he wanted—'

'Who?' Freya asked again.

'An old business friend of Alistair's, a pal from the golf club. He used to own one of the ferry companies here. Gr—'

'Graham Linklater?'

Kristin's eyes narrowed. 'Do you know him?'

Freya glanced over Kristin's shoulder at the open office door. 'I need to talk to you somewhere privately. I've … I've got something.'

'Got something? Chick, what's going on?'

Freya's hands balled into fists. Why wouldn't Kristin just listen? 'I've got something to show you and it's … it's big. Linklater, Ola, Liam, it's all connected. It's the same thing.'

'What's she saying now?' Gill piped up. 'Is she saying this is part of the Campbell girl story somehow? Because I swear to God, if she's trying to—'

Kristin silenced her with a scowl and a wave of her hand. 'Freya, we decided it would be best if you left the Ola and Liam matter alone. We agreed, remember?'

'No, we didn't agree. You told me to drop it because Alistair convinced you to, but you were wrong.'

Freya took out her phone, found the photo she'd taken last night of the doll and the mattress and the message scrawled on the wall of the Play Pen. She showed Kristin.

'Dear God, Freya, what am I looking at?'

'This is where Ola and Liam went the night they were killed.'

She watched the faces gawking back at her from the desk, each folded into a confused frown. Maybe everyone being here was a good thing. The more people who knew about this, the better.

'I think it's best if I show you.'

She took the computer nearest to her, the one next to Gill. Kristin stood behind her, Sophie joined her too. Gill rolled her chair next to Freya's.

The CD hissed as it started to spin. The first picture she showed them was the one of Liam and Scott.

'Is that—'

'Liam McDonnell, yes.'

'Where did you get this?' Kristin asked.

Without disclosing his name, Freya explained how Scott had contacted her yesterday, in response to her tweet from the press conference. 'They told me they were a close friend of Liam's. And they knew things to back it up.'

'What things?'

'Details about his nan, his parents, but they knew what happened at Harray. Remember I'd spoken to one of Ola's old school friends and they'd told me there had been an argument that night between Ola and Jason Miller?'

Kristin nodded.

'Well, her friend didn't know Jason's name, but this source did. Not only that, they knew what the argument had been about and where Ola and Liam had gone after. They said they googled my name, seen I'd written the story on the GP in Partick. That's why they felt they could trust me with this.'

She ignored Gill's scathing glance and continued to explain everything Scott had told her. Eastwynd Farm, Sigurd Holdings, Graham Linklater. The list of girls and the Talent Scouts, the go-between and the Play Pen. The whole sick story.

'The boys in this photo, they were paid by Linklater's go-between to bring the girls,' she said. 'Remember the BMW Liam drove, the one they found at Yesnaby? This is how he could afford it. It was how he first met Ola too.'

'How do you know that?' Gill asked.

Freya swallowed, knowing what would happen next. She took Ola's diary out of her coat pocket and opened it to the page where Ola and Liam had met.

She passed it to Kristin, who had been quiet the whole time Freya had been talking. 'This is what Ola wrote in her diary about the day she met Liam.'

'You took that?' Gill said. 'You stole it from Beth's house?'

'I didn't steal it, it was an accident.'

'What, it fell into your pocket, did it? I don't know if this is one of your methods from down south, sweetheart, but here we don't—'

'I put it in my pocket when you started yelling at me. I couldn't think straight with you—'

'I only yelled at you because you were being—'

'What does DI Muir say?' Kristin asked, cutting them both off. Her voice was calm, distant. Freya looked at her, but her gaze was lowered, fixed on the pages of Ola's diary.

'I haven't told him yet.'

'Why not?'

'Because …' Freya turned to Gill. 'Your story in the summer, the one that angered Magnus Robertson.'

Gill puffed out her chest. 'Aye?'

'What did it say?'

'Some hard truths, that's what. I said the Orkney force isn't led by the police, it's run by politicians who turn a blind eye to serious crime in these islands because they either don't want to scare off the tourists or they're too frightened and lazy to do anything about it.'

Freya opened the photograph of Graham Linklater and Allan Tait.

'Who's that?' Sophie asked.

'*Who's that?*' Gill repeated, wheeling herself closer to the screen. Freya felt her whole body tense up, a fog fall over her brain, as Gill leaned her weight against her, the smell of perfume and old cigarettes attacking her nostrils. 'Who's that? That man there …'

Gill put a finger on the monitor, over the man on the right.

'That's your man Linklater. And that …'

She moved her finger to the figure on the left.

'That's Chief Inspector Allan Tait, the man who was chief of police here before Magnus. Are you saying this was taken at one of these parties?'

Freya nodded.

'So this whole time, they've known about this?' Gill looked over her shoulder at Kristin. 'Oh, we've got to run this, Kris. No letting them off the bloody hook this time.'

Kristin didn't respond. She simply stared at the screen.

'Why now?' Sophie asked. 'I mean, why's the source only disclosing this now if they've known about it for seventeen years?'

Freya nodded. At the back of her mind, she had asked herself that too.

'Isn't it obvious?' Gill said. 'They say anything before now, who's going to listen? Nobody knew for sure those bairns were dead. Folk probably haven't given this story a second thought in years, and now it's all anybody can talk about. Seems the perfect time to me.'

Sophie nodded, but Freya didn't think she was fully convinced, and she wasn't either. Scott had had seventeen years to tell someone about Linklater's parties and had chosen not to. Fear might have been a factor, but speaking out hadn't become any less dangerous since the bodies had been found. If anything, it meant these men would be more desperate to hide what they had done.

Then there was Linklater's murder – his death had to be linked to the abuse of all those girls seventeen years ago. The message on the wall at Eastwynd Farm meant others in these islands knew what had happened there. Sophie's question applied to Linklater's killer too – if they had known all this time, why wait until now to act? The discovery of Ola's and Liam's bodies at Bay of Skaill had kickstarted something Freya didn't yet understand.

Unless, of course, the timing was a coincidence.

But as her dad used to say, *There's no such thing as coincidences, only connections you haven't made yet.*

Gill turned to Kristin again, who was still clutching Ola's diary. She was staring at its cover, but her focus seemed to be somewhere else. 'Well, boss? How do you want to play this? If we put this out there today, it might get lost in all the other coverage. We may be best holding on to it for a few days if we want maximum impact. But if there's a chance someone else could break it before we do …'

'There's something else,' Freya said.

Something that meant they may have no choice over what they did next.

Freya clicked on the photograph she had seen before leaving the library.

'My source told me that on the night Liam and Ola died, they'd seen Liam arguing with one of the men who'd paid to be at the party. One of the men who'd paid to have sex with the girls.'

Her three colleagues leaned in to look at the photograph of the man fighting with Liam. The man whose name had been on an envelope in Paul Thomson's house. One by one, they glanced up, looked over towards Kristin's office where Alistair Sutherland was standing in the doorway.

'Alistair,' Gill said, pointing at the screen. 'This is you.'

41

ALISTAIR LEANED AGAINST THE frame of Kristin's office door, his eyes sunken, his face ashen.

'What's me?'

'In this photograph,' Gill said. 'This is you fighting with Liam McDonnell.'

Alistair slowly pushed himself away from the doorframe and joined the others at Freya's computer. He looked at the photograph. Freya saw no hint of emotion cross his face.

'Well,' he said. 'I had a feeling we'd reach this point eventually. I never imagined it would happen this quickly.'

He sighed, releasing a breath it seemed he'd been holding for seventeen years.

He looked at Kristin. 'Didn't I tell you she was a gamble?'

Kristin looked at the floor and said nothing.

Confusion filled Freya's head with cotton wool. Was this a confession? What did he mean, *she was a gamble*?

'Alistair,' Gill said again. 'How do you explain this?'

Alistair pointed at the screen. 'Do you know who that is there?'

'That's Liam Mc—'

'Not him. The other man.'

'Gordon Tulloch,' Freya said.

Alistair fixed her with a tired glare. His powder blue eyes were riddled with spidery red veins. 'Gordon Tulloch, aye. Used to be the Dean of the archaeology department at the college here. A good man. He and I go back further than I care to admit. If I remember rightly, I was helping Gordon set up for a talk he was giving for a charity event at some hall or other that night in Stromness when that little cretin and his pals barged in, smacked off their heads, causing trouble. I remember it well, but I had no idea until now he was the same boy who had disappeared, nor did I realise his pal was taking pictures.'

Freya felt that fire in her belly again. 'You're lying. I've been in that room. I was there last night. It's a place called—'

'Aye, Eastwynd Farm, was it? Graham's peedie hideaway.' Alistair shook his head. 'I heard your story from Kristin's office there. It was quite a good one, I'll give you that.'

He pulled an empty chair from the desk and sat down.

'How about you tell us another, Freya. Tell everyone here the tale of how you lost your job at *The Herald*. Or should I tell it for you?'

Sweat blossomed on the back of her neck beneath her coat collar. She'd known this wouldn't be easy. She was ready.

'You can try and deflect all you like,' she said. 'I've got hundreds of these photos. And people know what happened. I've got sources who can place you there, who can tell everyone what you and your pals did.'

'Really? Who are these sources?'

'I'm not going to tell you.'

'Of course.' He smiled. 'After all, journalistic integrity is so important to you, isn't it?'

Freya glanced at the others. She saw the doubt creeping into their eyes.

'Why don't you tell us all about Damien Barber and what you did to him, eh?' Alistair said.

'That's got nothing to do with this.'

'A successful businessman you accused of abusing women without providing a shred of evidence? I'd say it has everything to do with this. It's almost as if this topic is some kind of sick obsession of yours.'

'I've got evidence, I've got—'

'Oh, these pictures, aye. And what do they show, exactly? Show me a single one where someone is getting abused, Freya. Show me the one that proves that thing you said about the … Talent Scouts, was it? Let me see the bloody proof.'

Something changed in Alistair's eyes then. He saw he'd struck a blow. These pictures supported what Scott was telling her, but they didn't prove it. All she had was Scott's word and he wasn't giving her the full story. Without others coming forward to corroborate this, she had nothing.

And Alistair knew it.

'I really had hoped for better from you, Freya. I honestly was rooting for you to turn things around. Remember when we spoke yesterday, I told you I'd had a chat with your old editor in Glasgow and he was highly complimentary about you?' Alistair said. 'Well, what I didn't tell you, because I didn't want to upset you further, is that I could tell something was off. You see, he was *too* complimentary, almost as though he couldn't wait to offload you onto us, so I pushed him a little harder.'

He leaned forward, knotted his fingers. Freya caught a whiff of that overpowering cologne and something else. It smelled like he'd been drinking.

'What he really said about you was that you'd had one big story a couple of years ago and you'd been trying to claw your career back ever since. He said the pressure was getting to you and the cracks were beginning to show. He said he reckoned …'

He paused, maybe for effect. Or maybe he really was considering whether or not to take the shot.

'He said he reckoned that accident of yours was no accident. He told me he wouldn't have been surprised if you had stepped out into traffic yourself.'

Those words were like a blade between her ribs, puncturing her lungs, pulling out the air.

'And what's worse,' Alistair went on, 'he was worried you might have been desperate enough to have done it simply to accuse Barber, because that's what you did, wasn't it? When you couldn't get the story you'd concocted about him to stick, you went and accused him of trying to have you killed.'

Freya shut her eyes, felt the warm tears roll down her cheeks. She never wanted to open them again because she couldn't bear to see the looks on the faces of the people around her. Not looks of anger, or disappointment, but a look she knew well. Pity. Pity for someone who clearly wasn't in their right mind.

'You said it yourself on Tuesday, Gill,' she heard Alistair saying. 'She obviously needs help, but we're not the ones to give it to her.'

When she did open her eyes again, Alistair was standing. There was a bite to his voice when he spoke.

'I will not sit here and listen to you slander a good man's name before his body's even cold. Coming out with the most sick, depraved nonsense I've ever heard in my life, in an effort to prove we were wrong to take you off a bloody story. How dare you do such a thing.' He shot a glance at Kristin. 'I need another drink. When I come back out here, she'd better not be.'

He strode away towards Kristin's office.

Freya looked at the others, hoping for support. Every single pair of eyes looked away.

She stood up. 'You can't stop this, Alistair. People know, and they've already got to Graham Linklater. How long before they get to—'

'Enough!'

Alistair spun around. His eyes seemed redder, burning with rage.

'You're right enough, I can't stop you from peddling your delusions, Freya, but I sure as hell don't have to pay you for it.'

'Meaning what?'

'Meaning you no longer work here. I cannot have a reporter on my books who's violent, insubordinate, untrustworthy, and, frankly, downright dangerous. You're fired. Now get the bloody hell out of my sight.'

42

IN THE SILENCE THAT followed, Freya could hear the click of the fluorescent lightbulbs. The tick of the clock. The constant, ever-present thrum of the building.

It reached a deafening crescendo, a ringing in her ears that was shattered by a hand on her shoulder.

'I'm sure your source made it sound very convincing, and with those pictures too, I have to admit, even I was nearly taken in by it,' Gill said. She spoke in the same cloying voice she'd used with Beth. She didn't seem to be gloating.

That somehow made it worse.

'Look, hen, if I was you, I'd take some time, get my head in the right place, then—'

Freya turned and ran for the door.

Outside, she got in her car, over-revved the engine as she floored the accelerator. She had no idea where she was going, she simply needed to get the fuck away. Terrifying thoughts were washing over her like a rising tide and she was struggling to keep her head above water.

How the hell was she going to tell Tom?

They'd just bought a house: they couldn't easily sell up and move away again. And they couldn't afford to live on Tom's wage alone – she *had* to work, and this job was all she knew. Reporter roles were hardly plentiful in Orkney, and, even if they were, Alistair would torpedo her chances. And he wasn't going to stop with her job – he and everyone else who had been involved in those parties was now well aware she knew about them. They were going to destroy her. She thought about what Paul Thomson had told her: *This could make them feel cornered, threatened. They'll come for you.*

She stood on the brakes as someone stepped in front of her car.

Kristin put her hands on the bonnet as Freya skidded to a stop. She opened the passenger door and got in.

'Take a left out of here,' she said, pulling on her seatbelt.

Kristin directed Freya the short distance to a food truck on the edge of the Hatston estate where she got out, bought them both black coffees, then told Freya to drive to the pull-in off Grainshore Road overlooking Kirkwall Harbour. They sat in uneasy silence together for a minute that felt closer to ten, watching the water, condensation creeping up the glass before Kristin said: 'I can't do this in here. Let's take a walk.'

They crossed Ayre Road to the footpath circling the shore of the Peedie Sea. Lights in the shapes of snowmen and Christmas trees hung from the lampposts, and in the distance the spire of St Magnus Cathedral poked its nose above the rooftops. It was coming up to half one now, dry but fully overcast, and a bitterly cold wind was sweeping in off the harbour. Very few people were out. They passed a man in a baseball cap and a woman wrapped up in a hat and scarf, two dogs trotting calmly either side of her – a Labrador and a Labradoodle. The Labrador made Freya think of Luna, which in turn made her think of Tom, who she still hadn't spoken to since their fight last night, and that brought her back to what had just happened and her thoughts began to unravel and …

'I've worn the wrong bloody shoes for this,' Kristin said, pulling Freya out of her free fall. She looked down and saw the high heels Kristin was wearing. She had no idea what label they were, but she was sure they would be expensive.

There was a bench up ahead. 'Do you want to sit down?'

Freya surprised herself at how calm she sounded, as if the past half an hour hadn't happened.

Kristin shook her head. 'I prefer to walk. The movement helps me think.' She looked at Freya for the first time since they had left the newsroom. 'When I was going through my divorce, I used to wait until the kids were asleep then I would go out walking for hours through the London streets. Probably not the smartest thing to do, but I needed that space, you know?'

Freya nodded, though she had no idea what was happening.

'My ex-husband, I let him cheat on me three times before I finally divorced the bastard,' Kristin said casually. 'He had a knack for making me doubt what I saw with my own eyes. The first two affairs were just figments of my imagination. When I mentioned he seemed to be spending a lot of time with a particular woman at his office, I was being irrational. When I found receipts for dinners for two at fancy restaurants when he had told me he was working, I was being paranoid. Or overly emotional, that was another favourite of his. You see, the thing is, people tell you you're mad enough times, you start to believe it. Do you remember I told you yesterday that Jason Miller asked me out once and I told him to fuck off?'

Freya frowned. The question didn't seem related to what Kristin had just said. She wasn't sure she'd heard it right.

But Kristin continued: 'About a week or so later another boy asked me out. James Buchanan. Now he *was* hot, nothing like Jason Miller. Tall, beautiful dark skin and the sweetest deep brown eyes. I didn't even think he knew I existed.' She smiled. 'I thought I was on a roll, either that or the perfume I'd got as an early birthday present must have been really fucking good.'

She laughed, then wiped her cheek with the back of her hand. Freya glanced over and saw that she was crying.

'I tried to play it cool for, like, maybe a day or two, but in the end I had to say yes. He said he was taking me to a party.'

Freya stopped, but Kristin walked on.

'Please, chick, let's keep walking,' she said without looking back.

The wind picked up, sent a chill through Freya. It blew lines into the still surface of the water beside them, like worry furrowing a brow. Freya caught up with Kristin. She didn't say anything. She sipped her coffee, which was already going cold, and let her talk.

'I don't remember being at any party,' Kristin said when Freya got alongside her. 'I don't remember getting to the house or where it was, who was there, anything. All I know is James picked me up in his car, we started drinking – he had me on bloody snake-bite, for Christ's sake – and when I woke up the next morning I knew something wasn't right. I … everything fucking hurt and I knew something bad had happened. I'd never slept with anyone before then and I …'

She stopped walking then. A tired-looking woman with short, dark hair ambled past them. Unable to say what she wanted to out loud, Kristin covered her face with her hand and began to shake. Freya put her arm around Kristin's shoulder and as she did, Kristin sprung around, threw her arms around Freya and hugged her tight.

They stood there like that for a long time, Kristin silently crying on her shoulder, and Freya felt the tears well in her eyes too, but she tried to hold back. This wasn't her trauma to cry over and so she felt like a fraud, like she was somehow stealing Kristin's thunder by crying too, even though really she knew other people didn't think like that and the pain and anger she felt at what had happened to her boss was genuine.

When Kristin finally pulled away, she dried her eyes with her hand again and gave a sheepish glance around, perhaps hoping there was nobody nearby to see.

Freya dried her eyes too. Her mind was burning with questions. She had to ask: 'When did this happen?'

'Early July, 2003,' Kristin said without pause. 'I'll never fucking forget that. It was at the start of the summer holidays, eight days before my sixteenth birthday.'

A whole year before the first photos on Paul's CD. More than two years before Ola and Liam were killed.

How long had this been happening?

Kristin began walking again. 'I didn't speak to anyone about it all summer. James never called. And I couldn't tell my parents – I didn't even know what I would say. I wasn't that close to my dad, and my mam – well, I thought, if she knew her precious little daughter had been out drinking with boys, she would only have told me it was my own fault, what did I expect to happen? She'd say she'd warned me enough times. Then when I got back to school in the autumn, nobody would talk to me. I didn't understand it.'

She wiped her cheek with her hand again, took a sip of her coffee.

'It turned out Jason Miller and a few others had spent the summer telling everyone I was begging for it that night. He'd told everyone I was a slag and I'd been throwing myself at him and anyone else with a cock. But the thing was, I didn't remember. For all I knew, it was true, and James wouldn't talk to me, so …'

Kristin fell silent as they passed a young mother with a toddler in a pushchair who had stopped to watch the geese.

'My source told me that's what they did,' Freya said when they had passed her. 'They spread rumours about the girls to try and undermine them. They even invited other kids along to act as witnesses to how wasted they were. They called them decoys.'

Kristin shook her head. 'Decoys, Talent Scouts … sick fucking bastards.' She stopped, turned to face Freya. 'I believe you, you know. I believed you right away and I should have stood up for you in front of Alistair, but I was just so … I mean what if he was there, at the same party I was?'

'Who? Alistair?'

Kristin nodded. 'He could have been the one who …'

'No,' Freya said, and at first she thought it was the right thing to say but, the more she considered it, she realised it was probably true. 'I doubt he would have hired you if he knew you'd been at one of the parties.'

'How would he know? It's unlikely he would have remembered me. It was probably just another Saturday night to those dirty pricks.' Kristin turned towards the water, wrapped her arms across her chest and held herself tight. 'We're running this bloody story. I'll speak to Soph and the others. I'll get them on board. What's Alistair going to do, sack the lot of us? He'd have no paper.'

'He might try.'

Freya managed a smile, and Kristin smiled back. 'Well, fuck him. We've got those photos too. Maybe there's something we can do with them. Don't they have meta tags or something? Date and location stamps. Maybe they can prove Alistair was—'

'Fuck,' Freya cut her off.

'What?'

'The photos. I've left the CD in the bloody computer.'

Dread gripped her throat as she realised the one physical link they had that tied these men to the parties, to Ola and Liam, was still sitting in a CD-ROM drive at Hatston.

Back at the newsroom there was no sign of Alistair's Mercedes in the car park, but Freya still didn't want to go back inside. Kristin said she'd run up to check. She was back within two minutes.

'It's gone,' she said as she climbed back in Freya's car. 'Sophie says he's taken it.'

Freya shut her eyes. A feeling close to vertigo crashed over her, like she was standing on a very narrow ledge high on a clifftop and one wrong step would send her tumbling.

'Fuck, it's going to be harder to run the story without them,' Kristin said. 'We can still do it, though. It only takes one person to see it and come forward to back it up. But without those photos all we've got is the account of a single unnamed source. I take it another copy won't be easy to come by?'

Freya shook her head, but not in response to Kristin's question. She'd been here before and knew it didn't matter if they ran the story.

It wasn't going to work.

Men with power – men like Alistair, Linklater, Tait – they didn't leave getting caught to chance. They had money and connections and influence, and they would use every weapon in their arsenal to shoot this story down, no matter how many people came forward to back it up. There would always be a way to undermine the victims' accounts, inflict further damage on people whose lives they had already shattered into pieces and, when others saw that, they would be too scared to come forward and the story would wither and die like a flame without oxygen. It would simply be buried again, deeper and deeper each time.

Her mind was spinning with the things she'd seen and heard today. She knew the answer was in there somewhere, but they were failing to coalesce into a clear picture. One question kept returning to the forefront of her mind:

Why now?

When Sophie had asked that, she'd only repeated something Freya had been asking herself since this morning. When she had gone to Paul's garage, the way he had reacted to hearing Scott's name had distracted her and she'd almost missed something else he said – he had asked Freya how she found him. More specifically, he'd said: *Let me guess, he's come crawling out of the woodwork since they found those bodies at Skaill.*

Freya opened her eyes, took her phone from her coat pocket.

'What are you doing?' Kristin asked.

'Just … one minute, and I'll explain.'

She opened her messages to Scott. There were two new ones since she had last replied to him at the library: 'Do you recognise any of the others?' and 'Hello?? You still there?'

She scrolled up, found the one she was looking for from earlier: 'we never knew anything about the men themselves. I only knew Linklater's name because he was listed as Sigurd Holdings' owner, and I got the company name from the land registry. It wasn't hard.'

Dark thoughts began to creep up on her.

'Freya?'

She looked over at Kristin. 'Do you know where Alistair lives?'

'Why?'

Freya didn't answer. She looked at her phone. If she told Kristin what she was planning, she would be horrified. There was no way she would go along with it.

'Freya,' Kristin said again. 'I've just told you something I haven't told anyone in almost twenty years. Not my ex-husband, not even my own parents. When Gill was kicking off on Tuesday, you should've told me. When you were running around on your own this morning, getting those photos, doing … whatever caused this – she gestured at the scratches on Freya's face – 'you should have let me know. I understand what happened in Glasgow. I know the way you were treated. When I hired you, Alistair told me all those things your last editor had said about you. I can't imagine what it must have been like to work in that kind of environment, but you're not working for them anymore.'

'I'm not working for you anymore either.'

Freya tried a laugh, an attempt to diffuse the tension, but Kristin looked disappointed.

'Why did you hire me?' Freya asked. 'If you'd heard all those bad things about me, why give me a job?'

'Because I figured it was either complete bollocks and the men you used to work for were extremely threatened by you, or you were the type of woman who would go to extreme lengths to bring down a sick fuck you knew was untouchable.' Kristin grinned. 'Either way, you sounded pretty badass.'

Freya smiled. She wanted to tell Kristin that her former editor was half-right – she *had* stepped out into traffic herself that night. But she had not done it with the intention of framing Damien Barber. The thought had never entered her mind.

All she had been thinking in that lowest of moments was that she was utterly and truly alone.

'I've got Alistair's address upstairs,' Kristin said. 'But if you want it, you're going to have to tell me your plan. I'll not let you do this on your own.'

43

FREYA TOLD KRISTIN WHAT she intended to do, but only up to a point. If she shared the precise plan that was forming in her head, Kristin would never agree to it.

'I want to talk to him.'

'Don't you think it's better to wait? If you turn up on his front doorstep this afternoon, he's hardly going to invite you in for tea and scones.' Kristin sighed when she saw her words had made no impact. 'Listen, I want to nail these dirty bastards as much as you do. More, in fact. But do you have to do this now?'

Yes, she did.

Because … she just *had* to. If she dropped this now, it would be like having an itch she couldn't scratch. No, worse: she would feel it like a wound left to fester, spreading into her bloodstream. Eventually, it would leak into her organs and shut her whole body down. But she didn't know how to explain that to Kristin. The infection analogy sounded melodramatic, but it wasn't. That was how it felt when she had her mind set on something and there was a block in the way.

She tried to find words Kristin would accept. 'I can't go home. I can't face Tom yet, tell him what's happened. And besides, Alistair will be on the phone to his pals right now. They'll be readying their defence. We need to act now.'

'Come back upstairs,' Kristin said. 'I meant what I said. I'm running this story. At the very least we can print Linklater's connection to Sigurd Holdings and that farmhouse – that should be easy enough to stand up. We can say sources have told us that's where Ola and Liam went on the night they were killed. We don't have to link it to the whole sex party racket, but it'll be enough to get things started.'

It wouldn't be enough. Not for Freya.

'He's angry right now,' Freya said. 'If I talk to him alone, maybe I can get him to slip up. I can get him on tape.'

'How?'

Freya reached across Kristin's knees and opened the glovebox. There was a Dictaphone inside. 'I'll record him on my phone and on this. He'll suspect I'm recording him, so I'll show him the phone, act like I've been caught, but he'll never know there's a second device.'

'Seriously, Freya? That's one hell of a long shot.'

'You said that on Monday too, remember?' she said with a tentative smile, though secretly she agreed with Kristin. It was a stupid idea, and it would never work.

But it didn't need to. It only needed to buy her some time.

'If I get something, I can take it to MIT. Then they can take it further, investigate Alistair properly,' Freya said. 'You'll never get this story out while he still owns this paper.'

'Why haven't you told DI Muir about this yet?'

'I trust Fergus. I do. But he worked under Tait. He was involved in the original investigation into Ola and Liam's disappearance – he *has* to have known something wasn't right. I don't think he's caught up in this, but …' She looked at Kristin. 'It's like you said the other day, people can always surprise you.'

Using her own words seemed to work. Kristin sighed, looked up through the windscreen at the sallow light coming from her office window. 'If you go there this afternoon, he's not going to want to see you. You said it yourself, he's mad as hell just now. And … I can't believe I'm saying this, but we don't know what he'll do. I never had him down as the sort to pay to rape young girls, but who knows what he's capable of.'

That was precisely what Freya had been hoping she'd say.

'I'll let you know when I get there, and if you haven't heard from me in another hour, call the police.'

'Christ, Freya, you can't—'

'Call 999 and tell them you heard gunshots. Say you heard a woman screaming. Anything to get them to come.'

Kristin shook her head. 'A lot can happen in one hour.'

Freya was banking on it.

Kristin glanced up at her window again. She nodded. Then she leaned across the handbrake and gave Freya a hug, and Freya let her.

She got out, looked back through the open passenger door. 'I'll text you the address. But Freya, promise me you'll be careful.'

'I promise.'

* * *

The blonde-haired woman gets out of the car a second time, stands there with the passenger door open, talking.

I sip lukewarm coffee and watch her in my rearview mirror. The reporter doesn't make a move to join her. A good sign. That means she's heading somewhere else. I followed them both as they took a walk at the Peedie Sea and got the sense they were planning something. With any luck, it'll be something I can use.

So far, the reporter's worked out well – she's got the photos, and she'll get me the names of the people in them too. She just needs to do it fast. I've got the car radio tuned to the local station and it's been nothing but wall-to-wall coverage of Linklater's death. With every hour that passes, the police have something new. They were never this quick to act seventeen years ago, but when a fat, rich pervert dies it's clearly a different matter. Some detective, a woman named Macintosh, told reporters they had a promising lead, and, as soon as I heard that, I knew what she meant – I stood in the blood. When the dirty old fucker was bleeding out, I stood over him to watch the panic on his face, the life leave his eyes, and I left a footprint behind. I don't know what they can learn from that, or how quickly it will lead them to me, but I still pulled the car over and thrashed the steering wheel till I couldn't feel my hands.

A car door slams.

My gaze shoots to the rearview mirror.

The blonde-haired woman walks across the car park, disappears inside the building. I put my coffee in the cup holder, my hand on the ignition key, but the reporter's turquoise Hyundai doesn't move. She sits there for another ten minutes and the delay makes my skin itch. What is she doing? Has she seen me watching her? I'm recalibrating my plan when her brake lights come on and finally she drives away.

I start my engine.

The reporter takes a left at the junction onto the main road, heading towards Finstown. I put my car into gear, when in my wing mirror I spot a black Skoda several metres behind me pull out into traffic without indicating. It passes me and turns left at the junction too. And I follow.

We head west. The road stretches in a long sweeping curve as it clings to the shoreline around the Bay of Firth. I can follow the reporter from several vehicles back and still keep her in sight. The black Skoda is two cars behind her. Night is creeping in already and the vehicles ahead of me have their taillights lit. At Finstown I watch for a blinking orange light to indicate the reporter is heading left towards Birsay, but she keeps going, doesn't turn off the A965 until the signpost for Bay of Skaill and the road past Brodgar. The Skoda goes with her.

We pass the giant stones at the side of the road. I'm trying to decide who this second tail might be, and if the reporter knows they're there. As the landscape rises and falls in waves, I feel my adrenaline dip, my energy wane for the first time since last night. I've been on a high since my visit to Graham Linklater. I need to keep that feeling alive.

But what if this is somehow a set-up?

What if I've been found out?

That blistering rage burns in me again as I imagine being caught with only one of those sick fucks zipped up tightly in a body bag. I need more. The reporter indicates to turn up ahead, but the black Skoda continues straight and so do I. If I had followed her, she would have noticed. The black Skoda speeds away and I curse myself for being so fucking stupid, so paranoid. There are only so many routes anyone can take on this tiny spit of land. At the next junction I pull over – the turning the reporter took leads down a single-track road that comes to a dead end at the clifftops at Yesnaby. Wherever she's gone, down there, she'll be easy enough to find.

I'm about to turn the car around as my phone screen lights up on the passenger seat. The reporter has sent another private message.

An address.

44

SHE SPOTTED ALISTAIR'S HOUSE long before the robotic voice on her phone told her she was approaching it.

Alone in the sweeping moorland high above the North Atlantic Ocean, a building grew out of the half-light. It was approaching half past two but already night had struck a mortal blow on the day, light bleeding out of the sky at an alarming rate. From the single-track road, she could make out spires and chimneys clawing at the blackening sky like the fingers of an outstretched hand.

A dark feeling spread to her heart and she fought to keep the paranoid thoughts at bay. Before turning onto the Yesnaby road she had noticed the two cars behind her, thought they were following her, but when they had continued straight on she knew she was being stupid. Kristin's words had got to her:

Who knows what he's capable of.

It didn't matter; she wouldn't be alone with him long, then help would be coming. She had no intention of contacting Kristin again after she had told her she'd arrived. She needed the police to come, but she also needed time before they did.

Before leaving the newsroom car park, after Kristin had gone back inside, she had called Mr Henderson at Kirkwall Grammar. The first part of the plan she had decided against sharing with Kristin.

'This seems a rather underhand way to go about things,' Mr Henderson said when Freya had revealed who she was. She'd told the receptionist she was a concerned parent calling about a pupil.

'I'm sorry, I didn't think they'd put me through if I told them why I was really calling, and this is important.'

She asked if he'd known a pupil, a friend of Liam's, named Scott Connelly.

There was silence on the other end of the line. Freya didn't know why. Was he reacting the same way as Paul had? Was he racking his brains trying to think? She hated not being able to see what was happening.

'Mr Henderson?'

'I'm trying to place the name,' he replied. 'I don't recall Liam being friends with anyone by the name of Connelly. Do you happen to know what he looked like?'

Freya passed on the description Scott had given of himself.

'I suppose that could describe any number of boys, but it's not ringing any bells. And certainly not for anyone who socialised with Liam. Why do you ask?'

Freya explained that Scott had been providing them with information about Liam. 'I'm not sure how much I can trust it, not without knowing he is who he claims to be.'

It wasn't a lie.

She heard the sound of a text message arriving as Mr Henderson said: 'There was a boy here by the name of Connelly while Liam was with us, but I know for a fact his Christian name was Andrew. He was a black-haired boy, several years younger than Mr McDonnell. As I said when we met, Ms Sinclair, I tend to remember our students, and I can say with some certainty there was nobody by the name of Scott Connelly here during Liam's time. Is it possible this man isn't being entirely honest about who he is?'

'It's definitely starting to look that way,' Freya had said.

She indicated for the turning onto the private road to Alistair's house before her phone instructed her to do so.

A quick glance in the rearview mirror; there was nobody behind.

Gravel snapped beneath her tyres as, at the end of the road, she neared a set of double gates blocking the entrance to the grounds. She slowed as she tried to decide her next step, but as she did, the gates juddered into life and began to peel open.

A nauseating feeling rose in her throat.

He knew she was coming.

Or perhaps not. The gates could be automatic. She needed to calm down, keep a clear head.

The road opened into a large forecourt before steps rising to the vast house. The Sutherland family had no doubt been here since the landowning Scots had arrived at the end of Norse rule in Orkney six hundred years ago. The building was old and designed to look older – eighteenth- or nineteenth-century, Freya guessed. Gothic in style. If it hadn't been for the low dusk light, she might have seen gargoyles peering down from the rooftops.

She felt the wind rocking her car before she came to a stop. There were no other cars in the forecourt, but lights were on in some of the windows, a faint wisp of smoke blowing sideways from one of the chimneys. She glanced at the front door and her throat clenched again when to her horror she saw it was open, Alistair leaning against the doorframe. He still had on his smart grey trousers and a white shirt open at the collar, looked like he had a drink in his hand. He appeared relaxed, in control. Everything happening as he expected it should.

She didn't like that.

She had hoped to text Tom before going inside, but now there was no time. There was so much she wanted to tell him, but it would have to wait. Instead, she quickly fired off her text to Kristin telling her she'd arrived.

Remember, she wrote. **One hour.**

She then switched to the Twitter app and sent the message she had copied and pasted into it before leaving Hatston. A message to Scott.

This address.

There wasn't chance to get her Dictaphone from the glovebox either. Alistair would see her do it; there wasn't any point.

'Looks like I've lost a bet,' he yelled over the wind as she got out of the car. 'You don't know when to leave things well alone, do you?'

She didn't answer.

Her confusion made him smile. He shook his head, turned and walked inside the house leaving the front door open.

The wind, with nothing to block its path off the ocean, whistled through the forecourt. It whispered to Freya from the dark corners of the building, warned her not to go inside.

She didn't listen.

She locked her car, walked up the stone steps to the house, and closed the front door behind her.

45

FREYA STOOD ALONE IN a large hallway. Voices echoed from somewhere deeper within the house and Freya realised Alistair might not be alone.

'Are you coming?' he called to her.

The voices didn't stop when he did.

'No need to take off your shoes,' he shouted. 'I doubt you'll be stopping long.'

Strange how the mind works; his comment about her shoes reminded her of what Fergus had told her yesterday about Ola's body. The shoes removed. Her leggings ripped. Her underwear nowhere to be found.

The plastic bag over her head and her skull coming out in pieces.

A shiver trembled through her.

Alistair appeared in a doorway at the end of the hall. 'If you're trying to decide whether to stay or go, don't let me stop you. You can leave the same way you came in.'

She followed him into a sitting room lit by lamplight and the shifting glow of a fire in the hearth. Windows looked out onto the gravel forecourt and across the rolling landscape to the clifftops. The ocean wasn't far, she could still see it even in the gathering dark. It was flecked white with tumbling waves. Black dots of fulmars circled above it. A TV mounted on the wall was on – the source of the voices, she realised. It was playing the news, one of the twenty-four-hour channels, a story about a shooting on the US west coast. The murder of an elderly businessman in Orkney was never going to take the top billing, no matter how rare it was.

In the centre of the room, three plush sofas were positioned around an expansive, cream-coloured rug with a dark wood coffee table in the middle. The air smelled of the logs burning in the fire, and pine from a large Christmas tree in the corner. Alistair downed the drink in his glass then walked to a mahogany cabinet against the far wall.

'Drink?' he asked her.

'No, thank you.'

'Are you sure? I've a local whisky here bearing your name, a *Highland Park Freya*. Ever tried it? Fifteen years old and four hundred quid a bottle, but it seems appropriate, don't you think?'

'Because of the name or because you like fifteen-year-olds?'

He was grinning when he glanced over his shoulder. Her jibe hadn't hit him how she'd hoped. This was a game Alistair had no doubt played before and knew how to win.

'Careful, Freya,' he said. 'I may no longer be your employer, but I'm still not a man to cross.'

He gestured for her to sit at one of the sofas and she did. He joined her, taking a seat on the sofa opposite. Although she'd declined his offer of a drink, he brought two tumblers of golden brown liquid with him, slid one across the smooth tabletop to Freya.

He glanced at the TV. 'No word anywhere about Graham. These reporters don't seem to have got as far as you have. Maybe you should try asking these news channels for a gig, eh?'

He laughed at his own joke. Freya didn't.

He reached for the remote, turned off the TV. 'Speaking of which, if you've come to beg for your job back, you can forget it.'

'I haven't.'

'Then what do you want?'

'To offer you something.'

He laughed again, more raucously this time. 'Really? Well, now you do have me intrigued. What is it you'd like to offer me?'

'Protection.'

'I see.' He grinned, nodded. 'And I suppose this is the point where you offer not to tell anyone else about all those disgusting things you were blethering on about at the office, and, now that we're alone, I don't deny them. Perhaps I even open up to you about them a wee bit, and all the while you've a tape recorder running in your pocket, is that it?'

'It's not the Eighties. We don't use tape recorders, we use phones.'

She took hers out of her coat pocket, showed him it wasn't recording.

'And how do I know you've nothing else hidden under that jacket of yours?' he asked. 'Does that thing even come off? I've never seen you out of it.'

She unzipped and turned out her pockets, pulling out the unopened letter that had been in there for days. She opened her coat a little way and turned out the inside pocket too.

Alistair's face straightened. She had confused him – he'd guessed she was coming there to record him, the obvious plan, but now he knew that wasn't what she had in mind, his confidence withered.

'What's that?' he asked, pointing at the envelope.

'Nothing you need worry about,' Freya said, putting it back in her pocket.

Alistair leaned back on the sofa. 'So, what's the game here? If you're not here trying to catch me out, what are you up to?'

'It's like I said, I'm here to offer you protection.'

'From what?'

'Scott Connelly.'

That punch landed as intended. The red glow of his whisky-warmed cheeks leached away.

Freya said: 'He's been using me to try and find you and the others like you. And seeing as I now know where you live …'

She left the rest of her sentence dangling.

Alistair took the bait.

She saw the fire ignite in his eyes. 'You're saying Scott killed Graham? And you led him to him?'

'He found Graham himself, it's the rest of you he's after now. That's why he sent me looking for those photos you've stolen. He knew faces, he just needed the names.'

Freya didn't know for certain that Scott had killed Linklater, but it seemed to fit. She had started putting this together earlier, when Scott Connelly had turned out to be a real name. One that put the fear of God into someone as unhinged as Paul Thomson. But it was Sophie's question that had sharpened her focus.

Why now?

As far as Freya could see, if Scott's only motivation was revealing a scandal, he could have taken what he knew to any reporter at any time. He'd sent her to South Ronaldsay last night to gauge how eager she was, how far she would go to get what he was offering, then he'd pushed her to get those photos, even going silent on her once she had suggested other means of revealing the truth. And once she had got hold of the pictures, he'd only been interested in one thing:

Who is he?

Do you know his name?

Do you recognise any of the others?

Scott wasn't bothered about exposing the truth, he only wanted to know the names of the men at the parties. Freya wasn't sure at first why he'd sent her to get the photos from Paul instead of simply collecting them himself and sending them to her, especially as he hadn't minded her using his name, but, if he had murdered Linklater, it made sense he'd be lying low. He had admitted that he'd actively tracked Linklater down, that his was the only name he had been able to find, and now Graham was dead. And Freya was fairly certain that, now Scott knew their names, Alistair Sutherland and Allan Tait would be next.

And she had just given him one of them on a plate.

This brought her back to the question of why Scott had started to act now? But then she'd realised that Paul had answered that for her already: *He's come crawling out of the woodwork since they found those bodies at Skaill.*

'Scott Connelly killed Liam and Ola, didn't he?'

Alistair squirmed on the sofa. He sipped his whisky, ran his tongue over his lips. 'I genuinely have no idea.'

'But he was at Eastwynd Farm that night. He was the one who sent Jason Miller to Harray to lure them both there.'

Alistair closed his eyes, gave the slightest nod.

'He was your go-between,' Freya said. 'The man Linklater paid to recruit the boys to bring you the girls.'

She was certain Scott was the blonde-haired guy she'd seen with his arm around Liam's neck in the photos, the one in his early twenties. Too old to be a Talent Scout, too young to be one of the rich perverted pricks like the man in front of her. And when she'd had it confirmed by Mr Henderson that he had never been at Kirkwall Grammar with Liam, one of the final pieces fell into place.

There were still a few things that didn't fit, but she would get to them.

'I imagine he wasn't happy that Liam was protecting Ola, someone you and your pals had paid good money for, right? He needed to show people what happens when they don't do what they're told.'

'You're asking the wrong person,' Alistair said. 'Regardless of whether or not you believe this, that night at Eastwynd was actually only the second of those events I ever attended. I had very little to do with Scott Connelly directly. Graham and Allan were the ones who …'

He stopped himself. Freya noticed him glance at his watch, like he had somewhere else he needed to be.

'You still know who he is, though,' Freya went on. 'Nobody else in Orkney does, do they? Only those of you who were at the parties. I'm guessing he's not from here originally. You're the only ones who can give him away, so he's come back to make sure that doesn't happen.'

Alistair drained his glass. 'You sound like you've got this all figured out, so why are you here?'

'I told you, to offer you—'

'Protection, aye. But what is it you're wanting in return?'

A few things, but she decided to start with the easiest. One of those things she still couldn't make fit.

'What was happening in that photo of you with Liam and Gordon Tulloch? You and Liam seemed to be fighting.'

Gordon Tulloch's involvement was still a mystery. It was the only thing left making her doubt her theory about Scott. It was clear Gordon had somehow known about the bodies before the news had even been broken – he'd seen the SOCOs from the beach and gone on the run less than thirty minutes later. He was also the obvious person to have put them there, given his background. And why had Scott denied seeing him at the parties when they had clearly been at Eastwynd Farm that night at the same time? It was almost as if Scott was protecting him for some reason.

'We weren't fighting,' Alistair said. 'Or, I should say, he wasn't fighting me.'

Freya frowned. She didn't know what he was getting at and it pissed her off he was being so cryptic.

She took her phone out of her coat pocket again.

'What are you doing?' Alistair asked.

'Texting Scott your address.'

'I'm answering your bloody questions, what more do you—'

'Answer me straight, drop the bullshit. What were you doing?'

'I was dragging him off Gordon. The peedie scrote had tried to batter his lights out and I was pulling him away. That good enough?'

'Why?'

Another glance at his watch. 'Why do you think? Because Gordon was a friend of mine and—'

'No, why did Liam attack Gordon?'

There was a sound somewhere in the house then. Sounded like a door closing. Freya's head spun towards the hallway. She listened.

'Who else is here?'

'Nobody,' Alistair replied. And when Freya looked back at him he was checking his watch a third time. 'My wife's away in Edinburgh with our girls, Christmas shopping. It's an old house, Freya. Strange noises are par for the course. You get used to it.'

His phone pinged then at the same time as a bell rang in the hallway. He checked his phone, let out a long breath as he did. He almost seemed to deflate with relief.

'About bloody time,' he said, pressing something on the screen.

'What's happening?'

Alistair stood and picked up his glass. He pointed at Freya's. 'You not drinking that?'

'What's going on? What was that on your phone?'

Alistair picked up the glass of shockingly expensive whisky he'd poured for Freya, downed it in one. 'That was the gate. Someone's coming to join us.'

'Who?'

The sound of gravel crunching beneath tyres drew her gaze to the window. It was almost completely dark outside now, but through the glass she saw headlights nearing the house.

A black Skoda parked next to her car in the forecourt.

46

ALISTAIR LEFT FREYA AND went to answer the front door. She watched a man climb out of the black car and walk towards the house.

'You took your bloody time,' she heard Alistair say from the hallway.

'She was followed,' a rasping voice replied.

'By whom?'

'Best kens. Their car's parked at the end of the road there by the clifftops. No sight of who was driving. I've checked the grounds, not seen a peep. The lads will deal with it when they get here.'

'They're coming here?'

'On their way now.'

A door closed. The voices neared.

Instinctively, Freya stood up and backed away from the doorway, towards the fireplace.

Alistair entered the room first.

'Well, you only win half our bet,' he said over his shoulder to the person in his wake. 'She's not here to try and record me.'

'You sure about that?'

A man with a gaunt, grey face came through the doorway behind Alistair. The bald head flecked with liver spots, the closely cropped silver hair at the sides, made him look quite different from the photographs Freya had seen of him earlier, but she still knew who he was.

'Hello, Freya,' he said as he walked into the room. He turned to Alistair. 'You've searched her, then?'

Freya tensed. She felt her hands ball into fists. She noticed the poker out of the corner of her eye, just beyond arm's reach.

Allan Tait saw her clock it too. 'Easy. Let's not get too excited now.'

'Her phone isn't recording and there's nothing in any of her pockets,' Alistair said as he walked to the cabinet at the back of the room and poured three more glasses of whisky. 'Though I don't suppose it would matter, if the cavalry's arriving soon.'

Tait sat on the sofa nearest Freya, crossed his legs and folded his hands into his lap. He was a tall man but skeletally thin, both in his body and his face. Much thinner than in the photographs she'd seen of him this week. There was a croak to his voice too; Freya wondered if he might be ill. Something terminal, she hoped.

Alistair came back and handed Tait a glass of whisky, slid another to Freya. Four hundred pounds a bottle and he was pouring it out like pop. He sat down in the place he'd occupied before, but Freya stayed standing, watching them both.

Tait pointed a bony, sallow finger towards her. 'When Alistair called me earlier, asked me to keep an eye on what you were up to, I said you'd more than likely show your face here before the day was out.'

'You don't know me,' Freya heard herself say.

'True enough, but I knew your dad and this is exactly the kind of stunt he would have pulled. And look where that got him.'

Freya felt a chill creep through her.

Tait saw that too. A malignant grin spread across his lips. 'I remember him bringing you down to the station when you were a wean. You were a peculiar wee thing, even then. Alistair tells me you've not changed much.'

Freya said nothing. Tait's arrival, his mention of 'the lads', and, most of all, her father, had knocked Freya way off course and she was struggling to navigate her way back.

'What are you doing here, Freya?' he asked.

'She's here to offer us protection,' Alistair said, sipping his drink.

'Oh, aye? From what, exactly?'

'Scott Connelly.'

'Really? So, he *is* back? Was it him who did Graham?'

'She believes so.'

Tait turned to Freya. 'And what makes you think that? Is Scott this mysterious source of yours, by any chance?'

'She says he's been—'

There was a noise beyond the room again. Closer than before. Everyone heard it this time. All three of them turned to look.

Tait and Alistair shared a glance. For the first time since the former Chief Inspector's arrival, Alistair looked nervous.

'I'll go,' he said, standing. But instead of leaving the room he stepped towards the fireplace. Freya recoiled as he approached, almost felt relieved as he took the poker from its stand. 'Probably just the wind, but all the same …'

Tait nodded.

Alistair left the room and Tait turned to Freya. 'Why don't you come and sit down? You're making me nervous standing there like that.'

Freya didn't move.

She didn't say anything.

She was still fixating on Tait's earlier question: why was she here?

Why had she not gone home to Tom and Luna like Kristin had suggested and left this well alone?

But she knew the answer: she was here because she didn't trust anybody else to do anything about this.

Nobody *ever* did anything.

Freya's real plan, the one she hadn't dared share with Kristin, was to lure Scott to Alistair's house and hope she'd got her timings right. It needed to be perfect. If Kristin called the police and they arrived before Scott did, they might scare him away. And if they arrived too late …

There was always the chance Scott might murder Alistair before the police showed up but, after careful consideration, given the terrible things Alistair had done, it was a risk Freya had been willing to take. But, in spite of what she had confided in her earlier, Freya wasn't sure Kristin would have seen things the same way. Scott being arrested and being able to tell MIT the whole sick truth behind what had happened to Ola and Liam was now

Freya's only hope of exposing this scandal and getting her life back. It was gradually beginning to dawn on her that his arrival was also her only real chance of getting out of this alive.

A strange feeling began to fill her chest. It took her a while before she realised it was regret. She'd gambled her life on a murderer who had lured schoolgirls to rapists. And now, if he came, he was outnumbered.

'Someone knows I'm here,' she said. She could hear the tremble in her voice and she was mad at herself for it. 'If I don't contact them within an hour of arriving here, they're going to call the police.'

Tait checked his watch. 'I followed you here. I know when you turned up. I'd say that gives us at least another hour before they get here, if they come at all. There's no hurry.'

There was a grandfather clock against the wall behind the sofa where Alistair had been sitting. Freya glanced at it and saw Tait was right, she had been there a little under half an hour. There were still more than thirty minutes before Kristin would call the police – *if* she kept to her side of the plan – and God knows how much longer until they got here.

'Are you going to kill me?'

'Not me. I don't do the dirty work.'

'Then who?'

He took a slug of his whisky. She watched his Adam's apple rise and fall as he swallowed. He wiped his lips with his hand then patted the sofa beside him.

'Sit.'

She did, as far away from him as she could without perching on the arm of the sofa.

He watched her a long while – a sideways look through sunken eyes – before he spoke.

'You surprise me, you know, how naive you are. Given your family history, what your father did for a living, I thought you might understand the way of the world a little better,' he said. 'Alistair told me what happened earlier. You swanning back into his newsroom with your big discoveries, thinking you had it all figured out, when you don't even know the half of it.'

Freya stayed silent. She listened to the sigh of the old house in the wind, the ticking of the clock, the crack of the fire. She didn't need to respond – Tait seemed like he wanted to tell her everything, almost like he needed to gloat.

Or maybe he thought it didn't matter what he said because she'd be dead soon.

She tried to push that thought away.

'The Talent Scouts, the Play Pen ... that was all Scott. He loved naming things for some reason, but we never bothered with any of that. He was a show-off, that boy. Too big for his own boots. That whole operation with the schoolboys bringing us girls was far too complicated and it was never going to last. The old way was much simpler.'

'The old way?'

'Aye, the way we did things before your old man died.'

Freya felt a rush of pins and needles in her hands. She reached for her ear. There were so many questions she wanted to ask, but they were all drowned by the tidal wave of emotions crashing over her.

Tait got the reaction he had wanted. He gave Freya that grin again.

'Funny to think all of this can, in some small sense, be attributed to Neill,' he said. 'Long before Scott joined us, we had an altogether more elegant set-up. The girls came to us from Europe, stayed here a while afore journeying on south. Graham's boats came in handy with that. We had them at our parties, nobody knew they were here, then within a week or two they were gone again. Nice and clean. But when Neill got killed, that brought our colleagues from the south up here, poking around. Things got a bit too hot for some people and so, as is the way of all good things, it came to an end.'

Freya struggled to stay calm, make sense of this.

Just how long had this been happening?

She remembered when her dad had died, he had been on duty at the time. His car had blown a tyre and flipped over several times on a lonely road beside the Loch of Hundaland in the desolate Birsay Moors. It had been several hours before anyone had found him, yet he was less than ten minutes' drive from their home. For a long time when she was little, Freya had nightmares that he had been alive for much of that time, out there alone, calling for her. Hoping in vain that someone might come.

Because his death had occurred in the line of duty, an investigation was launched, and she did recall officers from the Northern Constabulary coming from Inverness to visit. They had spoken to her mother but not to her. They had concluded his death was a tragic accident.

'Did you kill my dad?' she heard herself asking.

Her voice sounded small. Distant.

Tait wasn't grinning now. His expression was as serious as the sickness that appeared to be ravaging him. 'There have been folk who have accused me of it. But no. Like I said, I don't do the dirty work.'

'So, someone else?'

'Your dad had his enemies. It's as I said, Freya, you're naive to think anyone in our line of work wouldn't have. The whole "safe island communities" thing is for the tourists. It's for politicians and putting on posters, but these are violent shores, always have been. Take it from me, as someone who policed these islands for more than thirty years, dark deeds have long been carried out here and no doubt always will. The people who trafficked those girls from Europe, they've moved on to other things now, but they're still here in Orkney. Still as mean and rotten as they've always been. Which is why your whole charade earlier, talking about me and Alistair, Graham and Scott, like you've stumbled on some grand conspiracy …'

The bell rang in the hallway again.

Tait didn't take his eyes off Freya. 'We're merely small pieces in a much grander puzzle.'

Tait forced his bony frame off the sofa and went to the hallway to answer the bell. Freya remembered it wasn't the one for the front door but for the gate on the lane. When he returned, the house was now in complete darkness save for this room.

'Where the bloody hell has that man got to?'

'He's here,' Freya said, more to herself than anyone.

Tait turned to look at her. 'Who's here?'

'Scott Connelly. I gave him this address when I arrived. He's been looking for you.'

Tait frowned. 'You gave Scott Connelly this address? Why?'

Headlights appeared in the now-blackened window. Freya heard the crunch of gravel again, louder than before. A heavier vehicle. Seconds later, a white Transit van, smeared with dirt and pocked with patches of rust, rattled to a stop facing the window, its headlights burning into the room, blocking out whoever was behind the windscreen. It sat with its diesel engine chugging. Freya felt her throat tighten as a dark figure got out.

'Why did you give Scott Connelly this address?' Tait asked again.

'Because, if the police won't do anything, and Alistair won't allow this story to get out, then I had no other choice. He's been using me to find out your names and your—'

'Scott Connelly knows my name all too bloody well. Who do you think it was who found him in the first place? He knew all of us. He doesn't need you to give him this address. He's been here before with me, for Christ's sake.'

There was a heavy knock at the front door.

'Have you spoken to him? Did you meet him?' Tait demanded. There was a desperation in his guttural voice now that Freya found both exhilarating and terrifying.

'No. We only spoke over text.'

'Then that's not Scott fucking Connelly you've been—'

Freya heard a scream as the lights went out; realised it was her.

Tait was yelling somewhere nearby.

A fist hammered the front door again.

The beams from the van filled the room with a harsh white light. They made Tait's skin appear even paler, almost translucent. She saw him turn towards the hallway. He was going to unlock the front door and let that figure from the van inside and she knew she had to act.

In the beams of light pouring through the window, she saw the whisky glass.

No time to think. She picked it up, ran across the room and swung it at the back of Tait's bald head where it exploded with a sickening crack. Warm liquid covered her hands, could have been whisky, could have been blood. His or hers?

Tait groaned, clutched at the back of his head, then he flew around and grabbed Freya by the throat. He was a sick man, but his strength hadn't left him. His cadaverous fingers closed around her windpipe. She felt her eyes bulge and a pressure in her head, and spots appeared in the white light in front of her as she kicked, bit, clawed, but nothing she did loosened his grip.

Her limbs grew heavy, then everything became still. Like she was swimming in a deep, warm pool and she had dropped her head beneath the water, sound beginning to fade, and she was looking upwards as she sank deeper, watching lights dance on the surface as they blanched and withered away.

Blood hit her lips as Tait's fingers let go.

It spilled onto her face, her hair.

Freya dragged a breath into her lungs that set her throat on fire. She opened her eyes – she was lying on the floor, Tait beside her, his eyes heart-attack wide as he clutched at a gaping slit across his throat and his dying breaths quivered in his open windpipe. A pool of blood – black in this light – grew between them.

There was a thundering sound. The pounding on the door. Someone yelling.

And a hand.

'Freya, come on!'

She looked up at the person standing over her, blood-stained blade in one hand, the other reaching out towards her.

'Freya, we've got to fucking move! Come on!'

In the shadows there was no face she could see, only a voice. But that voice changed everything.

47

THE SOUND OF BREAKING glass. The window. The men from the van were inside.

'Fuck!'

The figure standing over her started to run.

Someone was climbing in through the window. Freya heard the crunch of heavy boots stepping on glass.

'Wait!'

Freya was on her feet without realising she'd forced herself up. Then she was in the hallway without consciously leaving the room. Ahead of her a silhouetted shape ran into the darkness. Behind her, voices howled like a pack of hounds baying at the scent of blood.

She ran.

A kitchen. More broken glass. A door banging open in the wind.

Freya launched herself through it into the dying light. The biting air filled her lungs, gave her another yard of pace, despite the pain searing through her ankle. She found herself in manicured gardens, a long lawn unfolding into the distance where the silhouetted figure sprinted towards a gate in a wall. She went through it several seconds behind them and the horizon opened up and the wind took her breath away.

Her muscles burned. Her lungs filled with acid.

She kept running.

The dusk sky was overcast, burnt grey turning black, but there was a glow far ahead of her at the edge of the world where the clouds didn't reach the sea. The figure ran ahead of her across dark open farmland towards the light.

Towards the clifftops.

'Wait!'

The figure didn't stop. Couldn't hear her over this wind.

There were no voices behind her now, but she didn't turn to see if they were still coming. The wind thundered against her chest, forced her back, and a vortex of thoughts made her feel faint. But she didn't slow down. Couldn't.

Wouldn't.

Stop, and she was dead.

That voice. It was a voice she knew.

One recurring image kept sweeping past her eyes: the shoes. The shoes had been buried on top of the body.

Up ahead, the figure seemed to have come to a standstill before setting off again. As Freya tried to catch up, she found a barbed wire fence blocking her path. A piece of torn black cloth flailed wildly from it in the wind. Beyond the fence, farmland became moorland. Rough underfoot. The sky grew larger as the sea neared, and the thunderous sound of the North Atlantic making heavy landfall against the jagged walls of sandstone echoed in the air around her.

'Ola, wait!'

The figure slowed. It stopped.

Hunched over, hands on knees, spitting into the mud.

Freya caught up with her. She thought she must have dreamed it, but it was true. The figure was a woman dressed head to toe in black. Short, dark hair under a baseball cap. Covered in blood.

Freya would never have recognised her but for that voice. The same acid-laced voice she had heard on the Stromness quayside as a teenager.

Did you really think Harry could fancy a spaz like you?

Her mouth formed the only question her stupefied brain could muster.

'How?'

Ola Campbell looked up at her and when Freya saw those grey eyes, she knew it was true.

Ola didn't answer. She was panting heavily, clutching at her arm, and it was only now that Freya saw she was bleeding. She was hurt.

Freya looked back towards the house. The curve of the land and the rapidly encroaching night meant she could no longer see it. Nothing out there but the wind and the gathering dark. The relentless gale coming off the sea blew a chill into her bones as she realised she had no idea where those men were now, who they were, how many of them there had been in that van.

They needed to move.

As if reading her mind, Ola spoke again.

'My car's at the top here.' She nodded in the general direction of the car park at the end of the Yesnaby road.

'They know.'

Ola swallowed. She was struggling for breath. 'Who are they?'

'I don't know, he didn't tell me. He only referred to them as "the lads".'

'He? That one trying to strangle you? Was that the pig?'

'Allan Tait, yes.'

'Good.'

She spat again into the hard ground.

The ocean roared behind them. The land was wide open here. No place to hide.

'The shoes,' Freya said out loud as the thought occurred to her again. 'They didn't fit.'

'What?'

'The shoes didn't fit the body you buried in your clothes. That's why they were on top of it.'

In the half-light, Freya saw Ola nodding. 'Yeah.' She forced herself upright, still holding her right arm. 'Come on.'

Ola set off walking towards the car park.

Freya followed.

There was no escape from the wind here. Sea spray scattered over the clifftops. She had her breath back now, but her heart still hammered in her chest, her throat, her temples. Adrenaline coursed through her, making it hard to think of anything other than survival, but in her head, the picture of what must have happened that night at Eastwynd Farm was slowly beginning to recast itself.

For now, though, it remained tantalisingly out of focus. She watched the woman walking ahead of her, this woman who had come back from the dead. This woman who had tormented her teenage years. This woman who was now a murderer.

This woman who had just saved her life.

Ola looked back at her over her shoulder. Maybe she was trying to place her.

'We went to the same school,' Freya said.

'What?'

'I thought you were looking at me because you recognised me.'

Something about Ola's expression changed, but she didn't acknowledge what Freya had said. She glanced across the fields towards the house. Freya watched her as they walked and thought of the man she had seen in those pictures and the description Scott ... Ola had given of him. Five ten, skinny. She looked at how tall and thin Ola was. Once decomposition had started in earnest, a body of that description, dressed in Ola's clothes and with its head caved in, might fool investigators for a short while, but not for long.

'That's Scott who's buried in your clothing, isn't it?'

Ola looked over her shoulder again. She nodded.

There was the answer to the question: *why now?*

'You had to come back before the police figured out it wasn't you.'

'Can't believe it's taken them this long,' Ola said. 'Or maybe I can.'

The forensic examination of the remains had been delayed by the difficult excavation. Nobody would look at them too closely until they reached the lab in Aberdeen and had been unpacked and laid out on the table. And even that may have been put on hold if there was a more pressing case anywhere this side of Perth, such as Graham Linklater's. That was a fresh kill and, as DCI Macintosh had said on Tuesday, the first forty-eight hours would be crucial. The examination of his body would take priority over bones that had been in the ground seventeen years.

Freya knew it would be a lengthy process to identify the bodies, given what Fergus had said about the skulls being smashed in. That would rule out ID by dental records, and DNA was harder to do without tissue. But there would be simple ways to tell if the body was male or female from features on the pelvic bone, and she knew age could be fairly accurately determined from collarbone length. The minute anyone did the slightest analysis of those remains, they would know that body wasn't Ola's. If the police hadn't found out by now, they would know soon.

They reached the clifftop footpath, picked up the pace a little.

'The other body, is that Liam?'

'Yeah, it's Liam.' Ola stopped, turned. The wind rushing over the clifftops blew her a step sideways. 'Look, I know you're desperate to bag this story for your paper, but—'

'I don't care about a story. I want everyone to know the truth. I want justice.'

Ola looked Freya up and down, took her measure. Freya wondered what she saw.

'You've got to hand yourself in,' Freya said.

'What?'

'The police surely know by now that body isn't yours. They'll be looking for you. And what's your plan? You're just going to kill everyone who ever went to one of those parties?'

'Pretty much.'

'It won't matter. Tait's just told me it was bigger than that. It was going on for years before Scott showed up. Tait said it started out as human trafficking, that there are others here in Orkney who were—'

'Who?'

'He didn't say, but I'm going to find out. But the police need your testimony about the parties. There's no other evidence, nobody else is coming forward. They need *you*.'

Ola looked out to sea, at the rapidly fading light on the horizon. She shook her head. 'I think you've got it into your head we both want the same thing.'

'Don't we?'

'I don't give two fucks what went on before,' Ola yelled. 'I don't care about the truth, or justice for anyone other than Liam. All I want is to see those bastards who destroyed my life and Liam's life bleed the fuck out in front of me.'

'Help the police find them, bring them down. The detectives running this case aren't from here, they're MIT. You can trust them.'

Ola laughed at that.

'How are you even going to find the rest of them?' Freya asked.

'Without your help, you mean?'

Ola was still holding the knife. It suddenly dawned on Freya that she was the only witness who had seen Ola alive.

The only witness still breathing.

She took a step back and a rock gave way beneath her foot. She stumbled as a stab of pain pulsed through her ankle.

'Relax,' Ola said. 'I'm not going to fucking kill you. But you know, if I hand myself in, first thing they'll ask is how I knew to find my way here. They'll take my phone. You still so keen on everyone knowing the truth?'

'Yes.'

She meant it, even if it might make her an accessory to murder.

Ola saw that. 'You're a fucking piece of work, you know that?'

'I've been called worse. By you.'

Ola looked at her and, for the first time, Freya thought she saw a glimmer of true recognition in her eyes. 'Aye, well, I said a lot of dumb shite when I was younger. Don't take it personally.' She sighed. 'Listen, let's get to the car, then we can—'

A rock near their feet shattered into pieces, followed by a crack of gunfire. They both turned to look up the rising cliff edge. At the top was a squat, dark shape – one of the disused anti-aircraft gun towers from World War II. Someone was standing beside it.

There was a flash of light, a whistling sound as something flew past them. Another rock burst open behind her.

'Fuck!'

Ola took off running. Back in the direction they had come.

Another rock exploded at her feet before Freya realised what was happening. The men from the van.

She turned and ran.

Ola was way out in front. Freya hadn't recovered from the sprint from the house and her legs felt like lead. Like she was running through treacle. The stumble she'd taken over the rock had set her ankle alight again and she was struggling to put weight on it. To her horror, she was limping.

Another clap of gunfire behind her. Another whistling sound close past her head. Ola was pulling further away, disappearing into the night. Freya couldn't keep up. She wasn't going to outrun the men behind her. Keep going like this, and they would be on her in seconds. She needed to—

Another gunshot.

Away in the distance, Ola dropped to the ground.

Freya's heart froze. She stopped running.

She stopped breathing.

Another bullet thumped into the ground mere metres away, shattered her trance and she ran again. Towards Ola.

If anything happened to her …

She wrenched her phone from her coat as she ran, forced her fingers to dial 999 at the second attempt. She breathlessly yelled something into the receiver about gunshots … at Yesnaby … come quick!

Please, God, get here fucking quickly!

Ola was lying face down when Freya reached her, a dark pool of blood spreading across the smooth, red rock from her right shoulder.

'Ola!'

Nothing.

'Ola, get up! Come on!'

Freya looked up. The figure was running. Getting closer. Just the one. She scanned the black landscape around them and saw nothing.

The ocean thundered at her back. Spray from the waves drenched her neck. An idea filled her head and there was no time to think. No room for doubt.

She had to act.

She dragged Ola's limp body towards the clifftop. There was a groan as she did – a good sign. About two metres below the drop here, a narrow ledge in the layered sandstone jutted out before the island fell away into the churning black water beneath.

She left Ola perched on the edge and carefully lowered herself down the rocks as the wind tried to take her with it. Her foot slipped as she hit the ledge, her stomach launching into her mouth, but she managed to find her grip. She edged along the cliff face, the acrid stench of shit from the nesting birds stinging her tongue, increasing her vertigo. She forced herself through it.

Clinging to loose rock with her fingernails, she scampered around the curve of the cliffs before dragging herself back up to the top.

The man with the gun was to her right now.

She had come up behind him.

He stood over Ola's prone body, took aim at her head.

And Freya ran with every ounce of energy she could summon.

ONE WEEK LATER

48

SHE OPENED HER EYES, but it made no difference.

The room was dark. No way of knowing what day or how late it was. Freya lay looking up into nothing, letting herself slowly come back to life. There had been a sound, like a doorbell or a phone ringing, but, as the lingering fog of sleep began to lift, she realised she must have dreamed it. Funny, because she remembered her dream vividly. The same dream she'd had every night this week.

It must have been a week now since the events at Yesnaby. She had slept through Christmas and had no mind to do anything but sleep through Hogmanay as well. She knew what Helen would say about that, but she didn't have the energy to care. Tom would be upset too; their first Christmas in Orkney and she'd ruined it. That, she was more concerned about. Yet another crack she was going to have to fix. They still hadn't cleared the air and so it hung thick with the reek of everything that was rotting in their relationship. She wanted to reach out to him, wanted to say so much, but words were beyond her right now. Everything was. Her eyelids were beginning to draw closed again as a whining sound came from the hallway.

That dog always knew.

Light slipped under the door. It slid across the floor and over the walls as the door crept open. Tom poked his head in. Freya could hear Luna's strained panting – Tom must have hold of her collar to stop her from running in and licking her half to death.

'You awake?'

'No.' She hoped he heard the smile in her voice.

'There's someone here for you.'

'Who?'

The sight of Fergus sitting at the table when she went through to the kitchen sent a jolt of panic down to her fingertips. A body must have washed up, or somebody had come forward, having seen what she had done, and he was here to arrest her. But she soon realised that wasn't the case. Something about him looked different; his scruff was gone. He'd shaved and the bags under his eyes were less pronounced. He stood as she walked in, looked like he was thinking of giving her a hug but then thought better of it. He offered her a smile instead.

'How are you feeling?'

'Tired.'

'I called in on you a few days back, Tom here said you were sleeping. Said you had been ever since …'

Freya just nodded.

Her eyes were drawn to a cardboard box on the chair next to where Fergus had been sitting. It wasn't one of theirs from the move. It looked old, tatty. Even from this distance, she smelled it was engrained with dust, like it had been sitting in some forgotten spot in someone's loft a while. Fergus sat down and Freya took a seat across the table from him.

'I think I'll take Luna for a wee wander, let you two talk in peace,' Tom said.

Freya wanted to tell him there was no need, but the words never left her tongue.

Fergus didn't argue either. He nodded his thanks to Tom, who kissed Freya's forehead then grabbed his coat, torch, and the dog lead from by the back door and whistled for Luna who, after an uncertain glance at Freya, went scampering after him.

Fergus waited awhile after he'd gone out. 'You look like you could use a cup of tea.' He stood up, took the kettle to the sink. 'Thought you'd want to hear that Ola Campbell's awake.'

That aroused a slight spark in her. She looked up.

'Couple of days ago now,' he said, plugging in the kettle and opening the cupboards in search of teabags. 'Doctors say the bullet missed anything major. She'll be fine.'

'On the right.'

'Sorry?'

'Teabags,' Freya said, pointing. 'Cupboard on the right.'

That familiar knot in her stomach was back. What would Ola tell the police now she was awake? And would it match what Freya had said in her statement?

'Is she talking?'

'To some folk. Not to me.' Fergus chuckled but quickly fell serious again. 'Suppose I can't blame her, given the hit our reputation's just taken. Gill Irvine must be in her bloody element.'

Freya wouldn't know: she hadn't been back to work yet. Though she had briefly spoken to Kristin, who had come to collect Ola's diary and return it to her mother. She had told Freya a job would be waiting for her whenever she felt ready to return. Yet another conversation she was going to have to have with Tom that she was dreading.

'Nobody formally cancelled your contract. As far as our payroll people are concerned, you're still on our books,' Kristin had said. 'And seeing as the man who said you were fired is rotting in Hell just now, I think it's safe to say the job's still yours, if you want it?'

What would become of the paper now Alistair was dead was another matter, but not one Freya had the energy to concern herself with.

'MIT are handling everything now. We've officially been stood down. They're keeping me in the loop still, but …' Fergus sighed, rapped his fingers on the worktop as he waited for the kettle to boil. 'It's going to be an interesting few months ahead. Inverness will be sending someone in to keep an eye on us. Heads will roll, no doubt.'

'Yours?'

Fergus chewed his bottom lip. 'Who knows.'

'I'm sorry if anything I've done costs you your job. I really didn't mean for—'

'You've nothing to apologise for, Red. If anything, it's me that owes you an apology.'

He glanced at the cardboard box on the chair, looked like he was about to say something, but the kettle boiled. He set about making the drinks and didn't elaborate. He sat back down at the table and passed Freya her steaming mug of tea.

'What she's said so far corroborates what you told us. She murdered Linklater, Sutherland, and Tait, and she's coughed for Connelly too. She says you didn't know who she was when the two of you were exchanging messages.'

Again, Freya only nodded.

When the police and ambulances finally arrived at Yesnaby, Freya had been taken into hospital with suspected shock. Maybe it was, but it was a feeling Freya was familiar with. A feeling that lingered now. A complete and utter shutdown of her brain, like a computer that had overheated running too many tasks.

The following day, she had been interviewed under caution by a DS Danielle Devlin and DC Prakash Bains of MIT. Slowly, she had told them everything: that she had been in contact with Ola, though she hadn't known it was her at the time; that they had exchanged messages and she had given Ola Alistair's and Tait's names, and subsequently Alistair's address. She had lied, said she had simply wanted to see if Scott would turn up so she could bag herself a scoop, that she hadn't known what the outcome would be. She wouldn't have been able to read the two detectives even if she hadn't been so overwhelmed. She had no idea if they believed her.

Maybe Fergus could see the thoughts behind her eyes, because he said: 'Ola's told us she was following you when you went to Alistair's house. She would have turned up there even if you hadn't sent her the address. Nobody thinks you did anything wrong.'

Another nod was all she could manage.

'Besides, MIT have plenty else to be concerning themselves with.' Fergus blew on his tea, took a sip. Freya's throat was sandpaper dry, but she still couldn't summon the energy to lift her mug to her lips. 'Everything you told us about these parties, these … Talent Scouts, and what have you, Ola's said the same thing.'

Ola had told them that on the night of 1 October 2005, Jason Miller had arrived at the house party in Harray and lied about Hannah, Ola's little sister, being taken to Eastwynd Farm. That had led to Ola and Liam racing over there.

'We've spoken to Miller. He confirms it. Says Connelly sent him, told him what to say,' Fergus said. 'He's being cooperative too in the hope we go easy on him for his role in the whole Talent Scout business. He's told us Connelly was the link between the men and the boys – the one who paid them and gave them the "shopping list", as he called it. Beggars belief what went on.'

Fergus told her that once they'd arrived in South Ronaldsay, Liam had told Ola to wait in the car, keep it locked, while he'd gone inside the house to find Hannah. But Scott had caught on they were there and had come out looking for Ola. Liam had come back outside as Scott was about to put a rock through the window of Liam's BMW.

'A fight broke out and Scott used the rock on Liam's head instead. He killed McDonnell, so Ola killed him. The whole thing's bloody tragic.'

'Nobody I spoke to last week knew Scott was dead,' Freya said. 'They all seemed to think he'd been away somewhere, but nobody was surprised when I told them he was back.'

Fergus nodded. 'Ola says there were no witnesses. It all happened outside the house, away from everyone else.'

'And then she moved the two bodies to Skaill and buried them out there herself?'

A grin tweaked at the corner of Fergus' mouth. 'She's told us she didn't leave Liam's car at Yesnaby, and she can't have used that BMW of his to move the bodies because it was examined and came up clean. But she's not saying who helped her or why.'

The 'who' part seemed obvious to Freya.

It was the 'why' she was yet to figure out.

'She's told Macintosh pretty much everything else,' Fergus said. 'She's given us Paul Thomson. MIT got a warrant, searched his place, picked those photos up, and they've had him in for questioning.

'Ola says she and Liam were madly in love, and that's why he confessed everything to her. She reckons he only did what he did to get money to care for his sick nan, then the two of them were due to run off into the sunset together.'

Freya watched Fergus closely. She hated herself for it, but she still harboured those lingering doubts. All that time working with the man, could he really have been completely in the dark about Allan Tait?

Once again, he seemed to read her mind. 'I don't blame you for not coming to me once you found out about Tait.'

'Did you know about him?'

He weighed his words carefully. 'Remember I told you he'd put his man Shearer into your dad's job? Shearer was his peedie lapdog, did whatever was asked of him. So, for that reason, and others besides, aye, I suspected he was bent, but did I know the extent of it?' He shook his head. 'Maybe I should have. Maybe I've been lying to myself all this time, seeing only what I wanted. I think a part of me wasn't ready to admit it. I don't want to make that mistake again.'

'What do you mean?'

Fergus looked Freya in the eye, let out a deep breath. 'Last Monday, at that crime scene, we knew within minutes what we were dealing with. Even the poor boy, Kyle, knew, for pity's sake. The clothes, the jewellery, the plastic bag. I called Magnus, told him we had a murder case on our hands and to refer it to MIT. He told me I was being hasty, said we were best to wait and see what it looked like when the bones came out the ground.'

'But MIT were there the next morning. What changed his mind?'

'You did.'

Freya frowned.

'He didn't make the call until your story broke. Questions would've been asked if he hadn't. Macintosh has already queried the delay.'

A thought made it through the fog. Last Monday, when Freya had called Fergus to tell him she'd spoken to Kyle, she had asked him why he was being so forthcoming, why he hadn't just offered a 'no comment' to all their questions or simply declined to see them in the first place. He'd given her just enough information to learn the remains were recent while at the same time being able to deny it.

'You wanted me to find Kyle, didn't you?'

Fergus nodded, but it was so slight Freya wasn't sure if she'd seen it.

'And on Wednesday, everything you told me, it was to keep me fired up, make sure I stayed on the story.'

Another imperceptible nod.

'But when I offered to report Gordon Tulloch missing and you told me to leave it …'

'I didn't want him knowing you were involved. That you were on to something.'

'Him? You mean Magnus?'

'I've no proof of anything,' Fergus said quickly. 'Nothing I could take to anyone higher up. Nothing even I could mention to Jess this week that wouldn't make me look paranoid. But that man … I told you Jim Shearer was Tait's wee pet project, well Magnus Robertson was the same. That man shot up the ranks so quickly he got a nosebleed. He's the youngest Area Commander these islands have ever had. All because of him.'

'Because of Tait?'

This time Fergus' nod was obvious. 'Without your story, he would've delayed the call to MIT for at least a couple of days. Now I can't say why he would do that, but the only reason that makes sense to me is he wanted to give folk warning of what was coming.'

'He was golfing buddies with Alistair,' Freya said, thinking aloud.

'And others besides. I've no doubt MIT will be chapping on the door of a number of his pals over the coming weeks unless he can steer them clear. I've known Magnus attend charity events hosted by Linklater, Tulloch. He's tied to the lot of them.'

Fergus rubbed his freshly shaved chin. He suddenly looked tired.

'I'm sorry I dragged you into this, Red. If I had known how far it was going to go …'

'You didn't drag me into anything,' she said. 'I'd have chased this no matter what you'd said to me.'

He smiled. 'Your face told me as much that first morning. You remember what your dad used to say about his thinking face?'

She did.

When she was little, on their walks along the shore, sometimes they would go hours without saying anything to each other, and when they'd stop and Freya would search amongst the rocks for shells or sea glass, her dad would stand stock still with his gaze somewhere far off among the waves. Sometimes she thought he looked angry, but if she ever asked him if he was mad or upset, he'd snap back from wherever it was he had been in his mind and his face would soften in an instant.

'It's just my thinking face,' he'd tell her with a smile. 'I was miles away, Red.'

Fergus put his hand on the cardboard box beside him. 'Well, anyway, I've brought you something by way of an apology. But, if it's all the same with you, I'll take it away with me and bring it back in a few days. I wasn't really thinking when I brought it with me tonight.'

'What is it?'

'Just some things of your dad's your mam left with me, but it'll keep. I should've realised how much all this has taken out of you.'

'Whatever's inside there won't make me as anxious as not knowing,' Freya said. 'You might as well leave it.'

'Well, that's your call.' He glanced at his watch. 'But I've taken up enough of your evening already.'

Freya wasn't sure what day it was, yet alone the time. She looked at the digital clock on the microwave; it was ten past nine at night. For the first time all week she felt wide awake.

As he reached the front door, Fergus said, 'If I pass your man out there, I'll tell him to head away home.'

'Can I ask you something before you go?'

'Certainly.'

'Are there any leads on the men in the van?'

Fergus' brown eyes skipped between hers. She wondered if there was another message there he could read, and if he could, what he made of it.

Images from her recurring dream flashed through her mind again. The gunman standing over Ola. Freya running towards him. The whites of his eyes through his balaclava as she pushed him and he went backwards over the cliff edge, arms wheeling, into the abyss.

Fergus shook his head. 'My bet is they've gone to ground and will be lying low for a while.'

She nodded, thought about saying something else, but he stopped her.

'It's a small miracle you came away from Yesnaby unharmed. Ola Campbell's lucky to be alive, thanks to you.' He placed his hand on Freya's shoulder. 'I very much doubt we'll be hearing from those men any time soon. Try not to think on it, okay?'

After he had gone and she was alone in the house, Freya went back into the kitchen and sat at the table. Her tea was untouched, a cold, brown film on its surface. She looked at the box. Fergus was right; whatever was inside it, she wasn't in the right headspace for it now.

She opened it anyway.

49

SHE COULDN'T PUT THIS off any longer.

A few days after Fergus' visit, Freya sat cross-legged on the floor in front of the log burner, Luna lying beside her, her unopened gifts from Tom still sitting beneath the tree with the gap beside them where his should have been. She would make it right, and they would celebrate their own Christmas at some point, separate from the rest of the world, but first there was something else she needed to attend to. She tore open the envelope from her coat pocket before her nerve got the better of her.

There was a single folded piece of A4 paper inside:

> Thank you for referring Freya for an assessment of Autism Spectrum Condition (ASC). Freya attended initially on 30 November. The diagnostic assessment examined: social reasoning; the communication of emotions; language and cognitive abilities; sensory ...

She skipped ahead, scanning for important words, her heartbeat quickening with every line.

It was still early, still dark outside. Tom was having one of his last remaining lie-ins before starting his new job next week. She was alone, save for Luna, reading by the glow of the fire and the Christmas lights.

Turning the page, she found the paragraph she needed:

> Conclusion: the evidence provided for this assessment was discussed in a multi-disciplinary forum and it was agreed that Freya in all probability does not have an Autism Spectrum Condition. While Freya clearly displays some of the traits and ...

She read it again.

Then a third time.

Then she burst into tears.

50

THE LAST SUNRISE OF the year bruised the low clouds over Scapa Flow. Freya watched it turn them shades of burgundy and burnt yellow from their small garden, gripping a mug of coffee in her frozen fingers. She could imagine her mother muttering something about shepherds' warnings.

'Hey.'

Tom walked up behind her. Whereas a week ago he might have put his arms around her waist, nestled his chin into the nape of her neck, he simply placed a hand on her shoulder. She hadn't yet found the energy to talk about their fight, and Tom would never push it.

'You okay?'

Freya nodded, though she wasn't sure she was.

Luna was somewhere nearby too, making sure she found everything there was to sniff, not straying far. She'd clung to Freya these last few days, like she knew. She always knew.

'I saw the letter on the table,' Tom said.

'Did you read it?'

'No, but I saw the state it's in, so ...'

After she had torn the letter and thrown it into the fire, she'd had a rush of panic and retrieved it before it went up in smoke, singeing her fingers in the process.

Maybe she should have left it there. Reading the rest of it hadn't helped. 'Apparently, I can't be autistic because I'm married and I've got a job,' she said. 'They reckon I've got characteristics of being autistic, but they've not caused me persistent difficulties.'

Now the dust had settled, she felt more numb than annoyed. She'd read things like this sometimes happened, had heard stories of people not being diagnosed because they had managed to maintain eye contact with the clinician, or because they could speak in full sentences, or because they said 'please' and 'thank you'. And it happened more often with women than men. The odds had always been against her.

And it had got worse:

> ... The absence of any developmental history from a parent during the diagnostic process means we have been unable to accurately determine whether or not Freya's traits have been present from childhood or have developed later in life as a result of a mental health condition, such as Emotionally Unstable Personality Disorder ...

Freya hadn't wanted her mother involved in her assessment. It was none of her bloody business. And besides, Helen had always been so concerned that other people might think her daughter wasn't 'normal' that she was never going to tell a clinical psychologist that Freya had only eaten yellow and white foods for a while when she was little, or had burst into tears over the sound of a persistently dripping tap.

And why couldn't they have taken Freya's word for any of that, anyway?

'So, what now?' Tom asked.

'What do you mean?'

'I mean what do you want to do? Try again, get a second opinion?'

Ever the engineer, trying to fix things.

'Since you started looking into this, I don't know, it seems to have helped you.'

She nodded. It had.

Before, there would be times she'd feel overwhelmingly anxious and couldn't work out why, which only made things worse, but since learning she could be autistic, and beginning to understand what that meant, things had gradually started to make sense. It explained why being with people left her feeling like she was hungover, or why a sudden change of plan made her irritable and unable to think, but it also explained why she spotted things other people didn't, and why she threw herself into every single thing that piqued her interest. The possibility of being autistic had finally given her the language to describe the way she experienced the world, given her hope that maybe it was okay to be different, that she wasn't simply a 'fucking weirdo' after all. Now, all that had been snatched away.

'Those people don't have a sodding clue what you've been through,' Tom was saying. 'Saying just because you're married and you've got a job you can't have faced difficulties, I mean, I can't …'

'I know,' Freya said with a sigh. 'Clearly they're not married.'

Tom looked down, saw her smile. He wiped a tear from her cheek with his thumb and grinned too. 'It's the textbook definition of a persistent difficulty.'

Freya wrapped her arms around his waist, and they stood there holding each other for a long time, neither talking, the clouds of their collective breath rising into the frozen air. The wind was light and the islands seemed calm, still.

Freya rested her head on Tom's chest and listened to the sigh of the sea, the thump of his heart. He was right, the people who had carried out her assessment didn't know the first thing about what she had been through because she had hidden it from them.

Just like she had hidden it from everyone.

'There's something I want to tell you.'

She didn't look up as she spoke. She kept her cheek pressed to Tom's chest.

'Nobody pushed me in front of that car.'

Tom didn't move. He said nothing. She felt his breathing deepen.

'That night, I reached a point where I didn't know if I could keep going. I wasn't sad, or I didn't think I was, I was just … tired. So fucking tired of everything, of me and my thoughts and I just … I wanted the whole world to go away for a while and for everything to be peaceful.' She looked up at him. 'I didn't tell you because I was worried I would scare you. I thought you might think I didn't love you enough to want to keep living, but it wasn't like that, and I didn't know how to explain. I still don't.'

Tom pulled her in close to him. 'Thank you,' she heard him whisper by her ear.

'I'm sorry for putting you through this.'

His silence surprised her, if for no other reason than he usually protested when she apologised for anything. Especially of late. She was glad he hadn't, but she didn't know what it meant. Did other people just instinctively know these things? Did they know what you were supposed to say?

Her words, when they came out, surprised her too. 'Please don't leave me.'

He wrapped his arms around her all the more tightly. 'I won't ever.'

'Nobody would blame you. I've been so caught up in my own shite, I don't know why you put up with it. We've come all the way here because of me and I've fucked it all up already.'

'I thought you said it was my fault we were here.'

When she looked up at him, she was relieved to see him smiling. 'I didn't mean any of those things I said last week. I was just …'

Just what? Having a meltdown? How could she be, if she wasn't autistic? But maybe she wasn't, perhaps the letter was right. Maybe she was just selfish. Immature. Unable to control her emotions.

Sobs shuddered through her and she felt Tom kiss the top of her head.

'Coming here was a sticking plaster,' she heard him saying. 'You were right in a sense: I can't keep you safe. And it scares the hell out of me. I never want to lose you, but I can't …'

His voice tailed off, and they both said nothing then. They stood in silence in the weak morning light, holding each other. There was so much to fix, but the weight of it seemed too great to shoulder in this moment. It was going to take time.

When the biting dawn air drove them back inside, Freya made breakfast. She insisted she do it this time, not Tom. The sun was still shining after they had eaten and got dressed, so Tom suggested they take a walk at nearby Waulkmill Bay to clear their heads. They were putting Luna into the car when a black Passat pulled onto the track to their house.

'Heading out?' Fergus asked through the wound-down window. 'I'll come back another time.'

'We're going over to Waulkmill. You could come with us,' Freya said.

Fergus' eyes flicked towards Tom. 'Maybe it's best I catch you later.'

'If it's about the box you left, Tom's already seen it.'

'Afraid so,' Tom said. The slight tremble in his voice made Freya smile. It could've been because Fergus was a policeman or because he was the closest thing Tom had to a father-in-law.

'Right you are,' said Fergus. 'You lead the way.'

They parked in the pull-in at the side of the road, high above the beach. A footpath led down the steep heather-clad hillside to the huge expanse of flat, golden sand that at low tide stretched back over a quarter of a mile from the shallow edges of Scapa Flow to the salt marshes at the foot of the Orphir hills. Other than a concerned-sounding gaggle of long-tailed ducks, they had the place to themselves. They kept Luna on her lead until they'd passed them, then she went tearing off across the soft sand towards the water. Tom stayed with her, trying – Freya could tell – to give her and Fergus some space.

'They've found Gordon Tulloch,' Fergus said.

'Where?'

'Rangers in the forest park in Argyll found his van in a clearing off a logging road. Actually, they found his dog wandering the road. It led them to him.'

'Thorfinn? Is he okay?'

Fergus smiled at that. 'That's the dog, is it? Aye, he's fine. They've got him in a shelter down that way, if you're interested in giving him a new home.'

She might be.

'Anyway, they found Tulloch's body,' Fergus said. 'He left a note.'

In it, Fergus said Gordon Tulloch had confessed his role in the tragic case. He had left Eastwynd Farm that night to find Ola on her knees beside the two bodies and he'd decided to help her. They used his VW camper to take the bodies to Skara Brae. A place far from prying eyes. A place he believed they were unlikely to be found.

'He claims it was his suggestion to swap Scott's clothes for Ola's,' Fergus said. 'The idea being she'd have a short window of warning before anyone came looking for her once the bodies were found. He then helped her head south, gave her money and the names of some people who might be able to get her set up in a new life.'

Freya had already guessed that. She only had one question left.

'Why?'

'Guilt,' Fergus said. 'He reckoned he was leaving the party early that night racked with shame at being a part of it. Says he was heading for the clifftops when he found her.'

'To kill himself?'

Fergus nodded.

'And he just changed his mind when he saw Ola, and decided to become an accessory to murder? I still don't—'

'He was the reason she was there in the first place,' Fergus said. 'He'd put her name on the list.'

The list Scott gave to the Talent Scouts. Freya felt sick. She tucked a strand of loose hair behind her ear and watched Tom throwing a ball for Luna a few metres away at the water's edge. She followed its curve through the air, took in the hills and the sea and this lemon-coloured sky that seemed to go on forever and she inhaled a deep breath of the invigorating air. It was hard to reconcile the horror of what she was hearing with the beauty of this place.

'Is this public yet?'

'There's a statement due later. It'll only mention a body being found in the search for a missing man, not the rest of it.'

'Can I give Kristin the heads up?'

'You're back at work now, are you?'

'Not yet.'

She would be soon, though. Tom would be starting his new job next week and she didn't want to knock around the house on her own. She needed the structure, the routine. The sooner going to the newsroom felt normal again, the better.

'You can tell her,' Fergus said. 'Though I'd appreciate it if you could leave out the details about his note. Jess is bound to know where that came from.'

Freya nodded. She doubted they needed it anyway. Since last week *The Orcadian* had been breaking the news about Ola, Sutherland, and Tait ahead of anyone else. It was another reason she was keen to get back – she felt bad knowing how much they had on, and she wanted to help. She had told Kristin everything that happened at Alistair Sutherland's house before burnout had got the better of her, and Gill and Sophie had been taking care of it. Kristin told Freya she would get a byline on every piece. At the time, she could not have cared less, but already she was beginning to feel differently. The key piece, though, had been an editorial written by Kristin about her own experience. Three other women had come forward since it had gone to print. More would follow.

Freya turned and faced the salt-laced breeze coming off the sea, buried her chin into her coat. 'What happens next?'

'With Gordon?'

'With everything?'

'Ola's given MIT several of these so-called Talent Scouts. They've given up others in turn. Jess tells me they've got names of some of the men. Now it's a question of getting the evidence watertight before they make their move.'

'They haven't arrested any of them yet, then?'

'It'll come. But it takes time.'

'What about the rest of it?'

'What rest of it?'

'What Tait said, about the trafficking. About them being small parts of a bigger puzzle.'

Fergus nodded, but he didn't answer.

Freya turned to him. 'And what about the men in that van?'

She still saw flashes of the whites of the gunman's eyes as he went over that cliff. She knew that was guilt, though she didn't feel the slightest hint of remorse for what she had done. In some ways, it was like it hadn't happened. And given the chance a thousand times, she would act the same way without blinking. He was about to kill Ola, who had just saved her life. And no doubt he would have killed her next. She had to do what she had done.

She *had* to.

But that wasn't what worried her.

She was done with secrets. It was burning her insides and she was certain Fergus and the likes of DCI Macintosh could see it. She planned to tell Tom the truth of what had happened, and she wanted to tell Fergus too, but, as he had the other night, he seemed to read her thoughts and he gave her the same look he'd given her at Bay of Skaill last Monday.

That look that said, *Don't.*

'Whoever they were, they're long gone. And nobody's going to miss them,' he said. 'If I was you, I'd try to put them out of my head.'

A long silence passed between them before Freya said: 'Tait said he wasn't going to kill me, that he didn't do the dirty work. Then those men arrived. They worked for him.' She looked at Fergus. 'Do you think they're the ones who killed my dad?'

Fergus glanced at her. 'How soon after I left the other night did you open that box?'

'About five minutes.'

'Did you read everything in it?'

She had.

Inside, Freya had found several small notebooks, not unlike the ones in the drawer in Ola's bedroom. The box had the musty smell of dried paper and, when Freya had opened one of the notepads, she'd felt a small pulse of electricity rush through her arms, making the hairs on her skin stand on end. She had recognised the scruffy handwriting, much like her own.

The pages were filled with notations. Places, times, dates. And initials.

- *AT uses phone box c/o Cragiefield and Work, 31/03*
- *AT meets SC @ Windwick, 22:49, 04/07*
- *TDL @ Burwick, AT, SC, GL present, 00:19, 07/07*
- *AT uses phone box c/o Cragiefield and Work, 31/04*
- *AT meets SC @ Evie Sands, 23:30, 10/07*

'How long have you had that box?'

'About six months,' Fergus said. 'Helen was doing some clearing out last summer and she came across it in the attic. She thought it was police stuff, things from Neill's work, so she asked me to take it.'

'And you haven't told anyone?'

Fergus' expression hardened. 'Who would you have me tell?'

'DCI Macintosh. I mean, the initials AT are all over those pages. That has to be Allan Tait, right?'

'Possibly.'

'My dad was watching him, wasn't he? He knew Tait was involved in something and he was investigating him on his own.'

'I don't know.' His voice was laced with sadness. 'But, aye, that's my guess too.'

'And GL, that's Graham Linklater. And SC is mentioned almost as much as Tait. Surely that's Scott Connelly.'

'Linklater, maybe. But Connelly …'

Fergus glanced at Tom, who was still at a distance, playing with Luna. He took a folded piece of paper out of his coat pocket, handed it to Freya.

'Those notebooks go back to 1997. Your dad had been a DS a little more than twelve months at that point, and I'd only recently taken my detective's exams, just to shut him up. Scott Connelly was fourteen years old.'

He pointed at the piece of paper. Freya unfolded it. It was a printout of Scott Connelly's criminal history. She scanned the page, reading a bleak history of a life spent in and out of foster homes before graduating to juvenile detention centres and prison.

'I ran that off last week when I first heard Connelly's name,' he said. 'I thought the same as you, but between '96 and '99 Connelly was doing a stint in Polmont. There's no record of him showing up in Orkney until 2003. It can't have been him.'

'Then who?'

'There's a few spring to mind. A fella named Seamus Cleat your dad put away years ago. He's as slippery as they come. Sean Cotterill was a drug lord from the south who used to operate here. Then there was Simon Cooper, remember him?'

Freya shook her head, though she thought maybe he did ring a bell. Something about these names struck her as familiar but she couldn't place it. Perhaps it was simply she had overheard her dad talking about them when she was a kid.

'He was a local councilman,' Fergus was saying. 'He was taking bribes, pushing through dodgy contracts. It was big news at the time, though you would only have been seven or eight. Your dad had a hand in taking him down too. These are just the few I've been able to think of since I saw those notebooks.' He nodded at the piece of paper in Freya's hand. 'Take a look at that sheet again.'

'What am I looking for?'

'Scott's arrival in Orkney.'

Freya ran her gaze down the A4 sheet until she found it. Scott had been arrested in March 2003 for dealing Class C substances to schoolchildren, taken to Kirkwall police station, but all charges had been dropped. There was nothing on him since.

The sheet noted the arresting officer. 'PC M. Robertson,' Freya read aloud.

'The same man who found Liam's car at Yesnaby.'

They were silent awhile, listening to the waves lapping the sand. At the time of his death, her dad had been carrying out a secret investigation into the then head of the Orkney police force, a man now known beyond doubt to have been corrupt. Freya was certain it had cost him his life. If Chief Inspector Magnus Robertson was in any way linked to Tait, he could never find out they knew.

'These notes Neill made, I think they mean his death wasn't an accident, but they're not evidence of that. They're not evidence of anything,' Fergus said. 'Neill never showed them to anyone, including me, for a reason. If I take these to Jess Macintosh now, one way or another it'll get back to Magnus. All we'd be doing is giving him and whoever he's connected to notice we're on to them. And I guarantee he'll do everything he can to burn whatever trail is left to what really happened to Neill.'

'So, you want to investigate it on your own?'

'No, I want you to investigate it with me.'

She looked at him. She had never seen him as serious, as intense as he looked now.

'There'll be bigwigs from the North Command watching us like hawks the next few months,' Fergus said. 'Every time I've an itch on my arse they'll want to know which finger I used to scratch it. There'll only be so much I can do. If I get caught doing things like printing off folk's records without a good reason, I'll be shown the door in no time. I know I've asked too much of you already, Red, but I can't do this properly without you. And *only* you. Nobody else can know.'

Freya looked at Tom, who smiled and waved before launching the ball across the sand for Luna; she tore away after it, never tiring of the repetitive game. Even after everything they had spoken about this morning, was she really going to do this?

She reached for her ear, counted the piercings forward and backward.

One, two, three, four, five. Five, four, three …

'Take your time,' Fergus said. 'Give it some thought.'

Truth was, she didn't need to.

ACKNOWLEDGEMENTS

DESPITE THE TITLE (WHICH was, in truth, inspired by a nice afternoon at the Orkney Brewery!) there was nothing solitary or isolating about writing this book. It has very much been a team effort, meaning there are a lot of people to thank …

First of all, I owe a huge debt of gratitude to my amazing agent, Ella Kahn. Ella signed me for a different book, and didn't freak out when I asked her to pull it from submission because I'd come up with another one which I really wanted to be my debut. The faith she showed in me and this story is the main reason you have this book in your hands now, and I cannot thank her enough.

In Daisy Watt and the team at HarperNorth, I've been so lucky to find an editor and a publisher who really understood Freya and the story I wanted to tell. The first time Daisy and I chatted, I knew she was the right person to bring this book to life. Thanks too to Taslima Khatun for the awesome graphics I've been spamming social media with, and Megan Jones for sorting out the map, which was very important indeed! (Got to have a map!!)

I have the most amazing pals in the world who just so happen to be incredible writers too. I'm afraid I'll miss someone, but thanks to Anita Frank (No, no, no, NO!!), Bev Jandziol, Wiz Wharton, Corin Burnside, Simon Cowdroy, Mark Left, Kate Galley, Pushpinder Kaur, Suzanne Ewart, Kate Foster, and Danielle Devlin for beta reading (go buy their books!!). Particular thanks go to Danielle for sharing her knowledge of police procedure, including an incredibly detailed explanation of what happens in custody, which was brilliant stuff but got cut from the final draft (Sorry!). Any mistakes I've made about police work are clearly all her fault!

Everyone in our Virtual Writing Group (VWG) has shown me so much support it feels cruel to pick certain people out … but I'm gonna! So, thanks to Neema Shah (who's been cheering me on since 2017, and beta reading the stuff it took to get me here), Fí Scarlett, Jenny Ireland, Rebecca Netley, Julia Kelly, Sarah Smith, Lucy Hooft, and Manolita Foster (buy their books too!) for various acts of kindness and help along the way.

A big thank you to Sarah Gilmour, the real life chief reporter at *The Orcadian* (and nothing like Gill Irvine!!) who answered my many questions about her job; to Nick Clark Windo, who was my mentor for six months, and taught me so much about getting emotion into my storytelling, despite my constant fanboying; and to Debi Alper and Emma Darwin, who run the Jericho Writers Self Edit course (if you want to be an author, do this course!!). Debi was one of the first people to give me feedback on my writing, and her words of encouragement made me believe for the first time I could actually do this.

Finally, a huge thank you to you, the reader, for picking this book up and hopefully getting this far, and to the people of Orkney for always being the loveliest, most welcoming folk when I visit. My words could never do your majestic islands justice, and I hope you'll forgive me for turning your home into a crime scene. If you're reading this and have never been to Orkney, do go visit. There is far less murder and mayhem there than this book makes out, I promise!

AUTHOR'S NOTE

THIS IS NOT A book about autism. It's not even really a book about being autistic. I simply wanted this to be a book with a neurodivergent main character, because we exist.

Around 1 in 10 people in the U.K. are autistic, but barriers to diagnosis mean the true figure could be much higher. Sadly, women and girls are still far less likely to be diagnosed than men and boys, at a rate of 13:1 in some places. Autism, ADHD, and all forms of being neurospicy (my favourite term for it!) are still woefully understood, and rarely explicitly portrayed, which is why I wanted Freya to be like me. I hope I've adequately captured the challenges and the joys that come with having a neurodivergent mind, but I would hate for anyone to think Freya's story is a definitive portrayal of what it's like to be ND, because there's no such thing. There's a saying in the autistic community: 'If you've met one autistic person, you've met one autistic person.' Freya's experience is simply a version of my own.

I was referred for an autism assessment in August 2020, around the same time I started working on this book, and was diagnosed as being autistic with ADHD in 2022. Writing *Dark Island* was a kind of therapy for me, and if Freya's experience feels familiar and you want to know more, get on social media and search the hashtags *#ActuallyAutistic, #ADHD*. Look for ND authors and creators (there are a bunch of us!) and read their work, watch their shows. I hope it helps you realise there is absolutely nothing wrong with you either. In fact, like Freya, you're fucking amazing.

And you are not alone.

Harper North

would like to thank the following staff and contributors for their involvement in making this book a reality:

Fionnuala Barrett

Samuel Birkett

Peter Borcsok

Ciara Briggs

Sarah Burke

Alan Cracknell

Jonathan de Peyer

Anna Derkacz

Tom Dunstan

Kate Elton

Sarah Emsley

Simon Gerratt

Monica Green

Natassa Hadjinicolaou

Megan Jones

Jean-Marie Kelly

Taslima Khatun

Sammy Luton

Rachel McCarron

Molly McNevin

Alice Murphy-Pyle

Adam Murray

Genevieve Pegg

Agnes Rigou

Florence Shepherd

Eleanor Slater

Emma Sullivan

Katrina Troy

Daisy Watt

For more unmissable reads,
sign up to the HarperNorth newsletter at
www.harpernorth.co.uk

or find us on Twitter at
@HarperNorthUK

**Harper
North**